Praise for
THE LAST TRUE VAMPIRE

"Full of sexy vampires, strong women, and excitement."
—*Fresh Fiction*

"The chemistry is electric . . . Kate Baxter has done her job, and masterfully." —*San Francisco Book Reviews*

"A jackpot read for vampire lovers who like sizzle . . . brimming with heat!" —*Romance Junkies*

"Mikhail and Claire's love story ha[s] that combination of romance, steam, and suspense."
—*Book-a-holics Anonymous*

"If you like the Black Dagger Brotherhood . . . pick up *The Last True Vampire*, you won't be disappointed."
—*Parajunkee Reviews*

"Kate Baxter has done a remarkable job of building this paranormal world." —*Scandalous Book Reviews*

Also by Kate Baxter

The Last True Vampire
The Warrior Vampire

NOVELLA
Stripped Bear

THE DARK VAMPIRE

KATE BAXTER

St. Martin's Paperbacks

This is a work of fiction. All of the characters, organizations, and events portrayed in this novel are either products of the author's imagination or are used fictitiously.

THE DARK VAMPIRE

Copyright © 2016 by Kate Baxter.

All rights reserved.

For information address St. Martin's Press, 175 Fifth Avenue, New York, NY 10010.

ISBN: 978-1-250-05377-0

Our books may be purchased in bulk for promotional, educational, or business use. Please contact your local bookseller or the Macmillan Corporate and Premium Sales Department at 1-800-221-7945, ext. 5442, or by e-mail at MacmillanSpecialMarkets@ macmillan.com.

Printed in the United States of America

St. Martin's Paperbacks edition / May 2016

St. Martin's Paperbacks are published by St. Martin's Press, 175 Fifth Avenue, New York, NY 10010.

10 9 8 7 6 5 4 3 2 1

For Chelsea. Thanks for being my cheerleader.

ACKNOWLEDGMENTS

Thanks to infinity go out to the readers for taking a chance on my crazy vampire world and embracing it. You're the best!

Thanks also to my family for putting up with my crazy deadlines and stints of disconnect while I live in an imaginary world. And to my agent, Natanya Wheeler, for believing in me and continuing to support me. Huge thanks to my awesome editor, Monique Patterson, whose enthusiasm continues to convince me that I might actually be getting the hang of this whole writing thing.

Another big thanks to everyone at NYLA, as well as Alex Sehulster and the wonderful copy editors, cover artists, proofreaders, and marketing team at SMP that continue to support me. You guys rock!

As always, I take full credit for any and all mistakes. If I've missed anyone here, I'm going to accredit it to my post work-out brain haze. But you know who you are and what you mean to me.

CHAPTER
1

"Jenner . . . you're *insatiable*."

Wasn't that the fucking truth.

He sealed the punctures in the female's throat. A slow sigh slipped from between her parted lips as he rolled her limp body off of his chest and onto the mattress beside him. He hadn't even bothered to get her name, but she sure as hell knew his. Came with the territory when you were one of only a few vampires in a sea of hopeful dhampirs.

Was it so bad that he'd used her body and taken her vein? As a dhampir, she nourished herself from his life force. Whether intentionally or not, she'd used him as well. Besides, he'd made sure she'd gotten off. A few times. He doubted she'd be complaining anytime soon. Hell, he doubted she'd be doing much of anything for a good, long while. Over the course of the night he'd exhausted her body and nearly drained it of blood. In hindsight, he should have gone easier on her, but there wasn't a whole hell of a lot he could do about that now.

Jenner pushed himself up and swung his legs over the side of the bed as he cradled his head in his palms.

The female reached out for him, her arm flopping onto the mattress beside him, hand groping lazily.

"Don't leave. . . ." The words were barely coherent. "Spend the day with me."

The day? Jesus. The thought of being trapped there with her past sunrise caused Jenner to break out into a cold sweat. He wasn't a stay-over sort of male. And he didn't want to give her the impression that what had happened between them was anything more than what it had been. Did that make him a heartless son of a bitch? Probably. He was already soulless. He couldn't feel regret over his recent whoring ways if he'd wanted to. He fucked. Fed. Survived. There was little else to his existence at this point.

"Gotta jet, honey." What the fuck was her name, anyway? He really needed to start nailing that shit down from the get-go. "Mikhail has strict rules about being away from home base once the sun's up."

That wasn't entirely true, but she didn't need to know that. Security had certainly become the king's priority over the past few months. Especially with Gregor—the berserker warlord hell-bent on the vampire race's destruction—still unaccounted for and Mikhail's mate, Claire, at the end of her pregnancy. So yeah, he wanted Jenner close, but it's not like he had a curfew or some shit.

"Mmmmm. You wiped me out, baby."

At least, that's what Jenner thought she said. With her muffled words she could have muttered anything. He glanced over his shoulder at her, all naked willowy limbs and bronze skin. Well, it'd been bronze when they'd started their play earlier in the night. Now her complexion bore an ashen pallor as a result of the amount of blood he'd taken from her. *Gods-damn it.* Jenner let out a gust of breath. Leaving her weak and helpless would be a class-

A dick move. Feeding her from his vein would help to replenish her strength, and he hadn't drained her to the point that doing so would trigger her transition. He really would have his ass in a sling if that happened. Mikhail had some very strict—not to mention archaic—rules about which dhampirs would be turned. Jenner snorted. By trying to keep the growth of their race under control, his king had inadvertently resurrected a classist system that was sure to enrage more than a few dhampirs. Not to mention rally others to Siobhan's cause.

Siobhan. Fuck. He'd assured Mikhail that he'd drop in on the female before sunup. In his haste to fuck and feed from the female currently lounging beside him, he'd forgotten all about Siobhan. Time to GTFO.

Jenner leaned back on the bed and scored his wrist with his fangs. He brought his arm to the female's mouth and her eyes drifted dreamily from his face to the four droplets of blood that formed on his wrist. A lazy smile settled on her lips before she sealed her mouth over the punctures and began to suck. Jenner's cock stirred, and for a moment he considered doing as she'd asked and staying right there for the duration of the day. She moaned against his flesh and a shiver raced down his spine and settled in his balls.

Damn.

"Gotta go, sweetheart." As much as he wanted to bury his cock in her one more time, he had things to do and pissing off Mikhail wasn't on the list.

Her tongue passed over the punctures—gods, it felt good—and she pulled away with a sensual moan. "Your blood is like a drug, Jenner. Just a sip and I'm wired."

He wished he knew what that felt like. His own addiction to blood and sex had been reduced to a base need that found no satiation or satisfaction. The thirst was an unquenchable fire in his throat, his body ached for release, and it didn't matter how much he drank or fucked. The desperate need never went away.

He was empty. Soulless. And nothing he did served to make Jenner feel full.

"Get some sleep."

Her bottom lip protruded in a pout. "Isn't there anything I can do to convince you to stay?"

His eyes wandered down the length of her naked body, pausing at the swell of her breasts. Jenner swallowed down a groan and reached for his jeans. "Short of an order from my king, no." He leaned down and placed a quick kiss on her cheek. "I'll see you around."

"Don't be a stranger, baby," she purred after he finished dressing and headed for the door.

Jenner paused, his hand on the knob. *Stranger.* She had it spot-on. He didn't have a fucking clue who he was anymore. He made his way through the tiny apartment, closed the door behind him, and stepped out into the cool spring night. With a long, exhausted breath, he straddled his bike and reached for the handlebars when his cell rang. He fished it out of his pocket and answered, "I'm on my way to Siobhan's now. Tell Mikhail to hold his horses."

"That can wait." Ronan's tone was all business tonight. "Meet me at my office first."

"I'll be there in ten minutes." Luckily, he was close to downtown.

"Good." Ronan disconnected the call without another word.

Great. Looked like it was going to be a long night. Jenner took another deep breath and stretched his neck from side to side. He'd been reckless tonight. Taken too much of the female's blood and let his control slip too far. A single thought resonated in his mind and he shuddered: *Monster.*

* * *

Jenner walked into Ronan's office, half-expecting to see Mikhail there as well, intervention-style. Only Ronan knew the truth of Jenner's worries, and the male would be stupid not to share in them. The past several months of his transition had only served to prove that Jenner was everything he'd ever feared he would become. For weeks, he'd been expecting the hammer to drop. For Ronan to confront him or for Mikhail to pronounce his death sentence. He wanted to feel relieved for yet another stay of execution, but as Jenner took note of the dhampir male sitting opposite Ronan a strange tingle of anticipation raced down his spine. The male gave Jenner a sidelong look and barely concealed the curl of his lip as he regarded him. *Awesome*.

"Now that we're all here," Ronan said in the down-to-business tone that made him the consummate professional, "why don't we get down to brass tacks. Jenner, this is Thomas Fairchild."

A coven master. *Fucking great*. That's all Jenner needed. Some aristocratic asshole looking down his nose at him. Jenner opted to skip the formalities and gave the male a slight nod. Fairchild didn't seem to notice—or care—as he straightened in his seat and adjusted the sleeves of his suit jacket. Straightlaced. Stuck-up. Obviously rich. And probably as classist as they came. Fairchild's coven resided on the outskirts of Los Angeles and its members were secretive and reclusive. No one knew much about them. As far as the thirteen covens were concerned, Fairchild's lot were outcasts. Some thought them zealots or separatists like Siobhan's coven.

"As I told you on the phone, I've heard that you're a male who solves problems," Fairchild began in an equally crisp and haughty tone. "I have a problem. I assume that in your current condition, you can help me."

"Current condition?" Ronan cut Jenner a look as he smiled wide enough to showcase his dual sets of fangs. Jenner swallowed down his amusement and folded his arms across his wide chest as he waited for Ronan to bring on the charm. "Are you uncomfortable with the term 'vampire,' Mr. Fairchild?"

The male cleared his throat nervously and Jenner's mouth quirked at the corner. The scent of Fairchild's anxiety and fear perfumed the air. It shouldn't have pleased Jenner so much to see the aristocratic male in distress, but he couldn't help himself.

"My niece," Fairchild continued without responding. "She's in need of protection."

Again, Ronan glanced Jenner's way, his brow cocked curiously. "From what?"

"A witch," Fairchild replied.

A palpable wave of concern wafted from Ronan. His mate, Naya, was a witch. He scooted to the edge of his seat as he leaned farther over the desk. "I'm afraid you're going to have to be more specific."

Fairchild cast another glance Jenner's way as though he couldn't be trusted to hear the delicate details. *Please.* Jenner had been forced to suffer the prejudices of assholes like Fairchild his entire life. That he had to suffer them now—in his own place of employment—dug into his skin like a tick.

"You see that big, scary-looking vampire right there?" Ronan apparently sensed Fairchild's distaste as well. "He's the one who's going to be protecting your niece. So I suggest whatever issues you have with him you get over. Quickly. Otherwise, you can take yourself out the way you came."

Jenner appreciated the solidarity, but he suspected that Fairchild saw what Jenner saw every time he looked in the mirror: a creature that should have been put down a long damned time ago.

Fairchild gave an almost indiscernible nod. "A dark witch has been searching for my niece for centuries. I've kept her hidden—protected," he amended. "But she's headstrong and no longer content to accept that she must exercise caution at all times. I suspect that she's been exercising her freedom, sneaking out of the compound at night. She's quite resourceful, you see. I need someone who can track her. Watch over her and keep her safe."

"So you want us to follow her around without her knowledge?" Ronan asked. "Provide personal security when she's out and nothing else?"

"Not exactly," Fairchild said. "I also want you to find the witch. And kill her."

"For what reason is she hunting your niece?" Ronan asked, his eyes narrowed with suspicion.

"Reasons that I don't care to share," Fairchild remarked in his insufferably stuffy tone. "Surely someone in your line of work can appreciate discretion. All you need to know is that my niece is in danger. I want that danger eliminated if possible."

"How do you expect us to do that?" Ronan said.

"If I knew how," Fairchild remarked, "I wouldn't have come to you for help, would I?"

"We can offer her protection," Ronan said. "But until I have more details about this witch I can't help you with finding her or killing her."

Fairchild gave a thoughtful nod. "Trust has to be earned, I suppose. We'll start our relationship with protection only. If I deem you trustworthy, I'll explain more of the situation and we can move forward from there."

"Fine," Ronan replied.

Jenner swallowed down a derisive snort. Males like Fairchild were all the same. Stuck-up, self-righteous, covetous sons of bitches. Like he didn't have enough on his plate, now Jenner was going to have to babysit some prim and snotty female who had more money than sense. She probably crawled out of her window at night and headed straight for the club district. He'd rather fall on a slayer's stake.

"We'll work out the details, and Jenner can start Monday."

"Why Monday?" Fairchild's tone hitched with annoyance. "That's three days away."

"Because Jenner has *other* responsibilities," Ronan stressed. "Monday. Or nothing."

"Very well." The male reached in his jacket pocket and pulled out a checkbook.

Jenner didn't need to be here for this part. He knew how his time would be spent after this week. *Gods.* As though his existence weren't tortured enough. "You need me for anything else?" Jenner asked. "Otherwise, I can take care of that other bit of business we have."

Ronan's brow puckered as though he'd forgotten all about Siobhan. The lightbulb came on and his mouth puckered. "Yeah. Might as well get that out of the way, too."

The idea of dealing with the female was as unsavory to Ronan as it was Jenner. She was a raging pain in the ass. One who had to be dealt with whether they wanted to or not. Would this night ever end? For once, Jenner couldn't wait for the sun to rise.

"You look like shit, Jenner." Siobhan never was one to mince words. The female's tongue was as sharp as a well-honed blade. Jenner couldn't disagree, though. It had been one bitch of a long night. "I can't imagine that *your king* appreciates how much time you've dedicated to whoring your way from one end of the city to the other."

Her disdainful tone didn't go unnoticed. There was no love lost between the self-proclaimed dhampir queen and his king. If it was possible, she'd gotten even nastier since the race's resurrection. No doubt she was attempting to bait Jenner with her insults, but he wasn't biting.

"Have you managed to find out why the werewolf is so interested in you?"

For months a rogue werewolf had been tracking Siobhan's every move. Jenner suspected he was on the Sortiari payroll and that the guardians of Fate were using Siobhan as bait to coax Gregor into the open in much the same way Mikhail had been. Jenner had no idea what the female's history was with the berserker. All he'd been told was that it had been violent and bloody. He doubted the Sortiari knew any of the details, either. Where Mikhail had intimate knowledge of Siobhan's history, the Sortiari used seers to guide them in the right direction. Fucking fortune-tellers and fanatics. The Sortiari were nothing more than a pain in the ass.

"As if I'd tell your king anything."

She sat on her makeshift throne, legs tucked daintily beneath her. She painted a lovely image, prim and delicate. A convincing illusion, to be sure. There was nothing soft or helpless about her.

"What makes you think I'm not asking for myself?"

She answered with a derisive snort.

"Who is he, Siobhan?"

She deflected like a pro, "How much longer is Mikhail going to keep Chelle from me?"

"Mikhail isn't keeping anyone from you."

"Careful, Jenner. I can smell the lies on your skin."

"I'm sure you like to think so."

She smirked.

The truth was, Chelle was being kept from *everyone,* not just Siobhan. Ronan's twin had been turned not by the bite and blood of a vampire, but through the power of a magical coffin that, according to legend, was the origin of the entire vampire race. Not even Ronan was convinced that his sister was harmless. Chelle was volatile. Her thirst still raged and her new vampiric existence was unnerving as hell. As was her disconnection from the Collective. She'd become secretive since her turning. No one but Chelle had any knowledge of the extent of her power, her physiology, or her abilities. Unleashing a variable like that on the world could be a dangerous thing indeed. Jenner knew that the only reason she'd allowed herself to be hidden away was because Ronan had asked her to cooperate. It wouldn't be long, though, before she tired of captivity and left Mikhail's guesthouse of her own volition.

Every vampire living shared in the collective memories of the race. Interconnected like a grove of aspen trees, their blood, their memories, were one. But Chelle appeared to be a species unto herself, an offshoot of the original line, and it served to reason that any dhampirs she changed would become as saplings to her bloodline. Not exactly something that Mikhail wanted to become common knowledge so early on in the race's infancy.

Especially when Siobhan possessed the very chest that had transformed Chelle.

Ronan had traded the chest for his freedom from a blood troth made to the female and Jenner admired the male's ingenuity. Knowing that Siobhan disdained all of vampire-kind, he'd been confident that by placing the chest in her safekeeping it would be hidden away where no other dhampir would find it or use it. Mikhail was dubious. Placing power like that in the hands of a female who might as well be his enemy was risky. Which was another reason why Jenner had been stuck to her like glue for months. Mikhail was determined to stay one step ahead of her at all times.

"I'll make a deal with you." Siobhan's lips spread in a

calculating smile. "Let me see Chelle, and I'll be more than happy to share everything I know about the rogue with you."

Intel on one rogue werewolf was going to cost Mikhail a face-to-face with Chelle? "That's not going to happen."

"Too bad," Siobhan responded on a wistful sigh. "That is my condition for sharing information. Quid pro quo. Tell your king he can take my offer or leave it."

Jenner didn't have to offer her terms to Mikhail. He already knew what his king's response would be. "Take care you don't back yourself into a corner, Siobhan. An island is a lonely place to live."

"I neither want nor need your counsel, Jenner. Now get the hell out of my sight before I have Carrig throw you out."

Another useless conversation, and still chasing his tail. He would've been better off staying with the lusty female in her apartment. Jenner inclined his head to Siobhan ever so slightly. "May the day treat you well, Siobhan."

"I'm sure it will," she said with a dismissive flick of her wrist. "Sun's about to rise; I suggest you run to your hole, *vampire*."

Gods, she was bound to cause all of them a shitload of trouble.

Bria Fairchild balanced on the ledge of the high-rise and stared down at the city below. The wind whipped at her long ponytail and she pulled her dark hood up over her head to shield her not only from prying eyes but also from the chill. Under the cover of night, she was free to do as she wished without her uncle's rigid rules and obsessive protection weighing her down. He'd gone out tonight, which was rare, but she'd used the situation to her advantage. Over the years she'd become an adept escape artist and could circumvent the locks, high-tech alarm systems, and high fences that protected his coven from a witch who had hunted their family for centuries.

Atop the high building, Bria didn't fear a threat she'd never seen. She didn't fear *anything*.

She tightened the backpack against her body and took off at a full run. The wind whipped her hood from her head and her eyes watered. She ran like the traceurs—the free-runners and parkourists—who used the urban city-scape as their personal playgrounds. Bria had studied their movements for decades, long before parkour be-came an Internet sensation. Her dhampir physiology was perfectly suited for free-running. She could jump high, run fast; her movements were agile and fluid.

These stolen moments in the dark of night were her only taste of freedom. Once per month she allowed her-self to leave the confines of her uncle's coven, and for that night she was *free*.

Bria negotiated a large roof vent. She braced her hands on the metal dome and launched her body over it in a graceful arch. Her feet came down silently and she whis-pered through the night as quiet as the breeze that stirred around her. With the edge of the building's roof in sight, Bria pushed herself harder. Faster. Her arms pumped and her breath sawed in and out of her chest. A quick hop sent her up onto the ledge and she used her speed to pro-pel herself into the air.

For a moment she was weightless. Floating. She soared across the space from one building to the next as though hopping over a puddle. When her feet made contact with the roof of the building she let her knees give out and landed in a roll before she came to her feet once again. The landing did nothing to slow her down. She contin-ued to run, vaulted off of another roof vent, and propelled herself into a front flip. Bria ran, dove, twisted, and turned until her muscles ached and she was out of breath. But still, she didn't stop. She'd achieved the flow state, where the parkourist's confidence outweighed everything else. Caution, fear, doubt, no longer existed. Her body was perfectly in tune with her mind and focus. The world melted away.

Bria once again breached the space between one roof and another, and this time when she landed she came to rest. She pulled the GPS from her backpack and checked the coordinates. *Perfect.*

The members of their coven were forbidden outside relationships. It was too dangerous, the world too uncertain. Slayers had come to Los Angeles and attacks on dhampirs had become more common. The vampire race had reawakened and the slayers had taken up their ancient cause of eradication. Not even the dhampirs were safe. Of course, the slayers were the least of Bria's uncle's worries. What Thomas Fairchild truly feared was wielders of magic. Witches. They were the reason his coven lived in a nearly impenetrable compound. All for his and Bria's protection. In all of the nights she'd ventured out over the centuries, she'd yet to encounter a single witch, let alone one who had a vendetta against them. Though, when leaping from rooftop to rooftop, Bria supposed the chances of running into another living creature—witch or otherwise—were slim.

She'd never had friends who didn't belong to her coven. Had never known any other creatures but her own kind. But Bria had found a way to reach out to the outside world. The invention of the Internet had saved her from a life of desperate loneliness. And tonight's outing was a part of one of her latest Internet obsessions.

She pulled a long metal tube from her backpack and

unscrewed the lid. She tucked an ancient ring, a gold coin, and a length of antique lace inside along with a pencil and logbook before closing it. Bria tucked the tube behind an air-conditioning unit and logged the coordinates for the location of the container into her GPS. When she returned home, she'd leave the coordinates on the geocaching Web site's message board for another treasure seeker to find.

A smile curved her lips as anticipation coiled tight in her stomach.

These stolen moments of freedom might not have been the life Bria had hoped to live, but she made the best of it. She'd thought about leaving the coven. Of finding another group of dhampirs to take shelter with. She still might, someday. Each time she left the compound her hunger for independence grew. It wouldn't be long before her uncle could no longer keep her there whether it was for her protection or not.

The first streaks of dawn made their appearance in the eastern sky. Sunrise was an hour, maybe two, off and she needed to return home before anyone realized she was gone. She raced back through the city the way she'd come, across the rooftops where no one would notice her. When she reached the outskirts of the city she kept to the shadows and slowed to an easy jog. Miles melted away under her feet and in the space of an hour she'd managed to find her way back to the compound. Bria came to a halt just outside the chain-link fence that surrounded her home as the cacophony of frightened screams and the sounds of a fight reached her preternatural ears.

Bria's heart leapt into her throat. The coven was under attack. Whether from slayers or witches she didn't know, but she didn't have time to consider her options. Her uncle needed her. Her coven needed her. She dug deep and found that place inside of herself where fear did not exist as she searched for a weak spot in the fence where she could circumvent the razor wire. She quickly scaled the links and vaulted herself to the other side, where she landed on her feet without a sound.

She would fight whatever creature awaited her inside the walls of her home. To the death if that's what it took to protect those she cared about.

CHAPTER
2

"Help us! Please!"

Bria hung limp in her uncle's arms. She didn't share in his panic or desperation, which was strange considering she was the one who was dying.

"My king, I implore you. Save her!"

What if she didn't want to be saved? True, the slayers' attack on their coven had been both unexpected and horrific, but it had also been . . . fortunate. For her, at least.

Her lids cracked, and through the slits of her eyes Bria made out the shape of a tiny guard station, manned by three hulking males. One held a phone to his ear, while the other two tried to calm her uncle, who shouted not at the guards but into the lens of a camera that was mounted just to the left of a wrought-iron gate.

As though the vampire king would concern himself with one pathetic dhampir's death.

"She's not healing!" Blood, warm and sticky, trickled from the wound at Bria's throat. She'd been cut by a slayer's blade, likely infused with Sortiari magic. She might have healed otherwise. "She'll bleed out in a matter of minutes. My coven is yours if you save her. You have my troth here and now!"

Let me bleed out. I want to die.

Before the slayer's blade had pierced her flesh, Bria had felt truly alive. There was no greater honor than to die protecting others. Wasn't that what her father had done? He'd died protecting his family from the Sortiari slaughters. Her uncle had ordered her away from the fight, told her to run and hide. But she'd refused to cower as member after member of their coven fell under the slayers' blades. For all of her life she'd been sheltered. Kept. A bird in a cage and made a prisoner for her own protection. Forced to sneak out under the cover of night and steal every scrap of freedom she could find. She'd lived a lifetime in a matter of hours tonight, first as she'd run through the city and later as she'd hacked and stabbed at her attackers. None had fallen under the dainty leaf-blade sword, but she'd given it her all. And her valor would be rewarded with blissful death.

Freedom.

Bria's world blurred out of focus and her mind drifted. The scrape of metal grated on her ears and her uncle rushed forward, jostling her in his arms. With any luck, the vampire king's guards were about to escort them off the property. She wanted to make a plea of her own. To beg her uncle to let her go. She wasn't in pain. To the contrary, she felt *nothing*.

I want this. The words formed on her tongue, but her lips refused to move. *I can't live this life anymore.*

Her uncle's step faltered and Bria's eyes snapped open. A house so large it might as well have been a museum loomed above her, shadowed and foreboding in the gray light of dawn. A tall door swung open and Bria's gaze came to rest on a female with long wheat-colored hair and brilliant gold eyes. Concern marred the female's forehead as she ushered Bria's uncle inside the house. *No!* her mind screamed. *Send us away. I don't want to be saved.*

"Please, take me to the king!" her uncle's panicked shout rang in Bria's ears.

"Claire, step away."

A deep, commanding voice that vibrated with power echoed in the large foyer.

That powerful voice was answered with an exasperated sigh. "Don't get your panties in a bunch, Mikhail. Can't you see that they need help?"

Bria didn't need help. All was right in her world.

The female must have been the vampire queen. Only the king's mate would have the audacity to speak to him in such a brazen way. Bria admired the fire in Claire's voice, the fearlessness she exuded in her tone. Bria had always wished she could be a female like that: fierce and commanding.

"Claire, wait for me upstairs." It appeared that the king wasn't too pleased with his mate's fire. Bria shivered at the chill in his tone. He was a male who would not be defied.

"The hell I will." For a brief moment Bria willed herself to hold on to life. If only to hear how this power struggle would play out. "Look at them, Mikhail. This isn't a trap or a trick. She's bleeding to death all over your overpriced marble floors. If you won't do something to help them, then *I* will."

No! Of course, she admired the queen's fire, but Bria didn't want any favors from her. Not when she was so close to leaving this miserable world behind.

Silence stretched between the two and Bria's uncle held her tighter against his chest, his own breath and heart racing with distress. He would mourn her, but in the end her death would be better for all of them. She would be free of his protection and he would be freed of having to protect her.

"Claire, I can't help anyone if I'm worried for your

safety." Had Bria not been dying, she would have swooned at the king's gallantry. To have a male love her like that! "So step away, love, and put me at ease."

"Help her, Mikhail, and put *me* at ease."

The vampire queen was obviously a female who didn't know how to lose. Bria admired her.

"There's only one way to help her," the king responded.

"Yep. And the sun is going to rise in less than an hour. Time's wasting, so let's get her upstairs and get to work."

Another stretch of silence followed and Bria drifted further toward darkness. Her uncle let out a shuddering breath, much too relieved for her peace of mind. It didn't matter, though. She was fading quickly. She'd lost all sensation in her limbs and the chill of death settled over her skin. It wouldn't be long now. Her body was jostled as someone helped her uncle to remove her pack from around her shoulders and off of her back, but Bria barely felt it. They could race her upstairs but it wouldn't change the fact that her heart was about to beat its last. Blood no longer trickled from the wound at her throat. It was time to let go of this lonely existence once and for all.

Thank the gods.

Darkness penetrated the periphery of Bria's vision as her heart stuttered in her chest. So close. So near that dark abyss that called to her. Her mouth went dry and her tongue stuck to the roof of her mouth. Her senseless hand flopped out and she managed to grip the queen's arm. They had to let her die. "P-please . . ." The word died on her tongue and a soft smile curved her lips as she toppled over the ledge and into infinite darkness.

Death was painless. The fire that raced through Bria's veins was anything but. A scream ripped from her throat as she thrashed against the sensation that she was burning from the inside out. What was happening to her?

"Try to stay calm, Bria. You're almost past the worst of it."

How long had she been in this state? The voice that spoke low next to her ear belonged to Mikhail, the vampire king. She remembered the commanding timbre and she stilled as the memories of what had happened came rushing back to her.

The queen. Her mandate that the king help them. It couldn't be possible, could it?

Memories swirled in Bria's mind, visions of lives that had been snuffed out centuries ago. Dhampirs in her coven whispered about the legends of a collective vampire memory. She'd always thought it was a myth. . . .

Scents reached her nostrils in an assault that overloaded her senses. The artificial light of the bulb beside the bed nearly blinded her and a riot of color swirled in her vision. Strength unlike anything she'd ever known surged within her and Bria choked as she tried to suck in a sharp breath. Her lungs refused to inflate with air and the sound of her own heartbeat was now absent from her chest.

As was any sense of herself. An empty, fathomless chasm opened up inside of Bria and she clutched at her chest as though she could somehow fill the void. *Gods.* The vampire king had turned her!

Not her soullessness, the assault on her senses, or her past isolation and loneliness troubled Bria in the wake of her transition and newfound strength. It was more than she could have ever imagined. Ever *hoped* for. Surely now her uncle wouldn't keep her shut inside the compound. Not when she was so strong. So utterly capable of taking care of herself. She hadn't found freedom through death. Instead, she'd been freed in her rebirth.

"She'll need to feed soon." A male whom she didn't recognize spoke. The timbre of his voice was deep and rich and sent a pleasant shiver over Bria's skin. Maybe they'd let her feed from him. He sounded good enough to eat.

"It's taken care of." Her uncle spoke, but his voice sounded different to Bria's heightened senses. "I've called in a member of my coven."

"Good idea," the male said. "She might go easier on someone she knows."

Were they worried about her? Surely she could feed without killing someone. Fire raged hot in her throat and Bria reconsidered her control. Her fangs throbbed in her gums and she was possessed with a need to sink them deep into yielding flesh and glut herself on blood.

"Bria? Can you hear me?"

"Claire, for the love of the gods, would you please stay clear of her fangs? There's no telling what she'll do in the grip of bloodlust."

"Pfft. You worry too much, Mikhail." A smile curved Bria's lips. She liked this female. "Bria? Listen up; let's show these boys that they have nothing to worry about. Whaddya say?"

When Bria turned on the mattress to face Claire, she was greeted by a feral gold stare that would have stalled the breath in her chest had she any to fill her lungs.

"Claire?" Bria asked.

"Yup. You got it. Now, do you know what's happened to you?"

The events of how she'd gotten there were hazy. Bria remembered that she'd wanted to die. That her life balanced on a razor's edge. "I've been turned." Even her own voice sounded strange in her ears. It distracted her thoughts and would take some getting used to.

"That's right. How are you feeling?"

"I think I'm all right." The words rasped in her too-dry throat. "The thirst . . ."

"We're going to take care of that," Claire replied. Her

gaze slid to the vampire king. "Think you can hold on and not bite anyone until your dinner shows up?"

Bria smiled at Claire's teasing tone. "I can."

"Told ya," Claire said to Mikhail.

Bria searched the room for her uncle and found him tucked away in a far corner, watching her with a wary gaze. The fear that glistened in his dark blue eyes twisted her heart. Did it matter that she was no longer a dhampir? She was still his niece. Still the only blood relation he had left. That hadn't changed. And now that she was stronger, she could protect them both. There would be no need to hide and cower in their coven. Surely he knew that?

A soft knock came at the door and the male whom Bria didn't recognize crossed the room. "Looks like you don't have to wait," he replied as the door swung wide. "Dinner's here."

Claire snickered and Mikhail pinched the bridge of his nose as though he'd had his fill of the both of them. Bria had heard rumors of Mikhail Aristov's temper. That he was withdrawn and prone to violence. Cold and unwilling to lower himself to interact with lowly dhampirs. She had no doubt that he was severe and that his very presence intimidated. But he'd saved her life. Given her the gift of his bite. There was nothing heartless about the vampire king.

"Bria?"

She shot an accusing glare in her uncle's direction and he averted his gaze. He could have asked anyone else to come, but instead he'd summoned Lucas. This was not the time for a power play. Lucas was a formidable warrior and strong in his own right. But in their present company the male would be as helpless as a newborn babe.

"Whoa there, buddy. Slow your roll."

The fair-haired vampire placed a sturdy palm on Lucas's chest to stay his progress. A low growl rumbled in his throat and Bria sensed the impending violence as the tiny hairs pricked on her arms. Her uncle remained in his corner of the room, eager enough to have orchestrated this disaster and yet unwilling to do anything about it.

"If you have a care for your life, dhampir, you will be mindful of your behavior in the presence of your king."

Claire rolled her eyes, the only one in the room who seemed unfazed. "There's way too much testosterone in this room. Ronan, take a hike. Mikhail, behave yourself or I'll bounce you, too."

The handsome vampire called Ronan flashed an amused smile. "You're the boss, Claire. Holler if you need me, Mikhail." He gave Lucas a hearty smack on the back before he exited the room.

"Not much better," Claire groused. "All right, Bria. Obviously, your friend has been brought here to feed you. It's tricky the first couple of times. Tough to control all of that strength when you're in the grips of burning thirst, know what I mean?"

Bria nodded. Already the scent of Lucas's blood drove her crazy. So much so, she'd begun to doubt her ability to control herself.

"Mikhail and I are here to make sure that you don't go all bloodlust crazy on your friend. This isn't something to be taken lightly, Bria. You have to be gentle. Careful. Mikhail won't have it any other way."

Her gaze wandered to the king, who looked at his mate with love and respect. No matter what the others thought, Mikhail Aristov had to care for his people. All of them. Otherwise, he wouldn't have cared how Bria fed from Lucas, who was nothing more than a stranger to him.

"I understand," she replied through the fire in her throat.

"Good. Then I think we're ready to roll, don't you?"

Gods, yes. Bria needed blood in the way that she used

to need air to breathe. As Lucas stepped toward Bria, Claire took several tentative steps back, tucking herself close to Mikhail's side. For the first time Bria noticed the swell of the other female's belly. The queen was pregnant. No wonder Mikhail had been so fiercely protective of his mate. It was a wonder that he'd allowed so many unknown dhampirs into his home at all. They were all lucky to be alive.

Lucas took a seat next to Bria on the bed. His blue eyes shone with wonder and not a little fear as he caught a strand of her hair between his thumb and finger. Bria sensed that had her soul still been intact she would have been filled with a resounding sadness. Lucas had been her closest friend since childhood. It had become obvious over the past few years that he'd wanted more than a friendship with her. But the continued absence of her soul only proved that Lucas was not meant for her or she for him. She'd learned enough about vampire-kind to know that only her true mate could return her soul to her. She and Lucas were not a tethered pair.

She wasn't sad, though. She wasn't anything, really. Her single-minded thought was focused on the vein that pulsed at his throat and how badly she wanted to sink her fangs into his flesh. It was forbidden, though. The first rule of their coven: Never take blood from the throat. Bria wanted to, though. Gods, she could think of little else. She wanted to feel ashamed for that wantonness, but there was only her need and gnawing thirst. Instead, she focused on Lucas's wrist and took it in her grip.

"You're stronger than he is, Bria. He might look unbreakable, but you could easily kill him." She noted the warning in the king's tone and gave a sharp nod of her head. She couldn't think clearly, couldn't force herself to speak when all she wanted was to drink. "Be gentle. And be mindful not to take too much. Do you understand me?"

Again, she nodded. The knowledge that she could easily kill her uncle's most formidable warrior filled Bria with a sense of euphoria. The power she now possessed rushed through her, as heady as any drug. But she knew that if she disobeyed the king's command her punishment would be severe and she had no intention of disrespecting his generous gift by accidentally killing her oldest and closest friend.

Bria wasn't senseless. She could exercise self-control. But as her fangs broke the flesh of Lucas's wrist and his warm blood flowed over her tongue she doubted everything. Most of all, her ability to stop.

Jenner leaned against the heavy oak door as he closed it behind him. Against his better judgment, he'd left Siobhan's lair only to prowl the streets for a willing vein. Willing veins became willing flesh, and before Jenner had decided to come up for air three nights had passed. Three fucking nights without returning to Mikhail's. Without at least checking in. The past seventy-two hours were a blur of blood and sex that barely registered in the recess of Jenner's mind. He'd behaved like an addict on a bender. Worse. An *animal*.

After he checked in with Mikhail—and took the ass chewing he was likely to receive—he'd need to get ahold of Ronan. Tonight was supposed to be Jenner's first night of playing bodyguard to Thomas Fairchild's special snowflake of a niece. Jenner cupped the back of his neck as he tried to rub some of the tension away. The last thing he wanted to do was follow a spoiled, entitled little brat around the city while simultaneously taking care of business for his king. *The things I do for money* . . .

The ground level of Mikhail's mansion was abandoned, and Jenner let out a sigh. He climbed the staircase slowly, hopeful that his king wouldn't go too hard on him for going AWOL yet again. With slayers running rampant throughout the city it was still dangerous for a vampire to be caught alone and defenseless. Jenner needed to get a fucking grip on his lusts before Mikhail bypassed the slayers altogether and put him down for good. He was wild. The very monster he'd hoped never to become. It wouldn't be long before he became rabid and out of control, too. His king would have no choice but to run a stake through his heart.

Jenner's step faltered on the stairs and he gripped the banister for support as a delicious aroma hit his nostrils. It awakened his bloodlust with a ferocity he'd never known, and the fear of this new, desperate want shook him to his core. Jenner thought he'd experienced lust, but the primal need that rose up in him now paled in comparison.

Three stairs at a time, he raced up to the second-floor landing in search of the tantalizing scent. His secondary fangs punched down, throbbing in his gums, and his cock hardened to stone in his jeans. He clamped his jaw shut, puncturing his lower lip from the force. Blood welled in the seam of his lips and Jenner licked it away as a low, feral growl built in his chest. He'd gone mindless with need, wild with it. As though he had no control over his own body, he followed the path of the scent that called to him, pausing for the barest moment in front of one of the guest bedrooms before throwing open the door.

Mine.

Seated in a wing chair in the corner of the room, her legs tucked beneath her, she started as the door bounced off the wall from the force of Jenner's entry, nearly dropping the book she cradled in her hands. Her eyes glittered like amethysts, fringed by dark lashes. Raven hair framed her face, the silky tendrils curling softly to caress her shoulders. Twin sets of fangs scraped the full swell of her bottom lip, coaxing the blood to just below the surface of her skin.

A vampire. Who was she? Who had turned her?

The deep flush on her skin only served to further awaken Jenner's thirst and his gut clenched painfully as he took a step forward only to crash to one knee. Her scent enveloped him, and power that rivaled taking blood from the vein surged through him. The dark, empty chasm inside of him filled to bursting and Jenner dragged in a ragged gulp of breath as his soul slammed into the center of his being like trees bending to the will of a gale-force wind.

Gods. This female had *tethered him.*

A roar built in Jenner's chest, and the female stared at him, wide-eyed. She'd fed recently; the sound of her heart thundered in his ears and her chest rose and fell with her quickened breath. The roar quickly transformed into a snarl. He'd tear the throat from any vampire or dhampir who'd dared to offer her a vein.

She belonged to *him.*

"You're . . ." The word died on her tongue, but gods, the sound of her voice was a lick of heat down his spine.

He had to have her. To take her vein. Glut himself on the sweet blood that called to him while he pounded into her tight heat. Jenner's thoughts clouded as a desperate growl built in his chest. "Mine." He'd become a mindless animal without reason. A creature of raw lust and tangled want. Reason was impossible with her so close, her scent filling his nostrils and the sight of her so delicate and yet fierce, a temptation he couldn't resist.

A temptation he didn't have to resist.

Jenner pushed himself up from the floor and rushed at her. She scrambled from her perch in a blur of motion toward the bed. The predator in him surged. Driven by hunger and lust, his brain refused to comprehend her

drawn brows and tightly pinched expression. His lack of
reason refused to acknowledge the fact that her fear
scented the air. That despite the tether, he didn't even
know this female's name. Knew *nothing* about her or why
she was here. The only thing that made sense was that he
wanted her. *Needed her.* And he was going to have her.

"Jenner, have you lost your fucking mind?"

Before he could claim his prize, Ronan took him down
in a full-body tackle that knocked the air from Jenner's
lungs. A snarl tore from his throat as he struggled to free
himself. Ronan was like a brother to him, but Jenner would
kill the son of a bitch before he let him get in the way of
what he wanted. The female leapt up onto the mattress, her
gaze wide and curious as she stared down at him.

"Mine!" he roared as he threw back an elbow and
caught Ronan in the face.

"You broke my fucking nose!"

"What in the hell is going on here?" Mikhail shouted
as he entered the room.

Not even the presence of his king could thwart Jenner's
efforts to get to her. He lashed out, fangs bared, as he freed
himself from Ronan's hold.

"A little help here, Mikhail?" Ronan grunted as he
pinned Jenner's arms in a bear hug.

Mikhail joined Ronan to crash on top of Jenner and
a bellow of rage echoed in his ears as he fought to free
himself.

"Jenner, control yourself or I'll put you down!" Mikhail
pinned him in place with a knee and wrenched one arm
behind his back. "Jenner!" His commanding shout served
to clear some of the lust that fogged Jenner's mind, but
his actions were still nowhere within his control.

"She's mine!" he bellowed.

"He's lost his mind, Mikhail." Ronan struggled to pin

Jenner's other arm down and forced his face to the hard-wood floor. "Mad with bloodlust."

"We've got to get him out of here."

No! Instinct spurred him and Jenner bucked against Mikhail's hold.

"The two of us can barely subdue him," Ronan grunted. "Bria, get Claire. Tell her to call the guard station and let them know we need some help up here."

Jenner surged against the big bodies holding him down. No one and nothing was going to keep him from her. Mikhail could try to put him down. He'd like to see the male try.

The female scooted to the edge of the bed. She took her bottom lip between the dainty points of her fangs and Jenner roared. He had to take her vein. Claim her. Now.

"Don't hurt him!" The female's impassioned shout stilled three aggressive vampires in an instant. "We are tethered."

"Holy shit," Ronan said as he slumped fully on top of Jenner.

"Indeed," Mikhail agreed.

"Get the fuck off of me," Jenner growled. "The female is *mine.*"

Neither male obliged. Their combined weight further pressed Jenner onto the floor. He struggled beneath them and it was a long moment before he felt the weight of Mikhail's body lift. Ronan took his time, exerting a little too much force as he shoved off of Jenner's body. He grunted under the push and filled his lungs with air. His thigh muscles trembled with a rush of adrenaline, and when he could finally get his shit together to stand he listed to his left and didn't fall over again only because Ronan had seen fit to brace him upright.

"Her uncle isn't going to be happy to discover his

sheltered, virginal niece is mated to this charmer," Ronan murmured.

Her uncle? Who was this female who'd tethered his soul? *Virginal? Christ.* What had Jenner missed over the course of a few days?

"Take me away from her." The words grated like gravel in his throat. Miles, hell, continents between them wouldn't keep Jenner from her. What made him think a simple wall would prevent him from ravaging her? "Before I do something I'll regret."

CHAPTER
3

"Who is he?" Bria breathed.

"Eric Jenner," Claire answered with a laugh. "But everyone just calls him Jenner."

"Jenner." Bria liked the smooth way his name rolled from her tongue. Enjoyed the soft sound of it. Though there was nothing smooth or soft about the vampire who'd burst into her room and rushed at her as if he dared anyone or anything to come between them. Bria's heart raced in her chest and a riot of butterflies took flight in her stomach as they fought their way up her throat.

Her soul had been tethered by the wild male who'd fought to get to her with a ferocity the likes of which she'd never seen. Not even Lucas could compare, and his reputation was famed in their coven. Jenner was violent, hulking, stacked with muscle. Bria recalled the bright silver that lit his eyes when he looked at her, the way his full lips pulled back to reveal the sharp points of his fangs as his attention wandered to her throat. The intensity of his gaze, the deep rumble that vibrated in his chest, had frightened her. Frightened . . . and *excited*.

A thrill chased through Bria's body, the sensation as foreign to her as her new vampiric existence. She belonged to this male. This *stranger*. "I can't believe this is happening."

"Trippy, isn't it?" Claire stretched out on the bed and groaned. "I swear, this baby is trying to kick his way out." She rubbed a hand over the swell of her belly. "He's like a little karate master in training and he's using my ribs to practice on."

Bria smiled. "What's going to happen now?" Bria's uncle had been insistent that once she could control her thirst she return to their coven. She was too weak, too frail, to live outside of the protection of their walls. They were still in danger. Still threatened by an unknown witch with a vendetta against their bloodline. When he looked at Bria now her uncle didn't see her as a vampire, strong and fierce. He still saw her as a helpless creature. A kept thing. And it soured Bria's stomach to know that he continued to perceive her in such a way. Was that what Jenner had seen when he first laid eyes on her? Something fragile and breakable? Too pathetic to properly care for herself? *Take me away from her. Before I do something I'll regret.* Bria's cheeks grew warm with indignation and shame. She was *not* weak. And she wished that someone would give her the chance to prove it.

"I don't know," Claire replied. "But whatever happens, I doubt your uncle's going to be thrilled."

His overprotectiveness bordered on manic. It was a wonder he'd left the safety of the coven to seek the king out in the first place. "I never expected the tether to be so immediate."

Claire snorted. "Takes the term 'speed dating' to a whole new level, doesn't it?"

Bound for eternity to a male she didn't know. It certainly was an extreme version of speed dating. Bria swallowed down the worry that gathered in her throat. "Is he a cruel male?"

Claire's brow furrowed and she placed a comforting hand on Bria's forearm. "No." She drew her lip between her teeth and Bria studied the single set of dainty fangs. There were differences between the queen and other vampires. Her eyes, her fangs. Her very demeanor. She was indeed a mystery. "I'm not gonna lie, Bria. Jenner can be brutal. Not to mention intimidating." Bria thought about his sheer size, the dark archaic tattoos that covered his skin. The sharp angles of his face, his chestnut hair, and the intensity of his dark brown eyes. He wasn't simply intimidating. The male was *overwhelming.* "He's loyal, though. Fierce. He'd die to protect Mikhail, or Ronan, or even me. We can add you to that list now, too. He's not cruel. But to the wrong people, he's definitely dangerous."

Dangerous. The one word encapsulated Jenner.

"Does he frighten you?"

"No way," Claire said. "And don't let him frighten *you,* either."

Easier said than done. Claire had Mikhail to protect her from dangerous males. Would Bria be safe with Jenner? Or was she destined to live in fear of the male who'd tethered her? "He needs to feed." She'd seen the bloodlust in his gaze when he'd burst into the room. The pain that marred his brow when his gaze lingered on her throat. She swallowed and looked up to find Claire studying her. "I want to offer him my vein."

"You sure about that?" Claire's incredulous tone bristled and a growl rose in Bria's throat. "Oookay, sounds like you are sure," she said with a smile. "I'm not saying you shouldn't. It'll probably help to level him out. But you've only been a vampire for a few days, and from what I heard, Jenner was a little out of it when he busted in here. Do you think you can keep him from going off the rails?"

If she was going to prove to everyone that she was a capable female, Bria needed to start by taking charge of her own life. "Yes, I can."

"That's good," Claire remarked. "You'll need to keep that attitude if you plan on giving this a go."

"My uncle expects me to leave with him when my bloodlust is under control." Already Bria had begun to master her thirst. What would happen when her uncle returned to fetch her? Her voice dropped above a whisper. "I don't want to go with him."

Jenner was brutish, yes. But also strong. Fierce. Two vampires, both built like warriors, had barely been able to subdue him. Even her uncle couldn't argue that she'd be safer in Jenner's care than hiding within their coven. In Jenner, Bria saw a chance at freedom. That is, if the vampire would have her. Tether or not, he could reject her. She simply had to make sure that wouldn't happen.

"You don't have to." Rumors had circulated for months about Mikhail Aristov's mate. That she was a heartless ice queen whose thirst for blood rivaled that of the first vampire. And that she could walk in the light of day without burning to ash. Some said she was a goddess who'd come to resurrect the race; and others, a demon who heralded their destruction. Bria had seen the differences in Claire with her own eyes, but largely, the rumors were false. Claire was a kind, strong female and Bria hoped that they would be friends.

"Thank you," she said. "But the king—"

"I'll take care of Mikhail." Claire flashed a conspiratorial grin. "You'll learn soon enough that these big, bad vampires are nothing but teddy bears once they've been tethered. Well, as far as their mates are concerned anyway."

To have power over a male such as Jenner would be a heady thing indeed. He looked to be the sort of male who would be mastered by no one. "I'd like to see him now. Can you arrange it?"

"Arrange it?" Claire said with a laugh. "I'm surprised he hasn't knocked the door down again to get to you."

"This is a monumental clusterfuck."

Ronan wiped the remnants of blood from his nose with a damp cloth and Jenner groaned, the scent of it burning in his throat like cinders. He thought he'd known hunger, but that gnawing, insatiable need was nothing compared to what he felt now. He was weakened by his want. Crippled by it. Convinced that he'd shrivel up and die if he didn't take the female's vein. Her vein and her body—

"Hey!" Ronan snapped his fingers in front of Jenner's face, shaking him from his reverie. "I need you square."

Square? He wasn't going to be close to having his shit together until he fed, and Jenner had no intention of feeding from anyone but the female in the next room. "Who is she? What's her name?"

Ronan looked to Mikhail. The king shrugged his shoulders as if to say, *The damage is done; why keep anything from him now?*

"Bria Fairchild."

Jenner's eyes went wide. "Fairchild. As in . . . ?"

Ronan nodded. "His niece."

Jenner rolled his shoulders in an effort to release the tension that pulled his muscles taut. He'd been tethered by the very female they'd been paid to protect. This went far beyond clusterfuck proportions. "How was she turned?"

"Thomas brought her here just before sunrise, three days ago." Mikhail did nothing to hide the accusation in his voice and Jenner cursed his own foolishness for staying away for so long. "She'd been injured in an attack on their coven and she was bleeding out."

Jenner's gut bottomed out as a rush of adrenaline raced through his veins. She'd been attacked the same night he and Ronan had met with her uncle. Coincidence? Had she died, Jenner's soul might have remained in oblivion for an eternity. While he'd been on yet another bender, glutting himself on blood and eager flesh, his mate had been on the verge of death. He was a fucking bastard. A lowlife son of a bitch who didn't deserve the honor of being tethered to any female, let alone one so seemingly delicate and beautiful.

"I'll gut the slayers responsible."

"Easy," Ronan replied. "We don't need you going all Hulk smash on anything quite yet. You know as well as I do that Fairchild is a twitchy bastard. We're investigating his claims about the attack, though for now they seem legitimate and Bria corroborated her uncle's story."

"We know the slayers haven't left the city," Jenner replied. "L.A. reeks with the stench of berserkers. Do you think it was something else?" *The witch, perhaps?* "What reason would he have to lie?"

"He has his secrets," Ronan said with a shrug. "Your guess is as good as mine."

Ronan had that right. Hell, Fairchild wanted protection for his niece but hadn't been willing to divulge the details of why. He could've lied about the slayers. Hell, he could have lied about the witch. Gods, if only he weren't so preoccupied with his thirst, Jenner might be able make sense of all of this. For months they'd been vetting dhampirs, rallying covens to swear fealty to Mikhail. The Sortiari had backed off, leaving them in relative peace, so what reason would they have to unleash their berserkers to wage war on the vampires once again? Thomas Fairchild's coven had yet to be contacted, but not for lack of trying. In fact, his meeting with Ronan had been the first contact anyone had had with the male in decades.

"Stop growling," Ronan complained. "It's off-putting."

"I'll remember that the next time someone looks at Naya sideways."

Ronan grumbled under his breath but didn't bother to argue. The male was as fiercely protective of his mate as Mikhail was of Claire. So why condemn Jenner for a reaction that was as much biological as it was . . . what? Emotional?

For fuck's sake, he didn't even know Bria.

A knock came at the door and the hairs stood up on the back of Jenner's neck. He was wound so fucking tight he might spring through the ceiling at any moment. Claire peeked her head into the study, her golden eyes alight with mischief. "How's it hangin', fellas?"

Mikhail gave her a look. "How's Bria?"

"Right as rain," Claire replied. "She's worried about big, bad, and broody over there, though." She jutted her chin in Jenner's direction and he scowled. "For some reason, she's under the impression that he's starving to death and she wants to do something about it."

"She's offered to feed him?" Ronan choked.

Jenner glared a hole through the other male. Was it so far-fetched that she would be concerned for him? They were tethered after all. "She asked for me?" Ronan's incredulity aside, Jenner couldn't help but be surprised. He'd all but attacked her not an hour ago.

"Uh-huh," Claire said with a grin. "Think you can behave long enough for a snack?"

That Bria had offered him her vein was enough to bring Jenner to his knees. How could he possibly exercise control when all he wanted to do was open her vein and glut himself on her blood?

"No," Mikhail said. "He's not even close to being in control."

"Mikhail, you were fangs deep in my neck thirty

seconds after we met." Claire turned to Ronan and added, "How long was it before you were latched on to Naya and slurping like your life depended on it?"

He gave her a rakish smile. "Your mate has a point, Mikhail. Did either of us have comparable control upon our tethering?"

"Feeding is bound to calm him down," Claire suggested. "I'm no vampire expert, but it does wonders for the both of you."

"Keeping them apart is only going to compound the situation," Ronan agreed. "And yeah, her uncle's going to need to know, but it's not like Bria is some teenager caught in the back of her boyfriend's car. Thomas has to acknowledge that a tether trumps even familial obligations."

"Someone should go with you, Jenner." Mikhail obviously wasn't convinced that Jenner could control himself. Hell, Jenner wasn't even sure he could. "At least for the first time."

"Bria can handle it." All eyes turned to Claire, and Ronan raised a skeptical brow. "They can both handle it. Have a little faith, would you?"

Mikhail gave a sharp nod of his head. They were a bunch of hopeful fools if they thought Jenner could keep his shit tight. But Mikhail also knew that the longer Jenner waited to feed, the more mindless he'd become. And if that were to happen gods help them all.

Claire swung the door open wide and stepped to the side. "We're close if you need us." The queen might have championed him, but that didn't mean she wasn't without doubt. *Great.* They all knew—including Jenner—that he was nothing more than a mindless, starving beast. Maybe they'd all be better off if Mikhail put him down.

With mechanical steps, Jenner climbed the stairs to the second story. By the time he reached Bria's room, his hands shook and the fire in his throat raged with thirst.

He knocked on the door—which seemed asinine considering how he'd barged in earlier—and waited.

"Come in."

Gods, the sound of her voice. As smooth and sweet as honey from the comb. Jenner turned the knob and slowly eased open the door, his breath still in his chest. The sweet scent of her blood slammed into him and Jenner's fangs throbbed in his gums as the bloodlust once again swept him up in its frenzy.

How in the hell could he possibly exercise control when he wanted her so badly?

She didn't say a word, simply rose from the chair and crossed the room toward the bed. A lump formed in Jenner's throat and he swallowed it down. Tight cotton pants that were more like a second skin than a garment clung to her legs and a long wispy shirt swayed with her movement, camouflaging the curves underneath. She was taller than he'd first thought. Strong, yet soft and curvy with pert, full breasts that Jenner knew would perfectly mold themselves to the palms of his hands. His cock stirred and he willed the bastard not to further betray his arousal; he was sure his own scent was already doing a bang-up job of that.

Bria settled on the mattress, her legs tucked beneath her, and swept the length of her dark hair over one shoulder, baring her throat to him.

Fucking hell. This was *torture.*

Jenner's throat went dry, his thirst igniting like dry kindling. One foot shuffled in front of the other as he made his way to the bed. Toward the scent of blood that called to him like no other could.

Mine. The word echoed in some primal part of his brain over and again. His hands balled into fists at his sides as he inhaled deeply. His gaze settled on the pulse point of her delicate neck throbbing gently under the skin.

A low growl rumbled in his chest. He could think of nothing but taking her vein.

Words formed and died on Jenner's tongue. He'd fucked and fed from females without exchanging a single syllable, and yet the thought of treating Bria with the same casual indifference cut through him like a well-honed blade. The sudden return of his soul was doing a serious number on him. Anticipation thickened the air, and had Jenner needed to breathe he was sure he would have choked on the intake.

"Please, sit."

Her eyes met his and Jenner's step faltered. Delicate and refined, this female was everything that Jenner wasn't. How could Fate have bound their souls together? He was a harsh, barren desert compared to her dewy petal softness.

The mattress gave way beneath his weight as he settled down beside her. She released a slow, shuddering breath and her scent soured with the citrus tang of her fear. Jenner's heart clenched as he shot to his feet. She was afraid of him. He was nothing more than an animal to her.

"No, don't leave." Bria reached out and caught his hand in hers. Her satin-soft touch coaxed a low growl to Jenner's throat.

"You're afraid." The words grated like sandpaper. He couldn't bear to look at her. To see the evidence of that fear on her face.

"I'm anxious," she said. "No one has ever taken my vein."

Jenner turned to find her soft expression guileless. Dhampirs drank blood, though less frequently than vampires. It seemed impossible that she'd never offered her vein to a member of her coven. "Never?"

"My uncle wouldn't permit it. We're tethered, Jenner.

You need to feed." She looked up at him from lowered lashes. "And so do I."

Jenner sat back down beside Bria. He turned her wrist in his grasp, but she pulled away. "No." Once again, she swept her hair away from her throat. "From here."

Sweet gods. As Jenner leaned in and inhaled the tantalizing fragrance of her blood he sensed that this delicate female would surely be his undoing.

CHAPTER
4

Bria's body came alive in Jenner's presence. Tiny currents of electricity that traveled the length of her spine, tingled at the tips of her nipples, and settled as a low thrum between her legs. She was painfully aware of him. His sheer size overwhelmed her. Yes, the prospect of having his fangs at her throat frightened her. She wanted to be afraid, though. To push past that fear and *live*.

Jenner reached out to cradle the back of her neck in his massive palm. The heat of his skin seared her and at the same time coaxed gooseflesh to the surface of her skin. With his thumb at her jaw he angled her head to the right, and Bria clutched her hands in her lap to keep them from trembling. Time seemed to slow as Jenner lowered his mouth to her throat, his breath a heated caress that caused her stomach to clench. His lips sealed over her flesh with a shock of wet heat and his tongue flicked out at her skin before he sucked gently.

Oh, gods. A rush of wetness spread between her thighs and Bria sighed. Her sex pulsed in time with her heartbeat and her eyes drifted shut as Jenner bit down, piercing her flesh with his razor-sharp fangs.

A moan slipped from between her lips with the first deep pull of his mouth. Fiery heat raced through Bria's veins and her fists uncoiled, only to wind in the fabric of Jenner's shirt. Feeding had always been perfunctory for Bria. And she'd only taken blood when necessary, four or five times a year and only from the wrist, since drinking from the throat was forbidden in her uncle's coven. She'd never realized that the act could be . . . *sensual.*

Jenner groaned against her throat, a sound that bordered on pain.

Bria's own thirst ignited and she swallowed against the searing heat. She'd never known such raw, urgent need. Her bloodlust had been difficult to manage over the past few days, but now she found it nearly impossible to control. Her gums throbbed as her secondary fangs elongated and her mouth became dry.

Jenner gripped her tighter and pressed his body close to hers. The male was a wall of muscle, hard, unyielding flesh that Bria yearned to touch. He bit down harder and a whimper escaped her lips. She'd never felt so *good,* so in tune with her true nature. Jenner's hand flexed at the back of her neck, the blunt ends of his fingertips digging into her flesh. Her limbs grew deliciously heavy and her lids drifted shut. She would sit like this for hours, with his mouth on her throat, if it pleased him.

So quickly it made her head spin, Jenner laid her body out on the mattress and settled himself between her thighs. Bria gasped as the hard length of his erection pressed against her core through their clothes and another shock of heat raced through her body. A brazen male, to be sure. He rolled his hips in slow, shallow thrusts as he fed and a low growl rumbled in his chest.

Bria's breath came in quick pants and her hands abandoned Jenner's shirt to grip his massive shoulders. Swept up in sensation, in bloodlust, and in the tether that inextricably bound them together, she met every thrust of his hips as pleasure built to a fevered pitch inside of her. Her own innocence became a burden with the mounting friction of Jenner's movements. She'd pleasured herself before, knew her own body. But the need for release that built inside of her now bordered on desperate. Wild. Everything about this moment was foreign to Bria. As though she'd never truly known her own body—herself— until this moment.

"Please, Jenner." She fought the urge to plunge her hand into her underwear and pleasure herself. She knew that the orgasm would pale in comparison to what Jenner could give her. She wanted him to end the desperate want that swelled within her. Wanted the length of the erection that brushed her through their clothes deep inside of her. Her thirst raged and she pierced her bottom lip with her fangs, lapping at the blood that welled there. It wasn't enough to satisfy her. She needed more. She needed *him*.

His thrusts grew wilder, harder, and Bria gasped. Her body coiled tight and she sensed that in a few short moments Jenner would shatter her completely. Anticipation swirled in her stomach, her heart raced, and her muscles contracted. *So close*. Gods, she wanted—no, *needed*—to come.

Jenner pulled away with a snarl, eyes alight with silver, brow furrowed in pain, and mouth stained with her blood. Bria had never seen a fiercer creature. Fierce and *magnificent*. Unanswered need crested within her and tears sprang to her eyes. She willed them not to flow. Refused to let this powerful male see even an ounce of weakness in her. Her breath raced in her chest as Jenner's gaze locked on to her mouth. Hunger shone in his expression and Bria brought shaking fingers to her bottom lip and wiped away the droplets of blood that formed there.

"I'm sorry," he said through pants of breath. "I didn't mean to—" The furrow in his brow deepened and a low growl vibrated in his chest. He didn't mean to . . . what? Show her how much pleasure could be found in offering her vein to another? "I didn't mean to handle you so roughly."

Roughly? Gods, he hadn't been rough enough. Bria tried to push the words past her lips, but they wouldn't budge. What would he think of her if she told him the truth? That she wanted him to strip her clothes from her and take her like some wild thing with mindless abandon. *You're a naïve fool, Bria. You know as much about wild abandon as you do about being a vampire.*

Jenner pushed himself up on the mattress and helped Bria to sit. Did he think her so weak and pathetic that he should treat her as though she were made of glass? "I took too much from you. You need to feed."

She did, but Bria needed so much *more.*

Jenner's wild gaze settled on her throat once again and another delicious rush of pleasure shot through her. That he drank deeply of her and still wanted more filled her with a sense of power. He didn't move to take her again, however. His body stilled and his nostrils flared with breath. Jenner was obviously a male with ravenous appetites but even stronger self-control.

If only Bria could be so strong.

She rose up on her knees. He was so tall, she almost couldn't reach his neck. Her thirst blazed hot in her throat and his scent swirled in her head: a clean, masculine musk that caused her breath to quicken. This was the most intimate moment she'd had with any male. *Anyone,* really. Her uncle's stern overprotectiveness kept even the members of their coven at a distance, and over the years it had made Bria feel empty and isolated. She'd lived more in three days as a vampire than she had in all of the previous decades of her existence.

Leaning over Jenner's body, she angled her mouth toward his throat. His body stiffened and his hands came up to grasp her wrists in iron. He eased her slowly away from his body and a slight tremor vibrated from his clenched fists through Bria's body. Jenner's Adam's apple bobbed in his throat and his eyes flashed bright silver as his gaze met hers. "No. From my wrist."

His wrist? Rejection stung at the center of Bria's chest. Did he not want her close? She'd fed from the wrists of dhampirs in her coven. From Lucas. Tethered, yet little more than a stranger to Jenner, she'd bared herself to him. Offered her throat to him. If he'd lingered at her vein much longer, she would have given him her body as well. Now that the frenzy of feeding had left him, he treated her with cold indifference.

Really, what did she expect? The tether bound their souls but not their hearts. It hadn't formed an instant affection between them. She'd misinterpreted his arousal. There was pleasure to be found in the drinking of blood. Bria knew that now. Pleasure could be emotionless. Detached. If this was what Jenner wanted from their tether, then that's what Bria would give him.

Searing pain radiated in Eric's gums as one fang, and then the other, was ripped from his mouth. His own blood coated his tongue and a growl gathered in his chest that was just as much hunger as it was anger.

"They'll grow back." His mother's assurances did nothing to comfort him. "It's only temporary."

"Temporary." Edrik Salo, the vampire lord who ruled their territory, did nothing to hide the sneer

in his voice. "It's unfortunate that the female your son drained can't claim her death as such."

His mother would be wise to hold her tongue, lest she be punished alongside him.

"My liege—"

"Silence!"

His father bowed his head at the vampire's command. To see his father, a powerful vampire warlord, bow in shame tore at Eric's meager composure. It would do his father no good to plead his son's case. He had killed the female. Drank her to the point of death. His guilt was unquestionable. The act itself, unconscionable. At only sixteen years of age, he knew the severity of what he'd done. His parents thought to explain it away. He was simply a young dhampir who hadn't known better. But Eric was fully aware of what he'd done. He'd been seized by lust. Mastered by it. Driven mad by the taste of her blood on his tongue. And once his fangs had broken the skin he'd been unable to stop.

Even now, he craved more. With his gums bleeding, his fangs gone, beaten by Lord Salo's guards— Eric's father's own brothers-in-arms—and brought to his knees, he wanted more. Needed more. A thirst such as his was unheard of among dhampirs. They needed to feed four or five times a year, and even then, those feedings lasted seconds. He had feasted on the female for long minutes that seemed to last for hours. He'd taken pull after pull on her vein until her heart ceased beating. Her lungs no longer took air. She'd gone limp in his arms and still he hadn't pulled away.

A shudder passed over his body. He'd always known it would come to this. Not even the newly turned thirsted like he did.

The vampire's eyes flashed angry silver as he regarded Eric. "You will never be turned," Lord Salo said with such finality that Eric felt the words vibrate in his very bones. "Your body will be marked so that all of vampire-kind knows never to offer you the gift of transformation. I see your soul, Eric Jenner, and it is dark and black and unfathomable. As a vampire, you would become a monster. Uncontrollable, insatiable. Dangerous to our kind and others." The vampire lord turned his attention to Eric's father. "You and your family are banned from this and every other coven. You are outcast. Do you understand me?"

Eric's father's hurt expression caused a fissure of pain to spread across Eric's heart. His mother wept silently beside him and a sorrow so heavy weighed upon him that Eric didn't think he would ever walk tall again.

"I understand, my lord."

From the corner of Eric's eye, he watched as two vampires readied their needles and ink. He would be marked. Branded as a warning to anyone who looked upon him. He was, as the vampire lord decreed, a monster.

Jenner gave a rough shake of his head as he dislodged the unpleasant memories that darkened his soul even centuries later. The tenuous hold he had on his control slipped away with every second that passed. The taste of Bria's blood, rich and sweet, lingered on his tongue. The scent of her arousal drove him mad with desire, stirring his own body into a state of unfulfilled want. It was the taking of his vein that affected her, Jenner told himself. Nothing else. The inability to control her lusts a result of being newly turned.

Jenner knew all too well how difficult it was to master those urges. Even now, the darkness within him roared, demanding to be freed.

Ronan had called her virginal. She'd admitted that she'd never offered her vein to another. If no one had taken her vein, Jenner suspected her body was untouched as well. That he was the first to drink from her sent a surge of male satisfaction roaring through him. No other had tasted her. Taken that heady nectar on their tongue. Put his mouth to her delicate throat.

Her jeweled eyes became rimmed with silver and Jenner's gut twisted into a painful, hungry knot as she sealed her mouth over his wrist. Without preamble she bit down, sinking her fangs into flesh, and his cock pulsed hot and hard behind his fly. Her bite was a sweet torture he'd endure over and again. A pleasure unlike anything he'd ever known. The rush of delicious heat had no equal. An effect of their tether? Or perhaps a reflection of his own unceasing need.

Bria's lids fluttered and her blissful expression commanded Jenner's attention. Her nails dug into his wrist as she held him tightly against her mouth. The deep suction sent a wave of sensation from his wrist down the length of his torso, and it settled in the base of his sac. Jenner shuddered. His want of her was absolute. He didn't know a damned thing about this female, but he was certain that she didn't deserve to be tethered to a miserable bastard like him.

Time slowed to a standstill. She fed for mere minutes, but to Jenner it might as well have been years. When her fangs disengaged, his chest tightened. As much as he didn't think he could endure another minute of physical contact with her, neither did he want it to end. He pulled away too quickly, nearly jerking his wrist from her grasp. Dark brows pulled down over her eyes and

Bria's tongue flicked out at his blood that painted her full bottom lip.

"I can close the punctures for you."

"No need," he grunted through a renewed surge of lust. He didn't think he'd be able to endure her tongue gliding over his skin without tossing her back on the mattress and fucking her until the sun rose. Didn't think he could stop himself from ripping open her vein and drinking her dry. "They'll close on their own."

"Oh." Her disappointment sliced through him. "I didn't realize."

Vampires and dhampirs both possessed a venom that kept wounds in quickly healing supernatural skin from closing immediately. But vampires healed much faster than dhampirs did. The closing of punctures was a courtesy and sometimes an act of affection.

"Who did you feed from after your transition?"

Her expression grew wary. "Lucas," she said slowly. "A member of my coven."

The thought of her tongue sliding over the flesh of another male filled Jenner with an instant and violent rage. His hand snapped out and seized her wrist. "You will feed from *no one* but me," he said low. "From this moment on."

Bria's eyes widened a fraction of an inch and a citrus tang infused the space between them. She gave a shallow nod of her head and her jaw took on a stubborn set. "And you will feed from no one but *me*."

Jenner hadn't expected her to counter his mandate with one of her own. She didn't realize what a dangerous bargain she struck. The dark need within him surged, hungry, greedy. He should feed from anyone but her, anyone at all. Jenner's lips moved against his better judgment: "Agreed." Despite the danger to them both, he knew he'd never bother with the blood of any other after tasting her.

His thumb circled the petal-soft skin on the underside of her wrist where her pulse beat a steady rhythm. A frustrated growl built in his chest and he released his hold before pushing up from the bed.

"Where are you going?"

Jenner kept his back to her. If he stayed another second he'd ravage more than her throat. "I've been away for too long and I need to talk to Mikhail." He paused, his hand on the doorknob. Should he offer her something? Hell, he had no fucking clue. "I'll stay close. In case you need to feed again." He wanted to say something else. Something *more*. Jenner wasn't good with words, though. Violence was his forte. Destruction his only talent. "Come find me if you need me." He stepped through the doorway and closed the door behind him.

He stood out in the hallway, his fingers wrapped so tightly around the doorknob, he was surprised it hadn't snapped. Bria's scent swirled in his head; the skin at his wrist still tingled from the wet warmth of her mouth. The contact had been so innocent, and yet Jenner felt it over every inch of his body. She'd wanted him. Her legs had fallen open the second he settled between her thighs. He could have easily taken her. Fucked her until he collapsed on top of her and sated the lust that burned through him like fire.

Jenner wouldn't have thought twice about taking her had his soul still been vacant from his body. He would have rutted over her like the animal he was had she been any other female. Despite her innocence, Jenner had never beheld a more seductive female. Maybe it was because of that innocence. Her wide eyes and soft mouth had beckoned him. The softness of her skin begged to be touched. Sullied. Even now, Jenner considered turning around and going back in there to tear her clothes from her body. He wanted her bare to him. He wanted to bite her again and again. *Gods.* Claire had thought that feeding would help to calm him? Instead, he felt less in control than ever.

It took a surprising amount of effort to let go of the doorknob. He'd promised he'd stay close—hell, he'd been paid to keep Bria glued to his side—but with each step he took away from her Jenner didn't think he'd be able stay under the same roof without doing something rash. Bria could easily learn to hate him if he allowed her to see that selfish side of him. The side that didn't give a shit about consequences. The side that needed, *craved* without reason or restraint. If he didn't ease himself into their tether, he'd ruin them both. Jenner's soul wouldn't bear the burden of hurting someone as delicate as Bria. He had to get the fuck out of there.

"How'd it go?"

Jenner hit the top of the stairs to find Claire smiling up at him from the first-floor landing. He averted his gaze, too damned ashamed of his own wicked thoughts to look her in the eye. She'd championed him and he'd barely made it through feeding Bria without ripping her clothes off and fucking her senseless.

"Fine," he grunted as he headed down the stairs. "I need to get out of here for a while. Can you keep an eye on her?"

"Sure." Claire turned as he brushed past her in the foyer, her brow furrowed. "Everything okay?"

"Yeah. Just gotta jet."

"Jenner."

He paused, halfway out the door. So close to putting some distance between him and Bria. Claire needed to wrap it up before he changed his damned mind and rushed back up the stairs. "Call me when her thirst mounts again," Jenner said as he headed out the door. He turned to face Claire and shame flared in his chest at her disapproving stare. "I don't want her feeding from anyone else."

Her frown turned to a wry smile. "Gotcha. It's going to be okay. You know that, right?"

Did he? Jenner gave her a crisp nod and closed the door behind him. Right now he felt as though nothing would be okay ever again.

CHAPTER
5

Bria rubbed at her wrist. The ghost of Jenner's gentle suction still lingered on her skin. For days he'd kept his distance, only coming to her when they both needed to feed. And then it was all very polite and civilized. He was always present in the house, though. She felt him like the brightest light burning in the center of her soul. As though he watched over her from afar, he kept his distance until their hunger crested and they could bear the separation no longer.

Once again, they sat together in the guest room—never on the bed as they had the very first night—on a short love seat that allowed them no room for anything but sitting. They exchanged equally polite conversation before and afterward before Jenner inevitably made an excuse for his continued absence. The exchange of blood had become so routine.

And Bria hated it.

Their first night together, Jenner had given her a glimpse of what her vampiric nature truly was. She'd become a creature of intense appetites. But since that night Jenner had proved to be no better than her uncle. Jenner didn't treat her as his tethered mate but more like he was a steward who'd been entrusted with her safekeeping. She hadn't given up hope that things might change between them, though. She simply needed to give them both some time. She was sure that once they got to know each other better Jenner would loosen up.

Well, as loosened up as a male like Jenner could get.

"What did you do last night?" Bria's curiosity burned to know how Jenner had spent the night. It had been the first time since their tethering that she'd sensed he'd left Mikhail's property.

"Ronan has a client who's got a stalker," Jenner said. "I provided extra security for a charity event he attended."

"I didn't realize you worked with Ronan."

Jenner averted his gaze. Nervous? No. Almost . . . guilty. "Yeah. He's sort of a risk management consultant for the rich and famous."

"It sounds exciting." Bria had always found it sad that she lived in one of the most adventurous cities in the world and had never fully explored all it had to offer. "Is it dangerous work?"

Jenner flashed a feral smile. "Only for anyone who crosses Ronan."

Or Jenner, she surmised. "Does he live here with Claire and Mikhail as you do?"

At first Bria had assumed that both Jenner and Ronan lived with Mikhail. But it had become apparent that Ronan had a place of his own. Did Jenner? Did he have another home somewhere, but he chose to stay here close to her instead? Bria's stomach did a backflip at the thought. Getting information out of Jenner was like pulling teeth. His reluctance to talk about himself only caused Bria's

curiosity to eat away at her. Where did he go when he
wasn't here? Whom did he spend his time with? What was
his coven before he came to serve Mikhail?

"I have an apartment downtown," Jenner remarked. He
stood from the love seat and paced the confines of the
room as though his proximity to Bria made him uncomfortable. "I haven't been there in a while, though."

"Oh." She tried not to be hurt that he'd never offered
to take her to his apartment. They were tethered, true, but
he'd never made any pledge to her otherwise. It wasn't as
though they were required to live together.

"What did you do last night?" Jenner turned the intensity of his stare on her and Bria tried not to lose herself
in it.

His eyes were fathomless and soulful. Gold flecks
glinted in their depths that shone even brighter when his
irises gave way to silver. Like when he fed. A thrill raced
through Bria's body at the memory of his silver gaze
and the way it had focused on her throat moments before
he'd taken the vein at her wrist just minutes ago.

"I read," Bria said with a shrug. She regarded Jenner
from the corner of her eye as she tried to gauge whether
or not he picked up on the lie. "Watched TV with Claire.
My life isn't quite as exciting as yours."

Jenner's stare burned through her. Bria didn't know
why she felt the need to hide what she'd done from him.
She certainly wasn't a prisoner in the king's home, but
she'd still snuck out without telling anyone. Last night had
been a particularly adventurous treasure hunt. Not all canisters contained more than a logbook and pencil, but the
geocache she'd found near a police station in the valley
contained a baseball card, an old pocket watch that no longer worked, and a tiny bottle that had at one time contained perfume. Nothing valuable per se, but she'd had fun
anyway. Only when the sky began to grow light with the

coming dawn had she raced back to the house and snuck in just as silently as she'd left.

After a long, quiet moment, Jenner glanced away and cupped the back of his neck with one large palm. Tension sizzled in the space between them and his voice grew tight. "Have you talked to your uncle?"

"No. He's called a couple of times, but I've told Mikhail to tell him I'm not up for talking."

"Why?" Jenner turned to her, curious. "You've mastered control over your thirst. Do you still feel volatile?"

"I don't want to talk to him because he's going to try to convince me to go home with him," she said. "And I don't want to."

Jenner's eyes flashed feral silver. "Why would you have to?"

"It's complicated," she said low. In truth, Bria was ashamed to admit to Jenner that she'd spent decades inside of the stronghold that housed her uncle's coven with little freedom save the moments she'd stolen for herself under the cover of darkness. She was doing her best to show Jenner that she was strong, and that knowledge would only undermine that. "He's very protective of me."

"I can protect you," Jenner said.

She didn't doubt it. She'd never known a male as innately fierce as Jenner. But she didn't want his protection. She didn't want anyone's protection. All Bria had ever wanted was the opportunity to prove that she was capable of standing on her own two feet. She wanted Jenner to see her as an equal, not a stone around his neck.

Bria knocked her chin up. "I can protect myself."

Jenner's arrogant smirk coaxed a swarm of butterflies to take flight in Bria's stomach. "You think so? Maybe we should put you to the test."

She'd be up for any test as long as it ended with his mouth at her throat and his big body between her thighs.

Her transition had awakened Bria's desires to the point that she could think of little else lately. She used Jenner's words against him as she infused her voice with what she hoped was sensuality. "I'm up for the challenge. Try me."

Quicksilver flashed in his eyes and a low growl gathered in his chest. Bria loved that sound. He was an animal and he'd awakened the animal in her. She wished he'd give her the opportunity to show him just how he affected her.

"Will you take me out?" she asked. "Tonight?"

"Out?" His brow furrowed. "Where?"

"Anywhere." Excitement gathered inside of her at the prospect of being let loose in the city with him at her side. A night out with Jenner would surely prove to be more of an adventure than geocaching. "Are you working? I could come along. I'll stay out of the way."

"I'm not working tonight," Jenner replied. "Mikhail has tasks set out for me, though."

"Oh." Bria fought to keep her expression passive, but the air soured with his words. *A lie?* "What are you doing? I could help."

"No." Jenner's harsh voice cut through the quiet like a blade. "That's not a good idea."

"That's fine." Bria was quick to mask her disappointment. "I've never really seen the city, that's all." She risked another lie. Her occasional jaunts into the city had been her own private secret for decades. She wasn't ready to share that part of her with Jenner. Not when he insisted on treating their relationship as though it were nothing more than a casual acquaintance. "I thought it might be fun."

The crease cut deeper into Jenner's brow. "You've never seen the city?" he asked. "At all?"

"Not for more than a quick glance. And never alone. Like I said, my uncle is very protective."

"Why?"

Jenner's intensity should have frightened her, but it instead caused a rush of excitement to race through her veins. She didn't want to admit to Jenner that a vindictive witch stalked her. Maybe he wouldn't want to bother with a mate who needed constant looking after. Not that Bria expected him to. She could take care of herself now. How could a witch possibly be a match for a vampire?

"Both my mother and father were killed," she said. "I was entrusted to his care and he takes my protection seriously. He loves me."

Jenner took a step toward her and delicious anticipation gathered in Bria's stomach. The world melted away when he looked at her with such singular focus. She wondered, was it the same for him? He stopped just short of the love seat when a loud knock came at the door.

"Yeah?" Jenner barked

Ronan's voice came through the wooden panels: "I need you for a sec."

"All right!" Jenner called back. His lips pursed as though he wanted to say something, but instead he turned to leave the room. "I won't be far if you need me," he said, as he closed the door behind him. "Just call."

So close and yet so far away. Bria gave a rueful laugh. Did Jenner realize how his very presence made her yearn for him as he left her with nothing but longing night after night? If so, he was a cruel male indeed.

"Jesus, you look like shit."

Jenner strode down the hallway beside Ronan. He was getting tired of everyone making the same observation about his appearance. Ronan's expression grew serious and the male stopped mere feet from the door that separated Jenner from Bria. Frustration and want pooled in his gut, creating an acid that ate away at him. She'd lied to him tonight. More than once. Bria was hiding something from him, and the need to uncover her secrets caused his stomach to churn and his blood to pump in his veins. She'd claimed to have spent the evening with Claire, but that wasn't true. She claimed her uncle protected her for no other reason than love, but Jenner had smelled that lie on her skin. She said she'd never seen the city, but that was a lie as well. Or, at the very least, a white lie. Her duplicity piqued his curiosity. The fact that she'd left the house the moment he'd been away proved her uncle had been right in assuming she'd need looking after. Jenner had told her he had duties for Mikhail tonight, but it was his job to watch over her. Protect her. Tonight he planned to do a little recon on his mate.

Jenner met Ronan's curious stare head-on. "She's fine," Jenner said with a sneer. "Fairchild's getting his money's worth."

It had been days since Jenner had first fed from her and he had proved that he could play nice despite the dark urges that reared their ugly heads whenever he was in the same room with her. Ronan didn't need to know that Jenner's control was tenuous, though. His every waking thought was of Bria. Keeping his distance from her slowly ate away at him. With each passing day he grew more disdainful of piercing the vein at her wrist. He played nice to honor the bargain struck between Ronan and Fairchild as well as to preserve what innocence she had left when all he wanted to do was defile her. Ronan knew everything about Jenner's history. His friend had every right to be concerned, and yet Jenner couldn't help but feel the sting of Ronan's suspicions. "Do you really still think I'd harm her?"

"No," Ronan said, and Jenner raised a dubious brow. "All right, maybe. We both know about your control issues. And you have to admit you've been off the rails for the past several months. I'm concerned, that's all."

Over the course of Jenner's transition, Ronan had gotten a glimpse of the monster even the vampires had feared. His unchecked need was a living, breathing creature that writhed beneath the surface of his skin, desperate to get out. For months Jenner had fucked and fed from every eager female from one end of the city to the next in an effort to appease that dark need inside of him. He hadn't harmed a single one of them. He'd yet to drink any dhampir—or even Bria—dry. In fact, he'd left most of his blood donors begging for more. Did that not show some measure of control?

"My shit's tight," he growled. It wasn't too far from the truth. He still fought the urge to barge back into the guest room and strip Bria bare, to bury his fangs deep into her soft skin. But despite those urges, his thirst no longer burned in his throat. For the first time in months, one of his cravings seemed to be under control.

"Good," Ronan remarked. "Because Thomas Fairchild has requested a meeting with us as well as an audience with Mikhail. He'll be here tomorrow after sundown."

Great. "Why?"

"I assume he wants to kill two birds with one stone. You have to admit our arrangement with him has become complicated since Bria's transition. We're not simply hired to protect her anymore. She's sort of a member of the secret club, know what I mean? Aside from our deal with Fairchild, Mikhail thinks he's genuinely concerned for his niece, but you and I both know that Fairchild is a tough male to gauge. I guess Bria's been dodging his phone calls? Apparently it's given him cause for alarm. He probably wants a status update."

Ronan posed the question about Bria dodging her uncle's calls as though Jenner should know why Bria distanced herself from him. In truth, Jenner kept their interaction to a minimum. The more he knew about her, the more interested he became, and his interest only served to further ignite his attraction. The intensity of that attraction was a threat to his carefully maintained control and Jenner couldn't afford to slip.

Ronan wasn't the only one who didn't fully trust Thomas Fairchild. Bria was wary of her uncle and her claim that he was overprotective caused Jenner's hackles to rise. He'd hired them to follow her, protect her, take out her alleged stalker. Was that all there was to it? "Mikhail told him about the tether?"

Ronan nodded.

Super.

"The members of his coven are recluses. Some say as fanatical as Siobhan's coven. If he knows about the tether, I'd assume he's probably pissed."

"I don't know why he would be." Ronan continued down the hallway and Jenner fell into step beside him. "I mean, he might ask for a refund since you're technically his family now, but it's not like you knocked his niece up at the prom or some shit. You're tethered. It's as much a part of our biology as drinking blood."

Part of the family? Jenner snorted. He doubted an entitled male like Fairchild would ever lower himself to allow someone like Jenner into his coven. "That might've been true a few centuries ago," Jenner said. "I'd say there's a bit of a disconnect between our world and theirs, wouldn't you? What if her uncle doesn't buy it?"

Ronan shrugged. "Doesn't change anything. Fairchild will just have to accept it. Besides, he's sworn fealty to Mikhail. If he says you're tethered, you're tethered. Fairchild can't dispute a royal mandate."

Jenner wasn't so sure. "What bought Mikhail Fairchild's allegiance?"

"His niece's life," Ronan said with a smirk. "He begged Mikhail to turn her. Offered him everything he had in return."

Exactly. It had been an offer made out of desperation, which made his allegiance dubious. The tether that bound him to Bria tugged from the center of Jenner's being and his step faltered. Ronan gave him a sidelong glance. "Thank gods you've been tethered." Ronan continued down the stairs and Jenner followed. "That female is going to be your salvation, my friend."

Right now he felt anything but saved.

The tether gave another tug and Jenner stopped dead in his tracks. Ronan turned to look back at him, his brow raised in question.

"Tell Mikhail I'll be here at sundown tomorrow to meet with Fairchild."

"Can't you tell him yourself?"

A sense of urgency expanded Jenner's chest and he let out a gust of breath. His mate was up to something and he was going to get to the bottom of what it was.

"Gotta deal with something right now."

"All right," Ronan said slowly. "Anything you need help with?"

"Nah. I've got this." The urge to sprint back down the hall to Bria's room consumed him. "I'll see you tomorrow night."

Ronan's brow furrowed. "Call me if you need anything, okay?"

Jenner paused in the foyer as though he was headed out the door. "Yeah. Sure."

Ronan hung a left and headed toward Mikhail's study. As soon as he rounded the corner, Jenner flew back up the stairs and down the hallway. He threw open the door to find Bria's room empty.

"Gods-damn it," he said under his breath.

Bria was certainly full of surprises.

CHAPTER
6

Bria wondered if Mikhail realized how easy his security system was to circumvent. Of course, it's not like the king was trying to keep anyone in, just the slayers out. Once outside the perimeter of the fenced property, Bria paused to check her bag. With tonight's treasure safely stowed away and no one to miss her she should have felt a sense of elation.

Instead, loneliness weighed Bria down.

She'd never felt it as acutely as she did now. Her transition had brought her freedom from the oppression of her coven, but in exchange for that freedom she'd found herself tethered to a male who seemed to want nothing to do with her.

That wasn't entirely true, though, was it?

She'd sensed Jenner's desire. Smelled the rich, musky scent of it each and every time he took her vein. Whatever mystical force that bound them pulled taut whenever he walked into the room and the tension remained until they'd both sated their thirsts and he left her to spend the day far away from her once again. Jenner was an enigma.

Bria had never met a male like him. She was bound and determined to push his buttons until she discovered what made him tick.

Bria strapped her pack to her back and took off at a slow jog. It had been tough to get used to her new vampiric speed the first couple of times she'd snuck out of the house, but now she had the necessary control to keep her pace to what would be considered quick for a human. Bria hopped up onto a tall stone pier that marked the entrance to a gated driveway a few miles from Mikhail's property. The maneuver would have taken considerable effort before, but now she could easily leap thirty feet or more without even exerting herself.

Bria was drunk on her own power and strength. Not even the most adept traceur could compete with her now. She was a parkour *ninja!* Her flow state was supreme. There wasn't an obstacle she couldn't hurdle or flip over. She could practically leap tall buildings in a single bound. Hell, Spider-Man had nothing on her now. An elated, "Whoop!" escaped her lips and Bria laughed long and loud. With every passing day she thanked the gods that the slayer's blade had pierced her throat. She'd never felt so—

Bria spun in a blur to her left. Something tugged from the center of her chest and giddy anticipation surged within her. It was the same sensation that stole over her when Jenner was near. She usually felt that way moments before he knocked on her door and strode into the room. Bria turned again, this time sensing a presence to her right. She let out a shaky breath and rubbed at her chest. The only sounds to fill her ears were those of cars in the distance and insects as they buzzed nearby. Through the darkness, her keen eyesight found nothing out of the ordinary. No movement to betray watching eyes or a body about to pounce.

Perhaps all of that power had gone to her head.

She hopped down from the pier and landed with barely a sound. Rather than allow her hypersensitive senses to distract her, Bria turned her attention to the task at hand. She'd never hidden a treasure in a place like this before. She wouldn't want to place the canister anywhere it might get someone into trouble. While she searched for an appropriate spot to log her GPS coordinates, Bria ran alongside the paved road. She concentrated on fluid movements as she jumped into the air and twisted before landing on her feet. She dove and tucked into a roll before propelling herself upright without a break in her stride. She cartwheeled, flipped, and ran along the narrow ledge of a concrete wall before throwing herself into a front tuck and touching back down to the ground.

In the distance Bria caught sight of an enormous house tucked away in the trees. She doubted it would bother anyone if she left her canister at the base of the property, close to the road and as far from the actual residence as possible. She slowed to a walk, all the while marveling that her lungs didn't strain with each breath. Her heart hadn't even begun to race from her exertion. She might as well have been out for a pleasant walk, not running and throwing tricks up and down Mullholland.

Bria found a suitable spot for her cache and used her hands to dig a shallow hole in the dirt. She gathered several large rocks and set them beside the hole before she retrieved her pack from her back and pulled out the last canister she'd had with her and the few insignificant baubles that remained.

She peered over one shoulder. The sense that someone watched her hadn't gone away and a string of fear threaded through her rib cage. She'd never doubted her uncle's warnings that something evil hunted them even though she hadn't seen any proof of it. Did any of that matter now? Maybe she didn't have to be afraid anymore. Of anything or anyone. A witch might have had a mysterious vendetta against their family, but Bria was a vampire now. Powerful in her own right.

She was practically indestructible.

"Flown your cage, little bird?"

Bria dropped the canister on the ground. She turned whip quick toward the sound of the dark, rough voice that reached out to her through the darkness. Silver glinted in Jenner's eyes as he stepped from the shadows toward her. The invisible cord that tied them together gave a tug. He'd been following her and she'd stupidly ignored her own warning instincts.

Way to go, Bria. Stealthy, much?

"You shouldn't be out alone at night."

She cocked her head to one side and studied Jenner. Gods, he was a magnificent male. He was even more menacing, his body more imposing, when shadowed by darkness. She should have been angry that he'd followed her, but she could only muster a deep sense of appreciation. He'd known she lied about what she'd done the previous night. *Clever male.*

"I'm a vampire," she replied without guile. "Night is the only time I can be out."

Jenner scowled. Her humor was obviously lost on him. "Slayers are still attacking covens. Are you so anxious to meet their blades again?"

Jenner's anger snapped out at her through their tether. For someone who seemed not to want to have anything to do with her aside from feeding, he was certainly showing his overprotective side. Bria let out a huff of breath as she squatted down to retrieve her canister and the bracelet she'd dropped.

"I can take care of myself."

His dark laughter rippled over her, coaxing chills to the surface of Bria's skin. "You think so?"

She raised her chin defiantly. "Of course I do."

Jenner moved like the shadows that surrounded him. Fluid, fast, and silent. Before Bria registered that he'd shifted, he had her flat on her back and pinned to the ground. He captured both of her wrists in his large hands and secured them beside her. She struggled to free herself, to move even one small inch, but Jenner's strength held her immobile. He straddled her waist and she tried not to notice the heat that coiled low in her belly. His eyes glowed silver and the twin tips of his fangs glistened as he bared them and bent over her.

"Not so in control as you thought you were. You're trapped. Completely at my mercy. I could do whatever I wanted to you right now. I could drink you dry if the whim struck."

The dark timbre of his voice sent a trickle of fear into Bria's bloodstream. She sensed he wanted to do just that: sink his fangs into her flesh and drink until she had nothing more to give. He wanted to frighten her with his threats, but the gods help her, beneath that fear Bria felt a thick, hot wave of desire. "I'm not afraid of you, Jenner."

He leaned down so that his lips brushed the outer shell of her ear. "You should be."

Was it possible to burst into flames from unfulfilled want? Jenner was dangerous. Dark and violent. Since the day they'd met he seemed to balance on the razor's edge of his control.

And Bria wanted him more than she'd ever wanted anything in her entire life.

Jenner blew out a frustrated breath. The scent of Bria's arousal wafted around him, more fragrant and intoxicating than any perfume. He'd followed her from Mikhail's house, and for the past hour she'd held his attention unlike anything or anyone else ever had. Without even knowing, she'd put on a show for him with her acrobatic maneuvers and her graceful stride as she ran. She'd given herself over to the moment with an abandon that Jenner knew all too well. But where Jenner's abandon was typically reckless, Bria's was somehow practiced. Like a bird in flight.

Gods. He still couldn't believe that the female pinned beneath his thighs had tethered him. He'd thought her delicate. Breakable. Tissue paper entrusted to his bullish care. And while Bria was still an innocent, still naïve and too overconfident for her own good, there was strength in her that Jenner couldn't help but admire. She was extraordinary.

And he wanted her so badly he didn't think he could take another breath without her.

"What are you doing out here, Bria?" She'd dressed in a black sweatshirt with her black leggings that were more like a second skin than a pair of pants. A low growl rose in his throat as he thought of the soft curves of her ass on display for anyone to see. He wanted to peel the fabric away and explore that soft skin himself. She'd dug a long metal canister out of her backpack and been about to stow something inside of it when he'd confronted her. Was she sending messages to someone that she didn't want Mikhail—or maybe even him—to know about? Perhaps she sent secret messages to the male who'd fed her upon her transition. Jenner's grip on her wrists tightened. He'd kill the fucker if he came within a mile of her again.

Mine. Minemineminemineminemine.

The way Jenner coveted Bria bordered on fanatic. They'd only been tethered for a few days and already she occupied his every waking thought. There was no need for Fairchild to pay him to watch over his niece. Jenner was more than willing to be her shadow for free.

Her amethyst eyes sparked with defiant silver and Jenner bent over her until her gentle breaths brushed his face. "Answer me, Bria. What are you doing out here?"

She bucked her chin up and met him look for angry look. "Geocaching."

Geo-whatting? Jenner straightened. He released his hold on her wrists but kept her pinned between his thighs. "You're sending messages? Who to?"

Bria's brow furrowed. "I'm not sending messages to anyone."

"Then what's in the container?"

Bria sighed. Jenner didn't appreciate the long-suffering sound, as though she couldn't be bothered to deal with someone with such a low level of intelligence. As a coven master, Thomas Fairchild was an aristocrat of the dhampir social structure. Jenner was afforded a glimpse of that aristocratic air in Bria now and it did nothing to cool his quickly mounting temper.

She opened her right hand and raised her palm for Jenner's inspection. A delicate silver and turquoise bracelet rested against her creamy skin. "I'm leaving treasures." Her bashful tone caused Jenner's gut to churn. "A geocache is a container that you hide somewhere for someone else to find. You log the GPS coordinates and leave them on a message board. Some geocaches just have logbooks that you sign when you find them and you leave the canister there for the next geocacher to find. Some people leave treasures in their canisters. I think it's more fun that way."

This was why she'd snuck out night after night. A game had caused all of her uncle's worry. "Treasure hunting?"

She glanced away. "Yes."

A smile tugged at Jenner's lips. "You're like a pirate, then?"

Bria's gaze reluctantly met his. Her own lips curled at the corners and Jenner's heart stuttered in his chest. Gods, she was beautiful. "I don't pillage or plunder."

Jenner bent over her, if only to fill his lungs with her delicious scent. "Doesn't mean you wouldn't if you had the chance."

Her smile grew. Who needed to see the sun when he beheld something a million times more brilliant? "Maybe."

"How long have you been doing this?"

"A while," Bria said with a shrug. "Ten or twelve years."

A while indeed. Much longer than the few months her uncle assumed she'd been going out. "Who else knows that you go out at night, seeking and abandoning treasure?" He wasn't ready to reveal to her that her uncle had caught on to her little field trips.

Her voice dropped to a whisper. "No one. Only you."

Only him. He'd been the first to take her vein. The first to be deemed worthy to know one of her secrets. Would he be the first to claim her body as well? A hot wave of lust crested over Jenner and he sucked in a sharp breath. He could have her. Now. He could strip her flimsy excuse for pants from her thighs and fuck her right here on the side of the road like the animal he was. He could slake his desire for Bria here and now. Jenner had never been afraid to take what he wanted. Why should this moment— this female—be different from any other?

Because you know if you allow yourself to have her you'll lose all control and become the monster everyone feared you'd be.

"I know you want me, Jenner," Bria said in a breathy tone. "Why don't you do something about it?"

Gods the way she talked. Brazen, despite her innocence. Jenner ran his nose along the column of her throat. Bria let out a shuddering breath that Jenner swore he felt vibrate at the base of his sac. "Is that what you want, Bria? For me to ram my cock into your tight, virginal pussy right here and now? You think it's a good idea to tempt me with your beautiful body and heady scent, but I warn you, if I take you now, I won't be gentle. I'll fuck you good and hard. Is that what you want?" A hungry growl built in his chest. "Answer me."

Her scent soured with a hint of fear. *Good.* She might have claimed not to be afraid of him, but she didn't have a gods-damned clue what sort of male he was. Jenner fucked for pleasure. *His.* He took Bria's vein because it pleased him to do so and the taste of her blood had no equal. He was a selfish son of a bitch and that would never change whether his soul was intact or not. If he took her like she dared him to, she'd hate him. Would never be able to bear the sight of him again. If he took her like she dared him to he'd hate himself because he would surely destroy her.

"No," she said so quietly he had to strain to hear her.

His heart clenched in his chest and he wished he could take back the words. He pushed her away for her own protection, though. When she realized how far beneath her station he was—how utterly out of control—she'd regret being tethered to him. And her regret—her disdain—would break him.

"But I also think you're nothing more than a lot of talk."

Jenner's temper flared. *Insufferable female.* He bared his fangs as he met her gaze. "Would you care to test me?" He plucked at the thin fabric of her leggings. He could tear them as easily as rending paper. "I don't even have to take these off of you to get to what I want."

Bria's jaw took a stubborn set. "Do your worst, Jenner. I'm not worried."

He pushed himself off of her in a flash. His heart hammered in his rib cage, his breath heaved in his chest, and his cock was so gods-damned hard it caused him pain. She pushed Jenner to the very edge of his control and he held his balance just barely.

"Hide your treasure!" he barked from between gritted teeth. "And be quick about it, because I'm taking you back to Mikhail's."

Another heated word from Bria and he'd do every vile thing he'd promised her and more. He needed to get away from her. Before he did something he'd surely regret.

CHAPTER
7

"You've got to be one of the *un*luckiest bastards I've ever met, Whalen."

Christian should have known better than to use a bookie who was also a demon. Supernatural henchmen were a hell of a lot tougher to shake than human thugs. Not to mention more violent. Cars on the street below resembled Matchbox toys as he dangled over them. They wouldn't seem so small when his dome crashed through one of the hoods, though.

"I've had a kink in my back for a month," Christian remarked. "Hanging upside down is doing wonders. I should have gotten a hold of you guys a long time ago."

"Shut the fuck up, asshole." Demons never did appreciate snark. "You're thirty grand deep and Marac wants his money. No more excuses."

Christian made a show of patting his pockets as he dangled from the high rise, held tight by the ankles. So clichéd. "You know, I think I left the cash in my other pants. Why don't we go back to my room and check? Minibar's stocked."

One of the henchmen let go of one of Christian's ankles and his heart lodged somewhere in his esophagus. Supernatural resilience aside, he doubted he'd survive a fall from thirty stories. "I can get it to you by the end of next week." He had ten grand on an MMA fight scheduled for next week and it was a sure thing. Payout was five-to-one and he'd be flush.

"If Marac's gotta wait that long, it'll be forty grand."

Of course it would. Fucking bastard. "Fine. Forty grand. By the end of next week."

The demon still holding Christian's ankle hauled him up as though he weighed nothing more than a bag of sugar and deposited him on the asphalt roof. He stumbled as all of the blood drained from his brain and he tried to stand. His head pounded like a motherfucker and his vision blurred as his world righted itself.

"If you don't have Marac's money the next time we come to find your sorry ass, you can bet we won't be dangling you off of a building, Whalen."

No. The next time, they'd take their payment in blood.

"I'll have it." Christian dusted off his slacks and straightened the cuffs of his shirt. "Tell Marac not to get his shorts in a wad."

"Don't think about leaving town, either, asshole. Because we'll find your sorry ass."

Before he could respond, the pair of demons evaporated in a cloud of sulfuric smoke. *Creepy sons of bitches.* Christian listed to the side, his equilibrium still off, as he left the hotel roof and ventured back to his room on the fifteenth floor. McAlister and the Sortiari's bottomless expense account was footing the bill for the spacious suite, but Christian wasn't sure how long it would be before the director threw him out on his ass. There was always another job in another city. The Sortiari had their hands in everything. He didn't mind bouncing around; it kept loan sharks and bookies off his back. He wouldn't be able to dodge the demon, though. Christian's blood was on the money he'd put down on the Blackhawks' play-off game against Pittsburgh. Demons could find anyone, anywhere if they had your blood.

Fuck.

Gregor had gone to McAlister like he'd promised, which had put some cash in Christian's pocket. Not enough to get himself out of the hole he'd dug, though. The berserkers had yet to come to an agreement with the Sortiari, and for that reason McAlister kept Christian in the city. Rat bastard demon bookies aside, Christian didn't mind his extended stay in Los Angeles. Especially since his new favorite pastime had become stalking a certain sexy dhampir.

Siobhan.

Even her name exuded sex. He hadn't wasted any time learning as much as he could about the feral dhampir. Christian was obsessed with the female beyond her relationship with the vampire he'd been tracking. He didn't need to keep tabs on either of them anymore. Not since he'd managed to find Gregor. Still, Christian went out night after night, making the rounds at clubs he knew she frequented in the hopes of getting a glimpse of her. Neither of them even pretended to be unaware of the other anymore. It was a game. Cat and mouse. Christian the voyeur and Siobhan the exhibitionist, ready to perform for him.

The tension that sparked between them only made him want her more.

When he got to his room Christian searched his pocket for the key card. *Motherfucker.* The damn thing was in the room. Through the door his cell phone rang, and he knocked his head against the heavy door. What a monumentally fucked-up night. He'd be damned if he let it go completely to shit, though. He needed a night off. From his life, his debts, his gods-damned obligations. When the Sortiari paid your bills, however, there wasn't such a thing as a day off. He'd have to get a new key from the front desk so he could grab his phone. Then he'd go looking for a little distraction.

Onyx had just started to heat up for the night. The laid-back atmosphere of the club, a preferred hangout for supernaturals, put Christian at ease. No pretense, no hiding. No humans. Christian bellied up to the bar and ordered a bourbon, straight up. Until he scraped together the cash to pay Marac off, the top-shelf liquor was off-limits. He sipped from the glass and wrinkled his nose. This piss wasn't going to go down very smooth, but it'd sure as hell get him drunk.

Christian had swallowed down his third drink of the night when the scent of jasmine hit his nostrils. He spun in his seat, his eyes darting from one end of the club to the other. Through the press of bodies he spotted her, living, breathing sin wrapped in black leather and green satin. The miniskirt hugging the curves of her ass was damn near indecent. He hadn't seen her in anything like that before. Siobhan usually opted for a pair of tight pants, and though they covered her shapely legs, they were no less revealing. She'd never struck him as a miniskirt sort of female, but Christian approved.

Their eyes locked and a sly smile curved her bright red lips. She'd brought an entourage with her tonight. Several dhampirs whom Christian often saw her with—probably members of her coven. He checked for any sign of the big-ass vampire who'd been tailing her. *Huh.* The scary bastard was nowhere to be seen. Christian's lip stretched in a sneer, however, as his gaze lit on a male who never seemed to be far from Siobhan's side. He suspected that the dhampir who was stuck to her like glue was more than a casual acquaintance. Christian's wolf rose to the surface of his psyche, itching for a fight. The females didn't belong to them, though. Their relationship with Siobhan was strictly look, but don't touch.

Christian ordered another drink and settled his back against the bar. They'd been playing this game for a while now. He suspected that she went out night after night simply to be seen. Not that he minded. Watching the dhampir had become more fun than a trip to the race-track. He didn't even lose any money in the process.

Her emerald green eyes met his and Christian did nothing to avert his gaze. Her tongue played with the tip of one dainty fang and he swallowed down the groan that rose in his throat. She never drank when she went out. Didn't snort anything or pop pills. She never let her guard down. Siobhan was always in control. Everything she did appeared carefully calculated. Christian wanted to be the one who tipped her over the edge of that control. To be the first to show her how perfect abandon could be.

Siobhan pulled the male close and Christian's gut twisted like a damned pretzel. Her eyes stayed glued to his as she hopped up on a high stool and spread her legs, giving Christian a fleeting glimpse of her black lace underwear before the dhampir settled between her thighs. She got off on being watched, and for now Christian was more than happy to give her what she wanted.

She swept the length of her dark hair aside and the male lowered his mouth to the junction between her shoulder and neck. When the male bit down, Christian swore he could feel her flesh give way under his own teeth. His wolf surged to the surface once more with a predatory growl. The dhampir lingered at Siobhan's vein for far too long, and when he pulled away bright crimson stained her creamy porcelain flesh. Christian's nostrils flared. The scent of her blood carried to him. Drinking blood wasn't exactly his thing, but if she asked him to he'd bury his canines into that flawless, soft skin.

Her lids became hooded as the male reached between her legs and Christian locked his body down even though it wanted to shoot up off the stool. She didn't close her eyes, didn't look away. Jealousy burned through Christian's veins as he watched that fucker fondle her for anyone to see. Her lips parted and her head rolled back on one shoulder as she took her pleasure. All the while, her eyes never left Christian's.

She was playing with him. Taunting him. And he didn't like it one fucking bit.

Oh, who in the hell are you kidding? She's got you right where she wants you and you love *it.*

He was mesmerized by the sight of her. Cheeks flushed with passion, irises rimmed with silver. Her luscious mouth, parted and inviting. A sensual smile curved Siobhan's lips, revealing the sharp points of her fangs. She reached up and pulled the male's shirt to one side. Her tongue flicked out at his skin and Christian sucked in a sharp breath. His cock was as hard as marble in his jeans, and when she bit down and sealed her mouth over the male's neck he thought he'd come just from the sight of her.

She fed from the male in a soft, languorous way that lent a sensuality to the act. Christian downed his bourbon and slammed the glass back down on the bar before scrubbing a palm over his face. He didn't know how much more of this he could take. Her lids fluttered and her hand came around to grip the back of the male's neck. Christian noted the way her body grew taut and the slight tremor that rocked her body. The male might have given her the orgasm, but she'd come for Christian alone.

Gods, her sway over him was more powerful than the moon's.

His wolf snarled and scratched in Christian's mind,

enraged that another male would claim something that
belonged to them. *Dumb fucking animal.* His wolf had
laid claim to something that abso-fucking-lutely did *not*
belong to them. Nothing good would come of this—

Christian's cell buzzed in his pocket and he almost said
a silent prayer of thanks for whoever had the shitty
timing to interrupt his enjoyment of Siobhan's performance. He dug the phone out of his pocket and glanced
down at the text message: **Meet me at Rock and Reilly's
in West Hollywood. Twenty minutes. Come alone and
don't be late. —Gregor**

Yup. Shitty timing. But Christian needed to get the hell
out of there before he did something he'd regret.

The trendy Irish pub seemed a little boisterous for the
brooding berserker. At any rate, Christian might get a
Guinness out of the deal. He slid down from the bar stool
and headed for the exit, amazed he could walk considering the wood he was sporting. From the corner of his eye
he caught Siobhan watching him. Her dark brows drew
down sharply over her eyes and her lips thinned. He
should have ignored her. Put an end to whatever this was
between them right then and there. But Christian had
never had an ounce of gods-damned sense.

His eyes locked with hers and he mouthed the word
Magnificent. Her expression softened and her lips parted,
the only outward show that she was pleased with his
reaction. This would happen again. And again. The game
would continue until he couldn't bear to keep his distance
any longer. What then? Whatever this was between them
would play itself out or it would combust.

Either way, Christian was as good as fucked.

Siobhan was the ultimate gamble. And he was enough
of an addict to know that once with her would never be
enough.

CHAPTER
8

After taking Bria back to the house, Jenner spent the remainder of his night in agony. His thirst blazed, his cock
remained as stiff as a fucking steel rod, and his want of
Bria intensified with every minute spent away from her.
He left her in Claire's care and wandered the club district.
He hit Onyx, The Dragon's Den, and Ultra in the hopes
of finding a female whose body might tempt him away
from Bria, whose blood tasted sweeter than hers. But all
Jenner realized when the horizon showed the first signs
of sunrise was that Bria had no equal. No other creature
could compare. No other female had tethered his soul. No
other had such absolute sway over him.

He wandered into Mikhail's house and fell into bed in
the room next to hers moments before the sun rose. The
crisp, clean sheets on his bed smelled of fabric softener
and not the scent he longed for. The perfume of Bria's
arousal in the face of his crudeness earlier in the night had
burned itself into Jenner's memory. And it only made
him want her more. As the exhaustion of daytime sleep
weighed him down he laid the flat of his palm on the wall

behind him in the hopes of feeling the gentle brush of her presence along his senses. The tether tugged at the center of his chest and Jenner let out a deep breath. That small reassurance was enough. For now.

Not even in the void of daytime sleep could Jenner find respite. Instead, he was plagued with dreams of Bria. Her sweet voice, glittering amethyst eyes, and full pink lips haunted him. In his dreams, she ran from him, always just outside his reach. Graceful, quick, her movements precise, Jenner watched in appreciation as she dodged a wide sweep of his arms before her giddy laughter rang out around him. His throat raged with dry fire. His body burned with want. In his dreams, he latched on to her throat, ripped open her vein, and glutted himself on the sweet nectar of her blood until Bria's body went limp in his arms and the light left her glittering eyes.

When he woke at sunset tremors rocked Jenner's body. His balls were too tight and his cock stood out straight from his hips as though taunting him. A cold shower cooled his lusts a small amount, but Jenner knew the relief would be short-lived. His thirst still raged, as did the knowledge that even in his dreams he couldn't trust himself with Bria. Rather than exile his family centuries ago, their lord should have run a stake through Jenner's heart. At least then Bria would have been safe. At least from one of the monsters who wanted her.

Jenner groaned as he buttoned his jeans and pulled on his boots. Thomas Fairchild would be there by now and he needed to get his shit together, ASAP. *Gods.* Another night of being close enough to touch his mate. Another night of torture as he fed from the vein at her wrist and not her throat as he wanted to. Another night of fighting the urge to only take what he needed and not a fucking drop more. Jenner had hoped he'd find salvation in his tether. But he was beginning to realize that it would surely destroy him.

He spent the trek from his room down the stairs to Mikhail's study self-coaching himself to remain detached. He couldn't let Bria get under his skin. Couldn't let her know how deeply she affected him. The gods only knew how much her uncle had said to her already tonight. If the male was as elitist as Jenner suspected he was it wouldn't take much for him to convince Bria to leave Mikhail's protection and return to her coven. He might have already convinced her that, tethered or not, Jenner wasn't even close to being good enough for her.

He knew it wasn't fair to covet her. To keep her here as though she had no other choice while holding her at arm's length. But until Jenner could get his head on straight that's how it was going to be. He'd be damned if another male—especially the dhampir who'd fed her— ever tried to claim her. Bria belonged to *him*.

Jenner walked into Mikhail's study already wound so tight, he wasn't sure he'd get through the night without springing into the stratosphere. Claire sat in one of the chairs on the other side of the desk, the two of them deep in conversation. They'd always seemed to have a rapport. As though they'd known each other for a lifetime. Jenner didn't feel any such connection with Bria. He wanted her. Craved her blood. Her scent nearly drove him mad with desire. All physical responses triggered by their tether. Would that be all they'd ever share?

Jenner stiffened as Mikhail's gaze met his. Claire turned as well, a self-satisfied smile curving her lips. "So . . . how's it going?"

"Fine." He wasn't interested in talking about Bria—or his tether—with anyone. Fairchild obviously hadn't shown up yet and Jenner used the opportunity to steer the focus away from anything or anyone who had anything to do with Bria. "I've put it off, but we need to talk about Siobhan, Mikhail. She's—"

"Thomas Fairchild should be here any second," Mikhail interrupted. "He expected to take Bria back to his coven days ago, so I can't say that he'll be pleased about what's happened."

Jenner didn't give a fuck all what Thomas Fairchild was or wasn't pleased about. "Oh yeah? What do you expect me to say to him about it?"

"Nothing," Mikhail replied. "What's done is done. The tether is absolute."

"Any idea why he wants her back so badly?" The tiny hairs on the back of Jenner's neck stood on end. They all knew that Fairchild was reclusive, not to mention secretive. He'd refused to let Bria offer her vein to any member of their coven and apparently rarely let her leave the safety of their compound. Hell, he'd hired Ronan to keep a constant eye on her. To kill whatever it was that threatened her. And now the male was on his way to fetch her. There were many secrets between Bria and her uncle; Jenner wanted to know what they were.

Mikhail hiked a shoulder.

"She's not leaving with him." Jenner folded his arms across his chest. "If she can't stay here, I'll take her to my place."

A wry smile tugged at Claire's lips. "Atta boy."

"Claire."

"What?" She threw a narrowed gaze Mikhail's way. "Even you have to admit the guy is shady. And Bria doesn't want to leave." Her voice dropped an octave. "Mikhail, she's never been away from her coven until he brought her here."

Not entirely true. Jenner knew at least one of her secrets and it was something he held close to his heart. But he was also certain that Bria snuck out on her "treasure hunts" because her uncle never let her far from his grasp. Jenner's lip curled and a growl rose in his throat.

"The way she made it sound, she was practically a prisoner," Claire remarked.

"Let's not jump to conclusions." Mikhail leaned back in his chair.

Mikhail didn't realize how close to the truth Claire had hit.

"Jump to what conclusions?" Ronan entered the study all cocky grin and confidence. Jenner averted his gaze. Yet another male who'd settled into his tether and was as happy as a pig in slop.

"That Thomas Fairchild was keeping Bria a prisoner," Claire said.

Ronan cut him a look and Jenner finally met his friend's gaze. They'd yet to fill Mikhail in on their first time meeting the coven master, but not because it was some big secret. Rather, since Bria's transition and tethering it had seemed a moot point. She was Jenner's to protect whether he'd been paid to or not. And there was no use getting Mikhail riled up over a witch who may or may not be a threat until there was reason to. Especially while Jenner still needed Bria safely under his roof. Perhaps tonight he'd get some answers.

"I'm with Mikhail on this one," Ronan replied. "Let's not jump to conclusions."

Jenner tried not to let his eyes bulge too far out of his head.

"Bria doesn't want to return to her coven," Jenner said from between clenched teeth. "That's proof enough for me."

"Let's try not to make any assumptions until after we've met with Fairchild," Mikhail suggested.

"Yeah," Ronan agreed. He flashed Jenner a shit-eating grin. "You know what happens when you assume, right?"

If the male weren't like a brother to him Jenner might have considered popping him in the face.

The doorbell rang, followed by Alex's voice as he let Thomas Fairchild into the house. One of the benefits of supernatural hearing, no one ever got the jump on you. Jenner locked his jaw down and his fangs dug into his bottom lip.

"Try to get a grip," Claire advised as she rose from her chair. "I'm going to go check on Bria and let her know her uncle is here. Play nice, boys."

A moment later Alex showed Thomas Fairchild into the study. Mikhail's human assistant looked a little nervous when his eyes met Jenner's and he tried to soften his expression. A second male entered the room behind Thomas, large for a dhampir, fair-haired, with light blue eyes. Jenner's nostrils flared as he breathed in deeply of Bria's honey and lilac scent. The male reeked of her. *Lucas?*

A feral snarl ripped from his throat as he took a step forward. Jenner was going to rip the fangs from the bastard's mouth.

"Hey, I thought you were level," Ronan said nervously from the corner of his mouth. "What the fuck?"

"That male"—Jenner stabbed his finger in the dhampir's direction—"is going to find himself without his fangs if he doesn't take his ass outta here. *Now.*"

Thomas Fairchild looked from Lucas to Jenner, shocked as recognition lit his expression. "Excuse me?"

"You heard me," Jenner said to Bria's uncle from between clenched teeth.

"Jenner." Mikhail's tone was a warning that Jenner couldn't heed.

He took another step forward, ready to throw the bastard out himself if he needed to. The doors to the study swung wide and Bria walked in. Her smile quickly faded as her eyes darted to Jenner. The blond bastard stepped in front of her and took her by the arm, angling his head to hers as he spoke low. "Bria, you might want to give us a second."

He dared to put his hands on Jenner's mate? Rage clouded his vision and his need for violence surpassed his need for blood. "If you care at all for the peace Mikhail is trying to forge, get him out of here," Jenner growled.

Because all hell was about to break loose.

Bria's jaw hung slack. An aura of violence surrounded Jenner and his eyes flashed brilliant silver as his gaze landed on the hand Lucas had wrapped around her arm. She knew little of vampire nature, but Bria surmised that a switch had been flipped in the massive male. Tension vibrated off of him to the point that she swore she felt it in her own chest.

"Lucas, let go of me."

She spoke low, but a whisper was as good as a shout in a room full of vampires. She kept her tone free of distress, her face impassive. After escorting her back to the house last night with a not-so-gentle order to not go out alone again, Jenner had all but dismissed her. Now, however, he seemed ready to rip into Lucas's throat.

"What are you talking about, Bria?" Lucas seemed more concerned for her welfare than the enormous vampire staring a hole through him. "Is everything okay?"

It wouldn't be if he didn't get his damned hand off of her. Jenner's brows were dark, sinister slashes over his silver-rimmed eyes. His lip curled back to reveal the wicked points of his fangs. Instead of backing away, Lucas drew Bria closer. And Jenner's nostrils flared.

Uh-oh.

Bria pulled free and crossed the room to where Jenner stood. Her fingers itched to reach out and touch him. To soothe him somehow. His scowl and the curve of his lip told her that he neither wanted nor needed her comfort. Disappointment wrung Bria's heart. She didn't understand this new life. Didn't know what to expect of her tether to the hulking male standing beside her. It wasn't fair that she'd been thrown into any of this. He professed not to want her, but that didn't stop Jenner from behaving as though she were somehow his property. Bria couldn't seem to escape captivity, no matter her situation.

"Uncle Thomas." She greeted him with a kiss on the cheek.

His eyes narrowed with suspicion, but he returned her affection with a gentle smile. "You look well, Bria." She wanted to laugh. Was he surprised that her transition hadn't made her into a monster? He turned to Mikhail. "From the sound of your tone when we spoke, Your Highness, I thought something grave had happened to her."

Mikhail bristled with the use of the formal title. He lowered his elbows to the rests of his chair and clasped his hands in front of him. "Please, sit."

Her uncle dropped into a nearby chair. A musky scent settled on the air, so bitter that she wrinkled her nose. Bria canted her head as she tried to make sense of it. With little over a week as a vampire under her belt, she still couldn't identify some of the new scents that filled her head.

"As you can well imagine, the reemergence of the vampire race has brought with it occurrences that have perhaps faded from the minds of dhampir-kind."

"What kinds of occurrences?" Lucas's demanding tone coaxed a growl from Jenner's chest and Bria cringed. "What in the hell is going on? You give him some cryptic message about Bria and now you're trying to smooth out some unknown situation beforehand for what reason?"

For the three-hundred-pound vampire currently glowering at you, you silly fool.

Lucas was strong. A dhampir worthy of respect and

fear. But in their present company he was nothing more than a lamb amongst lions. His arrogance was bound to spawn nothing but violence.

Mikhail cocked a brow as his silver gaze met Lucas's and even Bria felt the power contained in his level stare. "Bria has been tethered," he replied without preamble.

Thank gods. All of the drama building up to the announcement was about to drive her mad.

"Bullshit! I demand to know to whom." Lucas wasn't in the position to make demands. His ego was going to get him killed.

He rushed forward, but Jenner cut him off before he could reach her. In the blink of an eye Jenner had Lucas pinned against the far wall, his arm stretched across Lucas's throat. "To me," Jenner growled not an inch from his face.

"No," Lucas rasped. His expression was part fear and part disbelieving shock. His arms went slack beside him as he looked to Bria for confirmation. The hurt that glistened in his eyes sliced through her. "I don't believe it. This male is an animal." Lucas all but growled the words in Jenner's face. "What did you do to her, you bastard?"

"What's going on here?" Bria had hoped her uncle wouldn't intervene, but his notion of privilege wouldn't allow it. "For the love of the gods, let go of him!"

Jenner ignored her uncle and instead tightened his arm over Lucas's throat. He drew in a ragged breath, but Lucas didn't show an ounce of weakness in the wake of Jenner's storm. Lucas met Jenner look for look, his lip pulled back in an angry sneer. The blue of Lucas's eyes gave way to silver and Jenner snarled in response.

"Jenner!" Mikhail barked. "Let him go."

Jenner's nostrils flared. He continued to bare his fangs, all but ignoring the command. Tension thickened the air to the point that Bria felt it constrict around her. Silence stretched out to an uncomfortable pitch that prickled along her skin.

"Jenner," Ronan said low, "dial it down."

Jenner's gaze remained locked with Lucas's and he did nothing to release his hold. Bria stepped up and laid her hand on his arm. "Don't hurt him, Jenner. Let him go. Please." Jenner's eyes narrowed with anger, but slowly he released his hold. Bria let out the breath she held in her lungs and her body relaxed with a shudder. Jenner was a violent male. Quick to temper. And whereas his display should have frightened Bria, it quickened the blood in her veins.

Mikhail pinned Jenner with an icy stare intended to wither him where he stood. Instead, Jenner took a step back from Lucas and folded his arms across his massive chest as though they exchanged polite conversation.

Bria's uncle turned to her, his expression pinched. "Bria, is it true? Has this male tethered you?"

Her gaze darted to Lucas, who watched her, rapt. "Yes," she said on a breath. "It's true."

The grief on her uncle's face knocked the air from Bria's lungs. She'd never seen him look so utterly destroyed, and she wondered at his reaction.

"I see now," he said with sadness, "that I have made a great many mistakes over the course of the past week. I shouldn't have brought you here."

"Let's all try to calm down." Ronan, it seemed, had adopted the role of diplomat. Mikhail scowled at her uncle's words and a low growl gathered in Jenner's throat. Only Ronan seemed interested in keeping the peace. "This isn't the big disaster everyone is making it out to be."

Jenner snorted and Ronan cocked a sardonic brow.

"Surely you knew this could be a possibility, Thomas,"

Mikhail remarked. "Fate has a way of righting itself once misaligned."

"So my niece's near death, her forced transition, and tethering are all a part of some greater plan?" her uncle asked. "You'll forgive me, Mikhail, if I don't subscribe to your notions of fate."

"It's a lie," Lucas interjected. "I refuse to believe it's true."

Jenner bared his fangs once again. "She's *mine*." His grating tone would have terrified death itself. "And if I smell her scent on you again, I'll take your head from your shoulders, dhampir."

So much posturing. Bria didn't think she could take much more of it.

"Whether or not you accept it, Thomas, it has happened," Mikhail continued. "The tether is absolute. And as you can see, a mated male is . . . temperamental."

Her uncle gave a disdainful snort. "Do not think to educate me on the temperament of a mated male, Mikhail. I know far too well the sort of havoc a tether can reap."

Bria cast a questioning look at her uncle. This was the first time in her life she'd heard him talk of tethers. Bria's mother had been turned by her father and both had died when Bria was just an infant. The bitterness in her uncle's words betrayed his emotions. For the first time since her transition, Bria wished she could better manipulate the Collective. To get a glimpse of her parents through their memories might have shed light on so many questions that her uncle had refused to answer.

Ronan and Mikhail shared a questioning look but said nothing. Jenner hadn't seemed to have heard or didn't care what her uncle had to say. He kept his attention focused on Lucas, who in turn chose to center his attention on Bria.

Foolish males!

"I'd like to speak to Jenner. Alone," her uncle said after a moment.

"That's not a good idea," Mikhail responded.

"I trust he's not so much of an animal as to attack his mate's own family," Thomas replied coolly. "As her only living relative, I think it's my right to have a word with the male who has tethered her."

Bria wanted to roll her eyes. You would have thought they still lived in the nineteenth century, the way her uncle behaved. So proper and civil. She wasn't property to exchange hands, for the gods' sake! There was nothing for him to discuss with Jenner. Bria's life belonged to herself no matter who or what had anchored her soul. That Mikhail would even entertain her uncle's request kindled her indignation.

"Jenner?" Mikhail deferred to him to decide. *Ugh.* Bria doubted this would end well.

"Sure," Jenner said with an unconcerned shrug of one shoulder. His eyes slid to her uncle's for a brief moment. "I promise not to bite."

CHAPTER
9

Bria followed Mikhail and the others out of the study and cast a nervous glance Jenner's way, but he refused to acknowledge her. Wouldn't offer her any reassurances. She'd protected the dhampir. Pleaded with Jenner to not hurt Lucas. Though had she not, Jenner might have been tempted to tear out the male's throat whether Mikhail had wanted him to back off or not. Lucas wanted Bria. He reeked with desire for her. The scent of her skin clung to him even though it had been days since he'd fed her post-transition. Jenner might not have known her for as long as the other male had, but she belonged to *him*. In Mikhail's own words, the tether was absolute. Any male who tried to take her from Jenner would meet a violent and bloody end.

"What sort of game are you playing at?" Fairchild asked the moment they were alone. "I've already paid your employer a mint for his services. Services I've yet to collect on thanks to this recent turn of events. Do you seek to fleece me by insisting that you've somehow tethered Bria?"

Fairchild didn't mince words. Jenner had to give him props for that. "See, your first mistake is in assuming that I need a red fucking cent from you," he sneered. "Your second is by thinking I give a single shit about how you feel about my tether with Bria."

"I'm her only family," Fairchild replied stiffly.

"Not anymore," Jenner growled.

Fairchild pursed his lips as he studied Jenner for a silent moment. His eyes narrowed and his mouth quirked with amusement. He possessed the same quiet calm as his niece. "You were a member of Siobhan's coven. An enforcer, if I'm not mistaken."

"I was."

"And now you serve the king?"

"I do."

Thomas regarded Jenner with a shrewd gaze that made him feel as though every particle that constructed him was being individually examined. "I've often found that a male of few words is also a male of action. Would you agree?"

To break it down, he shared the common opinion that Jenner was nothing more than a mindless brute. *Join the club, buddy.* He could think whatever the hell he wanted. Jenner didn't owe him a gods-damned thing. "Perhaps a male of few words is simply wise enough to think before he speaks."

Thomas chuckled. "True. Did you know that Bria had never known a single vampire—was too young to even know her own parents—before her turning?"

That didn't surprise Jenner. Mikhail had been the sole vampire inhabiting the planet for two centuries. There were only a handful of dhampirs in the world old enough to have known a true vampire. The rest were orphaned offspring, like Bria, left to fend for themselves.

"The notion of a tether is as foreign to her as is her own vampiric nature. Your souls are tied and now you think that gives you ownership of her. That you can drink from her and rut upon her as you wish?"

Jenner growled. He knew dick about Thomas Fairchild, but his second impression wasn't any better than his first. Obviously, he was concerned for his niece's welfare. That didn't mean Jenner appreciated Fairchild making assumptions about the sort of male Jenner might be. The way Fairchild spoke of Bria, as though she were nothing more than a possession—something for Jenner to use at his leisure—rankled. "You know fuck all about me," Jenner snapped. "Or what I think." He didn't owe the bastard anything, least of all an explanation.

"How do we know that this tether isn't a lie constructed to keep Bria here?"

Seriously? Bria's uncle wasn't just secretive. The suspicious son of a bitch had a serious hard-on for conspiracies. Jenner hiked a shoulder. "Bria confirmed it. Ask her again if you doubt it."

"I'll speak with my niece soon enough. Lucas is unhappy, and with reason. He expected me to promise Bria to him."

A surge of anger crested inside of Jenner. Fairchild accused him of seeing Bria as a possession when he was the one who'd planned to give her away. Jenner's lip curled as he leaned in close. "Life is full of disappointments. I suggest you tell Lucas to suck it up and get used to it."

"Mikhail Aristov saved my niece's life and I'm grateful for it," Thomas said. "But that does not mean that I don't hold him responsible for the slayer attacks on my and every other coven in the city."

Harsh words from someone who'd sworn fealty to Mikhail. It amazed Jenner how easy Thomas found it to condemn Mikhail for the attacks on his coven, yet he did nothing to acknowledge the fact that without him they would have died out centuries ago.

"What you think is irrelevant. Be glad Mikhail doesn't have a choice in nourishing your kind. His strength is yours. And now"—Jenner flashed a feral grin—"my strength is yours. *Your niece's* strength is yours. How do I know those attacks weren't orchestrated by the witch that you claim hunts you?"

Fairchild's feathers were nearly impossible to ruffle. Jenner wished he knew that sort of calm self-possession. "I can assure you, Jenner, that when Astrid comes for Bria, it won't be with a violent clash of swords. When she comes, she'll take Bria and kill her before anyone knows she's even there."

Icy shards of dread speared Jenner's chest. He understood aggression. Appreciated outright violence. Stealth and subversion would only serve to further tighten his already-coiled nerves. With Bria's penchant to run free at night, he'd have to keep her closer than he felt comfortable doing in order to protect her.

"If that's true, then why keep her a prisoner for so long?"

Fairchild bristled. *Good.* Jenner was glad to have finally gotten under the male's skin. "I love Bria as though she is my own daughter. You claim to be tethered to her. If you're so *temperamental,* as your king suggests, what wouldn't you do to protect her? Or perhaps I'm wrong in assuming the tether is as all-consuming as rumor suggests."

The bastard could goad Jenner's temper all he wanted. Jenner refused to take the bait.

"You might not understand what's happened. You might not like it. But that doesn't change the fact that Bria has tethered my soul and, in turn, hers is tied to me. The tether is absolute. Unbreakable. Your niece won't be leaving here with you. She's staying here. With me. You don't need Ronan any longer and you can keep your godsdamned money. She has me now."

"You're certainly capable of protecting her, aren't

you?" Nothing seemed to faze Thomas Fairchild. His scent was clean and didn't betray even an ounce of fear. Strange, considering the way he'd shut himself away from the world like a coward. "And you would, wouldn't you?" Thomas studied him as though trying to worm his way into Jenner's thoughts. "Protect Bria."

The male was shrewd. Calculating. And undoubtedly working an angle. Until Jenner could determine his loyalties, he'd have to be careful around Bria's uncle. He struck Jenner as the sort of male who played to whatever side could benefit him most. With Mikhail's kingdom still in its infancy and fragile, he needed to be wary of an ally like Thomas. Someone who could easily switch sides if he saw a greater benefit.

"I want to know more about this witch and why she wants Bria so badly." No one lived like Fairchild did— locked away and afraid—unless they were crazy or had made a dangerous enemy.

"How old are you—Jenner, is it?"

Good gods. Thomas Fairchild could give a Siobhan a lesson or three in the art of deflection. Jenner rolled his massive shoulders and cracked his neck from side to side. This beating-around-the-bush bullshit was starting to get on his nerves. "Old enough."

Thomas gave him a wry smile. "I made the mistake of allying myself with a vampire lord. When the Sortiari began their campaign in London, I had no idea the measure of their strength. I'd never desired to be turned, but my sister Anna did. I lent my army to the cause because it's what she wanted. She'd fallen in love with the vampire and he turned her. It was a mistake I would not make again given the choice. I should have taken her away. Done whatever was within my power to keep her from him. The immortal hold their grudges," he said with a dark edge. "Vendettas can span centuries."

Cryptic. Though his little story gave Jenner a little insight to the male. He'd probably sympathize with Siobhan given the chance. Jenner sensed that Fairchild's fealty to Mikhail carried as much water as a rusted-out bucket.

"Are you going to tell me why Bria needs to be protected or are we going to continue beating around the bush until sunrise?"

"I don't know you," Thomas said. "And you know nothing about me, my niece, or my coven. If you treat her with kindness and respect, if you can refrain from cruelty, you'll prove to me that you can be trusted not only with Bria, but with my secrets."

Jesus. It looked as though the rumors were true. Thomas Fairchild was mad. Being tethered to Bria might prove to be a disaster. Was this Jenner's punishment for months of disconnect and out-of-control behavior? To be saddled with a mate whose uncle was out of his mind and who might be crazy herself?

"Treat her with cruelty?" The insult bristled, but Jenner wasn't about to do anything to assuage the male's worries. "I'll treat her however the fuck I please. She is *mine*." A total dick thing to say, but he didn't care. He hated opportunists like Thomas.

The male swallowed hard and squared his shoulders. "I could take her out of here now. Back to her coven where she belongs."

Jenner had about a foot and a half and 150 pounds on him. "Your niece is no longer a dhampir. She doesn't belong in your coven anymore." When Jenner was pushed he pushed back.

"We would welcome her back home with open arms."

Jenner snorted. "She's no longer yours to care for. She is home."

Thomas's eyes narrowed, but his expression bore not a hint of malice. Instead, he seemed . . . pleased. "I have other business with the king," he said. "And then, I'll say good-bye to Bria."

Effectively dismissed, Jenner marched for the door. He already had too much on his plate to deal with Thomas Fairchild's insanity.

"Jenner."

He paused at the French doors and turned to face Bria's uncle.

"I look forward to our next conversation."

That made one of them. Jenner gave a slight incline of his head and left. Whatever Thomas's secrets were, Jenner knew they'd bring them all nothing but trouble.

"Come home with us, Bria. Please."

Lucas was distraught and Bria didn't want to add to that by disappointing him. She wasn't going to go home with him, though. She didn't belong in that place anymore.

"I need to stay here. Where I can learn about being a vampire."

"What's to learn?" He didn't hide his disdain and his scent soured. Jealousy perhaps? "Vampires and dhampirs aren't that different. Your life doesn't have to change at all."

"It's already changed, Lucas."

"Because you're *tethered*?" His voice quavered with rage on the word. "What does that even mean? What does it even matter?"

"You know what it means and why it matters."

"I don't. Neither one of us has ever seen a vampire until now. How do you know what this tether is? He could be lying to you. He's a shady-looking bastard. What if he's tricked you in order to take advantage of you?"

Why did everyone think she was stupid and weak? It was Bria's turn to be angry and indignant. "*I am a vampire*. Don't you think I'd know?"

"How? Tell me, how are you tethered to that male?"

Bria let out a slow breath. Putting words to something that was both magical and deeply personal was harder than she thought it would be. "The transition is painful," she began. "I wasn't sure I'd survive it. So much worse than the slayer's blade when it cut my throat. There's pain and then . . . there's *nothing*."

"What do you mean?"

They knew so little of their heritage. Even now, Bria didn't know what to expect. "My soul, it disappeared. As if something had sucked it right out of my body. It opened up this hole inside of me. It's dark, cold, emotionless, and *so* empty. But it doesn't hurt. What's left in the soul's absence is a sort of apathy."

Lucas's brow furrowed and he raked his hands through his hair. "It sounds horrible."

"It's not." She gave him a soft smile. "There's strength. And power. I can see and smell and hear things that I couldn't before. Everything is sharper. More intense." The memory of her fangs breaking the skin of Jenner's throat for the first time caused chills to race over her flesh.

"And the tether?"

"When I saw him, it all came rushing back. The emptiness was gone, the gray apathy vanished. I felt full to bursting. Even without knowing what it was, I recognized it. I recognized him for what he was to me."

Lucas averted his gaze. "It doesn't mean anything. It doesn't mean he loves you. You don't have to stay here with him."

She wanted to say that she wasn't staying for Jenner, because of him or anyone else. But as the words formed on her tongue she tasted the lie. "I'm staying here for myself," she said at last. "To learn more about what and who I am. And because in my soul, I know I can't turn my back on our tether."

"And you can make that determination after a matter of days? Bria, I've known you for *centuries*."

She couldn't explain her sudden loyalty to Jenner any more than she could the intricacies of their tether. "You really want me to go back there?" Angry tears stung her eyes. "Knowing that I'm nothing more than a prisoner?"

"At least you're safe there," Lucas countered. "There's no telling what he'll do to you. He looked as though he could barely control himself."

Bria averted her gaze as her fingers wandered to her bare wrist. Her cheeks flushed and her body heated at the memory of the things he'd said to her the night before, the heady scent of his arousal, and the hard length of him that had pressed against her belly as his big body leaned over hers.

Lucas's expression fell and his eyes flashed silver. "He's fed from your vein." The words left his mouth in a pained choke. "Hasn't he?"

The rules of their coven were strict. Her uncle didn't allow members to drink blood whenever the whim struck. Feedings were only permitted when necessary, and intimacies such as feeding from the vein at the throat were prohibited. And Bria had never been allowed to feed another member of her coven. Not even Lucas. To Lucas, letting Jenner take her vein was the equivalent of letting him take her virginity.

"He won't let you stay," Lucas said with renewed confidence. "Not when you're still at risk."

Bria rolled her eyes and threw herself down on the couch. For as long as she could remember, her uncle had feared an ancient enemy. A witch who wouldn't be satisfied until everyone in his bloodline was dead. Bria had been told that her father had died in the Sortiari wars and shortly afterward her mother had been found dead at the bottom of a ravine, leaving Bria's uncle as her sole guardian. After that, he'd become a recluse. Convinced that the only way to protect them from the evil that hunted them was to hide away from the world.

"I'm a vampire now. I can protect myself."

His pitying expression only fueled her ire. Always perceived as weak. Incapable. The one who needed to be cared for and watched over. Bria was stronger than her uncle or Lucas thought. She was braver than the most stalwart member of their coven. She'd simply never been given the opportunity to prove herself. Well, that part of her existence was over. And through her transition—and now her tether—she was going to live her life on *her* terms.

"Can you really leave us so easily, Bria?"

Us or him? Bria knew what Lucas expected. What her uncle had promised him. But she'd never seen him as anything more than a friend. Lucas was like a brother to her. And her tethering to Jenner proved that Lucas was not meant to be her mate.

"You make it sound as though I'm abandoning you."

Lucas scoffed, "Aren't you?"

"That's not fair. I deserve to make my own choices. To take my own risks." Bria rose from her chair and crossed the living room to where Lucas stood, one arm braced on the mantle of the enormous fireplace. "This isn't a prison transfer. It's *freedom*. Finally! And instead of being happy for me, you want to return me to my cell."

Something tugged at her chest and Bria felt Jenner's presence even before the sound of his footsteps reached her ears. She pulled away from Lucas with a start, not wanting a repeat of Jenner's earlier display of temper. One sharp fang pierced her bottom lip and a drop of blood welled from the wound. Lucas's gaze locked on her mouth and Bria took another step back as Jenner strode through the living room, his rolling gait as graceful and full of purpose as any predator.

He looked from Lucas to Bria, his brow arched curiously. The male had murder in his gaze as he reached out and brushed the pad of his thumb over Bria's bottom lip. He looked pointedly at Lucas before bringing his thumb to his mouth and licking her blood away.

Dear gods. The simple act nearly caused her knees to buckle. Jenner exuded power and sensuality without even trying. Lucas's anger became apparent in the change of his scent and the sudden tension that vibrated through him. She didn't understand Jenner's territorial show. He'd refused to let her feed from his throat, ushered her back to the house last night like an errant child, and rejected her advances despite his obvious desire for her. Now he taunted Lucas with his perceived ownership of her. What sort of game was he playing at?

"Your uncle wants to see you before he leaves." Jenner's deep, rumbling voice brought chills to the surface of Bria's skin. "He's waiting for you in Mikhail's study."

She hesitated. The quicker she said good-bye to her uncle, the quicker she could get Lucas out of there. Then again, saying good-bye would require her to leave Jenner alone with Lucas.

"All right," she said slowly.

"We'll speak again soon, Bria." Apparently Lucas had lost his mind, hinting that he'd be back. Jenner looked ready to tear Lucas's arms off and beat him with them. She just hoped he'd wait until she was out of the room.

Bria made her way down the hall to Mikhail's study. A sense of elation swelled within her and not an ounce of guilt. Jenner wouldn't hurt Lucas; somehow she knew that beneath his violent, growly exterior was an honorable, decent male.

And though she wished that she could make Lucas understand that what he saw as a curse had been her salvation, she wasn't about to bend over backward to make it happen. This was *her* life. Finally, she had a chance to live it.

"Jenner said you were leaving?"

Her uncle stared at some unknown point before bringing his gaze to hers. "I am. How are you feeling?"

"I'm fine." She was better than fine. *Amazing!* Rubbing it in her uncle's face, however, wouldn't do anyone any good.

"I'm glad. And Jenner. He's been kind to you?"

The way her uncle made it seem, she was a pet being transferred from one owner to another. Her stomach twisted into an angry knot and Bria fought for composure. "We haven't known each other long enough for him to be anything other than cordial."

Her uncle gave a sad shake of his head. "The notion of a tether . . . it's savage."

How could he think that? "It's our nature," Bria said.

"It's *their* nature."

"It's *mine*."

His eyes shone with sadness as he stood and went to her. "Did I make the wrong decision in bringing you here?"

If he'd asked her that question a couple of weeks ago she might have answered with a resounding yes. But now . . . "No," Bria said. "You didn't."

He let out a slow sigh. He took her in his arms and held her tightly. "I'll be back in a few days. Should you need *anything,* call."

"I will. Don't worry; everything will be fine."

"You might be right, Bria," he said. "You might be right."

CHAPTER
10

Jenner seriously needed something to take the edge off. His brain buzzed with Bria's scent, the taste of her blood still lingered on his tongue. That one drop taken from her lip had only served to reignite his thirst. He'd sought to make a point with Lucas. In doing so, he'd only managed to torture himself. Gods, how could he possibly crave her so badly after knowing her for only a short time?

"You didn't have to do that, you know." Bria came into the room like a vengeful wind once her uncle and Lucas left, her eyes flashing with quicksilver. "It was nothing more than a childish power play."

Jenner liked that behind her naïve, sheltered façade was a fiery disposition. He didn't have to ask her what she was talking about. Obviously, she was trying to look out for her boy. Save his feelings and all that. "It was a power play," he admitted without an ounce of chagrin. "Hardly childish, though."

"You heard us talking, didn't you?"

Jenner hiked a casual shoulder. He wasn't going to deny it. Lucas had sounded like a brokenhearted sap when he found out that Jenner fed from Bria's vein. The smug sense of satisfaction he'd felt at claiming something no other male had pushed Jenner to further goad the dhampir. If anything, to gauge his reaction.

"You're sort of an ass, you know that?"

Yeah, he did. A selfish, undeserving son of a bitch. "He would have broken you down. Convinced you to leave with your uncle. I made sure that wouldn't happen."

Bria's eyes narrowed. They were lovely rimmed with silver, but Jenner liked the natural amethyst color even better. "By rubbing our tether in his face?"

"By showing him that you no longer belong with your coven."

"You listen to me; I've spent my entire life under someone's thumb. I did not escape that unbearable control just to answer to some other high-handed male who thinks he should make my decisions for me. Do you understand?"

Jenner suppressed the smile that threatened. Such a surprise, this female. He admired her show of strength and declaration of independence. That didn't mean he didn't take her uncle's warnings seriously, though. Crazy or not, Thomas had been concerned for Bria's safety. Concerned enough to hire a couple of ruthless vampires to protect her. Jenner wasn't about to discount that. "I get it. But like I told you last night, there's something *you* need to understand. The attack on your coven wasn't an isolated incident. The city is swarming with slayers ready to kill us and you are one of six vampires currently inhabiting the earth. Freedom is one thing. Carelessness another."

She canted her head, sending the cascade of dark hair over her shoulder. Jenner's fingers itched to reach out and touch the silky length. "You think I'm careless?"

"I think you have a lot to learn."

Bria bucked her chin in the air. "You don't know anything about me."

"I know your thirst is mounting. And that if you don't feed soon, your control is going to slip."

She swallowed and Jenner found his gaze drawn to the delicate column of her neck. He sensed her thirst, but it was his own that raged like an inferno. The thought of piercing her flesh consumed Jenner. Before his tethering, any vein, any willing body, would have taken the edge off, albeit temporarily. Now he could think of nothing but Bria. Anyone else's blood would surely sour on his tongue.

"I'm not ashamed to admit it," Bria replied. "Claire says it's common in the first few weeks."

Ashamed? "There's nothing shameful about an act that's wired into our biology, Bria."

She averted her gaze. "Then why won't you let me feed from your throat?"

Fuck. Jenner raked his hand through his hair. She might not have thought she was naïve, but the female was painfully innocent. So much so that it only served to reinforce Jenner's decision to keep her at arm's length for now. "Can you manage your thirst? For a few hours, at least."

"Yes." She studied him with an intensity that caused Jenner's breath to stall in his chest. "Why?"

"Because we're going out."

"Out. As in *out* out?"

Christ on a crutch, what are you thinking? "Yes. Get whatever you need and let's go."

She hid her excitement well, though Jenner didn't need an outward show to know how she felt. A twinge of anxiety tugged at his chest and he hoped he'd made the right decision.

Bria smoothed her hair back and glanced down at her

tattered T-shirt and leggings. "I'll be back in a couple of minutes." She rushed toward the staircase, pausing at the first step, and said, "Don't leave without me," and headed up toward her room.

"Thomas Fairchild is going to have your ass if you defile his niece." Ronan strode into the room with a shit-eating grin on his face. "You're taking her out? As in *out* out?"

Jenner growled at his friend's mocking tone. "You want to keep her locked up in this house the way her uncle did?"

"No, but she's newly turned. She's barely got a couple of weeks under her belt. Sort of like taking a starving person to an all-you-can-eat buffet, don't you think?"

When Jenner told Bria that she would feed from *no one* but him he'd meant it. "I'll make sure her thirst is managed," Jenner remarked. "Her sheltered existence is the reason she should leave this house. She needs to understand that her newfound freedom doesn't allow for carelessness."

"'Sheltered' is a bit of an understatement if you ask me." Ronan crossed the living room to the bar and poured himself a scotch. "What did Fairchild say to you?"

"For starters, we're out a paycheck."

Ronan snorted. "I figured. Why pay you to protect his niece now that you'll do it for free? Did he tell you anything more about his witch problem?"

"Nothing that made any sense. He hinted at some old vendetta from centuries ago. He didn't offer me any specifics, though. I had a feeling I was being vetted."

Ronan tossed back his drink. "He's an odd son of a bitch, I'll give you that. And there's no doubt that Bria is as innocent as the driven snow." He chuckled into his glass as though it amused him to see a male as soiled as Jenner with a female like Bria. "Vetted, huh? Think you passed?"

Jenner leveled his gaze on his friend. "Would it matter?"

"Not a damned bit." Ronan's fangs glinted in a feral smile. "What's going on with Siobhan? She manage to stir up some shit again?"

Jenner had wanted to fill in Mikhail first, but Ronan needed to know that the female had shifted her focus. "She wants to see Chelle," he said. "She's offering to trade intel on the werewolf for a face-to-face."

"Fuck." Ronan poured himself another drink. "I was afraid of that."

"You know how she gets. She's like a dog with a bone."

"More like a tiger with a carcass," Ronan remarked. "Why do you think she wants Chelle?"

"Proof that Set's chest is the real deal?" Ronan suggested as he swirled the amber liquid in his glass. "It could be a power play. She and Chelle are friends. As much as anyone can be Siobhan's friend. Maybe she wants to form some sort of alliance."

"She'll find a way to use Chelle if she can," Jenner agreed. "Something's coming down the pipes, but I'll be damned if I know what. She's not going to lead us to Gregor, though. I've been following her around for months. I think she'd rather he stayed as far away from her as possible."

"I agree. Siobhan is going to cause us trouble, but she doesn't give a shit about Gregor," Ronan said. "Until he shows up at her door, she won't bother worrying. I've suggested to Mikhail that he should reach out to the Sortiari, instead."

"And he didn't lay you flat on your ass?" Jenner asked with a laugh.

"Only because Claire wouldn't let him. She agrees with me that it's best to keep your enemies closer."

"That's the fucking truth." As much as he didn't trust

Thomas Fairchild, Jenner knew that something seriously evil had its sights set on his family. No matter how much Bria wanted to break from that part of her life, Jenner needed to keep him close. If only to uncover his secrets.

Ronan set his empty glass down on the bar. "All right, I'm outta here. I feel like I haven't seen Naya in a week and I need some downtime."

Guilt stabbed at Jenner's gut. "I shouldn't have stayed away for so long. You know, before Bria." No doubt Ronan had been picking up his slack while he'd been on yet another bender. "It won't happen again."

From the corner of his eye Jenner spotted Bria coming down the stairs. Ronan gave him a sly smile and said, "I know it won't. Not now that you've got a reason to stick around. I've got a couple of clients lined up for this week, so I'll be a little scarce. Call if anything comes up."

"You need me to field anything?"

"I think your hands are going to be pretty damned full for now. I've got this." Ronan strode from the living room as he said over his shoulder, "Try not to kill anyone tonight."

"Yeah." Jenner's gut tied into a series of knots as his gaze locked on Bria. Ronan said something as he walked out the door, but Jenner couldn't be bothered to pay attention. Not killing someone might be a tough promise to keep, and they both knew it.

Jenner had never been the sort of male who found innocence alluring. He liked it rough, dirty, and messy and the females he'd chosen as bedmates always fit the bill. There was something decidedly sinful about Bria, though. A seductive purity that made Jenner ache to defile her.

Fresh-faced and dewy, she didn't appear very different from earlier except her hair that she'd piled high on her head and gathered in a ponytail. Not an ounce of makeup marred her natural beauty and she wore the same

tight-fitting pants but had swapped her T-shirt for a bil-
lowy blouse. The knee-high black leather boots she'd put
on gave the ensemble just enough of an edge. "Is this
okay?" She looked down the length of her body. "The
boots are Claire's."

Not for long. Jenner would pay any amount Claire
asked in order for Bria to keep them. He imagined what
she'd look like wearing nothing but those boots, her raven hair cascading over her shoulders, the rosy points of
her nipples peeking through that dark veil.

Gods.

Jenner scrubbed a hand over his face. He should have
stayed away. Merely sleeping in the next room was becoming too great a test of his mettle. At least offering to
take her out added the buffer of curious eyes and crowds
of people to keep him from reaching out to touch her. Public displays hadn't bothered Jenner in the past, however.
Maybe it wouldn't deter him now. *Fuck.*

At a little past midnight, the clubs would be starting to
heat up. His plan wasn't to ease Bria into anything.
Throwing her in the deep end was the only option, and
taking her to some tame, out-of-the-way place frequented
by humans wouldn't do anything to teach her a lesson in
exercising caution.

"Let's go."

He didn't comment on her appearance and her expression fell a little. Bria could have been wearing a fucking
trash bag and she would have ignited Jenner's lust. Flow-
ery compliments weren't exactly his thing. Thomas Fairchild's sheltered niece wanted to hear that she was
beautiful. And Jenner's single-minded thought was that
the female couldn't look more tantalizing and fuckable.

A regular motherfucking Tennyson.

Bria came to a halt just outside the door. "We're riding on that?"

The Ducati didn't offer the most practical means of transportation. Jenner liked it because it was fast and maneuvered well in traffic. A quick getaway was a hell of a lot easier when you could weave through the string of cars clogging up Sunset. Ronan and Mikhail liked their flashy Aston-Martins and sleek town cars. Jenner didn't give a shit about the flash 'n' flare. He was all about stealth.

"We'll fit." He gave her a sidelong glance. "You scared?"

He couldn't help but taunt her. If only to see that fire spark within her once again.

"No." Gods, that defiant tone nearly brought him to his knees.

"Then get on."

As he navigated the winding path of Mulholland down into the city Jenner wished he'd reconsidered taking the bike. Bria's body pressed tightly to his back and her palms molded to his chest as she held on to him. The heat of her body permeated his clothes; her thighs resting against his sent a tremor through his muscles. Jenner gripped the handlebars tighter and accelerated. The faster he put a little distance between them, the better.

Bria's heart pounded as though it would break through her chest. The bite of the wind on her face and the sound as it rushed in her ears exhilarated her. The speed of the motorcycle as it raced down the steep, winding road thrilled her. And the male whose back was molded to her chest excited her beyond reason.

She wanted this moment to never end.

Beneath her palm, Jenner's heart beat a steady rhythm. Bria let her eyes drift shut and she focused on the *thrum . . . thrum . . . thrum . . .* that vibrated through her very soul. Their tether was still a mystery to her and Jenner himself an enigma. He was gruff and demanding. At times harsh and even lewd. He'd shown a side of himself with Lucas that was decidedly violent. Because of Jenner, though, she might finally be able to stop sneaking around like a thief shielded by night and know true freedom. Not even her uncle could expect her to return to the coven now that she'd been tethered. She'd only known Jenner for mere days and already he'd given her the most amazing gift anyone had ever given her. He'd never know how much this moment meant to her. Bria let go of his chest and threw her head back and her arms wide.

The bike swerved and Bria's stomach rocketed up into her throat. Jenner reached back and grabbed her arm, wrapping it back around his torso. "Are you out of your fucking mind?" he barked above the rush of the wind. "Do you want to crack your skull on the gods-damned pavement?"

Bria wrapped her other arm around him and held on tight. A secretive smile curved her lips as she rested her cheek against his back. Had the big, bad vampire been concerned for her safety?

As they made their way into the city Bria soaked in the sights with newborn eyes. She marveled at her vampiric senses. So much keener than they'd been before. Her uncle had always insisted that their biology was closer to humans'. That though their eyesight was sharper, their sense of smell more discerning, to a vampire their kind were just as mundane. Bria believed that now. Los Angeles pulsed with a vitality that filled her with wonder. A riot of colors and sounds and scents that threatened to overwhelm her senses and yet she couldn't get enough. Bria considered tonight a victory, no matter how small.

It was a new world and she was going to revel in every new experience.

Bria stared up at the gleaming red and gold sign that hung above the nightclub's entrance and the way the pieces were meant to resemble scales that formed the words *The Dragon's Den*. Music filtered from the club to her ears as Jenner maneuvered the motorcycle into a parking space. The heavy bass echoed through her, caressed Bria's skin with a ripple of decadent vibration. People waited impatiently in a long queue to be let in, some of them dancing and enjoying the music from the sidewalk. The energy was palpable. It made her come alive.

She couldn't wait to go inside.

"Not so fast." Jenner's arm flew out to stop her before Bria could dash across the street. "Time to go over the ground rules for tonight."

Ground rules? Bria knew little of how a tethered mate was supposed to behave, but Jenner treated her more like a ward than the female whose soul his was bound to. It sent a shock of agitation up her spine. "I'm not an incompetent child, Jenner."

He cocked a brow as though to challenge her statement. *Arrogant male.* "You will not leave my side tonight. Heed all of my warnings and don't reveal anything about who or what you are. Do you understand me?"

His ground rules spelled out pretty clearly for Bria that Jenner did in fact find her incompetent. Her earlier sense of elation sank like a stone in her stomach. She'd heard the same warnings from her uncle time and again. On the very rare occasions she was allowed to leave the protection of the coven with Lucas, he reminded her of how vital it was to be inconspicuous. To never let anyone know she was Thomas Fairchild's niece.

"I understand," she said, infusing a frosty chill into her voice.

"Good."

Jenner took her hand in his and led her across the street. Bria fought the urge to jerk her hand away. She didn't appreciate being shepherded like a toddler lest she be hit by a car. "If I'm not to leave your side or interact with anyone, what are we even doing here?" Did he think she'd be appreciative of their little field trip if he expected her to hide in a corner of the club and make herself invisible?

"You're here to learn a lesson, Bria."

Jenner bucked his chin at the bouncer and he moved the velvet rope aside. Grumbles of protest sounded from behind them and Bria couldn't help but wonder what sort of clout Jenner had that would allow them immediate entrance. It would stand to reason that Jenner would take her someplace where her safety would be ensured. For once, Bria wanted to rush headlong into danger without someone worrying or trying to coddle and protect her. Perhaps the freedom she'd seen in Jenner was nothing more than another shackle.

I suppose I'm about to find out.

Inside the club, the sensory overload nearly sent Bria racing for the door. The sound of the music, overlapped with myriad voices, deafened her. Under the press of bodies and layers of scents, her chest constricted as tiny pins pricked at her skin. Her attention caught on the individual dust particles dancing under the swath of bright laser lights until everything around her blurred. *Too much.* It was all too much. Bria swayed on her feet and Jenner steadied her, holding her body close to his.

"Lesson one: You have to learn focus, Bria." Jenner's lips brushed her ear and the warmth of his breath coaxed chills to her skin. "To weed through the sights and sounds. You don't need to breathe if you don't want to. Cut off the scents that assault you. What you see as strengths your enemies will see as a weakness. They'll exploit your keen senses and use them against you." He cupped the back of her neck and tilted her head to one side much like he had when he'd fed from her the very first night they'd met. A tremor raced through her as he slashed across her neck with one finger and whispered, "You're so distracted, I could easily cut your throat."

Bria cleared her throat and tried to quell the shaking in her limbs. Jenner was a deadly male. Dangerous and exciting. "I would heal if you cut me." The only way to kill her now would be to put a stake in her heart or take her head completely off.

In a flash of motion he angled her body until her back was against the wall. He brought his fist up and with a downward cut brought it down to rest above her left breast. "I cut your throat to weaken you." His fist relaxed until his hand splayed out across her chest. "And now you're dead."

Her silly bravado crashed and burned. In a single moment he'd shown her that that her vampiric immortality did *not* make her infallible. Jenner's point made, Bria had no choice but to admit a temporary defeat. "Never let my guard down," she said on a breath. "Understood."

Jenner's eyes reflected with brilliant silver. He pushed away from her slowly, his palm lingering on her chest for a moment too long. A cocktail waitress caught Jenner's eye and he motioned her over. He ordered a Belvedere on the rocks for himself and—high-handed male that he was—a red wine for Bria.

"Maybe I wanted vodka, too."

He raked the length of her body with his eyes and what she suspected was meant to be a disdainful appraisal only served to heat her blood. "You'll have a glass of wine, *viaton*," Jenner said. "I want your senses sharpened, not dulled."

"Viaton?" she repeated. "What does that mean?"

Jenner flashed an arrogant grin. "It means 'innocent,' in Finnish."

Innocent. He might as well have called her a dirty word. Indignation heated Bria's cheeks at the insult. He had suggested that she was naïve. Everyone thought so—Claire, Mikhail, Ronan, even the members of her own coven—and it laid Bria low with embarrassment. True, she'd been sheltered. Closeted by her overprotective uncle. But she wasn't some silly brainless twit who didn't know a thing about the world she lived in. She was more street-smart than any of them gave her credit for.

That Jenner brought her to the club not for a night out but to teach her a lesson should have angered Bria further. Instead, she appreciated that rather than lock her away in order to keep her safe, he was helping her to learn how to protect herself. He could call her *viaton* for now if it pleased or entertained him. She'd soon prove to him—to all of them—that she wasn't as innocent as they all thought.

They waited in companionable silence for the waitress to return. Bria used the opportunity to sharpen her focus. Instead of taking in the crowd as a whole, she narrowed her gaze to one person. And then she pulled back. Three bodies. Five. Ten. In the space of several minutes she'd trained her eyes to see the individuals within the whole, to separate each singular movement within the swarm of motion. A cluster of pinpoints contained in an undulating mass.

Jenner leaned his head over hers. "What do you see?"

While she'd been watching everything around her Jenner had been watching her. Her body flushed with warmth and she pushed the distraction of Jenner's presence to the back of her mind. "That woman over there in the far corner. Her heartbeat is erratic. I think she's taken some kind of drug. And our waitress"—she indicated the bar—"has a tattoo of a four-leaf clover just below her left earlobe. She tried to hide it with makeup."

"Very good." Bria's eyes drifted shut as she let the deep rumble of his voice wash over her. "Now, let your senses work as one. What do they tell you?"

A ripple of sensation danced over her skin. Her body responded to him as though it had been conditioned to do so. Despite his overbearing nature and the fact that he'd refused to allow her to drink from the vein at his throat, Bria sensed the connection between them growing with each passing day. The tether that bound them tugged at her chest and she leaned toward him as though she had no choice. He wanted her gaze to roam the crowded night-club, but all she wanted was to close her eyes. To lean into his body and let her palms travel the sculpted hills and valleys of his body as she committed each detail to memory.

"That's not what we're here for Bria. Focus." How did he know the path her mind wandered? "Those thoughts are just another distraction. Push them to the back of your mind."

How could she? The scent of his blood wafted around her, invading her senses even as she tried to shut it out. Thirst ignited in her throat, a dry, unquenchable burn.

"Bria!" Jenner's voice snapped out at her like a whip.

"I need a second." Curbing her thoughts was more difficult than she thought it would be. Especially when it came to Jenner.

"Center your focus and I'll reward you."

Her lips turned up in a smile. "What will you give me?"

"My vein."

CHAPTER
11

Bria's lips parted invitingly at Jenner's words and the urge to put his mouth to hers nearly broke his resolve to see this through. Her thoughts were so focused that it caused the bond between them to flare and he sensed the need building within her. Need that echoed his own. A little over a week ago he'd been in this very club, on the prowl for a warm body and a willing vein. Now the thought of any other female shriveled and died in Jenner's mind. The center of his universe had shifted. And there wasn't a gods-damned thing he could do about it.

"Okay. I'm ready."

Jenner watched, rapt as Bria scanned the club. For someone who had been newly turned, her focus was extraordinary. He'd already known that as he'd watched her run, flip, and tumble through the dark last night. This wasn't a treasure hunt, though. It was a crash course in survival. Bria didn't have the luxury of settling gradually into this new life. Her uncle hadn't even raised her as a proper dhampir, treating the drinking of blood—something vital to their survival—as a shameful act. And starting tonight, Jenner vowed that he'd do whatever he could to undo the damage Thomas Fairchild had done.

Just be sure you don't damage her yourself in the process.

"I thought they were human at first." She looked up at Jenner with wide, curious eyes that sparkled like precious stones in the dark shadowed corner of the club. "How could I have missed it?"

"You made an assumption based on what you know and your mind overrode what your eyes, ears, and nose told you."

Beside him Bria stiffened, and her scent soured with a wave of anxiety. "I know the dhampirs. I recognize the scent of werewolves. My uncle did business with one once." She brought her nose up to the air and inhaled deeply. Her expression pinched. "What's that tang? It burns my nose."

"Magic," Jenner replied. He angled his body closer to hers. He'd have to be wary of any magic wielders from now on. Any one of them could be the witch who hunted Bria. "Probably a mage. Or a white witch." At least, he hoped.

Fear punched through Jenner's gut, nearly stealing his breath. *Damn.* He didn't think he'd ever get used to the way the tether connected his and Bria's emotions. She was afraid of magic wielders, which indicated that she might have some insight as to the danger she was in.

"There's something else." Her voice quavered, but she recovered her composure well. "That female over there"—she indicated a lithe, willowy female who danced alone by the DJ booth—"there's the slightest glow to her skin. Almost imperceptible."

Jenner's chest swelled with pride and he pushed the unfamiliar emotion to the soles of his feet. Bria was extraordinary. Her senses were much more finely tuned than he'd thought. "Fae," he replied. "I'm surprised you can see the luminescence. I can't." Jenner wasn't the sort of male who enjoyed admitting any weakness, but Bria needed that boost to her confidence.

"You can't?" She turned toward him and Jenner fought the urge to smooth away the furrow that cut into her brow.

"Mikhail can. The fae are powerful and their numbers small. They can easily camouflage themselves until they appear as mundane as a human." That Bria saw past the disguise was remarkable.

"I had no idea," she said with wonder. "She's beautiful."

The willowy fae wasn't nearly as breathtaking as the female standing next to him. Against his better judgment, Jenner reached out and captured a lock of hair that dangled from her ponytail between his thumb and forefinger. It slipped like strands of silk through his grasp. Bria's gaze went molten and a tide of lust rose within him. He'd promised her his vein if she focused, but would he be rewarded for his instruction?

"Lesson two: The world is populated with supernatural creatures that are just as strong as or stronger than you. You're further from the top of the food chain than you think."

Jenner angled his head toward hers. The waitress returned with their drinks and he pulled away with a jerk. *You're a class-A hypocrite.* He preached the merits of focus and control when he had *none*. She set their drinks down on a long bar mounted to the wall. He dug a twenty out of his pocket and handed it to her. She shook her head and said above the din of music, "Already paid for."

Jenner followed her gaze to the main bar at the center of the club. *Fuck.* A female perched on one of the high stools held her glass up in a silent toast. Her name was Melissa. No . . . Marissa. One of many females he'd casually bedded over the past few months. Jenner pushed the bill into the waitress's palm. "Tell her thanks, but no thanks."

She shrugged and tucked his offered twenty into a tiny box on her tray. "Whatever you say, hon."

"A friend of yours?"

That focus he was teaching Bria to use had come back to bite him in the ass. Shame seared his flesh and Jenner averted his gaze. He didn't want Bria to know that he was nothing more than a selfish piece of shit who didn't have the strength to master his own lusts.

"Sort of."

"She looks disappointed."

Her expression was certainly crestfallen. Marissa took the money their waitress returned to her and tucked it in her purse. With a narrowed gaze she examined Bria, and Jenner sensed her bristle beside him. A territorial growl vibrated in her throat, and damn, the sound of it did *nothing* to cool the heat racing through his veins.

Jenner leaned in close to her ear and tried to ignore the way her scent swirled in his head. "Lesson three: You're not without power of your own."

Bria turned her head to give him a questioning gaze. Her mouth hovered dangerously close to Jenner's and he leaned back before he gave in to the urge to taste her lips. "What do you mean?"

Her proximity intoxicated him. A mere week into their tether and Jenner could barely keep his hands off of her. If he focused on teaching her what she was capable of maybe he could keep the lust at bay. Maybe he'd quit thinking about last night and how damned good it felt to have her soft body beneath his.

"You can bend others to your will, Bria. It takes time to master, to recognize the power and channel it. But once you've learned to manipulate your power, it will be an easy feat to compel a human."

Her brow furrowed. "Only humans?"

Jenner shrugged. "Humans are more susceptible to magic. It depends on the creature and their own level of personal power. Dhampirs, too. Witches and fae can't be compelled." *Unfortunately.* "I don't know about shifters; I've never tried. A werewolf's magic is largely controlled by the moon, so I would think that with concentration one could be compelled."

Bria studied him. The intensity of the attention she bestowed on him damn near made him sweat. Because of their tether, an instant attraction had been forged between them. Nature's way of securing a mate bond. Jenner wasn't simply drawn to her because of their tether, though. Her curiosity fascinated him. Her fire sparked his interest. Her beauty intoxicated him. Jenner found that he didn't simply yearn to know her body. He wanted to know her mind and heart as well. Thanks to their tether, he already knew her soul and the purity of it made his seem dirty in comparison.

"Have you ever compelled someone?" she asked.

He'd never compelled another supernatural, but Jenner had found the skill useful in his line of work for Ronan. As a "fixer" for many of L.A.'s elite, the ability to convince someone not to blackmail the A-lister he had dirt on was a hell of a lot easier when he didn't have to use a beat-down to get it done. He didn't want Bria to know about that aspect of his job. It only served to remind him that Bria was too good to be bound to a violent bastard like him, and he didn't want her to realize that fact quite yet.

"A couple of times," he said. "All humans. No supernatural creatures, though. I've never needed to."

"I want to try," she said, her eyes lighting with excitement. "How do I do it?"

Why had no one told her these things? If Jenner hadn't insisted on educating her, would Mikhail and the others have been content to keep her in the house, as ignorant to her own nature as she was to the blossoming supernatural world around her? For decades her uncle had conditioned her to fear. To quell her curiosity. To be content with her life within the walls of his compound. Nothing he'd said had managed to breed anything other than an insatiable curiosity and not a small amount of defiance in her. True, she was newly turned and not the king's—or anyone's—priority or responsibility. But what if Jenner hadn't taken it upon himself to give her this instruction? The power and strength she thought she'd gained through her transition would have meant nothing in the light of her ignorance.

"Don't get frustrated if you can't do it your first time," Jenner said. His lips quirked as though he wanted to smile but denied himself the pleasure of it. Bria wondered what joy would look like on Jenner's stern face. Would it transform him into a creature even more wildly beautiful than he already was? "It takes an immense amount of concentration."

She was determined to do it successfully, if only to impress him. "All right. How do I start?"

"First, you have to find the seat of your power." At Bria's questioning look he continued, "When you were a dhampir, you could sense Mikhail's power. You took sustenance from that life force."

"Yes," she replied. Her uncle had always complained that it was disgusting necessity that dhampirs needed vampires to survive. Without that life force to nourish their own, they would slowly starve to death no matter how much blood or food they ingested. "A warm glow in the pit of my stomach. But instead of that sensation being a part of me, it was like someone had put it there."

Jenner nodded. "Exactly. Look for that sensation now. This time, it's a part of you, not something placed there. It's more subtle. Harder to recognize. But once you find it, you'll always know how to call on it."

For the first time since her transition, Bria realized that she didn't feel that nourishing presence. She'd been so preoccupied with her new senses, the intensity of her thirst, the experience of being surrounded by other vampires, and of course her tether with Jenner that she hadn't taken the time to familiarize herself with her own body. In the pit of her being, she found it. A kernel of heat, so tiny she might not have ever noticed it if Jenner hadn't told her what to search for. Her eyes drifted shut as she envisioned her inner power as a bright gold bead. She urged it to grow. At first the power didn't respond and she nearly lost her mental grasp of it. She wanted to impress Jenner, though, and centered her focus, willing that tiny sphere to grow. By small degrees, it became larger and pulsed with warmth that radiated from her center outward toward her limbs. She drew in shallow breaths and her eyes opened to find Jenner studying her. The intensity of his expression and the heat of his gaze nearly stole her focus from her own power, and Bria put her attraction to him at the back of her mind. She could do this. "I found it," she murmured. *Vampire flow state, achieved!*

His lips curved into an almost smile. "Impressive. It took me weeks to find the necessary focus."

"Really?" Pride swelled within her and it rivaled the pulsing heat of her power.

Jenner nodded while his dark eyes drank her in. Bria stifled a shiver as the memory of his hard body pressing hers down into the soft earth overwhelmed her. *Focus, Bria. You can indulge your fantasies later.* "Now what?"

Jenner looked up and caught the eye of their waitress. She headed their way and he said, "Think of a thought that you want to plant in her mind. Something simple to start. When she gets here, hold her gaze. Draw on your power and lend it to the thought you want to compel her with. Speak the command out loud and with authority. Ready?"

The cocktail waitress sidestepped a couple who'd stumbled in front of her. Once the path was clear, she hustled toward them. "I'm ready," Bria said.

"What can I get for you two?" the waitress called over the din of the music.

Jenner inclined his head toward Bria and the waitress focused her attention on Bria, who took a deep breath into her lungs and drew on her power as she visualized the gold orb in the pit of her stomach. It flared with heat and light in her mind's eye and she locked her gaze with the waitress's. "Hop on one foot." She added, "And sing the theme song from *Friends*."

The waitress's pupils dilated and her gaze glazed over. Bria felt a rush from the pit of her stomach that cycled outward through her body and made her light-headed. Without preamble the waitress began to hop on one foot, her voice projecting over the DJ's music as she sang, "So no one told you life was gonna be this waaaay—"

Bria sucked in an astonished breath. "Stop."

The waitress immediately halted, though her dreamy expression remained. "How do I turn it off?"

Jenner chuckled. "Release your hold on the power. Let it shrink inside of you."

Bria let out a gust of breath and, with it, the hold on her power. The waitress's eyes cleared and she gave her head a gentle shake. "I'm sorry, what did you say you wanted?"

"Oh, just a couple of waters when you get a second," Bria said with a smile.

"Gotcha. I'll get you squared away."

As she turned and walked off, a sense of elation welled inside of Bria. She'd never felt such a rush of heady power in her entire life. She let out a squeal and jumped up and down in celebration of her success. Jenner had warned that she wouldn't be able to master such a skill on her first try and Bria had *rocked it out*! "Did you see that?" she exclaimed. "I totally did it!"

Jenner laughed and his wide smile stilled Bria in an instant. "The theme song to *Friends*? Really?"

Bria cringed. "It just popped into my head."

Dear gods, he was magnificent. Such a simple thing, a smile, and yet it transformed his features in the way she suspected it would. No longer hard and imposing, his smile lent him a charm that stole her breath. Females must have fallen at his feet when he looked at them like that. Bria certainly felt her knees tug her toward the floor. A sudden flare of jealousy burned in her chest. The thought that Jenner would look at any other female like that prompted her to thoughts of violence. They were tethered, yes. Their souls inextricably bound to each other. But Bria began to realize that she might want more from him. That she might want his heart to belong to her as well.

Bria averted her gaze lest Jenner see the want she knew she couldn't hide in her own expression. She took a sip from her glass and savored the rich hints of fruit and oak on her tongue. Bria never could have guessed how immediate and powerful the effects of being tethered could be. Her attraction to Jenner was undeniable. With every passing day spent in his company, Bria realized that she wanted to know more about him. What had his childhood been like? Who were his parents? Did he have brothers or sisters? How did he come to be in Mikhail's service and what had his transition been like?

But right now she wanted to put her mouth to the flesh

at his throat. To taste his skin before she sealed her lips around the vein and pierced the flesh with her fangs. She wanted his blood to flow over her tongue and quench the thirst that burned hotter in her throat the longer she was in his presence. She wanted to feel his hands on her again.

"You're adept at compelling someone," Jenner remarked. His expression became serious again as he studied her. "I bet with some practice you could compel a dhampir with ease."

"Good," she said. Her tongue darted out at her lip and Jenner's gaze locked on her mouth. He'd promised her his vein if she could center her focus. Her fangs throbbed with the need to pierce tried to buy. "Maybe next time I'll compel that female who tried to buy you a drink never to so much as look at you again."

CHAPTER
12

From the corner of his eye Jenner caught sight of Marissa, still watching them. Her longing gaze had obviously not gone unnoticed by Bria. The possessive edge to his mate's words caused Jenner's heart to beat wildly in his chest. The scent of her blood swirled in his head, as heady and intoxicating as the liquor in his glass. Her power astounded him. Her beauty stalled his breath. And her fire brought him to his damned knees. His secondary fangs throbbed in his gums and he resisted the urge to seize her in his arms and nuzzle his face against her fragrant throat.

Jenner squeezed his eyes shut as he tried to get a grip on his control. He wouldn't be content to simply nuzzle her. Inhale her scent. He wanted her blood on his tongue. To flow down his throat. He wanted to glut himself on Bria's blood. Beside him, she shifted. His eyes flew open as he turned toward her. Bria had hopped up on the bar, putting her height level with his. She reached out to rake her nails through his hair and chills broke out over his skin. Silver rimmed the amethyst depths of her irises. She leaned in close and Jenner breathed in her delicious scent.

"What are you doing, Bria?" his voice rasped, and he swallowed against the fiery thirst burning in his throat.

Her sensual response caressed his ear as she lowered her mouth to his neck. "Taking my reward."

Jenner groaned as Bria's fangs broke the skin. She buried her face in the crook of his neck, sucking greedily as her hand dove back into his hair. He'd refused her his throat, and for good reason. Mindless lust overtook him, a haze of need that clouded his mind and crippled any chances of coherent thought. He cast a sideways glance across the club, to where Marissa watched with narrowed eyes, her lips thinned. Bria sought to lay claim to what was hers and that knowledge only served to excite Jenner further.

Desperate need burned through him. He twisted in Bria's embrace to face her fully, urging her legs to part as he settled himself between them. With a guttural groan, Jenner wound his fist into the ponytail cascading from the top of her head and pressed her tighter against him. He wanted to experience the sting of her bite deep in his flesh, needed to feel her thirst and desperation in every deep pull of her mouth. For the second time tonight, he considered throwing caution to the wind and giving in to his desires.

Fuck. His cock ached in his jeans, pulsing in time with every wild beat of his heart. Bria was much too innocent for what he wanted to do to her. Too gentle for his pent-up and insatiable passions.

Jenner released his hold on her hair and slammed his palms against the wall behind her. Her nails bit into his scalp and he reveled in the pain. She fed from him with abandon, not as though she were ashamed. Bria was more in tune with her true nature than she thought. He wanted nothing more than to coax that wildness from her.

Her mouth at his vein had no equal. He'd fed others from his throat, his wrist. Mouths and lips had sealed over his flesh; he'd felt the sting of a dhampir's bite. Those experiences were gray in his memory compared to the vivid sensation that started as a tingle at the top of his scalp and trickled down his body to bathe him in warmth.

As Bria continued to feed from him Jenner fought the urge to tear at her clothes, to slide his hand inside of her pants and seek out the heat of her pussy. Euphoric bliss fogged his brain and clouded his thoughts. Any common sense he might have possessed—any shred of control—evaporated under the gentle suction of Bria's mouth against his throat. How would she react if he popped the buttons of her blouse, jerked the cup of her bra aside, and suckled her nipple to a stiff point? Would she push him away or would she cradle his head against her?

Viaton.

The reminder of her innocence should have cooled Jenner's jets, but all it did was heat him to the point of combustion. When he was through with her she'd be anything but the wide-eyed *viaton*.

Bria's fangs disengaged from Jenner's throat and all he wanted to do was guide her back, to urge her to bite him again. Harder. Her tongue lapped at the punctures she'd made and Jenner shuddered. Another act of defiance after he'd continuously denied her the pleasure of it when she fed from his wrist. So full of fight, this female. His thirst for her mounted until Jenner feared if he didn't take her vein now he'd surely tear her flesh in his haste to taste her.

His control hung by a single frayed thread. Jenner kept one palm firmly planted on the wall, and he gripped the back of her head with the other. In a forceful jerk he pulled her head to the side and buried his fangs into her throat.

Her blood was ambrosia. The sweetest thing he'd ever tasted. Bria went liquid in his embrace, molding her chest to his. A low moan of pleasure vibrated against Jenner's ear and he bit down harder, opening the wound to allow her blood to flow faster. His thirst for her raged. His desire pulled his muscles taut and hardened his cock to stone. He couldn't get enough. Memories—not that of the Collective but those of his own past—tugged at Jenner's mind as though in warning. He fell headfirst into the visions, gave himself over to the bloodlust.

He was lost to Bria. Lost to her blood and his own uncontrollable thirst.

"Again? You fed from me just yesterday."

Ronja smiled invitingly despite her chiding tone. She reached out and took his hand, guiding him into the barn where no one would see. For weeks this had been their secret meeting place. They shared blood, shared their bodies, and no one was the wiser.

"Eric," Ronja whispered. "You have to be gentle this time."

He nodded, his throat too dry to speak. He could be gentle. He simply needed to slake his thirst.

With gentle care he laid her down atop the fresh straw. He kissed her once and then again on her mouth before venturing down to her throat. Ronja let out a gentle sigh as he cupped her tiny breast through the stiff fabric of her bodice. At sixteen he was considered a man by the members of his coven. He was tall, strong. Bigger than many of the warriors who'd been selected to be turned by their lord. He was already as fierce as any vampire, his thirst just as intense. It rankled that he hadn't been selected despite his father's petition. In fact, the vampires watched him with wary eyes when he ventured into the lord's hall at night. They feared him. And rightly so. When he was turned he'd become the most fearsome warlord in their history.

Drunk on his own ego, his own supposed power, he bit down on Ronja's throat, all promises of gentleness forgotten . . .

Bria reveled in smug satisfaction. The dhampir who'd so obviously sought Jenner's attention glared her hatred as she watched him feed from Bria's vein. He bit down harder, his grip on her tightened, and she gasped. He was lost to the thirst as he suckled her, his grunts and moans of pleasure vibrating through Bria's bones and settling as a deep thrum in her sex.

Taking his vein—and offering hers—in such a public display was a scandalous act. One that would have brought a heavy punishment from her uncle had she still been a member of the coven. Taboo. Forbidden. And feeling the eyes of onlookers on them only heightened Bria's pleasure. It was a slap in the face to every rule she'd ever been forced to follow.

Jenner bit down harder still and Bria swallowed down a moan. Did he realize the effect he had on her? That his aggressiveness sent a rush of want through her that slicked her thighs and stirred her desire? *I've never wanted anything as badly as I do this male.* A result of their tether? Or something else entirely?

Did it matter?

Jenner's tongue flicked out to seal the bites and Bria shivered. She wasn't ready for this moment to end. She needed to keep him on the edge, reckless. Before the bliss of feeding wore off and he regained the good sense to put her at arm's length yet again.

Bria wanted to teach Jenner a lesson tonight as well: She was more than the virginal image that had been painted of her. *So much more.*

He disengaged from her throat and Bria stilled. He rested his forehead against her shoulder, his breath coming in heavy gasps as though he fought off some deep, internal pain. Worry replaced any schemes she might have been devising and she traced the tips of her fingers down his temple and across the rough stubble of his jaw. "Jenner?"

He pulled away with a tortured groan. A deep furrow marred his brow and his eyes were alight with brilliant silver. His full lips pulled away from his fangs with a snarl and he wrapped his arms tightly around her as his mouth descended on hers in a violent and urgent kiss.

Oh . . . gods.

Bria let herself be swept away in the moment. She didn't give a second thought to the dhampir and her covetous gaze, to the other supernatural creatures that surrounded them, or to the sizzle of magic in the air that sent a zing of anxiety through her bloodstream.

Jenner's lips were firm yet demanding, his grip on her, possessive and commanding. The wet heat of his mouth seared her as his tongue lashed at out at the seam of her lips, urging her to open up to him. The taste of his blood lingered and mingled with her own that still clung to his tongue. Exquisite. Heady, like an aged brandy that caused her thoughts to haze and her head to spin. *More.* She wanted more.

His mouth slanted across hers as his tongue thrust into her mouth. She released a pleasured moan at the silky glide and wound her fists into the fabric of his shirt, pulling him closer. Jenner gripped her hip in one strong hand and jerked her against him. The hard length of his erection brushed against her sex and Bria sighed into Jenner's mouth as delicious pressure built inside of her.

Jenner had brought her here tonight to teach her focus. To show her that danger was ever present no matter her strength. To make sure that she knew the scope of what she was capable of as well as her limitations. None of that mattered when his mouth claimed hers. When she was in his arms the world melted away. Sensations and sounds, scents, dissolved until there was only him. His taste on her lips. The rich, musky scent of his arousal. The grip of his large hand on her hip and his fist in her hair. He drew her focus like no other thing in this world could. As for the danger . . . Bria realized as she further lost herself to his kisses that the most dangerous thing in this world was the male in her arms and the way he made her feel.

She broke away and searched his face. His gaze was unfocused. Feral. His nostrils flared and his chest rose and fell with his heavy breaths. "Jenner." Her own composure crumbled to dust. "Bite me again. Please."

His lips pulled back to reveal his fangs and Jenner struck.

The force of his attack nearly laid her out on the bar. He released Bria's hair only to cup her ass in his palms. With a thrust of his hips he jerked her to the edge of the bar, and Bria groaned as his erection ground against her sex at the same moment his fangs broke her skin. Pleasure crested within her and Bria's body took over. She met every thrust of his hips and a shock of sensation pulsed from her clitoris as he ground his erection against her.

"Don't stop," she gasped. "Oh, gods, don't stop!"

Their glasses rattled on the bar top with every powerful roll of Jenner's hips, and Bria's head fell back as he drank from her. They'd drawn the attention of many of the clubbers, and curious eyes watched with heated expressions. Gods help her, she didn't care. Didn't feel an ounce of embarrassment or shame. She let her eyes drift shut and blocked out everything around her until there was nothing left but her body and his. The powerful suction of his mouth on her throat and the deep thrust of his hips that awakened every nerve ending in her body.

Need built within her. Jenner's fingers dove beneath her blouse and the flat of his palm ventured up her torso. Bria's stomach muscles twitched as intense sensation fired along her sensitive flesh. Jenner cupped her breast through her bra before jerking the fabric aside. He touched her not roughly, but with an edge of possession that caused Bria's breath to race. With a gentle flick his thumb brushed over her taut nipple, and a rush of sensation raced through her to settle between her thighs.

"Do that again."

Another sharp thrust of his hips accompanied the strong suction of his mouth. He plucked at her nipple and the sensitive tip tightened further under his ministrations to the point that Bria didn't think she could take another moment of the intense pleasure he gave her.

"Oh!"

Her world broke apart into a mass of infinite stars before her. Her muscles contracted as wave after wave of sensation stole over her. Bria cried out and Jenner released his hold on her throat only to seal his mouth over hers. He swallowed down her sobs as the pulses ebbed and faded away into a pleasant glow that left Bria flushed and without breath. He'd given her an orgasm in the view of anyone who cared to watch. For the first time in her life Bria felt recklessly alive.

Gods, the way he made her *feel*.

"Jenner . . . ," she whispered against his mouth.

Bria wasn't so naïve that she didn't know her own body. She'd pleasured herself, knew how to bring herself to orgasm. There had been stolen moments in her uncle's coven when she was young. Males who kissed her and whispered pretty words in her ear when they thought no one was looking. Bria had spent decades *yearning*. She'd existed on hope and fantasy for so long that she'd despaired of ever knowing true passion. None of her fantasies could compare to this moment, though. As innocent as it had been, Jenner brought her to new heights. And Bria wanted him to take her higher still.

Jenner's body trembled against her as though he was barely able to restrain himself. He backed away with a start and scrubbed the back of his hand over his mouth. "Gods, Bria." He sounded appalled. As though he couldn't believe what had just happened. "I . . . Jesus fucking Christ." Regret and fear shone in his silver-rimmed eyes. "The bathroom is over there. Go."

"And do what?" Her anger mounted. That he'd treat what had just happened as something awful left her soaring heart in tattered shreds. "I don't need to go."

"*I* need you to go," he said on a desperate growl. "I need a minute. To get my shit straight. And I don't want to leave you here in the open, unprotected while I do it."

"I don't need your protection!" Bria felt eyes on them once again. She could only imagine what this must've looked like.

"You don't know what you need," Jenner countered. He no longer looked dazed, his expression clouded with lust. The male was absolutely *furious*. "Go."

Without a word Bria rushed past him, through the press of bodies toward the restrooms at the far end of the club. How could he treat her so callously? She'd seen the lust in his gaze, felt his need reach out through their tether. Had he brought her here simply to humiliate her?

Bria burst through the bathroom door, thankful to find it empty. She turned on the faucet and took several cleansing breaths before she splashed the cold water on her face. It cooled the heat of embarrassment that colored her cheeks, but it wasn't enough to quench the hurt that burned in her chest or cool her rising temper.

Eric Jenner wasn't the male she'd thought he was. Even more disconcerting was the sense that this male she'd known for such a short time had already managed to break her heart.

CHAPTER
13

Jenner's breath heaved in his chest as he turned his back on the mass of bodies on the dance floor. His elbows came down on the bar while he cradled his skull in his palms. Gods, he'd fucked up. Big-time. He'd hoped that being tethered would help him to finally get a grip on his control. That he wouldn't be mastered by his fucking lusts anymore. What he'd learned tonight with Bria was that he was more out of control than he'd ever been.

Even now his want of her threatened to consume him.

Bria said she didn't need protection, but that couldn't be further from the truth. Thomas Fairchild hoped that Jenner could be that male. No one—except perhaps Mikhail and Ronan—stopped to think that perhaps Bria needed someone to protect her from *him*. How could he have treated her so carelessly?

His own tortured memories swamped him and Jenner gave a rough shake of his head in an effort to dislodge them. He could have drained Bria if he hadn't regained his damned senses. His bloodlust had raged as he buried his fangs in her throat. Her blood, so sweet on his tongue, was a nectar he couldn't get enough of. With each swallow he'd lost himself to the point that he wasn't sure what was memory and what was reality. A vision of Bria, limp and lifeless in his arms as Ronja had been, flashed in Jenner's mind and he shuddered. He could easily kill Bria and there was no one save his own fool self to keep his lusts in check.

Gods. He was a fucking train wreck and everything he touched turned to shit. It would be better for Bria if he sent her back to her uncle. Even as the thought took form Jenner banished it from his mind. Mere days in her company and he knew he'd never be strong enough to let her go.

His soul belonged to her.

"She's not enough to satisfy you." Jenner cursed under his breath and turned. Marissa stood so close he could smell the cheap tequila on her breath. *Gods-damn it.* This was all he needed. She traced a finger down between his pecs and he bristled. "Let's go back to my place. I can give you what you need."

He looked pointedly at her hand that had come to rest on his stomach. Marissa's expression fell and she took a tentative step back. "Your girl can join us if you want. You know I don't mind sharing."

"Not tonight, Marissa." *Not any night. Not ever fucking again.*

"Your thirst hasn't been quenched. It takes a lot of blood to sate you. Your eyes are still bright silver."

She spoke about him as if she truly knew him. Marissa knew fuck all about his thirst. As for his eyes, they flashed silver with lust for his *mate* and agitation for the female standing before him. "Go find someone else to warm your bed tonight. Because it isn't going to be me."

Above Marissa's head Jenner scanned the crowd for any sign of Bria. She'd been in the bathroom for longer than he'd expected and he cursed his own foolish anger for sending her away. Anxiety pooled in his gut. Acid burned its way up his throat. Marissa continued to talk about the gods knew what. Jenner could think of nothing but pushing through the mass of bodies. *Where in the hell is she?*

As one of the soulless he hadn't been bothered by emotions. Now he experienced the fallout for his apathy in the female who glared at him with open hatred and in his own gods-damned worry for Bria.

"You're a selfish son of a bitch, Jenner! That whore you brought here tonight will *never* be as good for you as I am," she spat.

The sting of her palm cracking against his face caused Jenner's anger to surface. He deserved every bit of her disdain, though. And she was an admirable female for standing her ground. Bria, however, did not deserve it. His anger crested with a feral snarl and he clamped his jaw shut, lest he bare his fangs. He was a predator after all. An animal. And when cornered he behaved as any animal would.

"Speak of her that way again," he snarled, "and I'll make sure you're banished from the city. Your own coven won't even give you shelter."

"You'll come back to me. When you're mad with thirst and your cock is aching you'll *beg* me to take you to my bed!" Fear glistened in Marissa's eyes and she turned on a heel, stumbling as she pushed her way through the throng of bodies on the dance floor.

Jesus. What else could he fuck up tonight?

Jenner whipped around, his gaze scanning the crowd. He sensed Bria's distress long before his eyes found her. A constriction of his chest and a sharp twist of his gut that left him shaking. His fangs throbbed in his gums and rage scorched a path up this throat. He plowed through the people crowding the dance floor, his arm sweeping out like a scythe as he pushed bodies aside. Her fear stole his breath. All thoughts of his own unquenchable thirst evaporated under the rage that clouded Jenner's vision as he pressed on. Some sorry fucker was going to bleed tonight.

Had Jenner not felt her presence he wouldn't have seen her. A big, burly son of a bitch had Bria pinned against the wall not far from the bathrooms. Jenner took the male's scent into his lungs—a shifter if he had to guess—and ripped him away from Bria. He spun the male around and put *his* back to the wall with enough force to crack the brick.

The shifter's dark beady eyes went wide and his scent soured with fear. A smug, feral smile stretched Jenner's lips, revealing the tips of his fangs. "You put your hands on my *mate,* shifter. I've killed males for less." Speaking the word aloud sent a jolt through Jenner's system. Bria was his mate. His to protect. From anyone or anything that meant to do her harm. Even from his own godsdamned self. The male swallowed visibly and his gaze darted briefly to Bria. "Don't look at her, you piece of shit!" Jenner rattled the male hard enough to shake his brain loose. "You so much as breathe in her scent again and I'll tear out your throat. You get me?"

The male nodded emphatically, but that wasn't enough for Jenner.

"Say it," he growled close to the male's ear.

"I-I get you."

Jenner let him go and the male slumped against the wall. "Fucking vampire," he muttered under his breath. "I didn't want your frigid bitch anyway."

Jenner brought his arm up and spun. His fist cracked as it made contact with the male's jaw and he went down like a felled tree. Jenner reached down and jerked the fucker up by his collar, took a deep breath, and held the shifter's scent in his lungs once again, committing it to memory. "If I see you in this place again, I'll kill you." He released his hold and the shifter sprawled back to the floor.

Jenner's breath sawed in and out of his chest with his rage. His hands shook and he clenched them into tight fists. The urge to commit violence burned through him. He wanted to open the shifter's throat. To watch as his blood pooled on the floor and—

Gentle hands settled on his biceps and Jenner stilled in an instant. He turned to find Bria beside him, her expression full of concern. One hand ventured up to his shoulder, and with slow, circular motions she eased the tension from his muscles. The pad of her thumb feathered over the pulse point at his throat and Jenner shuddered. Her skin glided against his as soft as satin. Her presence was the calming warmth to his cold cruelty. Her touch a gentle balm on his abrasive violence. He didn't deserve this female. Would only ruin her.

"Did he hurt you?" Jenner choked on the words as emotion welled hot and thick in his throat. He didn't trust himself to touch her. Not while his grip on his control balanced on a razor's edge. The slightest tremor vibrated through him from the tips of his fingers right down to his toes and Jenner bit down on the inside of his cheek until he tasted blood. Her fear turned him into a mindless animal. He'd do anything to assuage it.

"No," she said on a shaky breath. "He thought I was the vampire queen. When I told him I wasn't, he wanted to know who I was, how many dhampirs had been turned." She removed her hands from Jenner's body and the absence of her touch sliced an open wound in his soul. "He said he'd never fucked a vampire and offered to buy me breakfast afterward. When I told him he could go fuck himself instead he got a little cranky. That's when you showed up."

Jenner's control slipped another notch. The thought of that male's hands on Bria, his breath in her ear, resurrected thoughts of murder. He needed to get the hell out of here before he lost it completely. He seized Bria's upper arm and tucked her close to his body. They were too exposed in the club. Too many threats loomed. He'd been stupid to bring her here.

"Jenner, what are you doing?" Bria had to take two steps for every one of his, but Jenner couldn't make himself slow down. "Let go of me."

"We're leaving," he ground out.

"Because of one stupid jerk?"

"This was a mistake. One I won't make again."

Bria tried to pull away, but he held her fast. Even as he said the words Jenner knew he'd regret them. If he kept up with the bipolar, overprotective asshole routine she'd grow to hate him. Maybe that was for the best, though. If he allowed himself to feel anything for her he'd surely destroy her.

Jenner's unapologetic ferocity left Bria awestruck. That didn't mean she wasn't furious as hell with him. When she walked out of the bathroom and saw the dhampir with her hand poised on Jenner's lean, muscular torso, though, Bria's temper had snapped. She'd wanted to tear the audacious female's throat out. Her own violent urge had shaken Bria. It hadn't deterred her, however. No, the shifter had managed to stay her course when he'd put her up against that wall.

And now Jenner was intent on dragging her home and putting her back on the shelf. This male she'd only known for a short time had taken it upon himself to make decisions for her as though he actually had the right. "I said, let go of me!" Bria gave another hard jerk of her arm and managed to free herself from Jenner's iron grip. He rounded on her, his eyes flashing with quicksilver, his lip curled back in a snarl. He could try to frighten her all he wanted. She refused to cower. "We might be tethered, but you don't own me."

She steeled herself against the vicious glint of his icy stare. He leaned in close, his mouth hovering dangerously close to hers. "Don't I?"

Cruel, heartless male. "No." Her deadly tone matched his. "You do *not.* I'll find my own way back to Mikhail's house. I don't want or need your company for the rest of the night, Jenner."

He reached for her again and Bria bared her fangs. It felt good to stand up for herself and she quickly became drunk on her own power. She could be as ruthless as Jenner. His brow furrowed at the warning inherent in her expression, but the violent gleam in his eyes tamed. Music surged around them, a deep, pounding bass that drilled into Bria's skull. The crowd surged with the wild beat and she used the opportunity to slip through the press of bodies. A sense of panic swelled within her as she expected Jenner to chase after her. And though she felt the heat of his stare sizzle over her skin, she knew that he'd stayed put.

That he would let her walk away both empowered and saddened her. Despite her need for independence, she wanted to know that the need she'd sensed in him hadn't been imagined. That he felt *something* for her. Which was silly, wasn't it? How could he possibly care about her when he didn't really know her? Well, she'd teach Jenner another lesson tonight. One about *her.* If she was going to be tethered to this male he needed to learn now that Bria would no longer allow herself to be treated with indifference. What she wanted mattered. And the sooner Jenner recognized that, the better.

She took his advice to heart as she left the club and stepped out onto the crowded sidewalk. In order to be truly in tune with her environment she couldn't let her senses work against her. Likewise, it would be foolish to draw attention to herself, no matter if the streets were populated with droves of supernatural creatures or simply humans. Bria had become a member of a very small race of creatures. Notoriety wasn't something she could afford. Especially with her uncle's centuries' worth of worries scratching at the back of her mind.

The fine hairs on Bria's arms stood on end. Her body reacted on pure instinct and she spun, fangs bared and ready to tear into flesh. She slammed the muscular form of her assailant against the stucco façade of a storefront at the exact moment his scent hit her nostrils. As quickly as she'd reacted Bria pulled back on her immense strength, holding him still before her.

"Lucas! What are you doing here?" Was there no one who thought she could take care of herself? "Did you follow me?"

"I'm worried about you." Worried and afraid. The tang of his fear burned her nostrils. His clear blue gaze searched hers and a crease marred his brow.

"I could have hurt you." Lucas was foolish to have followed them. If Jenner saw them together he'd kill Lucas. Indignant fire sparked in Bria's belly. Jenner had rejected her yet again. Proved to her with his possessive outburst that she was nothing more to him than a *thing*. To hell with Jenner. She'd known Lucas for a century. He was her friend. Bria wouldn't cut herself off from her family simply because it didn't please Jenner to see Lucas put his hands on something that the vampire deemed was *his*.

Careful, Bria. This could be dangerous ground.

She still didn't fully understand the extent of her tether with Jenner. She certainly wasn't interested in putting Lucas in danger. But since she was confident that Jenner hadn't followed her from the club, she figured Lucas was safe enough in her presence now. Besides, when Bria walked out on Jenner she hadn't thought about how she'd get all the way across the city and back to the king's home. At least now she wouldn't be racing against the sunrise to make it back there.

"You could never hurt me," Lucas said in a too-gentle murmur. "Just like I could never allow any harm to come to you. Where's the bastard who's claimed to have tethered you? I'm sure Thomas would be interested to know that he abandoned you in this part of the city."

"Which is why you won't breathe a word of this to him."

Lucas's brow furrowed. "You'd defend the vampire?"

"Jenner didn't abandon me," Bria said. "I left him." A spark of hope lit Lucas's eyes and Bria held up a hand. "It's not what you think."

"No?" Lucas arched a brow. "If you felt any loyalty to him, if this tether is as all-encompassing and magical as the vampires suggest, then why aren't you at his side right now?"

"*I* am a vampire," Bria stressed yet again. "Stop pretending as though I'm not."

"You are the same," Lucas said. "Sweet. Loyal. Soft." He reached out to smooth a lock of hair that had escaped her ponytail from her face. "Beautiful. Gentle."

Bria's temper rose. She allowed a warning growl to build in her throat. Lucas might as well have called her helpless. Weak. Incapable. Obedient. "I am *changed*. I could kill you easily, Lucas, and you behave as though I'm too frail to walk alone on the street." His brow furrowed at her vehement hiss. "I have taken the vein at Jenner's throat." This time, Lucas had the audacity to look appalled. "And he has taken mine."

"Bria." Lucas did nothing to hide his shock. "That is forbidden."

He wrapped his hand around her arm and guided her down the street. A heated conversation on a crowded sidewalk was bound to draw attention, and apparently Lucas wanted their exchange to be private.

"Why is it forbidden?" She'd never questioned her uncle's laws, but now that she was free of the coven Bria had become more brazen. "Have you ever wondered what prompted him to set such mandates? Do you know of any other covens that are so regulated?"

"The other covens are wild," Lucas said with disdain. "Animals who feed at will and without restraint."

Bria stopped in her tracks. Lucas turned to face her, brow raised in question. "Perhaps we *are* animals."

He urged her to walk again and his scent soured with fear once again. The power she felt outweighed her concern for her friend. She wanted to prove to everyone that she wasn't *viaton,* as Jenner had called her. Bria was ready to show her teeth.

"Bria, we are above the sway of base urges. Giving in to them only serves to justify the Sortiari's slaughter of our kind."

Never had those words sounded so false to her ears. Indignation burned through her and Bria pulled away from Lucas's grasp. If Lucas and even her uncle weren't going to treat her with any more respect than Jenner had, Bria had no use for any of them. "You're wrong. My uncle is *wrong.* He is afraid of what we are. What we have the potential to become. And he's taught us all to share in his fear. I'm not afraid, Lucas. Not anymore."

Lucas stopped in his tracks and seized Bria's arm. He

pulled her to him and his free arm came around her waist. "Come home where you belong, Bria." His whispered words were a desperate plea. "Please. Stay with me."

"Bria is a vampire now. A *tethered* vampire. She doesn't belong with your coven, dhampir."

Damn it. Bria had been so preoccupied with Lucas that she hadn't sensed Jenner come up behind them on his motorcycle. His voice rippled over her, dark and dangerous. Lucas met his stare, so defiant that Bria almost felt sorry for him. He was no match for Jenner, yet he refused to back down.

"You might have tethered her," Lucas said. "But you don't *own* her."

Jenner cocked a challenging brow and it was all Bria could do not to kick him. *Arrogant males.* "Sunrise isn't far off," he remarked as though he couldn't be bothered to respond to Lucas. "Let's go."

Lucas implored Bria with his drawn expression. No matter how she felt about Jenner right now, he was right. She didn't belong with Lucas and the other members of her coven. That part of her life was over. There was still so much she didn't know about her new existence, and the only way she'd learn was to remain at Mikhail's. At least, for now.

"Go home, Lucas," she said as she walked toward Jenner's motorcycle. A resounding sadness hollowed out her chest as she climbed on behind him. "Where you belong."

Jenner pulled out onto the street without another word. Bria buried her face in his back despite her anger. She couldn't bear to see the look of hurt on Lucas's face as he stared after them. For the first time in days, Bria wished her soul hadn't been returned to her. She could've used a healthy dose of apathy right about now.

CHAPTER
14

Not even the rush of the early-morning air could cool Jenner's temper. He'd followed Bria from the club, careful to keep his distance, only to find that bastard Lucas had sniffed her out like a hound on the hunt. Jenner had watched from the shadows as the dhampir led Bria away from the club, his head bent close to hers. When they'd stopped to exchange heated words on the sidewalk Jenner's resolve had nearly broken. The sight of the other male's hands on his mate, the urgently whispered pleas . . . It had taken a physical effort not to succumb to his blood-lust as he listened to Lucas beg Bria yet again to stay with him.

It seemed the bastard was relentless in his pursuit of her. Jenner gripped the handlebars so tight that they creaked in his palms. The Ducati came to a screeching halt at the security gate of Mikhail's driveway and Jenner's body tensed as he waited for the guards to let him through. Behind him, Bria gripped the sides of his jacket, unwilling to put her arms around him as she had earlier in the night. He'd treated her no better than the uncle she sought to escape, and Jenner was rewarded for his dick-ish behavior with her cool dismissal.

When he pulled the bike to a stop in front of the house Bria hopped off and rushed under the portico for the front door. The door swung open and a swath of light cut across the shadows before it slammed closed. Jenner didn't move. Didn't take a single gods-damned breath. He leaned on the handlebars, his body vibrating with tension. He didn't trust himself to chase after her again. If he did he'd be tempted to pick up where they'd left off at the bar and she'd know once and for all to whom and where she belonged.

Instead, Jenner sought out his king.

He sat with Claire in the entertainment room at the back of the house. Tucked into one corner of the large sectional couch, she lounged against him while he idly caressed the swell of her stomach. A movie played in the background, something action packed, with myriad explosions. But the two of them seemed not to notice. They kept their heads bent close together as they spoke in hushed tones. Again, Jenner was struck by not only the intensity but also the intimacy of their relationship and it caused his chest to ache with a foreign and uncomfortable want.

"Jenner," Mikhail said without turning to see who'd entered the room. "Is everything all right?"

"A word?" he replied.

Claire eased herself up from the couch. "I need to get breakfast situated before I get Vanessa up for school." She placed a slow kiss on Mikhail's mouth before she excused herself. "Try not to look so bleak, Jenner," she teased as she headed out of the room. "You'll get the hang of it."

Gods. Was it that obvious that his tether was the source of his sour mood?

Mikhail sat up straighter and held out a hand in invitation. "Sit."

A space of silence passed between them. Jenner took a deep breath. Released it. "Siobhan is requesting that you let her see Chelle. If you allow it, she'll share whatever information she has on the rogue werewolf. I spoke with Ronan about it earlier tonight and he agreed that—"

"It's been little more than a week, Jenner. Give yourself time to adjust."

He didn't want to talk about his tether. Or Bria. Or the fact that he felt more out of control than ever. He didn't want his king to know that he was on the verge of becoming the mindless creature he'd always feared he'd be. "It's not a good idea. The rogue is inconsequential. Siobhan's obsessions have focused on Chelle. She doesn't give a single shit about Gregor. He'll lick his wounds before he refocuses his efforts. The attacks on the covens are what need our attention for now. That's how we'll find him."

Mikhail regarded him for a quiet moment. "Have you fed, Jenner?"

"Yes." His voice cracked on the word. He'd taken more than he should have from Bria tonight, and still his thirst raged in his throat as though he was newly turned. *Monster.*

Mikhail cocked a brow. "Recently?"

Jenner let out a derisive snort. "As though you don't know that I've glutted myself without an ounce of self-control every night for months."

Mikhail's lips formed a hard line. "And Bria?"

Jenner thought of her fangs at this throat and his cock stirred. Gods, how he wanted her naked, soft, and willing beneath him. "She has a remarkable grip on her control."

"You didn't come here to talk to me about Siobhan, or Gregor, or even your own lack of control. Perhaps you should get to the point before the sun rises."

Where to start? Could he admit to Mikhail that he wanted the tether broken? That if he could he'd send his soul back into oblivion so he wouldn't have to endure the torture of emotions he couldn't explain or manage? That he'd live for eternity as one of the soulless if it meant protecting Bria from him? "I know nothing about her," he said at last. "And she sees me as nothing more than a violent asshole."

"She said that?"

"No," Jenner admitted. "She didn't have to."

"The tether is a gift."

No. It was a fucking curse. Jenner thought he could speak openly with Mikhail about the emotions that crippled him, but he found that he couldn't admit his weakness to his king. "You were right to keep me from her that first night," he said. "I should be kept from her now. I know I have no right to ask, but can Bria stay here for a while longer?" Until Jenner could decide how best to proceed with Bria, he wanted her somewhere close. Where he knew she'd be protected.

"Of course she can. It's already been established. You're both welcome to stay as long as you'd like."

Jenner was always welcome at the house and had stayed often in the past. He'd made a temporary home here because it had been easier to be close if Mikhail needed him for anything. And then because of Bria. Now, though, it would be best if he kept his distance. "I'll stay at my place for a while." Mikhail's gaze snapped up and Jenner added, "If that's all right with you."

"You'll only further test your control by keeping yourself from her," Mikhail warned. "And you certainly won't forge a lasting bond with her."

Exactly. Forming any sort of bond with Bria beyond their tether would only bring ruin. "For now, I think it's best."

Mikhail pursed his lips and pinned Jenner with a powerful stare that damn near made him squirm. "Spend your days where you will, but mark my words, you'll come to regret the decision. Your nights, however, still belong to me."

Jenner inclined his head. "Of course."

"I want you to pay a visit to Fairchild's coven," Mikhail said. "Without Bria."

As if Jenner would ever consider taking her there. "He makes me twitchy," Jenner admitted. "He's got secrets, and not a few prejudices."

"I agree. Find out what those secrets are. I can't afford any surprises."

Neither could Jenner. Especially where Bria was concerned. "I'm on it. What about Siobhan's request? She'll expect an answer from me."

"I'll consider it," Mikhail replied. "Only because my cooperation seems to annoy her."

Jenner pushed himself off the couch. "I'll visit Fairchild's coven at sunset tomorrow."

"Good." If Mikhail had anything more to say he held his tongue.

Jenner made his way back through the house to the foyer, his feet like lead weights that refused to lend him speed. He gripped the door handle and turned it. His head slumped between his shoulders and his jaw clamped down. Fire raged in his throat and his sac ached with unspent seed. Pent-up aggression, want, lust, raged within him, overriding any shred of common sense he might've had left. With a growl he spun on a heel and raced up the staircase to the second-story guest room.

He burst into the room without preamble. She started, her eyes narrowed as he shut the door behind him.

"Unless you've come to apologize to me, I suggest you leave."

Bria might have appeared fragile, but she was made of steel. That contradiction in her fascinated him. Jenner crossed the room, careful to keep his pace slow. "I will not apologize for protecting what's mine."

"Was it protection or possession that prompted you to come after me tonight when you knew I wanted some space? From what I can tell, you're more concerned with not sharing your toys than you are with taking proper care of them."

Jenner snorted. "You're right. I *don't* share."

Bria's narrowed amethyst gaze raked over him. But all her defiance served to do was further heat his blood. "And yet you share yourself well enough."

Had jealousy lent a sharp edge to her tone? Jenner cocked a brow, unwilling to assuage her doubts. He liked to think that Bria might be jealous. That despite this situation they found themselves locked together in, she might be interested in him beyond their tether.

"If the dhampir so much as lays a finger on you again, I'll tear open his throat and drink him dry."

Bria's eyes widened and her jaw set with quiet indignation. "Is that a threat?"

Jenner gripped both of her arms and leaned in so close that his mouth brushed the shell of her ear. Bria shuddered in his grasp and her scent bloomed sweet around him. Unafraid. "No, *viaton,* it is a promise."

Jenner's dark tone shivered over Bria's skin. She hated that despite his harsh words all she wanted was to draw him closer. His lips brushed her ear with his heated breath and her lower abdomen clenched with want. The scent of his blood ignited her thirst, as did the frantic beat of his heart.

She refused to let him continue to treat her as though she were some fragile thing. Likewise, she wouldn't let him humiliate her like he had tonight when she came from the bathroom to find another female rubbing her body against his. Bria came up on her tiptoes. Jenner's height prevented her from getting any higher than his throat, and the sight of the vein pulsing there sent her thirst into a frenzy. "Then you should know that I don't share, either. If another female ever puts her hands on you with familiarity again, you can expect similar retaliation."

Jenner's body went taut.

"I've been dictated to for centuries. Don't think for a moment that I appreciate your mandates any more than I did my uncle's."

Jenner's grip slid to her wrists. He pulled away, his eyes brilliant silver as he slowly urged her backward. Bria's breath came in shallow pants as she angled her head up to look fully into his face. A deep crease marred his brow, the same tortured look of pain he'd worn the first time she laid eyes on him. Jenner transferred both of her wrists into one of his large palms and pinned them above her head as he backed her against the wall.

His need flared through their tether and Bria sensed that Jenner hung on to his control by the barest of threads. A sense of her own power flared through her and she angled her head ever so slightly to the right, giving him an unhindered view of the slim column of her throat. He struck with the speed of a viper, burying his fangs into the delicate skin she'd bared to him.

Yes! Bria's mind screamed with triumph that she'd managed to push Jenner over the edge. His grip on her wrists slackened and then fell away as he grabbed her around the waist and lifted her up to his height. Bria wrapped her legs around his waist and angled her hips so that her sex brushed the length of his erection. Jenner groaned against her throat, but he did nothing to stop her. Instead, he thrust his hips to grind into her.

Bria thought that nothing could rival the joy she'd found in the freedom of her rebirth, but she was wrong.

This moment, offering her vein to Jenner and knowing that he would do the same for her, was unlike anything she'd ever experienced before. What she didn't know about him didn't matter as the warm suction sent a zing of sensation through Bria's body. No matter what happened between them, she would always crave this gruff, high-handed male who held her with absolute possession. Tethered or not.

Jenner pulled away from Bria's throat with a roar. A warm trickle of blood ran down the column of her neck and he lapped it up with the flat of his tongue. Bria melted against the wall, gripped his massive shoulders in her palms, and dug in with her nails. A low purr vibrated in his chest as he licked her again, this time lower, passing over the swell of her breast.

Bria's skin pulled as the punctures closed on their own, but Jenner continued to lap at her skin as though the blood still flowed. Slow, languid passes that turned her to liquid in his embrace. The male was every bit an animal. Wild and untamed. Her head rolled back on her shoulders and Bria simply *felt*. Every nerve ending in her body fired, her skin tingled with awareness of Jenner's touch. When the wet heat of his mouth left her, Bria brought her head up to find him studying her, his irises flooded with silver. He reached up and brushed the pad of his thumb over Bria's bottom lip. She flicked out with her tongue and caught the salty taste of his skin. The pained crease returned to his brow and Bria reached up to smooth it away. Whatever his demons, Jenner fought an internal battle, and she couldn't begin to guess what it was.

Bria wanted to soothe him. To bear whatever burden weighed him down. She opened her mouth to tell him just that when he rasped, "Take my vein."

She cupped the back of his strong neck and buried her fangs at the pulse point. A grunt that was half pleasure, half pain escaped Jenner's lips as his arms went tightly around her. He held her as though he was afraid she'd fly. Bria threaded her fingers through the hair at Jenner's nape. The fire of her thirst subsided with every deep pull, but it did nothing to calm the frenzy of bloodlust that swept her up in its violent storm.

With one hand at the back of her neck Jenner pressed her hard against his throat while the other wrapped securely around her waist. With the wall at her back Bria was effectively pinned. The tease of his erection as he continued to thrust against her drove Bria to wild heights of desire. She wanted skin on skin, and the distraction of the barrier of their clothes was maddening.

A desperate growl built in his chest as Jenner spun her away from the wall and deposited her on the bed. Bria's fangs disengaged from his throat and the ribbon of crimson that rolled in beads over the sculpted hills of muscle to disappear beneath the fabric of his shirt held her rapt. Gods, she wanted to lick it away as he had done to her.

Jenner reached for the hems of her thick leggings and pulled them from her, along with her underwear, with a forceful jerk. Bria gasped as his hand cupped her aching sex. The heat of his skin set her on fire. Her arousal slicked her thighs and Jenner dragged his fingers over her slippery flesh before his fingertips settled at her clitoris.

"Oh!" Bria sucked in a breath at the sharp stab of pleasure. "Oh, gods."

Jenner leaned over her until her vision was filled with his fierce countenance. "Bite me again," he commanded, and Bria obeyed. She came up on her elbows and buried her face in the crook of his neck, biting down as he circled the sensitive knot of nerves. "Yessss." The word left his lips on a hiss. "Harder. Make me feel it." She bit down harder and his blood flowed faster, warm and thick over her tongue. "That's it."

He panted over her as though her bite was all the pleasure he required. His fingers slid over her clit in an artful dance, applying the perfect amount of pressure as he circled it with slow, gentle passes of his fingertips. Bria's muscles contracted and her thighs began to tremble. She'd never felt such raw, blinding pleasure. His skin on hers, rough where she was soft, drove her mad with want. He eased a finger inside of her and Bria bit down harder at the light sting of the intrusion.

Jenner groaned. "You're so tight, Bria." He eased out and back in, slowly. *"Gods."*

He continued to work her, slowly, and Bria shattered. She disengaged her fangs from his throat and cried out, raw, ragged sobs of pleasure that vibrated through her with every deep pulse of her sex. She threw her head back, unable to maintain even an ounce of composure as the pleasure ripped through her. Her body trembled violently, and when she didn't think she could take another moment of Jenner's onslaught his strokes became softer still. Gentle as he slowly brought her back to earth.

She'd never felt so good.

For long moments he loomed over her. He inhaled deeply, feathered his fingers from her temple to her chin. As though she were made of glass, he pulled her up to her feet. Anticipation coiled in Bria's stomach as she waited for what would happen next. Confusion quickly overtook her, though, as he gently guided her underwear back up her thighs. He considered this over? For her it had barely started. Her need for Jenner hadn't subsided. Instead, it swelled within her. Torturing her with its intensity.

"I'll be damned if you run off alone again." His breath came in pants, his chest rising and falling with each word. "But if you do, I want you to be able to protect yourself." A tremor shook his voice as Jenner took a tentative step back. Silver lit his gaze and a rich bloom of his musky scent clung to the air. He wanted her. She knew he did. So why did he pull away? "There are matters that demand my attention at sundown tomorrow. But when I return, I want you dressed and prepared for a workout."

He gave her a lingering appraisal as his gaze raked from her feet, up the length of her body, until it met hers again. The furrow returned to his brow and he stalked from the room without another word spoken.

Disappointment settled like a stone in Bria's stomach, and still a secretive smile curved her lips. She didn't know why or how, but she sensed that though she was far from winning the war, she'd won a battle tonight.

CHAPTER
15

"I told you *not* to be late."

Christian might have been eager to take Gregor's money, but that didn't mean he was eager to be his bitch. Berserkers could be insufferably uptight. "You're lucky I showed at all," Christian replied. "I don't respond well to mandates."

The berserker smirked. Black bled into his eyes, the only indication of his mounting temper. "As long as I'm paying you, you'll respond to whatever the fuck I say you will."

Gods. The things I do for money. "As soon as you come to an agreement with McAlister, he'll send me somewhere else. Whatever you need me for, Gregor, you'd better get your ass in gear."

"McAlister and I will come to an agreement when hell freezes over."

So negotiations were going good? Christian scoffed, "You know what happens to those who leave their fold."

Gregor fixed Christian with his empty black stare. "I'd like to see him try."

Battles were fought by armies and McAlister was a single general. Without the berserker warlords to act as their muscle the Sortiari would have to undergo a major overhaul. Who would they enlist as their enforcers? Most members of the supernatural community regarded the secret society with suspicion. McAlister's paranoia hadn't done him any favors over the years.

"I doubt you ordered me to meet you tonight to talk about Sortiari business. And I gotta be honest with you, Gregor. I don't enjoy being strung along. So shit or get off the pot."

Christian's wolf rose to the surface of his psyche. The wolf didn't cower in the presence of the beast and the animal tired of these games as much as Christian did. If he didn't need Gregor's money to pay off Marac he would have told the berserker to fuck off and call it a day. But in case he couldn't rely on the money he had on the MMA fight to pay out he needed a backup plan. It was either that or burn in the eternal hellfire of the demon's torture pit.

That sure as shit wasn't how Christian wanted to go down.

The same insufferable and arrogant smirk curved the berserker's lips. "I've attacked every coven in the city that I could find," Gregor said. "Ten of them. There are thirteen dhampir covens in L.A."

"Trying to rattle the vampire king

Gregor's expression grew dark a   is
irises. "I'll kill him soon enough
cific coven. A specific dhampi
wen. Her family name would
was smart, she'll have cha

Christian snorted. "I'
to work out your kinks

A snarl escaped
of the beast that l

animal side clawed at the back of Christian's mind, rallying for a fight.

"I made a vow four hundred years ago that I'd wipe out
Connall Réamonn's entire bloodline. I won't rest until I've
done just that."

Vendettas were dangerous things. Christian made it a
point not to hold grudges. Vengeance ate at the soul like
a cancer, spreading and corrupting until there was nothing left but a dark, empty chasm. No doubt Gregor's black
eyes reflected the darkness that had consumed his soul.
Four hundred years was a long gods-damned time to hold
on to his anger.

"If it's a single family you're after, why kill them all?"

The black tendrils retreated from Gregor's eyes, leaving nothing but deep green. "Don't you know? All vampires and dhampirs are connected by blood. That makes
them all a single family line."

He made a sound point, but in Christian's opinion
Gregor used that loophole to incite violence for the sake
of violence. "I take it you think Réamonn's heir is hiding
in one of the thirteen covens?"

"Aye. She's somewhere in the city. And I have unfin-
ished business with that bloodthirsty bitch."

Christian scrubbed a hand over the stubble on his
jaw. "Seems you would've seen her out and about since
you've been in the city. How hard can one female be to
track?"

"I don't know what she looks like," Gregor admitted
with chagrin. "She was a lass when I killed her father."

Gregor certainly took his vendetta to dizzying heights.
Christian wasn't a killer. Not anymore. He'd given up that
life became a tracker for the Sortiari after fleeing
He no longer wanted a hand in dealing
leaving to more ruthless souls.

senses and his gut gathered

into an anxious ball. "If you had to venture a guess, what would she look like now?"

"She was a fair child," Gregor said. "Took after her mother. The humans in the villages thought her a healer and a witch." He spat as though warding off some ancient evil. "Raven hair, fair skin, and eyes like emeralds."

Fuck. Christian's wolf snarled. "You want me to find her so you can kill her?"

"I want you to find her," Gregor said, "so I can make her *suffer.*"

A cold lump of dread settled on Christian's chest. If any dhampir in the city fit Gregor's description it was Siobhan. The hard edge of her beauty betrayed her otherness. She was every bit the witch, as well. She'd enchanted Christian with nothing more than a fleeting glance and the curve of her wicked crimson lips.

"Why not continue as you've been?" Christian asked. "Ferret out the covens and attack them one by one."

"It's bringing too much heat. McAlister wants a tentative peace, probably because Aristov has begun to rally. It won't be long before the bastard has an army of vampires, and I'm not ready for a war. Not yet."

At least Gregor was smart enough to know that his tactics thus far had been too rash. "I don't work cheap," Christian said. At the back of his mind, his wolf snarled its discontent, but he willed the animal to calm. "Infiltrating covens could be dangerous for me, as I'm only one male. And I'm not looking to invite the wrath of the vampire king, either."

"I'll make it worth your while," Gregor said. "More than enough to pay off the string of gambling debts you've managed to rack up. It's time for us to lay low. I'm not willing to let her slip through my fingers by generating the fear that will tempt the covens to flee the city. I need stealth. I'm confident you'll find her for me."

Arrogant bastard.

"I'll need a good-faith payment before I agree to anything." His wolf growled in retaliation, but Christian ignored the warning.

Gregor tossed a small duffel bag at Christian's feet. "A male whose loyalties are easily bought is a dangerous ally to make." He leaned in close and his lip pulled back into a sneer as inky black swallowed his irises. "Don't make me regret purchasing yours, wolf."

"You worry too much, Gregor." He hoisted the duffel. Judging by the weight, there was enough cash in the bag to cover the forty grand he owed Marac with maybe a little left over to play with. "I'll be in touch."

Gregor was a male who wouldn't accept anything less than complete loyalty. Could Christian be the loyal employee Gregor wanted him to be? Could he give up the one thing he craved more than the rush of the impetuous bets he made? Christian had a feeling that if anyone was going to regret what transpired here tonight it would be him.

Siobhan stretched across the silken sheets, enjoying the slide of fabric over her bare skin. Beside her, Carrig lay panting, one arm slung over his eyes. Since Mikhail's ascension her appetites had become more voracious, and where her lover seemed to be sated she was remarkably unfulfilled.

Restlessness gnawed at her, the walls closed in around her until her lungs ached with the need for more air. Her fangs throbbed in her gums, and though she'd never known the burning thirst that plagued the accursed vampires, she swore that if she didn't feed soon she'd dry into a shriveled husk.

Carrig rolled to his side and whispered sweet endearments close to her ear. *"Mae fy dduwies. Fy frenhines.*

Byddaf yn addoli chi dragwyddoldeb yn y gorffennol."
He called her a goddess. His queen. He vowed to worship
her for eternity and longer. Pretty words of devotion. But
not what she wanted to hear. Nor who she wanted to
hear them from.

She'd thought of no one but the werewolf for months.

Even now, he haunted her thoughts. Piercing gray eyes,
light brown hair that ran with veins of gold, sharp cheek-
bones, and a strong jaw. He was as perfect a male as she'd
ever seen. But Siobhan had known many similar males.
One lay next to her now, gently tracing a lazy pattern with
his fingers on her bare stomach. The werewolf sparked
something within her that she'd never felt before. A hunger that left her hollow and frustrated. A need that weakened her. Weakness was one thing that Siobhan couldn't
afford.

She lay still until Carrig's body relaxed into slumber
beside her. She slid out from underneath the cage of his
arm and strode naked through rooms and hallways of the
abandoned building that sheltered her coven. Never once
in her life had she known shame. Embarrassment. Her
mother had taught her to be strong, to draw power from
that which others found shameful. And from her father
she'd learned ruthlessness. The loyalty of her coven was
absolute. She walked the rooms as not just a queen but an
empress, and her subjects lowered their gazes in her
presence.

The werewolf never lowered his gaze. His open stare
pierced her chest and left her breathless and shaking.
What would it be like to master a male like that? To break
him. To make him *hers.*

The slap of Siobhan's footsteps echoed on the floor as
she rounded a corner to the space of the building reserved
for her treasures. She picked her way through the dark
corridor, her eyesight keen even in the absence of light.

Why did she need vampiric senses to be strong? To see in the dark. To scent her enemies. Why should she have to forfeit her soul in order to fortify her strength, to lend that strength to her coven? And why did it take becoming a slave to another in order to reclaim her soul from oblivion?

At the back of the room, she found her prize. With her fingertips she traced the intricate etchings, older than the oldest vampire in existence. Set's chest was indeed a priceless bauble. Crafted by a god and charmed by a sorcerer. It was the font from which they all sprang. That is, if the legends were to be believed. Would Ronan truly entrust her with such a relic?

The real question: Was there anything he *wouldn't* have done to secure a future with his tethered mate?

Not since the werewolf began stalking her had she given Ronan more than a passing thought. In time she might have released him from the blood troth without a bargaining chip. But his insufferable bond, that biological and spiritual binding to the witch, had prompted Ronan to give up the ultimate prize. Siobhan hoped she'd never be crippled by such a bond. Somewhere in the back of her mind a warning scratched. If she didn't tread lightly where the werewolf was concerned she might lose herself, mate bond or not.

Gods, he was a magnificent male.

Beneath her fingertips, the chest pulsed as though with its own heartbeat. That Mikhail kept Chelle from her was proof enough of its power. Siobhan had never wanted to destroy anything so badly in her entire existence.

Her chest heaved as unpleasant memories surfaced in her mind. How did one suffer the Collective when her own private thoughts were enough to lay her low? Fear wasn't an emotion that Siobhan could afford, and yet it squeezed the air from her lungs and chilled her blood until it slogged through her veins like an ice floe in a winter river. A foe she barely remembered hunted her, and with good reason. No doubt he would search to the ends of the earth to get his claws in her.

He'd never find her, though. There was nothing left to connect her to her father's name. Nothing to connect her to that life that came crashing down around her centuries ago when she'd been too young to comprehend the consequences of her actions. Even now, across centuries, her mother's screams haunted her.

"I see you've taken it upon yourself to keep tabs on me even in the confines of my own coven." Carrig had been silently watching her for a while, but she hadn't the energy to acknowledge him until now.

"I worry." His gruff voice carried to her from across the room.

"If any harm would come to me here, then I'm not deserving of my station."

"None here would dare to harm you." Carrig padded toward her.

"Then why worry?" She didn't turn to face him. Instead, she kept her gaze cast downward at the glyphs carved into Set's chest.

"You come here every night and stare at that thing. Why?"

It was a question she'd asked herself many times. "I don't know."

If she lay in the mystical coffin would it change her? Would she emerge with a second set of fangs? Would her heart cease its beating? Would the sun eviscerate her with its rays? Would an empty void swallow her soul? And if so, who would tether it and return it to her? Carrig? The werewolf? Perhaps no one.

"We should leave the city," Carrig said after a moment. "The vampires' numbers are growing. We can move farther from the epicenter of their existence and thrive."

"I should become a coward, then?"

"*No.*" Carrig's emphatic tone gave her pause. "You should live without fear of discovery."

"I can do that here. No one knows who I am. Not even Ronan knows."

Carrig stepped closer, the heat of his wide chest buffeted her back, and Siobhan shivered. "Mikhail knows."

"Mikhail is too busy dealing with his growing kingdom to worry about me."

"What of the Collective?"

Siobhan's temper flared at Carrig's needling. "What of it?"

"Ronan, Jenner, or even Mikhail's mate could find memory of your life there."

Siobhan had no idea how the Collective worked, but it was the least of her worries. She'd been a child when her parents died. Who would know her in those tangled memories? "Millions, maybe billions, of memories to weed through. I'm not concerned."

"Gods, I wish you were concerned about *something.*"

Gray eyes, intense as they watched her, flashed in Siobhan's mind and she shivered. Maybe that was the problem. For the first time in centuries, she might care. "Find the werewolf, and bring him to me."

Behind her, Carrig bristled. He'd grown more possessive of her over the past few months. It was a complication that needed to be rectified. He took liberties with her now. Gave counsel when she didn't ask for it. Came to her in the dark of night without being bidden. Watched her from the shadows. Siobhan's heart was as cold and dead as a stone in her chest. It would do him no good to try to soften it now.

Was her heart so cold? *The werewolf quickened your blood well enough.*

"He's dangerous," Carrig growled. "A rogue. You should let me put him in the ground and be done with it."

She kept her words void of emotion. "Should I?"

"Gadewch i mi diogelu chi. Os gwelwch yn dda."

"I can protect myself, Carrig. The werewolf. Bring him to me."

Carrig pulled away and Siobhan missed his heat. "As you wish, mistress." His stiff formality tightened her chest. Just as silently as he'd come upon her, Carrig left.

Siobhan hugged her arms around her body, suddenly chilled. For centuries she'd convinced herself that she needed no one. Was above petty emotion and weakness. But now she worried that she no longer believed her own lies.

CHAPTER
16

Jenner sat in a small sunroom situated at the south side of Thomas Fairchild's compound. Mikhail could have learned a thing or two from the male in the security department. Whereas the king preferred his mansion that looked out over L.A., Fairchild had situated his coven in a rural area, miles from anything in all directions. A tall chain-link fence topped with razor wire surrounded his compound, and no one was allowed in or out without his approval. It was a wonder Bria had managed to sneak out for her geocaching adventures. His mate was quite the escape artist, it seemed, and his appreciation for her skills only grew in light of her uncle's secure compound.

Bria's ability to slip away from the property undetected didn't change the fact that the place was a veritable prison, however. The hackles on the back of Jenner's neck rose at the thought of Bria, kept in this place for decades.

So far Fairchild had made him wait for almost a half hour, and Jenner was twitchy as fuck. He'd fallen into bed just before sunrise, his cock hard as stone and his body wound as tight as a gods-damned spring. He couldn't get the image of Bria, soft and responsive beneath him, from his mind or the sound of her cries as she came from his ears. It had taken every ounce of willpower in his stores to walk away from her when all he'd wanted to do was fuck her until he was too exhausted to even think about leaving her.

He tried to convince himself that it was the biology of their tether that made him want her. That beyond the mystical bond that tied their souls there was nothing between them. He couldn't lie to himself any more than he could deny his own thirst. Bria fascinated him. The fire that burned beneath her cool exterior, the bravery she showed even though she'd been raised to fear. The wanton desire she exhibited that was such a contradiction to her innocence. The calm she exuded that washed over Jenner whenever he was in her presence. He wanted to know her beyond their tether. Every little nuance. And what shook him to his foundation was the fear that once she knew him as well—knew the things he was capable of—she'd understand why he'd kept himself from her. That he was nothing more than a creature with an insatiable thirst and so far beneath her station.

What then? When she found out there was nothing more to him would she return here? Opting for an existence in this prison rather than staying with him?

"I'm sorry I kept you waiting."

Jenner's body stretched taut as a bowstring as he turned toward the sound of Thomas Fairchild's voice. So lost in his own tortuous thoughts, he hadn't even noticed when the male entered the room. Jenner stood from the chair and the dhampir motioned for him to sit. It would serve to gain the male's trust by offering all the respect due the coven's master. That didn't mean that Jenner didn't want to wring the bastard's neck for keeping Bria locked up in this place for the gods knew how long.

"Lucas tells me you had quite an eventful outing with my niece last night."

A growl built in Jenner's throat. Fairchild's spy was going to find himself bleeding out in an alley somewhere if he came between Jenner and his mate again. "You would be wise to instruct Lucas to keep his distance."

"Indeed." Fairchild didn't seem fazed by Jenner's warning. Instead, the male appeared to be pleased.

His calm façade did nothing for Jenner's temper. Fairchild was the epitome of civilized sophistication. His outward appearance would have put him at home in a room of scholars, with his tweed jacket, carefully coiffed hair and crisp white dress shirt. Jenner doubted the male owned a pair of jeans or a T-shirt and believed he probably rolled out of bed looking as he did now. It was a wonder Jenner had even been invited to sit in the pristine solarium, animal that he was. He swallowed down a derisive snort as he took in the delicate china poised on an antique coffee table and the silver, polished to a high sheen. So damned civilized.

Thomas settled into the chair opposite Jenner and poured a cup of tea. He held it out to Jenner, a challenge in his gaze. Jenner took the dainty cup, feeling utterly ridiculous as he cradled it in his large palm. "You're old enough to know better than to play these games."

Thomas gave him a cool but indulgent smile. "You're probably right. But after so many centuries, memories become as dreams."

Not to a vampire. The Collective guaranteed that the past would thrive. "Bria isn't a monster who only hungers for blood," Jenner said with a sneer. That distinction was for him alone. "She's the same female you've always known."

"Is she?" Thomas asked.

"We are all animals at our cores," Jenner growled. "It

is your *choice* that you've repressed that part of your nature."

"You are a contradiction." Thomas mused without acknowledging Jenner's comment. "Much more intelligent than I initially gave you credit for."

"I didn't come here to be insulted." Bria's uncle wasn't the first person to misjudge Jenner and he sure as fuck wouldn't be the last.

"I'm sure you didn't." Thomas added a splash of cream into his cup and dropped in a sugar cube before pouring the steaming tea over it. "You came to hear my secrets."

Thomas might have misjudged him, but Jenner had *his* number. The dhampir was shrewd. "Yes," Jenner said without guile. "I think you owe me the truth."

"You know that Bria had never even known a vampire before she became one," Thomas said. He brought the delicate cup to his lips and sipped. "She's too young to have any memory of the wars. Any memory of her parents."

Wars? The Sortiari campaign had been genocide. Jenner didn't bother to tell Thomas that Bria was now a part of the Collective. Whatever she'd been too young to know would be a part of her consciousness now.

"Her father, William, was a powerful vampire lord and wanted nothing more than to bring his enemies to their knees."

Jenner lent Thomas his full attention. Many vampire lords rallied dhampir covens to their cause. Now that he knew Bria's father was an aristocrat, Jenner was even more convinced that he was far out of her league. Jenner's family had been considered so low that not even a dhampir coven would take them in, let alone a vampire. Jenner had fought against the Sortiari slayers to buy an honorable name for his family. Bria had been born with hers.

Thomas gave him an indulgent smile, as though he'd

heard Jenner's thoughts, knew his insecurities. "William was headstrong and quite the zealot," Thomas continued. "Fiercely loyal to his people and determined to save them from slaughter. My foolish sister Anna fell in love with William and he seemed obsessed with her. Quite the fairy tale," he said with barely veiled disgust. "You'd think that would have calmed William's battle lust, but it only spurred him to fight harder against the Sortiari. He turned her before the bulk of the fighting made it to London and it wasn't long after that Anna became pregnant with Bria. By some miracle, the vampire managed to tether my sister's soul. She insisted that I lend warriors to the fight and I did as she asked despite my misgivings."

Jenner's lip pulled back in a sneer. "It sounds as though you condemn your sister as well as William for their allegiances and their love." If Thomas felt so much disdain for vampires Thomas's loyalty to Mikhail could have been nothing more than lip service.

"I condemn no one save myself for my own foolishness."

Thomas Fairchild's prejudice rivaled his arrogance. His admission surprised Jenner, if only because he doubted the male enjoyed showing any weakness. It was perhaps his only admirable quality. Jenner set the damned dainty teacup down on the table. It wasn't like he was interested in Earl Grey.

"I wish I'd taken my sister far away from William," Thomas replied. "Bria would certainly be safer if I had."

Thomas shifted in his seat and Jenner allowed the male a moment to gather his thoughts. He'd come here for Thomas's secrets and it wouldn't get him shit if he pressed the matter.

"There are monsters in this world, Jenner," Thomas said at last. "Some of them are of our own making." The fine hairs on Jenner's arms stood on end. "Anna made

William a monster. That is the true evil that hunts us. Bria's own father."

A sense of urgency rose like a tide within Jenner. Mikhail had been the only vampire left for centuries. How could Bria's father have survived to hunt them? The possibilities were many and frightening. When Mikhail found out would he risk his own mate and his unborn child's safety by allowing Bria to stay in his home? Or would Jenner be forced to finally take her to his place, where nothing would stop him from taking what he wanted? "My patience is wearing thin." Jenner's secondary fangs punched down from his gums. He continued from between clenched teeth, "Stop beating around the bush and get on with it."

"William was fatally injured in battle," Thomas said with disgust. "And his own men left him on the muddied field, his throat cut through to his spine."

The Sortiari attacks had been sudden and violent. The vampires had been arrogant in their sense of immortality and they'd been unprepared. Many hid behind armies of dhampirs while others met the slayers head-on. Jenner himself had bled for a vampire lord who'd promised him the gift of transformation only to have died at the pointed end of a slayer's stake. A brutal time in their history, but the blame lay at the Sortiari's feet, not the vampires'.

"Anna couldn't allow him to die. She loved him too deeply to let him go. His head was nearly severed, even his own supernatural healing couldn't save him at that point, but magic knows ways to cheat death."

Finally, Thomas's ramblings made sense. "So she sought a witch."

"She sought a necromancer."

Jesus fucking Christ. Jenner's heart pounded in his chest with the burst of adrenaline that shot through his veins. Necromancers practiced the darkest of magic and nothing good ever came from dealings with one. Jenner shifted in his seat, the urge to leave and go to Bria almost overwhelming.

"I've never known a witch more powerful than Astrid," Thomas continued. "And believe me, I've searched. Resurrection isn't easy, even for a necromancer, and Astrid required a blood sacrifice as payment."

"Your sister paid her price, then?"

"Of course," Thomas replied as though Anna's decision to take an innocent life had been a no-brainer. "She traded the life of a member of our coven, among other things, for that of her lover. She would have sacrificed tenfold that many lives for William's. But Astrid betrayed her. What she brought back was not William."

Fairchild's sister had been a fool to have dabbled in such dark magic. "You should have known better than to let her do it," Jenner managed to say through the rage clogging his throat.

"I should have," Fairchild agreed. "But you'll soon learn that reason has no place in matters of love or family. William became a wendigo. A servant to the magic that created him. His life force is tied to Astrid's and has been for over two centuries. Can you imagine the hatred centuries of slavery would breed in such a soul?"

Jenner could guess.

"And you think William hunts you out of some sense of vengeance?"

"William hunts Bria," Thomas corrected, "because Astrid wills it."

"Why?" Jenner's blood ran cold. "If your sister paid her price, why does she hunt Bria?"

"Anna didn't pay all of Astrid's price," Thomas said gravely. "She promised the witch the blood of a newborn as well."

Bria. Jenner shot up out of his chair. A haze of pure

panic clouded his vision. "You let your sister promise the life of her own daughter?" His voice boomed around him, and the glass of the solarium shuddered in its wake.

"I have protected Bria."

Thomas's emphatic tone only served to further enrage Jenner. "By turning her into a prisoner!"

"What I did was for her own good." The rationalization for Thomas's actions fell on deaf ears. Jenner tucked his hands behind his back and gripped them tightly together lest he knock the selfish asshole flat on his ass. He could have stopped his sister, talked some damned sense into her, and instead he allowed her not only to offer her own child as payment but also to put her in lifelong danger by breaking faith. "I've kept her as safe as I could in the only way I knew how." Thomas fixed Jenner with a pointed stare. "But she has you now, doesn't she? A male such as you should have no problem seeking Astrid out. You could kill her and free William from his eternal slavery in the process. Free Bria from the danger that has hunted her over the course of her entire existence."

He truly was an opportunistic son of a bitch. Mikhail's suspicions had been well founded. Thomas Fairchild's loyalty was as fickle as the Santa Ana winds. He made his alliances based on who could do him the most good. Bria would never come back to this place. Not *ever*. "Does Bria know that her mother offered her as currency to save a life that was already gone?"

Thomas averted his gaze. At least the bastard had an ounce of shame for what his sister had done. "She doesn't. I've kept the truth from her. She knows that we're in danger from a witch and that the vendetta is older than she is, but she doesn't know why or from whom exactly."

"You're a coward," Jenner bit out.

"I am," Thomas agreed. "So you can imagine my relief that she has found a mate who is not."

Jenner snorted. He was through with this place. "You gave an oath to your king," Jenner said as he headed for the doorway. "Your coven is his. And you will *not* go back on your word."

"I suppose you'll make sure of it," Thomas replied in a somber tone.

"You bet your ass I will. And I'll enjoy it." Jenner pushed open the paned French doors and strode from the room.

"Having a doctor come to the house for prenatal exams weirds me out. I mean, a home birth really wasn't on my bucket list. Mikhail won't budge on it, either. I tried to bribe him, wager with him, con him. Oh, and I tried to use sex as a weapon. But with this massive belly, my body definitely *isn't* a wonderland, if you know what I mean."

Bria laughed at Claire's overexaggerated waddle as she crossed the kitchen to the fridge. She pulled a couple of sodas out and passed one to Bria.

"I'm sure that Mikhail only wants you to be safe," Bria said. She popped the tab on her soda and sipped. She thought back to last night and the shifter who'd demanded to know if she was the vampire queen. "Slayers are still out in force. It's not worth the risk to be exposed."

Claire made a sour face. "Bastards. They're totally fucking with my birth plan." Her expression softened as she leaned against the counter. "I know it's a good idea. I might have to burn our bed after the baby's born, though. I don't know if I could sleep . . . or do other things on the same mattress afterward."

Bria swallowed down her amusement.

"I'm done with my homework!" a tiny voice called from the living room. "Can I play Wii now?"

"You're really done?" Claire called back. "All of it?"

"Uh-huh!"

"Okay, *one* hour!" Claire turned her attention back to Bria. "God. I sound like such a *mom*."

Bria didn't know much about the human girl who lived with Claire and Mikhail, only that she must be very important to the both of them. She had her own security detail that drove her to and from school and anywhere else she needed to go. "It's going to kill me when her mom gets out of rehab."

Bria gave Claire a questioning glance but didn't press for details.

"She was in a coma for about six months. Head trauma. She's making progress, but it's slow going."

"That's awful," Bria said. "Poor Vanessa."

"She's a tough cookie." Claire's brow furrowed with worry. "She'll get through this."

Thanks to her night out with Jenner, Bria had become more in tune with her senses. There was something about Vanessa that tickled at the back of Bria's brain. An otherness that she couldn't quite put her finger on. It wasn't unsettling per se, just . . . *different*. "She's lucky she has you."

Claire smiled. "We're kindred spirits, that's for sure."

Again, Bria didn't ask Claire to elaborate. It wasn't her business anyway. "Claire, can I ask you a question?"

"Sure." She took another sip of her soda. "Sup?"

The question formed on Bria's lips, but she couldn't make herself speak. She didn't want Claire to know about what had happened between her and Jenner last night. It embarrassed her to admit that her tether with him felt tight and tenuous. That she worried they'd never find common ground and that she would live for eternity bound to a male she might not grow to love.

"Nothing," she said on a breath. "Never mind."

Claire fixed her with a stare and pursed her lips. "Nuh-uh. You can't open up for a question and then clam up. Spill it."

"Jenner wants to teach me how to defend myself." It was as good a deflection as any.

"Really?" Claire smiled wide. "Cool. Mikhail treats me like I'll break if I so much as stub my toe. Think he'll let you play with guns and knives and stuff?"

Bria hadn't considered it. "That would be exciting."

"Exciting?" Claire replied with enough enthusiasm for both of them. "It would totally kick ass."

Bria smiled. "It would, wouldn't it?" She'd been worried about Jenner's ominous mandate that she be ready for a workout, but now the thought of truly learning how to fight, how to defend herself, sent a thrill through her.

"Bria," Claire said. "You're officially my hero."

She snorted. "Hardly."

"Just promise me one thing." Claire leaned over the counter as much as her stomach would allow and Bria bent toward her. "Keep Jenner on his toes."

He flipped her world on its axis, excited and frightened her, brought her to dizzying heights of pleasure and new levels of frustration. She doubted she'd get the upper hand on him. "I'll try," she said. "I don't know that I'll be successful, though."

Claire looked her over from head to toe. "Dude. You've already got him so wound that he doesn't know which way is up."

"Do you think so?" Jenner ran so hot and cold, Bria found it difficult to ever get an accurate read on him.

"I know so," Claire said with a smirk.

Bria hoped that Claire was right. He could try to withhold himself from her, to protect some silly notion of her innocence, but she wasn't willing to let Jenner go without a fight.

CHAPTER
17

"Don't let your guard down, Bria. Focus."

Every night for the past couple of weeks Jenner had been pushing her, training her, teaching her how to fight. With every passing night his instruction became more intense, more focused, as though her very life depended on her ability to protect herself. Training her had become his obsession. Bria suspected he used it as a distraction as well. Jenner hadn't fed from her throat since that night in her bedroom. He took the vein at her wrist and insisted she drink from his. Likewise, he hadn't touched her outside of the gym with anything other than casual contact.

"Bria!" Her head snapped up to find Jenner staring at her, his brows dawn sharply over his dark eyes. "Pay attention."

She blew out a frustrated breath. Every night he exhausted her, running through maneuvers, fight techniques, dagger play, until she had no choice but to fall into bed at sunrise. He left her alone and wanting morning after morning. At sundown his insistent knock forced her from her room. There were no longer spare moments in her nights to sneak out. She hadn't been on a single treasure hunt since the night Jenner had followed her. She had become as much of a prisoner in the king's home as she'd been in her own coven. Maybe more so.

"I don't want to pay attention," she spat. "I'm tired of this."

"All right," he said. "We'll switch to hand-to-hand combat, then."

Gods. No more of this! She was already proficient with daggers and had actually managed to best Jenner in a sparring match last week. He'd even taken her to a shooting range a few times and she'd proved she was a decent shot. She couldn't be more capable of protecting herself.

"No!" Bria tossed the practice daggers to the floor. "I'm done, Jenner. I'm not doing this anymore."

Jenner swooped down with a low growl to retrieve the discarded daggers and held them out to her. Bria refused to take them as she held his stare. Silver chased across his irises, signaling the flare of his temper, and Bria snatched the weapons from his grasp. She attacked without warning, swinging out with both arms as she put Jenner immediately on the defensive. He didn't hold back—he never did—and made her work for the advantage as he retaliated with wide sweeps of his arms and low thrusts aimed at Bria's thighs. Anger fueled every action and she pushed harder, faster, putting weeks of training and her own inherent tumbling skills to good use as she gained the upper hand in the fight. The fierce expression on Jenner's face heated her blood; the display of muscles on his bare chest as they gleamed with a sheen of sweat whetted Bria's appetite for so much more than another sparring session. She let her frustration feed her purpose as she jabbed, swung, and stabbed with the daggers until she'd managed to back Jenner against a wall.

"I'm not weak!" she shouted as she poised the tips of

the blades at Jenner's throat. "And I'm done being a prisoner. I'm *through,* Jenner!" Her temper waned as a deep sadness swelled within her. "I'm leaving."

His breath heaved in his massive chest and his nostrils flared. Bria tossed the daggers down yet again with disgust. If she ever picked them up again it would be too damned soon. She spun on a heel and marched for the door. She refused to let Jenner deposit her at her bedroom once again only to leave her alone until the sun set. If this cool detachment was what she could expect of their tether for the remainder of her existence then Bria wanted *none* of it.

"You're not going anywhere, *viaton.* Not without me." His voice was a low, dangerous rumble. Bria suspected that even stalwart males gave Jenner a wide berth when he addressed them like that. Good thing Bria was tougher than a stalwart male.

The endearment bristled. She was sick and tired of his perception of her as some pristine, untouchable thing. He cared nothing for her beyond the blood in her veins. "Watch me." She picked up her pace, sure as the sun would rise that he'd come after her. She could take care of herself now. Jenner had seen to that himself. So if he thought she'd let him waylay her he had another think coming.

"Where do you think you'll go, then?" His temper boiled under the surface of his words, but Bria didn't care.

"Wherever the hell I want!" Her thirst was under control. The Collective barely tickled at her mind anymore. She had mastered her senses, her strength . . . all of it.

"Bria, no."

Her step faltered at the hint of desperation that clung to his demand, but she steeled herself against it. "Why? Tell me why."

She placed her hand on the door to the small studio

space that Jenner rented for them to work out in. Silence stretched between them as Bria waited for his response, knowing what it would be before he had the chance to say it. "It's not safe."

The fire of her temper burned bright. She whipped around to face Jenner and shouted, "You sound like my uncle! If I'm truly in danger I deserve to know exactly from what. I'm tired of cryptic explanations and guarded warnings. I've lived centuries and a witch has yet to find me. If you know something about it, then tell me. If not . . ." She turned and yanked the door open.

"Stop."

His voice rippled through her and Bria drew in a shuddering breath. Gods, the effect he had on her without even trying. Jenner had become her only weakness. It took more effort to walk away from him than she thought she could muster. But if she wanted to retain even a shred of self-respect she had to do it.

"Did your uncle ever talk to you about William?"

Bria paused.

"How do you know about my father?"

The sound of Jenner's quiet footsteps reached her ears as he crossed the width of the soft foam mat toward her. Delicious heat engulfed her as he came up behind her. If she simply reached back she could touch him. Jenner's hand came over hers and eased the door closed. His hulking body loomed over her. Overwhelmed her. And Bria trembled with need. His proximity, the scent of his blood, and the sweat that clung to his skin intoxicated her.

"Your uncle went to Ronan before you were turned looking for help. He paid Ronan—and me—to protect you and to find the witch that hunted you. You were attacked by slayers that same night."

Bria's eyes went wide. "You've known about the witch all this time and said nothing?" She let out an incredulous bark of laughter. "You're taking his money in exchange for my protection?"

"No, Bria," Jenner replied. "The tether changed everything. I protect what's *mine*."

His. The possessive edge to his words almost made her laugh. As if Jenner ever behaved as though their tether were anything more than an inconvenience.

"So you knew all about me before you even met me?"

"I only knew that Thomas Fairchild's niece needed protection. Nothing else. I didn't know who you were until after we were tethered and Ronan told me."

Her uncle and her mate had conspired against her, it seemed. And already Jenner knew more about the danger she was in than Bria knew herself. Her temper flared and she faced Jenner, her hands balled into tight fists. "I want to know everything he's told you. I have a right to know, don't you think?"

"You do," Jenner agreed. "And I'll tell you everything I know."

Bria's chest ached with unspent emotion. Hurt sliced through her and stole her breath. "My father died only a few weeks before I was born," she said. "I never knew him, and my uncle rarely spoke of him." Bria's heart stuttered at the concern in his expression. "How old are you, Jenner? Old enough to have fought against the legions of slayers?"

Sadness replaced the concern. "I'm old enough, *viaton*."

Her brow furrowed. "What does my father have to do with the witch that supposedly hunts us?"

"What did Thomas tell you?"

Bria let out a frustrated breath. She wanted Jenner to get to the point. There was no need to ease her into anything. "He told me that that an ancient evil hunted our family. A witch. That she killed my mother and wanted revenge for something that happened during the wars. I wasn't allowed to question him. He said that the less I knew, the better." Her voice thickened with bitterness. "That it was for my own protection."

Jenner's brows drew together. His dark gaze held hers as he reached out and smoothed a strand of hair from her face. A wave of pity reached out to her through their tether and she flinched as though stung. It didn't matter how strong she was. How capable. Jenner would never see her as anything more than pathetic.

"What do you know?" Her tone escalated with the anger that burned a scorching path through her. "Tell me!"

Silence stretched between them. A sickening stillness that turned Bria's stomach. Hurt and regret reflected in Jenner's expression. As though he were about to break her heart. "William is the evil that hunts you," he said. His voice trailed off into an eerie echo in the empty studio space. "At the behest of a necromancer named Astrid that your mother made a bargain with. The witch resurrected William after he'd died on the battlefield, and in exchange your mother promised her the blood of a newborn. You." A growl rose in Jenner's throat and his jaw squared.

"No," Bria choked. "You're wrong. She wouldn't. . . . William is dead. My uncle said he was killed."

"He was. And your mother couldn't let him go. William serves Astrid. He's a wendigo. Your mother cheated the necromancer and your uncle fled with you after she was killed. For centuries Astrid has hunted you in order to claim what was promised to her."

Realization slammed into Bria's gut and she buckled. All of these years . . . *centuries* as a prisoner! All because her mother had traded Bria's life for her father's and refused to pay up when things hadn't turned out the way she'd expected they would.

Bria's stomach heaved and she swallowed down the

bile that churned with an acidic burn. "It's not true." Her heart hammered in her chest, thundered in her ears. Her vision darkened at the periphery and Bria swayed on her feet as realization quickly turned to shock. "My uncle told you this?" she screeched. "It's a lie!"

Jenner caught her against his massive frame and held her tight to him. He spoke the truth. His scent was clean and masculine, musky from the workout but without the sour edge that would betray the lie. "I'm so sorry, Bria." Jenner cupped the back of her head as he held her against him. "I wish to the gods it was a lie."

"I wish she'd given me to the necromancer," Bria whispered. She thought back to that moment when she'd bled out in her uncle's arms at the gates of Mikhail's property. "I wish she'd let me go."

Fear gripped at Jenner's heart with sharp claws. Bria's calm resolve shook him to his foundation. "Don't say that," he murmured against her hair. He held her tighter until his arms encircled her narrow torso. "Don't *ever* say it again."

"This is why you've been teaching me how to fight, isn't it? Why you won't let me go out alone."

Bria pushed herself away from Jenner's embrace and fixed him with her cool amethyst stare. The accusation in her tone shredded him as guilt settled on his chest like a stone. But Jenner knew something of Thomas Fairchild's obsession. Like her uncle he couldn't bear the thought of losing Bria, and so he'd done the only thing he thought he could do. He'd made her a kept thing.

"I can't lose you, Bria." He did nothing to soften his words. "I won't."

Her low, disbelieving laughter echoed through the gym and brought chills to Jenner's flesh. "I'm sure you could find a new sparring partner with ease, Jenner."

It was obvious she egged him on to coax him into a fight, and Jenner was enough of a hotheaded asshole to take the bait. "You know you mean more than that to me."

"Do I?" Bria scoffed. "You have your soul back and the vein at my *wrist* when your thirst mounts. Aside from that, I don't see that you have any other use for me."

"Is that what you want from me, Bria? To *use* you?"

Her glare burned through him. "Someone should, don't you think?"

The threat inherent in her words caused Jenner's blood to boil. When had this ceased to be about the threat to her life? He leaned in close, a snarl gathering in his chest. "I told you what would happen if another male ever put his hands on you."

"You don't seem all that interested in my body. What would you care if I gave it to someone else?"

Bria's goading slowly pushed Jenner to a very dark place. Visions of her naked beneath that bastard Lucas materialized in his imagination. "Careful, Bria." Jenner bit the words off before he'd say something he'd regret. Something that would push her away forever. The more she pushed, the more frantic he became.

Bria brought her wrist to her mouth and bit down, tearing the flesh. Jenner flinched as the scent of her blood hit his nostrils and his bloodlust cranked from one to a million in a split second. Gods, the scent of her drove him mad with thirst.

"I could drain it into a glass for you," she suggested with a sneer. Blood dripped from the punctures in her wrist, landing on the mat below with a *tap, tap, tap* that Jenner felt with the force of a sledgehammer to his gut. "That way you wouldn't have to put your mouth on me at all."

A vicious snarl tore from Jenner's throat. He rushed at her, mindless, overcome with need and lust and desperate to satisfy that part of him that had gone unfulfilled for too gods-damned long. Bria held up her hand to stay his progress and crimson rivulets of blood ran down her forearm in a swirling pattern that hypnotized him.

"Be mindful, Jenner. You wouldn't want to soil my virginal skin with your mouth."

Jenner snatched Bria by the wrist and hauled her to him. He ran the flat of his tongue up her arm to the punctures in her wrist, taking in his mouth every drop of the blood she'd wantonly spilled. "This is *mine*," he growled, fangs bared. "You are *mine*."

Bria met him stare for stare. "Prove it."

Jenner took her down to the mat in a blur of motion. When his fangs broke the skin at her throat Bria cried out, a sound that was as much relief as it was release. It tore at his composure until nothing remained but tattered shreds of want and need.

She demanded he prove to her that she was his? He'd prove that to her and more. Jenner seized both of her wrists. He gathered them into one hand and pinned them to the mat as he continued to drink. Bria squirmed beneath him; her breath came in sharp gasps that brushed the hair near his temple. He reached between them and shoved his free hand past the elastic waistband of her workout pants and into her underwear. She arched up as he cupped the heat of her pussy in his palm and a groan worked its way up his throat as he found her wet and ready for him.

Gods. Withholding himself from her had been *torture*.

Jenner wanted Bria more than he'd ever wanted anything in his entire existence. Maybe it was gods-damned time that he took her down from the ivory tower he'd placed her in and finally claimed what was his. Bria didn't care about her innocence. Her virginity. Or the fact that she'd been born well above Jenner's station. She wanted *him.* Her scent, her slick sex, and her quickened breaths were all the proof he needed. The weeks spent keeping himself from her out of fear had worn him down to the point that his own damned lusts mastered him. It countered everything he'd been trying to prevent. He'd had her blood every night since their tethering and hadn't lost himself to his thirst yet. He hadn't once lost control with her. Why couldn't he have her? What force on this earth save himself kept him from her?

He needed to fuck her now, before they both died from their want.

Jenner forced himself to disengage from Bria's throat and closed the punctures. His brain buzzed from the high of taking her vein, and her body, soft and willing beneath him, overwhelmed his senses. Bria whimpered and thrust up to press her pussy tighter against his palm. "Damn it, Jenner," she said from between clenched teeth. "Touch me."

Jenner slipped a single finger in her tight channel. Bria moaned, the sound echoing around them in the small studio. He looked up at the mirrors that lined the walls and his breath caught at the multiple images of Bria reflected back at him, her head thrown back in ecstasy. Her tight heat squeezed him and Jenner couldn't help but imagine the sweet torture of her inner walls clenching his cock. He moved his finger out slowly and plunged back in just as carefully. Bria writhed beneath him and he watched her many reflections, hypnotized by the erotic show.

"Deeper," Bria panted. "Harder. Please."

She thrust her hips up and Jenner pulled back. She gritted her teeth in frustration and her fangs pricked her bottom lip. Her hands clenched and unclenched in Jenner's grip, but he kept her wrists pinned to the mats beneath her. Her quiet moans grew to frustrated whimpers and deep sobs of pleasure as he continued to ease his finger in and out of her. If she felt frustrated by his gentleness it was nothing compared to what he felt throughout these weeks of celibacy.

"Stop treating me as though I'll break." Her sweet voice bit with an edge of anger. He looked down at her face to find her eyes bright silver and trained on his face. Bria's head came up off the mat and her chest heaved with her agitation. "Take me, Jenner."

This aggressive side of her personality drove him past the point of reason. Jenner's cock throbbed in time with his pulse; it fucking *ached* with the need for release. He wanted to rip her flimsy cotton pants from her body and pound into her. He wanted to fuck her until the desperate ache that clawed at his chest evaporated under her cries. Needed to feel her pussy squeeze his shaft and milk him dry.

He drove his finger a little deeper, slightly harder, and Bria's eyes rolled back as she let out a loud moan. Control became harder to maintain as he pulled out and thrust again, this time easing a second finger inside of her. Bria's eyes went wide and she gasped at the intrusion. A rush of wetness coated his fingers as he continued to pump them in and out. Bria's breaths grew shallow and she wriggled beneath him. "No," she said. "I don't want to come like this." A crease cut into her delicate brow. "I want you inside of me, Jenner. I want you to fuck me."

Gods, those wanton words from her lips . . . Jenner resisted the urge to sink his fangs in her throat once again. To sink his cock deep inside of her. His hunger for her knew no satiation. His want of her body drove him to the brink of his sanity. If he took her now he'd hurt her. His own savage need would ruin them both and she'd hate him for it despite her pleas. *No.* He couldn't give her what she wanted. Not until he had a better grip on himself. Instead, he put his mouth to hers to silence her and began to work her clit with the pad of his thumb as he continued to thrust with his fingers. He could still pleasure her. He could still break her apart.

A spasm traveled through Bria's body into Jenner's as she came. Her pussy pulsed around his fingers, holding him tight. Her hips thrust wildly beneath him and he swallowed her desperate cries as he continued to kiss her. When he pulled away, Bria's eyes were squeezed shut and she turned her head away. Through their tether, her anger and hurt funneled into Jenner's chest and struck his sternum like a fist. He couldn't give her what she wanted. Not yet. Not until he had a better handle on himself. How could he make her understand that he'd do anything to protect her? Even if that meant protecting her from himself?

"How much longer are you going to be?" A loud voice accompanied several loud bangs on the door. "We have an eight-thirty class and you're putting us behind schedule."

"In a minute!" Jenner's deep, gravelly voice boomed through the quiet studio. He released his grip on Bria's wrists and eased her underwear and pants back up. Her breaths heaved in her chest and her cheeks were flushed crimson with both passion and anger. She was the most beautiful thing he'd ever seen. "Come on, *viaton*," he said low. "Time to go."

She looked up at him, her eyes narrowed with anger. "You can't keep me at arm's length forever, Jenner."

He knew that. And he was terrified of what would happen when she'd finally had enough of his bullshit.

CHAPTER
18

"A necromancer, huh?" Naya let out a low whistle. "You're hunting some pretty big game, Jenner."

He let out a snort. Ronan's mate was a powerful witch. She could track magic and magic users by following a trail of music only she could hear. Truth be told, Naya put Jenner on edge. She radiated power and it made his fangs twitch in his gums. After talking to Thomas, Jenner knew that he'd never be able to find this Astrid on his own. Hell, they couldn't even pinpoint Gregor and he was without a doubt hiding somewhere in the city. If Jenner was going to free Bria from the prison her life had been the only way he could do it was with Naya's help.

"If she's in the city, could you find her?"

"No," Ronan cut in with a low growl. "Absolutely not."

Naya rolled her eyes at Ronan's overprotectiveness. "Are you saying you don't think I'm strong enough to take on a necromancer?"

Jenner waited for Ronan to take the bait. He raked his fingers through his tawny hair and blew out a breath. "I'm saying you'll never get the chance to find out."

"I don't need Naya to fight the bitch," Jenner interjected. "Just track her."

Naya looked a little put out. She pursed her lips in a petulant pout and fixed Ronan with her dark-eyed stare. "You worry too much."

"And with good reason." Ronan began to pace the breadth of his perfectly decorated living room. "You'd chase her down and take her on single-handedly if you were given the chance."

Naya smiled with pride and shrugged as if to say she couldn't argue the matter with her mate. Jenner looked out the large picture window that overlooked the city. Myriad lights twinkled, a veritable universe beneath them. Though it was rumored that all vampires were descended from a god, they were far from infallible. Jenner's gut clenched as he thought once again about Bria and his desperate desire to protect her.

"It's not the tracking that's the problem, Jenner. The only way to kill a necromancer is to cut out its heart. I don't know anyone who's ever gotten close enough to one to even try. Are you sure you want to take on that sort of power?"

It wasn't a question of him being sure. If Jenner had any hope of salvaging any chance of a relationship with Bria it had to be done. His worry for her would only prompt him to make her more of a prisoner than she already was or ever had been. And she'd hate him for it. He already hated himself for it. "I'm not concerned," Jenner said. "Black magic or not, if you can find her for me, I'll kill her."

"I don't want Naya involved," Ronan said again. "There has to be another way to find her."

"Naya is the only one who can track magic," Jenner said. "I need her, Ronan. You have my word that no harm will come to her."

"Luz could do it," Ronan suggested.

Another witch, Jenner suspected. And by Naya's angry expression, one she didn't want anywhere close to L.A. "Abso-freakin'-lutely not."

Power sizzled in the air. Ronan's eyes flashed with silver, but he didn't challenge his mate on the matter. Jenner didn't know what he found more frustrating. His inability to track the necromancer on his own or having to sit by and observe another tethered pair who'd obviously learned to balance their mate bond.

Jenner couldn't be in a room with Bria for more than an hour before his desires drove him from her presence. His thoughts centered on his need to fuck her or take her vein and he didn't know how much longer he'd be able to hold out before he stripped her bare and dove into her slick heat. Bria was so delicate. So very breakable in comparison to his harsh bulk. Last week in the gym he'd taken her vein with a ferocity that caused him worry, and afterward it had taken every ounce of his self-control to pleasure her without losing himself to his own desire. Given leave to enjoy her body, Jenner feared that the meager hold on his control would snap once and for all.

"Seriously, you've got to snap the fuck out of this maudlin bullshit attitude, man."

Jenner looked up to find Ronan regarding him with a scowl. Obviously, the male had been talking to him, but as usual, Jenner was too wrapped up in his own godsdamned thoughts to pay an ounce of attention. He couldn't think straight. Could barely function since the night he'd rushed up Mikhail's staircase to find Bria sitting, legs tucked beneath her, in the guest room. His mind was too full of her, his soul too aware of hers. He was losing his fucking mind and he didn't see an end to his madness in sight.

"I'm just going to give you guys a minute." Naya cast

a cautious glance from Ronan to Jenner and once again to her mate. She leaned in and kissed him on the cheek before leaving them alone in the room.

"Maudlin bullshit?" Jenner pushed the words from between clenched teeth. "If Naya was in danger, you'd move mountains to protect her. So don't fucking get up in my grill when I want to do the same for my—" The sentence cut off on an intake of air. Jenner rarely said the word out loud. Had never allowed himself to actually believe it.

"What?" Ronan challenged. His irises flashed silver and his tone escalated. "Your *what*, Jenner?"

"My mate!" His chest ached with the word. Burned as though he'd been run through with a stake. The truth of it blazed through him. Damn near brought him to his knees. The distance he continued to put between them was slowly killing him. Gods, he was a train wreck. "What sort of fucking male am I if I can't even protect the one thing that's been entrusted to me?" Jenner's breath heaved in his chest as his frustration mounted. "She's half of my gods-damned soul and for the past month I've done nothing but make her more of a prisoner than she ever was. I can't even bear to be in the same room with her, Ronan. I'm—" His voice cracked with emotion and shame seared a path up Jenner's throat. "Fate has made a mistake."

Ronan gave a sad shake of his head. "Don't be a fool, Jenner. Fate doesn't make mistakes."

He cocked a dubious brow. The Sortiari's mission wasn't shaped from that opinion.

Ronan knew Jenner's secrets. All of them. "You know better than anyone why I've kept myself from Bria."

Ronan let out a sigh as he raked his fingers through his tawny hair. "You were young—"

"*Don't* make excuses for me," Jenner cut in. He thought of Fairchild's words about memories becoming as dreams.

"I let the past fade too far in my memory. Mikhail never should have turned me."

"How many dhampirs have you killed since your transition?" Ronan demanded.

Jenner looked away. "None. But that doesn't mean—"

"Bullshit," Ronan said. "And how many times have you taken more blood than you should from Bria?"

"Never. But each time I feed from her I want more." The words rasped as Jenner's thirst flared. Simply thinking of Bria's blood drove him to the brink. "It takes every ounce of willpower I have to pull away from her."

"You've never hurt her," Ronan insisted. "You've never once allowed yourself to drink more than you should from her. You let one mistake and the declarations of some aristocratic asshole mold your entire existence. Have you ever heard of a self-fulfilling prophecy, Jenner?"

He refused to meet his friend's gaze. It was easy for Ronan to talk about shit like self-fulfilling prophecies. He'd never heard the last beats of his victim's heart in his ears as he swallowed the last drops of her lifeblood. He'd never experienced the abandon that accompanied such an act. He'd never been looked upon with disgust and fear by the very creatures that needed blood to survive and been called monster.

"I wouldn't survive it if I hurt her," Jenner murmured.

Ronan gave a sad shake of his head. "She's the other half of your soul. You have no trust in your tether if you think you could possibly hurt her."

"It doesn't matter. Until I find the witch, the tension between us is only going to get worse." Jenner couldn't talk about his control issues anymore. The self-reflection made his gut ache and his heart pound. Whether or not Ronan thought Jenner was capable of hurting Bria, she was still in danger.

"You were meant to find her, Jenner. And you and I

both know that you're a scary motherfucker who's more than capable of protecting her."

Jenner didn't share in Ronan's optimism. "You know everything about me," he said low. "Tell me, how can I possibly be what she needs?"

"That's the thing," Ronan said. "You think you need to change yourself to be worthy of her. To be a different male than the one you are. But if you were a different male, she wouldn't have tethered you. You *are* what she needs. Stop worrying about a past that no longer exists and allow yourself this comfort. Once you quit fighting the tether and actually let yourself fall into it, you'll be amazed at how easy everything becomes."

A lump the size of a fucking baseball lodged itself in Jenner's throat. He couldn't stay here and hash out his emotions with Ronan like it was a natural part of their relationship or some shit. He'd be glad when things got back to normal and he could focus once again on his duties for Mikhail and busting heads for Ronan. He'd had enough emotional turmoil in a month to last three lifetimes. "I'm out," he said through the thickness in his throat. "The fancy fucking interior decorating in this place is giving me a headache."

Ronan gave him a rueful smile. "Naya and I will help you track the necromancer." Jenner paused in the foyer and turned to face Ronan. "But when it comes to meting out her death, I can't let Naya be anywhere near that."

Jenner gave a sharp nod of his head. "I'd never ask her to be. All I need is help finding the necromancer. Once we do, I'll kill her myself."

"Tomorrow night?" Ronan asked.

"Yeah." Jenner turned to leave. "The sooner the better."

He headed down the hallway for the elevator. He needed to get the hell away from everything that was fucking with his head, which meant he couldn't go home, where he had only his thoughts for company, and Mikhail's house was out of the question. He needed music, lights, the press of bodies, and so much sound that it would drown out the thoughts that tortured him and sent him closer to the arms of madness.

He'd known from the first moment he stared into Bria's beautiful amethyst eyes that she would be the cause of his destruction.

"Claire, I'm going out."

Claire looked up from the lettuce she was tearing to make a salad. Her brow furrowed over her unusual gold eyes. "Do you think that's a good idea?"

Bria appreciated that the queen didn't order her to stay. Claire was giving Bria the option to make her own decisions, and that's all she'd ever wanted. A choice. To be able to walk out the front door whenever she pleased without having to sneak out while everyone was distracted. "I can take care of myself," she said in what she hoped was an airy tone. "Jenner has been training me in dagger play and hand-to-hand combat. I bet I could beat Ronan in a fight if I had to."

Claire laughed. "I'd pay good money to see that. So . . . where are you going?"

Claire wasn't going to tell Bria that she couldn't leave the house, but it was obvious she planned to keep tabs on her. "I'm not running away if that's what you think."

"I didn't say that you were." Claire turned her attention back to her salad and said, "You know, I ran away once."

"You did?" Bria couldn't imagine a female as confident as Claire running away from anything. "Why?"

Claire's eyes slid to Bria and she smiled. "Are you

kidding? These guys are goddamned intense. I'm beginning to think that there isn't anything more dangerous in the world than a tethered vampire."

Bria's lips quirked in a half smile. "At least your mate hasn't put you on a shelf to collect dust." Her voice cracked with emotion she tried so hard to suppress. "I think that Jenner wishes our tether was cut."

"It's not what you think, Bria." Claire abandoned her dinner preparations and turned to face her. "Jenner's had a rough go of it." Indecision marred her features as though Claire wasn't sure how much she should say.

Bria's heart clenched. "Because of me?"

"Because Jenner has an issue with control."

Bria didn't have to be told to know that. It was something that simmered just below the surface of his skin all the time. She felt it every time he looked at her. Every time he touched her. Even in the sting of his bite she knew that he teetered on the brink, ready to slip with the slightest nudge. But contrary to what everyone thought, it wasn't a lack of control that was Jenner's problem. No, he had *too much* control.

"He holds back in all things," Bria murmured. "And it has stretched our tether to the breaking point. We . . ." Bria paused. ". . . He rarely touches me. We haven't—"

"Whoa, whoa, whoa. Hold up." Claire leaned in close and brought her voice down to a whisper. "Are you saying you guys haven't done the deed?"

Bria averted her gaze.

"Holy shit, dude!" Claire exclaimed. "No wonder he's wound so tight."

Was he? Bria wasn't so sure. All she knew was that she couldn't keep going like this. Weeks of his aloofness followed by moments of intense pleasure. *Her* pleasure. Jenner didn't allow her to touch him, never bared his body past his chest. Did he not ache for satiation like she did? Was she so disappointing to him that he had no desire for her?

No. That wasn't true. Jenner wanted her. She felt it through their tether, smelled the musky scent of lust that clung to his skin. When he fed from her throat a week ago in the gym he'd been ravenous for her. His bite had been hard and each deep pull of his mouth demanding. The memory of it sent a thrill through Bria's body that settled low in her abdomen. She wanted so much more from Jenner, but the male's control was absolute. His will was iron.

Even iron could be made to bend, though.

"Jenner and I have something in common, Bria." Claire went back to her salad prep and kept her tone conversational. "We both have chips on our shoulders, but I guess his might be a little bigger than mine," she added with a laugh.

"How so?" Bria didn't know anything about Claire's life and it pained her to think that she didn't know much more about Jenner's.

"Let's just say I didn't grow up in the lap of luxury. Neither did Jenner. And he's way more hung up on class division than I am."

As the niece of a coven master, Bria could be considered aristocratic in the dhampir social structure. She'd grown up privileged, entitled, despite the fact that she'd be given no personal freedom. She'd never wanted for anything. It had never occurred to her that Jenner would consider himself below her station. In fact, labels like that meant nothing to Bria and never had.

"Are you saying he doesn't think he's good enough for me?" The idea seemed ridiculous. Bria could think of no male better than Jenner.

"I'm saying he's put you up on a pretty high pedestal and he doesn't have a ladder," Claire said. "Maybe instead of beating around the bush, you two need to have it out." A wide grin spread across her lips and she waggled her eyebrows. "A good fight might lead to some good makeup sex."

If only . . . Bria had never thought of herself as weak, no matter how her uncle, Lucas, or the other members of her coven had tried to convince her otherwise. Not until her tethering had Bria known true weakness. With a touch, a look, a heated command in his deep gravelly voice, her resolve crumbled. Jenner was Bria's weakness and she hated herself for it.

"You're right about one thing," Bria said. "It's definitely time to have it out." She'd reached her breaking point. She could no longer continue to go on day after day wanting him and suffering this crippling loneliness. She wouldn't allow Jenner to keep her at arm's length anymore. "I'll try not to wake Vanessa if I get in late," Bria said as she hopped down from her stool. It was time to have it out with Jenner whether he wanted to or not.

"Hang on a sec and let me call Alex," Claire said as she grabbed her cell from the opposite counter. "He can take you wherever you need to go."

"Thank you, Claire." Having a ride into the city would take care of one obstacle.

"He'll bring you home when you're ready, too," Claire added with a soft smile.

Home. Never had that word meant so much, especially now that Bria had the choice to decide where home was—and who she chose to share it with.

CHAPTER
19

Alex pulled up to the entrance of Ultra. A line had already begun to form down the sidewalk of the West Hollywood club, but Bria didn't plan on waiting in line. Vampiric abilities had their benefits after all. She got out of the car and slipped the cell phone Alex handed her into her back pocket.

"You call if you need *anything*. Understand?"

Bria leaned down to the open passenger side window. She smiled at the human and said, "I'll be fine."

"Oh, I know you will be," Alex said. "I just want to make sure you know I won't be more than a block away if you need me."

As far as human males went, Alex looked more than capable of taking care of himself. His hazel eyes wrinkled at the corners as he returned her smile. Under his good humor, though, Bria sensed a hardness in the man. She supposed that anyone who kept company with vampires and dhampirs needed to be made of stern stuff. Mikhail only surrounded himself with those he felt were

trustworthy and competent. Alex was no exception to that
rule.

"Got it." Bria stood and watched as the dark-tinted
window glided up before Alex pulled out into traffic. She
watched as the car rounded the block, and then headed
for the front of the line waiting to get into the club despite the protests that rang out behind her. A few com-
plaints from the crowd weren't going to stop her from
going inside.

The gatekeeper was a hulking man with bulging muscles that tested the limits of his too-tight T-shirt. He eyed
Bria down the length of his nose before turning his attention to the clipboard in his hand. "You on the list?"

Bria waited until he made eye contact once again. She
drew on her power and projected a command into the
man's mind. "I am on the list," she said sweetly. "Bria."

Without looking at his clipboard he moved the dark
velvet rope aside. "You *are* on the list. Have a good night."

Bria had the cash she needed to pay the cover, thanks
to a little help from Claire, and pressed the bills into the
dazed man's palm. Anxious to get inside, Bria didn't look
back as she walked through the entrance and into the club
proper. She'd shared blood with Jenner enough that he was
easy to track. His presence burned in the center of her being like a beacon. It rankled that he'd come here tonight.
While she sat at Mikhail's house—her newly appointed
prison—Jenner went about life as he pleased, hitting the
clubs as though he hadn't a care in the world. The knowledge that he could so easily set her aside stung.

Bria was made of much sterner stuff than Jenner ever
gave her credit for. Like Claire had suggested, Bria
planned to have it out with him. Tonight she was going to
make it clear to him that she would no longer allow herself to be closeted away. And likewise, she was ready to
make it plain to him that she would no longer accept his

dismissal of her. Jenner had tethered her soul. And it was time that he started treating her in the way that a mate should be treated.

Before leaving the house, Bria had tucked two short daggers into a sheath at the small of her back that were easily concealed by the long tunic-style shirt she wore over a pair of leather leggings that Claire had lent her. She'd told Bria that someone should get some use out of the clothes, since she wouldn't be wearing them for a good long while. Claire had acted put out, but Bria could tell that the female was ecstatic over her pregnancy by the way she'd smoothed a hand over the curve of her belly.

Would Bria ever get the chance at that kind of happiness? She'd come to the conclusion that if she wanted it she was going to have to go out and seize it.

Without Jenner at her side Bria felt exposed, and it sent an anxious tremor through her body to realize that she'd come to find his protection, however stifling, as a comfort. Now that she knew the full truth of what hunted her, every sight, sound, shift in the crowd gave Bria a start. The tingle of magic in the air caused her heart to beat a wild tattoo against her rib cage. She'd never seen a wendigo. Didn't even really know what one was. Would she recognize William if he found her? Would she have the presence of mind to defend herself if he did? She needed Jenner. Not because she was too afraid to be without him or because she was weak. But because as a united front they could overcome all of the obstacles that stood in the way of their happiness.

"Mmmm. You look good enough to eat, baby."

Bria stiffened as a body pressed up against her back. She turned slowly to find a large man towering over her, the only thing extraordinary about him his height. He swayed on his feet and his breath reeked of whiskey. His leering smile didn't bother her half as much as his wandering hands. Human. And drunk enough to be obnoxiously brazen.

She slapped away the hand he rested on her hip. "Not interested." Bria might not have appeared threatening to the man, but she'd yet to bare her fangs. "Step off," she added in an attempt to sound tough. If he couldn't take the hint she'd be more than happy to show him what he was up against.

"What's the matter?" He put his hand back on her hip, lower this time so that his fingers brushed over her butt. "Loosen up and let's have some fun."

Bria stiffened and reached to her back. Her hand found the hilt of one of the small daggers and she took a precursory glance around to make sure no one was watching before she slipped the blade from the sheath. The drunk human squeezed her flesh and she brought the dagger up, pressing the sharp tip to the skin beneath his chin. His eyes widened and his jaw went slack. She angled the blade and dragged it along his jawline. He swallowed audibly, the sound as clear to Bria's ears as the sound of the dagger rasping against his stubble.

"Come on, baby," the human blurted. "I thought you might want to have some fun. That's all."

Bria drew on her power. She caught the human's eyes and held his gaze. "Leave me alone," she intoned, "and don't ever come back to this place."

His eyes glazed over and his expression grew dreamy. The human gave a slow nod of his head, turned around, and walked away with measured steps. Bria watched as he followed her instruction to the letter, walking through the door with mindless, zombie steps.

Bria sheathed the dagger and turned in an excited circle, a smile stretching from cheek to cheek. For the second time tonight she'd successfully compelled someone, not to mention she'd effectively shut down the unwanted advance. She wanted to pump her fist up into the air. Jump. Celebrate her accomplishment as well as her confidence. No one could deny that Bria was a formidable vampire now, not even Jenner. There was no one to celebrate with, though. No one to give her a pat on the back or to tell her that she'd done well. No one present to be proud of her show of independence and strength. It was a hollow victory. One that left a sour taste in her mouth.

A deep ache settled in Bria's chest as the tether that bound her to Jenner once again pulled to its breaking point. The distance between them opened up like a wide cavern. And she didn't think she'd be able to live through the strain. Claire said that Jenner had put Bria up on a pedestal. That he saw her as something too pristine to soil and above his station. How could Jenner think so lowly of himself that he thought the best thing for Bria would be to keep himself from her? He had to feel the strain as much as she did. With every passing day it became harder to bear. Jenner had said it himself the very first night they'd met: *The tether is absolute.* It would do him no good to continue to fight it.

Bria wouldn't *allow* him to continue to fight it. He belonged to her as much as she belonged to him. And she refused to sit by and watch as he tortured the both of them for no damned good reason.

She scanned the nightclub once again and narrowed her focus to block out anything that might disrupt her concentration. Jenner was here, his soul fired in her consciousness, and his scent stood out among all of the others packed into the building. It ignited her thirst, a dry fire that would only be quenched when she buried her fangs into his throat. That's exactly what Bria was going to do. Through with playing games, with being discarded, with having others make decisions for her. She was going to make sure Jenner realized who he belonged to. And before the sun rose she planned to belong to him both body and soul.

She caught sight of him across the crowded bar, standing head and shoulders above most of the people present. Despair followed on the heels of elation as she spotted him. Beside him stood the female who'd pressed against his body the night he'd taken Bria to The Dragon's Den. Jenner's gaze was focused on the female's face and a deep groove cut into his brow. His hands were wrapped around her wrists as he held her to him. Bria's heart clenched. She stared at him, dumbstruck, while her heart shattered into a million pieces.

He bit down harder to further open Ronja's vein. Her blood flowed over his tongue and he took one greedy swallow after another. Their young passions had been sated, but his thirst had not. He'd fed from her again and again while he'd been inside of her, and now, in the aftermath, he fed from her once more.

"The world has fallen out from beneath my feet . . . Eric."

Ronja's words slurred. Her heart slowed its rapid beat and still he drank. Her body grew cold beneath his. Her breathing became shallow and her arm fell away from his shoulder. Power flooded him, a rush that had no equal. Virile, strong, he was as mighty as any vampire. His petition for transition had been denied because they feared him. Feared his strength, the power that coursed through his veins. There could be no other explanation.

"Errrkkk." The whispered sound of Ronja's voice no longer registered in his ears. Nor did the plea as she attempted to push his name past her weary lips.

He'd exhausted her, loved her so thoroughly that she could barely speak. Satisfaction roared through him. When he found a vampire willing to turn him he'd turn Ronja. They could drink from each other and enjoy each other's bodies for eternity.

Her fist flopped against his chest as she tried futilely to push him away. His throat blazed with unquenched thirst and his mind wandered as he continued to drink wantonly from Ronja's throat. He held her tighter to him, nuzzled against her throat, and bit down harder as the flow of blood began to slow.

"P-leassss . . ." Even her breath in his ear had grown cold and he shuddered. "S-s-t-t . . . p . . ."

Realization blew the haze of bloodlust from his brain. It wasn't blissful exhaustion that weighed Ronja down and slurred her words. He'd taken too much. Drained every last drop of blood she had to offer.

Her heart stuttered in her chest. Th-thrum, th-thrum. *A long, slow breath released from her chest and Ronja went limp in Jenner's arms. He released her throat with a tortured sob as a bolt of white-hot fear shot through him. "Ronja!" He gave her a gentle shake. "Ronja!" And again, with more force. Her eyes stared, sightless, toward the sky and her creamy skin had turned ashen. "No!" His shout rent the quiet. He bit into his wrist and opened the vein before bringing it to her lips. His blood flowed over her mouth, down her throat, and over her bare breasts in rivulets that decorated her body like bright crimson ribbon. "Drink! Drink!" He pressed his wrist tighter to her mouth, worked his palm over her throat to make her swallow. It did him no good.*

He'd drained her. Taken the last drop of her life-blood into his mouth and swallowed it greedily down. In his mindless bloodlust, he'd killed her.

Jenner downed his fifth vodka of the night, wishing like hell that his metabolism wouldn't burn the alcohol off before it could numb his overactive fucking brain and the memories of his past that haunted him. Despite Ronan's assurances that Jenner's past didn't define him, he'd nearly given himself over to his lusts last week in the gym with Bria and it had been nothing more than another cruel reminder that when it came to her his control couldn't be trusted. The scent of her arousal invited him, as did Bria's own passion whenever he allowed himself to slip. With every passing day, each minute of time spent with her, Jenner found his soul twining more intricately with hers. His want of her was absolute. Overwhelming. Just the thought of her caused him to shake like a fucking junkie in need of his next fix. If he didn't hit the release valve soon he was going to crack.

He'd come to Ultra tonight in the hopes that the myriad sights, sounds, and distractions would clog up his mind and prevent him from thinking of her. But his mood soured with every drink he downed, and all the crowds had managed to prove was that where Bria was concerned there wasn't a single thing in this world that could lure his focus from her.

"All alone, Jenner? Did you finally kick that meek and mousy female to the curb?"

A low growl vibrated in Jenner's throat at the sound of Marissa's voice. The female was gods-damned persistent, it seemed. Apparently his cool rebuff the last time he'd seen her hadn't been enough to deflect her unwanted attention. Jenner leveled his gaze on the dhampir and his lip curled back to reveal his fangs. There was nothing meek or mousy about Bria. His mate was fierce. Strong. A force to be reckoned with.

"Gods, I love that violent streak in you," Marissa purred. "You're a cruel male to leave me wanting, Jenner. I haven't been properly fucked since you last took me."

"You'll have to find someone else to properly fuck you." Jenner tried to keep his anger under control. "I've told you once already, it's not going to be me. Not ever again."

Silver chased across Marissa's gaze. Her eyes narrowed before she masked her annoyance with a seductive smile. "I've never known you not to accept a body or a vein when one was offered up to you." She gathered her long hair over her shoulder to expose her throat to him. "What's changed that you can deny yourself what you can't live without?"

Jenner knew what Marissa—and countless others—thought of him. That he was a mindless creature of uncontrollable lusts. Undiscerning of his bedmates or the veins that he took sustenance from. Disloyal for breaking faith with Siobhan to pledge himself to Mikhail. And yet it didn't stop Marissa from using him when it met her mood. It didn't stop her from sating her own desires with him. Hell, she hadn't even minded sharing him. The differences between the female who stood before him now and Bria were staggering. Bria refused to share him. Refused to take another's vein. She was loyal to him when she had no reason to be. Honorable when he felt anything but. She stood head and shoulders above any other female Jenner had ever known.

"Everything's changed," he said. "You don't know a damned thing about me, Marissa. Not anymore." In fact,

Jenner suspected that the only person who truly knew him was Bria, and he'd turned her away. Never again, though. Jenner was through being a stubborn asshole.

His words didn't faze Marissa. She reached out and ran her palms down his chest, stopping at his waistband. She curled her fingers inside his jeans and Jenner seized her wrists. "I said *no*."

Marissa's mouth hovered dangerously close to Jenner's and she pushed her body against his, forcing the contact. This was his own doing. He had no one but himself to blame for her rash and wanton behavior. There had been a time when he wouldn't have hesitated to hoist Marissa into his arms and fuck the female up against the wall with all of Ultra's patrons looking on. But Jenner was changed. Bria had changed him.

He should have listened to Mikhail. To Ronan and everyone else who'd tried to get their points through his thick head. If he were simply a creature who craved endless amounts of blood, any body, any vein would have sufficed. If he truly had no control, was the monster he'd been branded as, he would have killed dozens of dhampirs in the months since his turning. He'd been careful, though. He'd bound himself in invisible bands of restraint. Bria tested his control, his lusts, as no other had. And still he'd never hurt her. Never taken more blood than she could safely offer. Could it be that Ronan and Mikhail had been right? Bria was meant for him. *His.* Whatever obstacles he thought stood in their way were weak and inconsequential. And he was gods-damned tired of trying to fight his own instincts.

Jenner choked on an intake of breath as the heat of Bria's presence burned at the center of his soul. His head snapped up, the female he still held in his grasp all but forgotten as he searched the club for his mate. *She's here? How? Why?* He'd told her not to leave Mikhail's house without him time and again. His anger with her warred with the worry that clawed at his chest with razor-sharp talons. The necromancer could be anywhere. Standing in the midst of the dancers on the floor for all he knew. Panic welled hot and thick in Jenner's throat as his frantic gaze scanned the breadth of the club over and again—

There!

She spun a full circle, the expression on her face so blinding beautiful and full of elation that it caused Jenner's chest to ache. Her happiness melted away, however, to reveal a deep furrow in her brow and a sadness that seemed to suck every ounce of oxygen from his lungs. Her gaze roamed over the club, searching until it locked with his. Her jaw hung slack, her luscious mouth parted, and that sadness quickly transformed to a resounding pain that sliced through him like the sharpest of blades.

He'd kept her cooped up for weeks and Bria had sprung her prison only to find him in a club, apparently enjoying his freedom while another female pressed her body fully against his, her wrists held tight in what Bria might have seen as a possessive grip.

"Bria!"

She turned on a heel and fled, her speed a smudge of color against the other bodies that appeared to stand still in comparison. Jenner released his hold on Marissa and took off after Bria, shoving his way past the bodies that formed a barrier between him and the only thing he wanted. The only thing he *needed*. And because of his own stubborn stupidity, he stood on the precipice of losing her forever.

CHAPTER
20

Jenner burst through the doors and out onto the sidewalk in time to see Bria duck into one of Mikhail's black Lincoln Town Cars. The taillights flashed momentarily before the car pulled out onto the street and merged with traffic. At least Jenner could be assured that Bria was safe and in good hands. And that she was returning to the house. That didn't mean he wasn't going to race after her, though. He got his ass in gear and had backtracked a block down the street to where he'd parked his bike when a deep, musky scent invaded his nostrils.

Fucking hell. Of all the shitty gods-damned timing.

Jenner stepped into the shadows, careful to remain unseen. He needed to get to Bria, to explain himself, but Mikhail would have his head if he found out that Jenner had the one male they'd been searching for in his sights and did nothing about it.

Fucking Gregor. Jenner wanted to rip the male's head from his shoulders simply for the interruption. The pressure that had been building inside of Jenner for weeks reached its bursting point and he took a lunging step forward, ready to take every ounce of frustration he felt out on the male's body. His step faltered as a host of voices joined Gregor's, and Jenner stepped back into the protection of the alleyway.

Son of a bitch. The male had a small army at his back.

"McAlister's got his eyes on us." One of Gregor's men stepped up to him, his hands tucked casually in the pockets of his jeans.

"Aye," Gregor agreed. "I've got the werewolf by the balls now, though. He'll be one less complication as we move forward."

"And just how did you manage that?"

Gregor scoffed, "He was easy enough to manipulate. The bastard's got a mountain of gambling debts. He's a whore who'll do anything for a little money in his pocket."

"You paid him to turn on McAlister?"

Gregor turned to face his comrade. "I paid him to find Réamonn's daughter."

The berserker scoffed, "Foolish, if you ask me. Why throw away good money? If we continue attacking the covens, we'll flush her out eventually."

Gregor grabbed the other male by the throat and took him down to the sidewalk. The concrete cracked under the force and a growl echoed over the sound of passing traffic. Jenner strained to pick through the sounds for that of Gregor's voice. A snarl ripped from his lips as he went nose to nose with the male who'd dared to doubt him. "Question my methods again and I'll put you in the ground. Whalen might play fast and loose with his money, but he's a damned good tracker and his loyalty is easily bought. He'll find her while we shift our focus to overthrowing McAlister once and for all."

"We're three hundred bodies and the Sortiari are legion," the other male rasped. "How do you suggest we overthrow Fate?"

A sick smile twisted Gregor's lips. He straightened and dragged the other male up with him. "By using the bastard's fears against him. Have you forgotten that his own death was prophesized by the very seers he employs?"

"I haven't forgotten. I'd say you have your work cut out for you, Cousin, if you intend to find a single witch amongst all of the supernaturals that inhabit the earth."

Gregor cocked a brow as he regarded the male. "What makes you think I haven't already found her?"

"Where?"

Gregor paused. His eyes narrowed and he canted his head to one side, listening. A burst of adrenaline dumped into Jenner's system and his fangs throbbed in his gums. He didn't move. Didn't make a fucking sound. He was one vampire, unarmed, in the presence of a dozen berserker warlords, each trained to kill with frighteningly quick precision. Confronting them would be suicide, and Jenner had too gods-damned much to live for to walk into a fight he had no chance of winning.

"Check the alleys!" Gregor barked. "There's something out there, and whatever it is, I want it dead. Don't come back without a body."

Fuck. Jenner would have to ditch his bike, which riled him enough to cause a low growl to vibrate in his throat. He swallowed down the sound, but not before one of the berserkers heard it.

"There! In the alley." He drew a GLOCK from a holster under his arm and squeezed off five quick shots.

Jenner turned and took off at a run. He hadn't left quickly enough, though. White-hot pain seared across his biceps, the unmistakable burn of silver. Fucking slayers had modified their ammo to include a silver compound that would effectively put him down if one of them managed to strike his heart. Jenner's strength flagged; the bullet must have grazed the meaty part of his arm. He pushed himself, his feet pounding on the pavement as he put as much distance between him and the slayers as possible. Another succession of shots fired and another burst of heat burned through him. The bullet struck his left shoulder blade. He pressed his palm to his chest, only to find that the bullet hadn't gone through. Damned thing was lodged between his back and his chest and the silver burned him from the inside out. Jenner's step faltered as he ran, but he managed to dig his cell out of his pocket and dialed Ronan.

"You know," Ronan answered, "I can only give you so much love advice in one—"

"I'm running down Sunset headed toward North Fairfax," Jenner grunted. "Had to ditch my bike. At least twelve slayers are tracking me and I've got a silver bullet lodged in my back."

"On my way."

Jenner stuffed his phone back into his pocket. Gunfire echoed behind him and he ran in a crisscross pattern to avoid being hit again. He veered onto Fairfax so as to make it easier for Ronan to find him. There wasn't a single advantage Jenner had that the berserkers didn't share. Speed, strength, the ability to see even in the absence of light . . . the playing field had been leveled and then tipped as soon as that damned bullet buried itself in his chest. He snagged the edge of his foot on a crack in the pavement and stumbled, catching himself on a parking meter before he smeared his face on the concrete. Another bevy of shots cleaved the air and another scorch of pain came as a silver bullet grazed his ear.

The squeal of tires echoed from several blocks away and Jenner regained his footing as another bullet struck the sidewalk right where he'd almost fallen. He continued to run, dodged, and switched his course so that he ran down the middle of the street. Ronan's Aston-Martin came screaming into view and Jenner pushed himself into a sprint toward the car. It came to a skidding stop in the median and the passenger side door flew open. Jenner dove into the interior and Ronan took off at a tear before he could even get the door closed. The *pop! pop! pop!* of gunfire became muted in the interior of the car, and Jenner allowed himself to let out a shaking breath. *Fucking hell.* He could have bit it tonight. Died in a pool of his own blood on the street and left Bria to think that his last act before he'd died was to betray her.

"Hang on, okay?" Ronan placed a tentative hand on Jenner's arm. Ronan's eyes were wide with concern, his fangs bared. "Hit anywhere else? You're shaking pretty damned hard."

He really was shaking like a sonofabitch. His limbs quaked to the point that Jenner couldn't grasp the seat belt to buckle it. Not that it would do a gods-damned thing for him. "Grazes to my arm and ear," he said on a rush of breath. "The bullet's lodged somewhere between my back and chest."

"Gotcha." Ronan shifted and punched the accelerator. "Let's get the fuck out of here and get you squared away."

"To Mikhail's," Jenner rasped. The silver had begun to take its toll and Jenner's stomach twisted in a knot of nausea. Ronan would kill Jenner himself if he emptied his guts in the fancy fucking sports car that he loved almost as much as his mate. Jenner bit the inside of his cheek until he tasted blood and willed the heaving of his gut to still. "Bria," he murmured. His vision darkened at the periphery and Jenner slumped in his seat. "Have to get to Bria. To explain."

"Okay," Ronan said as he skidded into a sharp turn. "Okay. Just hang on."

The silver wouldn't kill Jenner; at least he hoped it

wouldn't. But if he didn't make things right with Bria, *now*, her hatred of him would get the job done.

Bria let herself out of the car when it pulled into the circular driveway. She wasn't going to run or throw a fit of rage and jealousy. She refused to burst through the doors and stomp up the stairs like a spoiled child. Jenner might have broken her heart, but she'd be damned if she let him steal her dignity. She thought about the vow she'd made to him. That if another female ever touched him with familiarity again she'd unleash the force of her rage. She let out a soft snort. So much for claiming what was *hers*. Bria was tired. Tired of trying to win Jenner's affection. Tired of trying to prove to him that she was worthy of their tether. Of *him*. She wasn't going to force him to care for her. To want her. For one thing she could thank him: He'd given her the skills she needed to protect herself. She didn't need him—didn't need anyone—and it was time to go out and live her life.

She slipped through the door and crossed the foyer. Voices carried from the back of the house, Claire and Mikhail chatting in conversational tones. How was their tether so different from Bria and Jenner's? Why did they seem to fall into their relationship with ease, while she bumbled through hers, never fully connecting with the male whose soul had tethered hers? Claire had suggested that what stood between them was Jenner's own belief that Bria was something to be put upon a pedestal. Too pure for him to soil. Too far above his station for him to be deserving of her affection.

Whatever Jenner's reasons, Bria was done trying to convince him otherwise.

She stepped into the guest room and her heart sank as she realized that when she left this place she'd essentially be leaving with the clothes on her back. Aside from her backpack, which contained her GPS and a couple of baubles she'd intended to leave at geocaches, most of her possessions had been left at the coven's compound. Her uncle had brought a few clothes and books, but he'd held on to the bulk of what she owned in the hopes that she'd soon return home. There was no way in hell she was going back there. No, Bria had lived under someone's thumb long enough. Jenner had taught her how to defend herself and to hone her senses. She could be vigilant. If the necromancer found her then so be it. She'd rather die on her feet, fighting for her freedom, than wither and die a prisoner, unloved and unwanted.

She gathered up her clothes and books and searched through the closet for something to pack her things in when voices shouted from downstairs. The sound of the front door as it bounced off the wall cracked loudly and Bria rushed from the room to the top of the stairs as she tried to get a glimpse of who'd burst into the king's home.

"Mikhail!" Ronan's voice boomed as he dragged Jenner through the doorway. Bria's heart lodged in her throat at the sight of Jenner, his big body slumped against Ronan's, his head bowed. Blood trickled from his arm and down the side of his face. Bria slapped her hand over her mouth to stifle a gasp. In the blink of an eye the king was in the foyer, Claire right behind him. A deep furrow cut into Ronan's brow as he said, "Attacked by slayers. There's a silver bullet lodged in his chest. He lost consciousness right before we pulled through the gate."

Claire took off at a clip, as though she knew exactly what had to be done. "Get him into the kitchen!" she called out. "Scratch that! The dining room. On the table. We've got to get that bullet out."

Bria's world careened as the tether that bound her to

Jenner slackened. The silver would slowly poison him, and he'd need her blood if he was going to survive this. He might have hurt her, but she refused to sit by and watch him die. She flew down the stairs. Panic choked the air from her lungs and caused her to tremble. By the time she made it to the formal dining room that adjoined the kitchen Ronan had laid Jenner out on the long table. Claire was poised and ready with a pair of scissors she used to cut his shirt away. Ronan and Mikhail rolled him over onto his stomach and she used a washcloth to clean the blood from his back to reveal a raw, gaping hole. The silver would prevent him from healing and Bria had no idea how long it had been or how much blood Jenner had lost.

"We have to get the bullet out," Claire said. "Mikhail, we need a knife, something to open him up."

"I can do it." Bria stepped forward, her dagger in hand. Her hands trembled and she willed them to still. She didn't trust anyone else to do it. Jenner belonged to her. Whether he wanted her to belong to him or not, she was going to do this.

"He's volatile," Ronan warned. "Delirious. We'll need to hold him down or he might attack Bria." His gaze slid to her. "He might not realize who you are."

Obviously, Ronan had no idea what had transpired between her and Jenner tonight. "When did this happen?" It couldn't have been long after she'd left Ultra.

"About an hour ago. I don't know the details. Just that he was on the run and bleeding." Ronan looked to Mikhail. "There were at least a dozen of them. Maybe more."

Mikhail swore under his breath and the room sizzled with his anger. "We can talk about it later," Bria said. "Right now, we need to get the bullet out."

The room went silent and Bria brought the tip of the

dagger to Jenner's flesh. "Careful," Mikhail warned. "I've been shot with these bullets. They'll liquefy under the skin."

"Okay," Bria breathed. "Then I guess I'll just have to be extracareful."

She brought the blade to the wound and Jenner jerked. Mikhail and Ronan held him down, but he thrashed against their hold. He rolled to the side and his eyes snapped open, unfocused and feral silver. "I have to get to her!" he shouted. "Let me the fuck go! Bria!"

Claire moved to hold down Jenner's legs and Mikhail barked out a warning: "Claire, don't test me! I can't hold his shoulders down and protect you at the same time. Get away before he kicks you."

As though she hadn't even thought of the possibility, Claire moved away, her palm resting protectively on her belly. Bria didn't blame her. The queen needed to keep a safe distance as long as Jenner was out of control. Besides, she could handle this.

"Jenner." She spoke with a calm she didn't feel close to his ear. He stilled on the table, his body rising and falling with heavy pants of breath. "I have to remove the bullet. Don't move. Do you understand me?"

"Bria," he said through a grunt of pain. "Don't . . . leave. Have . . . . to explain."

The tether between them further loosened and Bria felt him slip away. She poised the knife above the wound and said, "I'm not going anywhere. Now hold still."

CHAPTER
21

The dagger's blade sank into Jenner's flesh. He snarled, a feral, wild sound that echoed in Bria's ears, but he didn't move. Not a single muscle. She tried not to think about his words. He wanted to explain what? Why he'd allowed another female so close to his body when it was Bria who should have been held in his embrace?

"Do you see the bullet?"

She turned her attention to Ronan, who still held Jenner's right shoulder down. "I think so." There was so much blood, the rich scent an unwelcome distraction. Bria's thirst raged, a dry fire that she was desperate to quench. A steady rivulet of crimson ran from the wound high on Jenner's shoulder blade and down his back. "It's not going to be easy to get to. There's a lot of blood and it's embedded more than a couple of inches."

Black veins began to spread from the wound, tendrils that marred the perfection of his skin. Jenner's body seized violently and he let out a shout before he clenched his teeth down, piercing his bottom lip in the process. He slumped back down to the table, his cheek flush against the polished wood. Bria reached out and smoothed his hair away from his temple. *Hang on, Jenner.*

"Cut around it if you have to," Ronan said. "He'll heal once it's out. But we need to get the bullet out of there before the silver does any more damage."

Bria steeled herself for what had to be done. She thought of her own wounds at the slayers' hands when they'd attacked her coven, the blood that had gushed from her throat, and her own desire to float away and cease to be. Her uncle might have felt he had no choice but to orchestrate her imprisonment, but he'd loved her enough to do whatever it took to protect her. He'd brought her to Mikhail to save her. He'd been strong for her. And now she was going to be strong for Jenner.

She pierced Jenner's skin and cut a deep circle two inches wide and more than two inches deep. The sound of his pained shout boomed in her ears and shook the chandelier that hung high above the table. With the wound now gaping and open Bria used the dagger's tip to dig beneath the bullet and leverage it out. Using her fingers, she reached into the narrow hole and with the tips of her fingers gripped the mangled silver bullet as she pried it loose with the dagger. It was spongy in her grip, as volatile as the male who trembled with pain beneath her. Slowly, oh, so slowly, she drew the bullet from Jenner's back, gripping it as tight as she dared as his body fought to hold on to it.

The bullet released with a sickening wet gurgle of suction and Bria dropped it onto the table's surface. It broke down in an instant and spread in a puddle, bright against the dark polish of mahogany. Bria watched as the black veins faded from Jenner's skin and the wound began to close. The silver had taken its toll, as had the blood loss. If he was going to be okay, he'd need to feed before he lost consciousness.

"Help me turn him over." Ronan and Mikhail eased Jenner onto his back and he winced as his left shoulder touched down on the table. Bria bit down hard and scored her wrist on her fangs. She brought it to Jenner's mouth, but he'd become unresponsive. "Drink, Jenner." There was no telling what damage the silver had done or how much blood he'd lost. He responded with a low moan and his tongue flicked out at the rivulet of blood that coated his lips. "Damn it, drink!" Bria shouted the command and pressed her wrist against his mouth. His lips slowly parted and after a long moment sealed over her flesh.

A collective sigh of relief passed from everyone present, but Bria doubted any of them felt it as much as she did. She hated that her worry for him crippled her even after he'd rejected her. But the tether was *absolute*. Whatever happened between them, she could do nothing to change that fact.

Jenner's soft suction at her wrist became more powerful with every pull. His hands came up to grip her arm and his fangs bit down hard to pierce her skin. Bria swallowed down a gasp as a rush of heat cycled through her veins. How could she ever get Jenner out of her head, her heart, when his effect on her was so instant, so visceral and absolute?

Their tether could never be broken.

A satisfied growl rumbled in his chest as he drank. Bria raised a questioning brow to Mikhail. "How long until he stops bleeding?"

"It's going to take some time for the wound to completely heal. The bleeding should have stopped already, though. He should be fine by morning."

She could leave. While he rested. Healed. She could slip out the door and no one would notice. He might need more blood, though. Bria was hurt, but she could never be cruel. Could never abandon him when he needed her.

Jenner's fangs disengaged from her wrist and his head lolled to one side. A flash of fear radiated from Bria's stomach and she placed a palm on his chest. "Jenner?"

"He's unconscious," Ronan said. "But I think he'll be okay. Let's get him upstairs."

Mikhail and Ronan hefted Jenner's limp body from the table and headed for the staircase. Bria stared at the formal dining table, the pristine surface marred by pools of silver and crimson. Her emotions teetered on manic, at once relieved and panicked. She'd done her best to turn off the worry, the doubt that clawed at her while she'd dug the bullet from Jenner's back. But now that the numbing effect of the adrenaline rush had worn off, Bria found herself unsteady on her feet and shaking.

What if he'd died? Their tether would have been severed and once again Bria would have experienced the crippling emptiness as her soul abandoned her for oblivion. She let out a shuddering breath.

"Are you okay, Bria?"

Claire spoke from behind her. Bria appreciated the female's concern and turned to face her. "I think so. I'm a little shaken up."

"That makes two of us." For the first time since they'd met, Bria noted the fear in Claire's expression. The queen had always seemed so fearless, so confident. As though she'd never known doubt. "I hope Mikhail kills every last one of those bastards," she said with a ferocity that Bria not only understood but also shared. "I want him to show them what extinction really is."

Claire wrapped her hands protectively around her stomach and Bria reached out to place a comforting hand on her shoulder. "You should probably get some rest."

Claire gave a wan smile. "I'm fine. You'd think being

almost nine months pregnant would be wearing me down, but I've never felt better. If anyone needs rest, it's you. Do you need to feed, Bria? We could call Lucas. Or you can feed from me if you need to."

"No." She hadn't seen Lucas since the night that Jenner proclaimed he'd kill him for putting his hands on her. Jenner's possessiveness of her that night had stirred something in Bria. Made her feel as though he could possibly want her. So much had changed since that night and she didn't know how she'd recover from the sense of loss that stabbed through her. As far as feeding from Claire went, Bria doubted Mikhail would be happy whether Claire was trying to help or not. "I'll be fine." Claire gave her a dubious look. "Really. But thank you for offering."

"If you change your mind, let me know," Claire said. "You'd better get upstairs and check on him."

Bria's gaze wandered back to the table. She didn't know if she was ready to be alone with Jenner, unconscious or not. "The table," she said. "I need to clean it."

"Don't worry about that now," Claire said. "We'll get it squared away later. Upstairs. Now. Otherwise, I'll have to ask Ronan and Mikhail to pack *you* up, too."

Bria smiled. "All right. You too, though. I think we all need a few hours of rest."

"Word," Claire said. "Now go. Let me know if you need anything."

"I will," Bria replied. Claire truly was an extraordinary female. "Thank you."

By the time Bria made it upstairs, Ronan and Mikhail had left. Jenner lay on her bed, his arm, face, and torso stained crimson. She could only imagine what his back looked like. Her own hands and arms were sticky with dried blood. Bria's stomach turned as another crippling wave of fear weakened her knees and threatened to send her to the floor.

Exhaustion weighed on her. Sunrise wasn't far off, but Bria refused to sleep. Instead, she went into the bathroom and ran a sinkful of hot water. She grabbed several washcloths from the cupboard, wetted one, and wrung out the excess water. Jenner's chest rose and fell with even breaths as she settled down beside him on the mattress. With gentle strokes she washed the blood from his body and then eased him over to his stomach and cleaned his back, careful to avoid the angry gaping wound that had yet to fully close.

She tended him gently. Lovingly. After several trips to the bathroom to rinse the soiled washcloth, she had Jenner as clean as she could get him. She didn't bother to shower, just wiped the blood from her skin and stripped down to her underwear and a cami. The sun would be up in a matter of minutes. Its approach weighed down her limbs and fogged her mind. Bria eased herself onto the bed next to Jenner and tucked her body against his. For a few hours at least, she could pretend that he wanted her. That she belonged here, with him. Their bodies intertwined.

She could pretend until the sun set that he loved her.

Jenner woke with a start. His breath sawed in and out of his lungs and he clawed at his chest and then over his left shoulder blade where the bullet struck. Self-preservation kicked in as his secondary fangs punched down from his gums and he shot up from the bed, ready to defend himself from an invisible foe. Confusion fogged his brain as the details of Bria's room came into focus. He slumped against the wall and caught his breath as he tried to make sense of how he'd gotten there. The last thing he remembered, he'd thrown himself into Ronan's car.

Jesus.

The gray light of twilight shadowed the outline of a body on the mattress. Jenner pushed away from the wall, his limbs quaking with unspent adrenaline, to find Bria resting peacefully next to the indentation his body left on the bed.

Beautiful.

He brought his arm over his shoulder and felt for the bullet wound. Only a raw, angry welt remained of the hole the slayer had blown in his back. The grogginess that weighed Jenner down wasn't the hold of sunlight on his body but the aftereffects of the silver poisoning. He'd told Ronan to bring him here. Who'd taken the bullet out of his back?

Bria stirred and Jenner reached out to brush a lock of dark hair away from her face. She kicked the covers away and his breath caught at the sight of creamy skin exposed to his gaze. His body stirred, his cock grew hard in his jeans. He'd never wanted anything as much as he did Bria. Had he ruined any chance of making her truly his? Was it too late to take what he wanted after pushing her away time and again? The temptation of her body was almost more than Jenner could stand. He still wasn't sure if he could trust himself with her. He reached for the sheet and draped it over her, careful not to wake her.

"Why do you cover me?" Bria whispered in the low light. She didn't move, didn't open her eyes. Her stillness and the hardness of her tone sent a ripple of anxiety through Jenner's body.

She'd smell the lie on him if he told her anything other than the truth. "Because the sight of you"—he swallowed against the emotion that clogged his throat—"twists me into a fucking knot."

Bria opened her eyes and pushed herself up on an elbow. The amethyst depths flashed with angry silver, though she kept her tone level. "Is that why you had another female in your arms last night? Because I *twist you into knots*? Perhaps if you'd been with me—*where you belong*—you wouldn't have found yourself with a slayer's silver bullet in your back."

Her disdain peppered his skin like bits of gravel. He deflected the hurt of her accusation with a question of his own: "Why were you out alone last night? I told you not to leave the house without me."

"And I told you that I wasn't something you could simply place on a shelf until you found need of it again."

"You belong to *me,*" Jenner growled. His anger was unfounded, further proving that he was nothing more than a selfish asshole. But it was so much easier than telling Bria the truth: that he'd kept his distance from her because he couldn't bear for her to find out that he was unworthy of their tether. "Your safety is my only concern. You could have been killed last night, Bria. The slayers were right outside of Ultra."

"Yes, my safety," she agreed in a chilling tone. "Always my safety. And what about yours? Don't you care that you could have been killed last night? I'm sick of you worrying about my safety and nothing else. Not even my happiness. I asked you a question and I deserve an answer. How can I possibly have any effect on you when you seem content to cast me aside in favor of another's affection?"

If she only knew how irresistible she looked, propped up on the bed with the rumpled blankets around her, her cheeks flushed and hair a wild tangle that cascaded over her bare shoulders. Bria was sin and innocence, fire and ice. And too pristine for the things he wanted to do to her.

"You have no idea what I've cast aside," Jenner grated. He rubbed at the residual burn of silver that ached in his shoulder, but the pain was nothing in comparison to his need for Bria that slowly ate him alive.

"Is it because you think I'm incapable of passion?" Bria averted her gaze. "Have I not shown you how much I want you? That your touch sets me on fire?"

"Stop." Jenner couldn't hear those words from her. Every minute in her presence broke down his defenses. Hearing that she wanted him, craved him, was more than he could handle. "You don't know how hard it is for me not to . . ." The words died on Jenner's tongue and he raked his fingers through his hair.

"Not to *what*?" Bria pushed herself from the bed and Jenner nearly choked at the sight of her clad in nothing but her underwear and a strappy top that was so thin he could see the dark outline of her areolas and the tempting points of her nipples through the fabric. "What is wrong with me that you feel you have to leave me every sunrise? That the only contact you can have with me is when you're teaching me to fight? To protect myself from an enemy that I've never even seen? How can you give me pleasure, take the vein at my throat, and in the next moment put me at arm's length? Why, Jenner?"

Jenner kept his gaze straight ahead. The accusation in her tone stung. "The thought of losing you—" The words lodged in Jenner's throat. "Bria, you have no idea what I'm capable of. I don't know that I'd survive it, *viaton*."

Bria let out a soft snort. "I'd no longer be a stone around your neck."

A stab of pain shot through his chest. He'd worked Bria. Pushed her. Made her train until she was too exhausted for anything but sleep. She wasn't a burden but a *temptation*. One Jenner found harder to resist by the day. He bent over her smaller frame until his mouth hovered close to her ear. "I *ache* for you. The light of your soul scalds me with its brilliance. I feel you everywhere, but I don't trust myself to be near you. To touch you. To take what I've wanted since the night you tethered me. I'm the prisoner, Bria. I'm nothing more than your helpless captive."

Her voice escalated with her anger. "Those are nothing but excuses. *Why* have you put this unfathomable distance between us?"

"Because I can't be what you need," he rasped as he pushed away and took several steps back. "I'm not what you think I am, Bria."

"Why don't you let me decide what I need, Jenner?" She took a step closer to him, and another. He willed himself to back away, to put distance between them, but his legs refused to move.

"Do you want to know what I think every time I look at you, Bria?" Jenner bared his fangs as his gaze raked over her barely clad body. "I want to fuck every tight inch of you. I want to fuck your mouth, run my cock deep between your lips, and feel the back of your throat against my crown as I come. I want to devour your sweet, wet pussy. Lick and suck it until you scream my name." He took a step closer and another. Bria leaned toward him, her eyes alight with silver. He reached out and fisted the locks of her silky hair and forced her gaze to his. "I want to fuck you so hard and so deep that you ache for days afterward." Bria thought she could handle him? Crude and wanton as he was for her? She thought she could hear the lewd things he wanted to do to her? Wanted to be defiled by him? "I want to fuck your ass." Gods, the thought of having her that way nearly made him come without a single touch from her. "Slowly, until you beg me to pound into you. I want to stripe you with my seed. Mark your flawless tits with ropes of white and make you lie still while I admire my handiwork. Does that appeal to your virginal ears, *viaton*? Would you like your body to be the canvas for my pleasure?"

The rich scent of Bria's desire bloomed around him and it nearly brought Jenner to his knees. Gods, after he had admitted every vile thing he wanted to do to her she still wanted him? He released his hold on her hair and let out a sharp breath as he took a stumbling step back.

"Gods, yes!" Bria exclaimed. "I want all of that and *more*! I'm tired of standing on this damned pedestal. I'm sick of you acting as though I'm this naïve, virginal creature who can't be soiled. I *want*, Jenner. I need your body as much as you need mine. I'm not innocent. I'm not pristine. I lie in this bed in the hours before sunrise and ache for you! I touch myself. I let my hands wander over my naked flesh and imagine that it's you touching me."

Bria ran her hands up her torso. The flimsy top rose up on her hip as her hands moved to cup her breasts. Jenner scrubbed a hand over his face. His heart thundered in his chest and his mouth went dry. She was the most desirable creature he'd ever laid eyes on. Seductive without even trying. "Take me down from this place you've put me. Defile me; use me; do whatever the hell you want to me. I need you, Jenner. Do it, or I'll find someone else who will!"

Her ultimatum ignited his temper and Jenner growled, "The hell you will."

"Oh no?" Bria cocked a challenging brow. "You seem eager enough to share yourself with females other than your mate. I think it's high time I did the same."

"If you so much as touch another male, I'll kill him and make you watch." He wanted to be gentle with her. Whisper sweet, passionate words to her. But Jenner knew nothing of gentleness. His world had been crafted by hardship and violence. Rather than a slow simmer, his passions raged like an inferno. He feared for Bria to see that side of him, and yet he refused to let her go.

"Why bother?" Bria snorted. "I'm sure there are plenty of females waiting for you at Ultra to occupy you while I find my own entertainment. You can visit me when a dhampir's blood isn't enough to fortify your strength. I'd be happy to offer you *my wrist* when your thirst mounts."

"Unless you want to see the full force of my temper, you'd be better off not trying to push my buttons, Bria."

She looked him up and down, but all her narrowed gaze managed was to further harden Jenner's cock. Gods, how he loved this side of her. Wild and enraged, her eyes bright with an angry fire. Her duality fascinated him. Her strength when her very upbringing should have turned her into something weak and pathetic. Her innocence—because no matter what she thought, Bria was indeed naïve—and the wanton desire that sweetened her scent. She was magnificent.

"I'm not afraid of your temper," she seethed. "Do your worst, Jenner."

She'd called his bluff. He could no more let that storm loose than he could sever their tether. He blew out a gust of breath and she took another step closer. Another. Until the heat of her body caressed his.

"I should have left last night," she said. "I should have walked out the door and left Ronan to dig that bullet out of your back."

Her words lacked sincerity. Hurt reflected in her eyes. In the tight draw of her brows.

"Try to leave me," Jenner said, "and I'll hunt you to the ends of the earth."

"Stop playing these games, Jenner," Bria said in a sultry tone that heated his blood, "and you'll never have to."

Jenner grabbed Bria and hauled her against him. His

mouth descended on hers in a furious kiss that conveyed every ounce of pent-up frustration he'd been unable to release since his tethering. Bria melted against him and he wound his fist in the silken length of her hair. She was heaven and hell. His salvation and the cruelest of punishments. Her arms came around his neck and her nails scraped along his nape bringing chills to the surface of Jenner's skin.

He cupped her breast with his free hand, squeezed the flesh through the sheer fabric of her top. Bria moaned into his mouth and Jenner came back to himself as he put her at arm's length. His head swam with her scent; where her body had touched his Jenner's skin burned. Weeks of carefully reigned restraint unraveled under her heated gaze and the sight of her, undone, gasping for breath, her taut nipples straining against the thin fabric as though in want of his touch.

"I can't," he rasped. "I can't, Bria."

"Why?" she demanded. Her eyes flashed violent silver and she bared her fangs. "Tell me why!"

"Because I need to be gentle with you! And all I want to do—all I can think of—is to fuck you with the ferocity of an animal! I want to glut myself on your blood! I could kill you," he said low. "I could drain you before you even realized the damage I'd done. I have no control when it comes to you—to anything—Bria. And it scares the fucking hell out of me."

CHAPTER
22

Jenner thought he had no control? Bria stared at him, awestruck. Her lips throbbed from his punishing kisses; her body hummed with want. His lewd and heated words did nothing to deter her. In fact, they only made her yearn more for the pleasure he could give her. She wanted all that he offered and *more*. No control? Good gods, for weeks he'd been the epitome of control.

"How many times have you taken my vein and never once lost yourself to bloodlust? You could no more hurt me than you could hurt yourself. You have to trust me, Jenner. Trust *us* and the tether that binds us. It's right. We're right! Stop fighting it and let go. Give in. To me."

Bria banished the image of that female in the club from her mind. Whatever life Jenner thought he deserved, whatever evil he thought he was capable of, whatever choices he made in an effort to keep her at a distance, Bria could forgive him. If only he allowed himself to trust in their bond. Darkness swallowed twilight and they stood nose to nose in the shadowed room. Bria reached out to wrap her fingers around the solid muscle of his forearm and Jenner flinched at the contact.

"I want you to touch me, Jenner." She took a step back and shucked her underwear. Tension sizzled in the space between them and Bria straightened to strip her cami off as well. Jenner sucked in a sharp breath and his gaze reflected feral silver in the darkness. Bria swept her hair off her shoulders so that it cascaded down her back. "I'm not made of glass."

Jenner groaned. That same sound of half pleasure, half pain that both excited her and tore at her heart. "I don't trust myself with you."

"*I* trust you. Stop running. Stop pushing me away. Stop treating me like I'm something you have to watch over and be the equal I need you to be. It'll kill me to do it, but I'm ready to walk away if I have to. Make me stay, Jenner," Bria said with desperation. "Give me a reason not to leave!"

All Bria could think about was Jenner lying on the table, bleeding out as the silver poisoned him. She'd never been so terrified of losing something. *Someone.* She stood before him now, bared to his gaze, both her body and her heart. The vulnerability she felt at offering herself to him in this way filled her with fear that caused her limbs to quake. Another rejection would break her. He had to know that. And still he made no move to assuage her fears.

Tears stung at Bria's eyes and she bit back the traitorous flow. She was stronger than Jenner gave her credit for. Stronger than anyone gave her credit for. With a sigh of resignation Bria bent to scoop up her discarded underwear and top. She turned away from Jenner and strode toward the bathroom. She respected herself too much to continue to live this way.

Jenner's strong hand gripped her upper arm and he

whirled her around. He crushed her to him as his mouth claimed hers in a desperate kiss that left Bria weak and shaking. His hands trembled as he caressed from her shoulders down either side of her collarbone to her breasts. Bria's nipples hardened from the contact and a tingle raced from the sensitive tips to her sex.

"Tell me to stop." His growled plea tore at Bria's heart, but she refused to give him the easy way out. He teased her nipples, rolling them between his thumbs and fingers. Bria inhaled sharply and she reached out, gripping the muscled mound of his shoulder to ground her. His palms slid down her torso and his fingertips dug into her hips with barely restrained strength. "Tell me that you despise our tether." He reached down between her legs and cupped her sex. His breath shuddered out of him as Bria rolled her hips into the contact. "That you despise *me*. Tell me that I'm a fucking bastard, Bria. Tell me to get the fuck away from you. That I'm not good enough for you. Tell me that I scare the hell out of you." The tremor that shook his hands spread throughout Jenner's body and his own pain and doubt flared through the tether, stabbing at Bria's chest. "Say something, *anything* to keep me from doing what I want to do right now."

"No, Jenner." Bria released her grip on his shoulder. She allowed her hands to wander over the perfection of his muscled chest, down the ridges of his abs to the waistband of his jeans. She popped the button and the zipper groaned in the quiet of the room. "I've already told you. You don't frighten me. I want this. I want *you*. And I'm not going to wait any longer."

A crease cut into Jenner's brow. Bria shoved his pants and underwear over his hips and down his thighs. He kicked them off from around his feet as though the denim were on fire. Bria put a little distance between them as her eyes roamed greedily over his naked body. Intricate black tattoos decorated his skin. Archaic symbols that seemed to come alive with every slight movement. She reached out and traced a swirling pattern. He shivered beneath her fingertips and a rush of excitement whipped through her. Gods, the male was magnificent. A flash of anger flushed Bria's cheeks. That he'd kept the beauty of his body from her gaze for so long was a crime in itself. She drank him in, her breath catching as she paused at the hard length of his erection protruding proudly from between his legs. Her sex clenched around nothing and Bria's arousal slicked her thighs. She reached out and cupped his heavy sac in her palm before working her way up the silken flesh of his shaft.

Jenner trembled with restraint. His hands fell from her body and balled to fists at his sides. His jaw squared as he clamped his mouth shut and his nostrils flared with sharp breaths. Bria's lips curved into a smile as she brought her gaze to his. "And you think you have no control?"

She continued to stroke him. Jenner was steel encased in silk and she marveled at the way he felt in her palm. Her thumb brushed over the swollen head and she swiped a bead of moisture from the crown. Jenner hissed in a breath and his hips thrust into her grip. He let out a low moan and the sound caused Bria's clit to throb with anticipation.

She could have spent hours touching Jenner. With each stroke of her hand she watched with fascination at the play of muscles that twitched and flexed throughout his body. The sound of his heavy breaths heated Bria's blood and the low groans of pleasure sent her desire into a wild tailspin that pushed her to the edge of her own control.

She went to her knees before him. Jenner started and reached for her arm as if to stop her. "Bria." Her name left his lips on a harsh breath.

Bria leaned back on her heels and simply admired the strength and beauty of her mate's body. *Hers.* This extraordinary male belonged to her and no other. After tonight, Bria would make sure that Jenner's eye never wandered to another female ever again. She dragged the tips of her fingernails through the dusting of crisp hair at the tops of his thighs and he shuddered. She traced the winding pattern of the tattoo that curved from one of those thighs, around his hip, and up to his back. A sense of power flooded Bria, that she could affect him so completely with such an innocent caress.

She continued to acquaint herself with his body. Slow passes of her palms that mapped every hill and valley. No inch of him went unexplored. From the small of his back over the firm globes of his ass, and lower. When she reached the sensitive skin at the backs of his knees Jenner shivered. A secretive smile curved Bria's lips. She hoped that she was the only one who knew about that spot and what it did to him.

Jenner's breaths became increasingly ragged with every stroke. Bria purposefully avoided the one area she longed to touch, teasing herself as much as she did Jenner. She came up on her knees and reached up to run her hands over the bulge of his pecs. The delicious friction of his hard, flat nipples over her palms made Bria wonder what it would be like to lick them. Nip at them. Would he like it? She supposed there was only one way to find out.

Bria put her lips to the skin just below Jenner's belly button. The swollen head of his erection brushed the underside of her chin and the contact coaxed soft moans from both of them. His muscles tightened with the contact, twitching as Bria stood and kissed her way up his body to his chest. Her tongue flicked out at his skin. Jenner's salty taste and masculine scent enveloped her and her body hummed with awareness of this male who brought out such intense reactions from her. She kissed over the bulge of one pec until her mouth settled over his nipple. She circled it with her tongue and sucked, before taking it gently between her teeth. Jenner's hand twitched at his side and Bria bit down harder, eliciting a low growl of appreciation from her mate. She switched to the other side and this time, when she bit down, he wound his fist in her hair, holding her in place for just a moment longer.

"Bria." He spoke her name with such reverence, it caused a riot of butterflies to swirl in her stomach. "Gods, that feels good."

His words and the heat in his voice made her brazen. Bria ventured back down Jenner's torso and she let her nails scrape a path down the ridges of his abs. He sucked in a sharp breath and kept his fist wound in the length of her hair. He'd yet to push her. To treat her roughly or without care. Jenner might not have trusted himself, but Bria trusted him completely. He would never hurt her.

She stroked the length of his erection and he thrust into her palm. Bria brought the glossy head to her lips. Satin-smooth and hot, she wrapped her lips around the engorged flesh and let out a quiet moan. *Amazing.* She moved her mouth over his shaft, sucking gently as she took him as deeply as she could. He filled her mouth, her lips stretched over his girth. She could easily stay between his legs for hours. Tasting him, licking, sucking, reveling in the solid glide of him against her lips, tongue, and teeth. He wanted to fuck her mouth? To come against the back of her throat? A tremor vibrated through her at the thought. She couldn't wait to experience that with him.

Jenner shuddered against her and gave shallow thrusts of his hips. His growls of pleasure excited Bria and she ran the flat of her tongue over the underside of his shaft all the way to the engorged head. She swirled her tongue around the crown and Jenner hissed in a breath. "So good.

Bria. Suck me harder, *viaton*. Let me feel your fangs on
my cock."

His words sent an electric rush of excitement chasing
through her veins. Bria did as he asked, working her
mouth over him as she took him deep, sucked hard, and
increased the pressure of her jaw until her fangs dragged
over his delicate skin. "Yes. Like that. Don't stop."

Bria didn't intend to stop until Jenner made her. This
was the most erotic thing she'd ever done. The reality far
surpassed any fantasies she'd had of performing this very
act. Pleasuring Jenner aroused her almost to the point of
distraction. Her pussy had become so wet, it dripped down
her thighs, and her clit was so swollen that every slight
movement of her legs created a pulse of sensation through
her core.

Starting tonight, Bria planned to make up for every
minute of time they'd lost because of Jenner's stubborn
insecurities. He was hers and she wasn't about to let
him go.

Jenner threw his head back with a low growl as he continued to thrust past Bria's soft lips. He'd wanted this for
so long, his every waking moment possessed with thoughts
of Bria willing and naked on her knees before him,
spread out on the bed for him to taste, beneath him as he
drove his cock deep inside of her, and her on top of him,
riding as he cupped the perfect roundness of her breasts
in his palms.

The wound at his back gave a tug, but the pain was
nothing compared to the blinding pleasure that blazed a
path through him. Bria's responsiveness, her unashamed
desire, heated his blood and made him want her even
more than he thought he could. She was his salvation and
destruction in one.

"Bite down," he grunted. Jenner enjoyed a little pain

with his pleasure and Bria didn't shy away from his desires. Her fangs pierced the flesh and Jenner's body quaked
with such intense sensation that he feared he'd go off before he had the chance to properly fuck her. She sucked
at him greedily, her delicate cheeks hollowed as she
worked her mouth over his shaft. Since his tethering Jenner had denied himself the one thing he wanted more than
anything: Bria. She knelt before him, soft, beautiful, yet
fierce and wild. She truly was made for him. She was
everything he needed, the perfect balance to everything
he was. How could he have been so stupid as to deny them
both what they needed to be whole? Each other.

Jenner gripped Bria by the arms and brought her gently
to her feet. She met his gaze, bemused, and Jenner didn't
waste a second to scoop her up in his arms and lay her
down on the bed. Her lips were swollen and dark pink.
So inviting. Jenner leaned over her and put his mouth to
hers. She moaned into his mouth and his cock twitched
at the sound as though jealous it no longer had her full
and undivided attention.

His tongue slid against hers in a slow caress. Over and
again their mouths met and parted. A measured, sensual
dance that wound him as tight as a spring. Bria nicked his
lip with her fangs and she licked at the puncture before
biting down in earnest. The sting of sensation raced down
his spine and tingled in his sac. With every meeting of
their lips their kisses became more urgent. Bria gasped
against his mouth and her body trembled beneath him. He
seized her wrists in one large hand and pinned them high
above her head as he settled between her thighs.

"Oh yes," Bria mewled as she squirmed beneath him.
"Yes, Jenner."

"Not yet, *viaton*." He slid the length of his cock against
her slick pussy and Bria cried out. "I need to make sure
that you're ready for me."

"I am," she breathed. "I'm ready."

"Not yet. But you will be."

Her breaths came in quick pants. The flat of Bria's stomach twitched against his, little spasms with each shallow thrust of his hips that caused Jenner's cock to throb. He kept her wrists in his grip as he put his mouth to her temple, the shell of her ear. Down the line of her delicate jaw and the slim column of her throat. His barely controlled restraint caused Jenner's body to tense. The scent of her blood called to him, the thrum of her pulse just beneath her skin. He'd denied himself the pleasure of her body for so long that it took every ounce of willpower in his stores not to sink into her heat on a wild and forceful drive. He might not have deserved her, but Fate had deigned to give this remarkable female to him. No longer would Jenner fight this attraction between them, the tether that inextricably bound them. Bria was *his*. And godsdamn it, he'd control his own animal urges and take it slow if it fucking killed him.

But first, he had to taste her. Every inch of her. And Jenner would start at her throat. He sank his fangs into her flesh slowly. The skin gave way under the pressure and Bria's back arched off the bed. She let out a whimpering cry. Her blood flowed warm and sweet over Jenner's tongue and he drank from her with languorous pulls of his mouth. Bria thrust her hips in time with every gentle suck as she pleasured herself on the length of his cock. The stiff nub of her clit caressed his shaft, up and down, the delicious friction almost more than he could bear.

"Jenner," Bria gasped. "I'm so close."

The urge to impale her on his cock and pound into her while she came around him was almost too strong to resist. Her blood, the sweetest thing he'd ever tasted, lingered on his tongue and with each swallow he only wanted *more*. But Jenner locked his shit down. He wouldn't let his impatience get the better of him. He wouldn't let his urges master him. He continued to thrust against her, enjoying the soft slide of her swollen lips against his shaft while he drank from her.

Bria's hands released and contracted into fists in his grip. Her hips jerked as she rubbed against him and she let out sweet sobs of pleasure that tingled over Jenner's skin. Her body went taut beneath him and a violent shudder racked her body as she came. Still Jenner kept his measured pace, the suction of his mouth slow and steady—never taking too much—as he drew out her orgasm. The first of many he planned to give her tonight.

Such intensity and he hadn't even fucked her yet. Jenner had worried for weeks over his inability to keep himself in check. To treat Bria the way she deserved to be treated her first time. To master his thirst and not give in to the urge to drink from her more than her body could give. In truth, he'd never felt so utterly satisfied. So in control. Simply giving her pleasure had sated his own need to the point that he no longer felt the desperate and overwhelming urge to take her. He knew that he could never, ever hurt her and would never allow himself to succumb to bloodlust. Instead, he enjoyed the act of seeing to her needs. Sharing in this new experience with her. Her pleasure was his in this moment. It wasn't selfish or one-sided. He'd never had it better. Nothing could compare to Bria.

Jenner closed the punctures at her throat. Her heart beat a frantic rhythm that matched his own. He worked his way down her body, his mouth leaving a blazing trail across her collarbone and over the swell of one breast. She arched into his touch and her sharp pants of breath caused her breasts to quiver. Jenner sealed his mouth over one stiff nipple and Bria's legs drew up on either side of him as she arched into his touch.

"It feels so good, Jenner," Bria said on a decadent moan. "I don't know how much more I can take."

That he could make her feel so good made Jenner want to roar his satisfaction. He pulled away from her nipple and blew lightly on her flesh, causing it to bead even tighter. "You can take everything I'll give you," he growled. "You'll come for me again and again before you're ready for me to fuck you."

She trembled in his grasp as though his words alone could bring her to release. He gave her other breast the same loving attention. He licked, sucked, nibbled, until she writhed beneath him. He ventured lower, down the soft skin of her torso and over the curve of her hip. He released his grip on her wrists, but instead of bringing her arms down, Bria reached up and gripped the slats of the headboard.

Jenner eased himself down her body. The scent of her arousal caused his cock to throb to the point of exquisite pain. If he'd known he could derive this sort of pleasure from attending to his mate while putting his own needs second he would have seduced Bria the very first night of their tethering. With her he could be selfless, and he marveled at the effect she had on him.

Her pussy glistened, dripping with want. Jenner dragged his finger through the wetness that coated her inner thighs and Bria twitched. He traced a path upward, careful to avoid the sensitive skin of her swollen lips. Instead, he explored the crease of her thigh, the short nest of curls that covered her mons, the area just below her pussy that rounded into the perfect curves of her ass. He'd fuck her there just as he'd promised. Not tonight, but soon. Jenner planned to introduce Bria to every pleasure imaginable. He continued to pet her until Bria began to writhe beneath him with wanton impatience. To know he'd brought her once again to that state of mindless want filled Jenner with a smug sense of satisfaction.

He was about to make her more mindless yet. Jenner sealed his mouth over her sex. The first taste of her was heaven and he lapped at her greedily before settling into soft, easy passes of his tongue. Bria cried out and her hands left the bed railing to dive into the short strands of Jenner's hair. He was glad he hadn't bothered to cut it for a while as she gripped the locks and gave a not-so-gentle tug.

His mate couldn't have been more perfect.

CHAPTER
23

Bria floated on a cloud of bliss. She'd never known such intense pleasure. Jenner gave her what she needed even before she knew herself exactly what that was. Her want of him intensified with every touch of his lips, every soft flick of his tongue. She'd never felt such abandon, and it was a heady thing to give over her control to the male who spread his big body over hers.

One of Jenner's hands splayed out over her stomach while the other pressed against her thigh to open her up to him. The soft, slick pressure of his tongue as it passed over her clit in a swirl was enough to make her cry out. Her back bowed off of the mattress, but he held her still. He increased the pressure until he'd coaxed her to the teetering brink of orgasm only to pull back with soft, teasing flicks that heated her blood but refused to allow her release. He took the swollen knot of nerves into his mouth and sucked, the scrape of his fangs along her hypersensitive flesh almost more than she could bear. Bria brought her bottom lip between her teeth to keep from shouting her pleasure for the entire house to hear. Her fangs punctured the delicate skin and Jenner groaned against her sex, his thirst obviously awakened by the scent of her blood.

It was a cruel game, but rather than allow the wounds to close, Bria bit down again. Harder. Jenner's actions became more frantic. He lapped at her with the same vigor with which he fed from her. Bria's inner thighs twitched and her body felt as though it coiled in on itself. Tighter and tighter until she couldn't stand another moment of the building tension. Jenner turned to nestle the inside of Bria's thigh and she inhaled a sharp gasp as his fangs broke the skin.

"Jenner!" The orgasm hit her with an instant intensity that stole her breath. Bria trembled as wave after wave of paralyzing pleasure blasted through her. She could do nothing to quell the sobs of passion that slipped from between her lips. Her tongue lashed out at her bottom lip and the taste of her own blood only served to ignite the fire of her unquenched thirst in her throat.

As he had before, Jenner brought her down slowly with easy passes of his tongue as he closed the punctures. His hands roamed over her with soft caresses that turned her to liquid beneath him. How could he have ever feared that he'd handle her with anything other than gentle care? Jenner's control far surpassed Bria's. Even now she could think of nothing but sinking her fangs into his throat while he was deep inside of her. Bria longed for that joining of bodies. She needed it more than she needed blood.

"Jenner," she said through panting breaths. "I need you inside of me. I can't wait anymore. Please."

Jenner came up on his knees. His gaze locked with hers, feral silver. "You can wait." His fingers gripped her upper thighs before sliding down between them. Bria gasped and rolled into the contact. "You're not ready yet."

"I am!" Desperation tore at her voice. She didn't care that she'd resorted to begging. She needed him so badly

she thought she'd go mad if he didn't take her. Every inch
of her body tingled with electric jolts of pleasure and she
undulated on the mattress as though it would offer her
some relief. Jenner had brought her to orgasm twice and
it still wasn't enough to bring her even an ounce of relief.
Bria's fangs throbbed in her gums and she bit down on
her bottom lip again if only to coax him into doing something rash.

He loomed over her, put his mouth to hers, and lapped
at the blood that pooled in the seam of her lips. "You're a
cruel female to punish me with the scent of your blood.
You know I can't resist it."

She couldn't resist *him*! When it came to Jenner, Bria
had no resolve. Anything he asked of her in this moment
she'd gladly do. His sway over her, like the tether that
bound them, was absolute. He wrapped his large palms
around her hips and Bria let her thighs fall open in anticipation.

He graced her with an arrogant, very male smirk. "I
told you, you're not ready for me yet."

Jenner flipped Bria over to her stomach. He crawled
over her, his massive body dwarfing hers as he braced his
arms on either side of her and put his mouth to her ear. "I
want your pussy dripping for me when I fuck you. I want
you so mindless with want that the bite of pain you feel
when I enter you will fade to the back of your mind."

Yes! Yes to all of it! Bria thrust her ass up and the length
of Jenner's erection slid through the crease of her cheeks.
No male had ever said such heated, wanton things to her
and it sent a renewed rush of excitement through Bria's
bloodstream. She came up on her knees, her head still
resting on the mattress to feel the satin glide of him over
her skin once again.

Jenner reached beneath her and fondled the weight of
one breast. "This is mine," he growled in her ear. His hand

slid between her thighs to circle her clit and Bria moaned. "This is mine." He reached up to grip one rounded cheek. "This is mine." He finally showed her his rough edge in his words and actions and Bria couldn't get enough of it. She tilted her hips upward, a silent plea for more of the same. He took her in his palm and squeezed her yielding flesh. "Your body is mine to pleasure." His voice became rougher with every word spoken. "Mine to enjoy. Your cries are for my ears alone." He circled her clit once again, coaxing just that sound from her lips. "And my body, my pleasure, is for no one but you. *No one.* Do you understand me?"

Was he somehow trying to convey to her that she'd mistaken what she'd seen at the club?

"Say it, Bria."

"Yes," she murmured. "I understand."

He kissed between her shoulder blades, down her spine to the small of her back. He kissed the very cheeks he'd squeezed in his palms, over her hips, and back up. Bria reached up, gathered her hair, and swept it off her neck. He kissed her nape, scraped his fangs over her sensitive skin and Bria shivered.

Jenner gipped her hips and brought her ass up higher in the air. Bria gasped as his hard length slid between her thighs. He gave a sharp thrust of his hips, slid between her lips. A shudder of sensation went through her when the swollen head of his erection brushed over her clit. Gods, she didn't know how much of this she could take before she was nothing more than a quivering mass of nerves, begging him to fuck her.

In Jenner's embrace Bria felt no shame. No embarrassment. No doubt. She could say whatever she pleased, behave as brazenly as she pleased, and he would never judge her for it, would never belittle her for her passion. She'd known it from the moment she'd laid eyes on him and he'd rushed at her, crazy with thirst and hell-bent on taking her. Jenner freed Bria to think, to experience, to *feel*. The taboos of her upbringing evaporated under Jenner's touch until nothing remained but gossamer memories at the back of her mind.

He continued to fondle her, to pluck the beads of her nipples, kiss her shoulders, back, and neck. He continued to thrust between her thighs, a tease of what was to come and more than enough to whet her appetite. Low grunts gathered in Jenner's throat, adding to Bria's pleasure. She rocked against him as her body coiled once again in anticipation of release. "I'm close, Jenner. You're going to make me come."

With a jerk of his hips Jenner pulled away. Bria reached back to keep him right where he was. "Please don't stop." Desperation, want, and mindless need accented her words. "Please, Jenner. I need to come. I have to."

Jenner rolled Bria onto her back. Anxiety rippled through her at the realization that she was about to get everything she wanted. His size gave her pause. She expected a bit of pain; she just hoped that her inexperience wouldn't ruin the moment for Jenner. Would he find pleasure?

"Bria, look at me."

She only now realized that her eyes were squeezed shut. Her eyes came slowly open to find Jenner's gaze locked with hers. He reached between her thighs and stroked her. He kept his silvered eyes trained on her face as he rekindled the fire that had brought her to the edge of her control. Within moments she writhed beneath him. Bria's legs fell open and she rolled her hips up to meet him. "Take me, Jenner. I need this. I *want* this. You."

He took his erection in his fist and guided it to her opening. With easy, shallow strokes he entered her only as deep as the crown, pulling out and dipping back in until Bria's chest rose and fell with her panted breaths and her nails dug into his shoulders. Her body trembled with anticipation, her stomach muscles clenched, and her nipples tingled as his chest brushed up against hers with every thrust of his hips. "Tell me again that you want me, Bria." A furrow cut into his brow and his jaw squared. "Tell me you want this."

"I do." The words would barely form, she was so mad with lust for him. "I want you, Jenner. Need you inside of me. Now. Please. I can't wait any longer."

He buried his face in the crook of her neck and bit down at the very moment he thrust home. Pleasure and pain burst within her all at once. The sensations mingled into one, the combination so intense that she bit down hard on her lip to keep from crying out. Jenner stretched her, filled her completely, and he stilled inside of her as he sealed the punctures at her throat. He panted against her temple and his body shook with restraint. "Bria," he rasped. "Bria. Gods, I've needed this. Needed to be inside of you."

She reached up and raked her fingers through his hair. "Jenner, I'm yours."

Jenner's arms trembled under his weight. His thighs burned with the urge to propel his hips forward. He wanted to take Bria hard and deep, to fuck every ounce of this desperate, insatiable need from his system until there was nothing left but peaceful exhaustion.

Gods, she squeezed him tight. Jenner's cock pulsed against her inner walls as he stilled inside of her. He panted through the intensity of sensation, giving her the time she needed to adjust to his size, the pain, and this new experience. When her hips rolled up to meet his

Jenner buried his face into the fragrant tangles of her hair
and let out a low moan. His mate was exquisite. Responsive. Made for him and him alone.

Mine.

He moved over her with slow, shallow thrusts, careful
to keep the bulk of his weight off of her. Bria's thighs fell
open as her body accepted him and Jenner sank deeper,
eliciting a sweet, mewling sound from Bria's lips that tightened his sac and sent his blood racing through his veins.
He brought his head up to look at her. Her irises rimmed
with silver, eyes wide and full of wonder, Bria's expression painted a sensual image that further ignited Jenner's
lust. Lips parted, breath bursting in shallow pants, her
cheeks flushed.

"Harder," she pleaded in a quiet tone for his ears alone.
"Deeper. Please."

Jenner couldn't speak, couldn't focus on anything but
his own slipping self-control. When she spoke in that
smoky tone, so sweet and sinful at the same time, it crumbled the fortress of his resolve. He thrust deeper and Bria
gasped, a look of sheer bliss cresting over her soft features. Her back arched off the mattress, pressing her lush
breasts against his chest. Jenner slid out to the crown and
dove back in coaxing more of the same sounds from his
mate's lips. She held him rapt. He could watch her for
hours. He'd never truly found satiation through another's
pleasure before. But with Bria it was different. Her pleasure was his and Jenner's own wants and needs took a
backseat to hers.

He fucked her slowly. Pulled out and drove home with
a measured precision that tested his resolve. She became
wilder, more mindless with every thrust of his hips, her
head thrashing on the pillow as her nails bit into the flesh
that stretched across his shoulders. His muscles contracted, tightening to the point that they twitched, but

Jenner kept up his relentless pace. He wanted Bria to feel every inch of him as he slid in and out. He wanted to draw out her pleasure until the orgasm exploded through her. Gods, he could only imagine how beautiful she'd look when she finally came. A work of art painted in shades of unrestrained passion.

One of her slender legs hooked around the back of Jenner's thigh. Her voice was hoarse from her cries and her thighs twitched as she squeezed him tight. Close. So close that her inner walls began to contract around his cock, squeezing Jenner with tight pulses that brought him to the edge. He refused to go off until he saw her come, though. He needed to see her expression when she came apart as much as he needed his own release.

Her gaze locked with his, her dark brows drawn sharply over her eyes. "Come for me, Bria," Jenner grated. His pace increased and a purr of approval vibrated in Bria's throat. "Come, *viaton*. Let yourself go. Let me feel you come around my cock."

Bria's eyes flashed brilliant silver. She bared her fangs and her back bowed off the bed. Her body went rigid and then melted beneath him as she came. Jenner's own fangs throbbed in his gums, his need to drink from her while she came overwhelming. He kept his gaze locked on her beautiful face, at the gamut of emotions that flittered over her expression as the orgasm claimed her. Bria dug her nails into his shoulders and she cried out as she rode the waves of sensation. *Beautiful*. So gods-damned beautiful that the sight of her was like a stake through Jenner's heart.

Jenner brushed a thumb across her cheek as his own need built to a fevered pitch. He'd seen the look of bliss crest over his mate's expression, but there was still more pleasure to give. As the last pulses of her pussy began to ebb, Jenner buried his fangs in her throat. Bria let out a desperate sob and he thrust deep and hard, coaxing yet another orgasm from her. Jenner's sac tightened as the wave of intense contractions gripped him, but he refused to find his own release until Bria was fully sated. Her blood coated his tongue and he greedily swallowed it down. A more heady nectar he'd never tasted. More. He wanted more, couldn't get enough. The past and present mingled in Jenner's mind and he continued to drink. He wouldn't stop until he'd had his fill. Couldn't stop even if he wanted to. Pleasure coursed through him. Bloodlust held him in its grip. *Monster.*

"Jenner. Oh, gods."

The sound of her voice broke the spell in an instant. He was not that impetuous male any longer. And one mistake of his past would not dictate his future. The words of a vampire long dead no longer held any sway over him. Jenner's heart soared as a sense of freedom burst within him. His soul was tied to Bria's. The tether was absolute. He needed nothing more to make him whole. As long as she was his, no harm would ever come to her.

Bria gripped him around the neck and struck. Her fangs broke through the skin and obliterated Jenner's resolve. He came with such fervor that his fangs disengaged from her throat. His head snapped back on a roar as his cock pulsed and throbbed inside of her with the force of a wild summer storm. Intense sensation tingled from his balls and ran up his shaft to the tip of his cock. He pounded into Bria, any sense of self-control gone. He fucked her with punishing abandon, thrust after powerful thrust until he was utterly spent and nothing more than a boneless mass of muscle resting on top of her. Jenner had never known such satiation. Such a feeling of completeness. It rocked him to his fucking core and left him gasping for air and shaken.

Bria closed the punctures in his throat and pulled away. Blood trickled from the bites he'd left on her, beautiful ribbons of crimson against her porcelain skin. Jenner scored his tongue, laved her punctures to close them, and then licked the blood from her flesh, unwilling to waste even a drop. She let out a slow, sweet sigh and he pulled away to find her full lips curled at the corners, her eyes closed and expression soft.

"Jenner," she said with wonder. "That was . . ."

"Amazing?" he suggested. Though "amazing" was a pale word for what he'd just experienced.

The word left her on an emphatic breath: "*Unreal.*"

A knot of emotion lodged in his chest.

"Bria." There was so much he wanted to say to her. So much that he had no words to convey. But most of all, he needed to explain his actions at Ultra last night so that she knew once and for all that the only female in his life was *her*.

Her eyes fluttered open, shining amethyst gems. She reached up and brushed the pad of her thumb over his bottom lip. "Today is the first day of my existence," she said dreamily. "Nothing that happened before tonight matters to me."

Bria's capacity for forgiveness, kindness, and understanding seemed limitless. A more selfless female Jenner had never known. Such a contrast to his own single-mindedness and selfishness. He gave a shallow thrust of his hips and she let out another blissful sigh. "Mmmm. I've never felt so good. Not ever."

That he was her first only satisfied that selfishness in him. That he'd seen, touched, tasted Bria in a way that no other male had—or ever would—only strengthened the fierce possessiveness he felt for her. No other had heard her cries of passion, no other had taken the sweetness of her blood on his tongue. She belonged to him *completely*. He coveted her with a ferocity that blazed through him like hellfire. No matter what he did, there would always be an aspect of his personality that had no control when it came to his mate. A trait he couldn't switch off no matter how hard he tried. Jenner knew without a doubt that if any harm ever came to her he'd cut a bloody swath in his wake and he would *decimate* the creature responsible.

Jenner withdrew from her body and Bria reached for him as though to keep him with her. The absence of her heat punched through him, a loss that choked the air from his lungs. His want of her consumed him. Would he ever find balance?

"Don't leave me," she purred in a seductive tone that shivered down his spine.

Hours remained before sunrise, but Jenner had no intention of leaving this room in the meantime. "I'm not going anywhere and neither are you." He rolled onto his side and gathered Bria's body close to his. The skin-to-skin contact made him want to never leave the bed. "I plan to keep you naked and right where you are for the rest of the night."

"You do?" Her expression was half naivety, half seduction. And 100 percent irresistible.

"I've only just started, *viaton*." Jenner cupped her breast and Bria sighed. "I plan to fuck you until sunrise. I'm going to do such wicked things to you that you'll beg me never to leave your side."

Bria leaned up on one arm. She reached down between Jenner's legs and stroked the length of his cock. It hardened in her palm. He couldn't wait to take her again. "Maybe it'll be me who makes *you* beg."

"A battle of wills?"

Bria cocked a challenging brow, her mouth quirked in a half smile.

The female could unravel him with a look. She crawled down the length of his body, kissing, licking, and nipping as she settled herself between his legs. Her tongue flicked out at the head of his cock and Jenner hissed in a breath. *Dear gods.* If it was to be a battle of wills he was pretty damned sure he was about to lose this round.

CHAPTER
24

"Fear is a strange thing, isn't it?" Bria spoke in hushed tones in the darkened bedroom. She lay in Jenner's arms, her body completed sated, but her mind raced. Something had happened in the hours of their lovemaking that solidified their bond. The tether felt stronger than ever and it filled her with a sense of belonging and contentment the likes of which she'd never known.

"How so?" Jenner lowered his mouth to her temple.

"Our coven," Bria began. "*My uncle's* coven. He rules by fear."

Jenner's hold on her tightened. "He hurt you?"

"No," Bria said with a sad laugh. "But if you instill enough fear in someone, you squash their curiosity. We were taught not to drink from the throat. Not to drink wantonly. To keep our bodies pure and untouched. We might as well have been a coven of priests. No one ever questions my uncle. No one disobeys. He uses covens like Siobhan's as an example of the wild creatures we'd become if we gave ourselves over to our urges. He told us that the Sortiari wars were lost because of the vampires' mindless lusts."

Jenner's rumbling laughter vibrated over her skin. "It's a wonder he let Mikhail turn you at all."

"No one was more surprised than me."

Jenner's fingers combed idly through her hair. His breath brushed the outer shell of her ear and Bria shivered. "You weren't afraid?"

"No." It was the truth. Even when she thought she'd die Bria hadn't been afraid. "When I realized that I'd been turned I was angry. I wanted him to let me go, and instead my uncle had thrown me into a new existence. At first I felt more trapped than ever, but then I recognized the transition for what it was: Freedom. I saw it as an opportunity to see the world through new eyes and disregard everything I'd ever been taught to fear. And then you came through the bedroom door that night. . . ."

Jenner sighed. "And I scared the hell out of you."

"No." Bria turned in his embrace to face him. She cupped his cheek in her palm. "You were the answer to all of my questions."

He bent his head to hers and kissed her. Softly at first and then with more urgency. Time slipped through her fingers as they kissed. Their hands roamed; their touches explored. Bria sighed into Jenner's mouth as his tongue slid against hers. When he finally pulled away she was out of breath and light-headed.

"My uncle let fear rule him. Now that I know the truth, I realize that he must have viewed my mother's love for my father as something corrupt. A weakness. Maybe he sought to protect us from the sort of wild love that would prompt us to do reckless things." Her voice lowered to a whisper: "Like promising the life of a newborn to a witch to save the life of a mate."

"Bria." His eyes searched her face as though he wished he could take her pain away.

Bria kissed him once and smoothed the crease from his brow. "You were right about me, Jenner. I was naïve. The world isn't black and white. There are many shades of gray. We all do what we think is right at the time. She loved me," Bria said through the tears that threatened. "She could have given me to the witch and she didn't. My uncle loves me. I might not agree with the things he's done, but for him, his choices were the right ones."

"I'm going to kill the necromancer." The harsh conviction of Jenner's words chilled her. "When I find her, she'll pay for every day of your life she's taken away."

"Jenner, I meant what I said earlier. My life began tonight. Nothing that happened before matters."

"It matters to me," Jenner said. He brushed the pad of his thumb over her bottom lip. "I'm going to make sure you never have reason to fear again."

Such a male. Bria had never met anyone as honorable as Jenner. "I've acted like a selfish, spoiled child. I'm sorry."

Jenner grinned. "And I've acted like a stubborn pain in the ass. If I could make it up to you, I would."

"You taught me how to fight," she remarked with a wry grin. "I'd say that's atonement enough."

"You're a fierce fighter, *viaton*." Jenner's affectionate tone warmed her. "A natural warrior."

"How would you know?" Bria teased.

"I've trained my fair share," Jenner said. "You're formidable, Bria."

"You grew up in Finland?" Bria hoped to learn as much as she could about Jenner. He'd told her that *viaton* was a Finnish word. It must have been his native tongue. "How did you meet Mikhail?"

"Through Ronan," Jenner said. "We were both members of Siobhan's coven at one time or another and he's the closest thing I've had to a brother. When Mikhail found Claire, Ronan suggested that I be turned after him. That's when he brought me here."

"So soon?" Bria said. "I would have thought you'd known him for ages."

Ronan let out a chuff of breath. "The Collective," he replied. "And the blood. It creates immediate bonds."

Bria had never considered it, but Jenner was right. She'd felt an instant closeness to Claire and Mikhail, even to Ronan. The blood that turned them connected them all to one another and formed an undeniable kinship. They were Bria's family now. Her coven. And Jenner was her *home*.

"It does," she said after a moment. "I guess I didn't notice it because the tether is so much stronger. It overrides everything else."

"The strongest bond of all," Jenner murmured. "Unbreakable."

Jenner had never known intimacy like this. He took a female's vein. He fucked her. He moved on. Even when he'd belonged to Siobhan's coven he'd kept his distance from the others, too afraid of his own uncontrollable appetites. The only solid relationship he'd forged with his own kind had been with Ronan. Jenner hadn't been all that interested in sharing his feelings, the details of his past, or any other sappy bullshit. Until now.

Bria made him want to share everything with her. Every thought, feeling, memory. Hell, even trivial shit that didn't matter, like how he liked his steaks cooked or what his favorite TV show was. He wanted to know her inside and out and he wanted her to know him in the same way. It made him feel all too vulnerable. But with Bria, Jenner had found a safe haven.

Memories swamped him. Apart from the Collective, these painful memories belonged to Jenner alone. He idly stroked Bria's hair, marveling at the fine, silky texture. "Before the Sortiari began to pick us off, dhampir covens answered to the vampire lord that ruled their region. In turn, each individual monarchy answered to a council of kings. Mikhail's father was a high king. As was his grandfather. And now, Mikhail will become a high king as well. The highest since he's the father of us all."

"Eventually, you'll be a king, too," Bria remarked. "You're part of Mikhail's inner circle."

Jenner snorted. "My family name brings with it a heavy burden of shame thanks to me. I'm far from worthy of that title. Besides, if I had it my way, there would be no monarchy. No class division. Already Mikhail resurrects an elitist system that will do nothing but cause dissention."

"I'm sure he has the best intentions," Bria said. "Order is important."

"It is," Jenner agreed. "But there can be order without division."

"What was your coven before you came to Siobhan?" Bria asked.

Emotion clogged Jenner's throat and he spoke through the thickness: "I had no coven." The words bounced around his chest, hollow.

Bria's brow furrowed. "How is that possible?"

She was so accepting, she couldn't fathom anyone not belonging. "You see the good in everyone, *viaton*. Someone who's done the things I've done isn't worthy of your acceptance."

"How can you say that? Jenner"—the soft emotion in her voice gutted him—"I know your soul and it is *good*."

"I've killed." He blurted the words. Ripped the Band-Aid from his past and laid himself bare to her with two little words. "I've killed wantonly and without control.

I've kept myself from you for your own protection. My control, it . . . I'm volatile, Bria. I wouldn't survive it if I hurt you. I shamed my family, myself, and I will bear the marks of that shame for eternity. I couldn't bear to shame you—or worse—as well."

Bria's questioning gaze met his. She reached out and Jenner flinched as the soft pads of her fingertips traced the jet-black pattern that marked his torso. Her gentleness was almost more than he could bear.

"Someone did this to you to *shame* you?"

"It was a warning," Jenner replied. "To any coven that might've been tempted to take me—or my family—in."

Her voice was little more than a whisper. "Why?"

"I killed a member of my coven. I drained her. I gave myself over to the bloodlust and drank from her until her heart ceased its beating."

"Dhampirs don't experience bloodlust." The quaver in her words, the fear in her scent, seared Jenner from the inside out.

"I did," he replied flatly. "I've always had intense appetites. I wanted nothing more than to be turned. I was obsessed with it. I behaved as a vampire long before I became one. I lost myself to the moment, to the power I felt, the rush. I pierced her throat and opened her vein. I drank from her until her body became limp in my grasp. The vampire lord who governed our coven declared that if I was ever turned I would become a monster that would have to be put down. My family was banished. And as a warning to any coven that might seek to give us shelter, my body was marked.

"Because of my indiscretion, my father—a powerful vampire warlord—was stripped of his reputation. We were never wealthy, and if not for his prowess as a fighter our family would have been the lowest of the lowborn. Our banishment was a blow my father never recovered from. He walked into the sunlight and ended his life, leaving our mother to care for us. Our family name was considered below regard from that moment on. Even my sisters were cursed to remain dhampirs. Not a single one of them was granted the gift of transition, because of me."

Bria came up on one elbow to study his face. The concern that marred her brow speared his heart. "I've never heard of such a thing. How old were you when it happened?"

"Sixteen."

"Jenner," Bria said softly. "You were just a child."

"Not then," he replied. "Not in the eyes of the coven."

Bria reached up to stroke his jaw. "My uncle said you told him that we are all animals. I know the thirst, the urges that seize me without reason. I believe that we are creatures who are driven by instinct. You made a mistake and your entire family was ruined for it. It's so unfair."

"You're highborn, *viaton*," Jenner said with affection. "You've existed without struggle. And you're so young. I've always had issues with control. I might have been the monster they feared if I'd been turned all of those years ago. It was a just decision. One that your own uncle—your own father—would have made if he'd been in the same position. I was punished in order to protect the covens. "

"I was born at the height of the killings," Bria said. "I'm not so young."

Jenner smiled. He traced the pads of his fingers over her delicate cheekbone. "You're young enough. Without my father's reputation and standing to carry us we became destitute. No title, no land, no holdings of any kind. The Russians controlled Finland at the time, and likewise, the Russian vampires ruled the covens. We lived outside of vampire and dhampir culture. My mother and sisters worked for a wealthy human family. I took out a small fishing boat and sold whatever we could catch."

A crease cut into Bria's brow. "You must have felt so disconnected."

Jenner hiked a shoulder. "It wasn't bad. Life was hard enough back then. Survival became more important than worrying over where we did or didn't belong.

"The humans fought their wars and we fought ours. It was only when the Sortiari slayers tipped the scales in their favor that the very vampire who ordered that I be marked and banished sought me out. It made no sense to turn dhampirs who would be incapable of fighting for days. The thirst and the press of the Collective alone would make it impossible. I was already fierce. As deadly in battle as my father ever was. Many dhampirs of the lower classes were promised the gift of transition if they pledged loyalty and fought. If they survived the war they'd be turned. I was offered forgiveness. All of my sins would be absolved and my family welcomed back into the coven if I lent my sword—my strength—to the fight. I jumped at the chance. I saw it as an opportunity to elevate my family's station. To redeem my father's name and atone for his death. I was a natural warrior. I survived while everyone around me—even my own poor mother and sisters—was slaughtered. Our region was decimated by the slayers. Only a few dhampirs remained. I left not long after that. Sailed across the sea and wound up in Boston. That's where I met Siobhan and Ronan."

"To my uncle, Siobhan is a cautionary tale," Bria said. "He told us stories of her coven often. I wasn't frightened, though. I envied her strength, her wildness. She answered to no one. I dreamed of running away to join her coven when I was young. I wanted to be one of her free, wild things."

Bria didn't care about class. Her family name, her position in her coven's hierarchy, meant nothing to her. All were equal in Bria's eyes. Not even Jenner's admission of what he'd done caused her to shy away from him. She coveted freedom and strength—*abandon*—where Jenner had spent his youth longing for a better station, praying to the gods for forgiveness and the control he so desperately needed. In Bria he found acceptance and forgiveness. Through her he realized that he could finally accept himself for the male he was. He could finally forgive *himself*. This female in his arms was his salvation.

"Jenner, I'm so sorry." Her fingers stroked up his arm and over his shoulder. So gentle. "You are not a monster. You lost yourself for an unfortunate moment. But you learned from it and you've more than atoned for it. You have more control than anyone I've ever known. You're fierce, yes. Insatiable, true. I feel your desires and your thirst as my own and they don't frighten me. I understand them because they echo my own. You protect the ones you care about. You are loyal. I've never known a more honorable male. Ever. I wouldn't want you any other way than you are. I forgive you for killing that poor dhampir. You should forgive yourself."

Emotion swelled in Jenner's chest and he had to clear the lump from his throat before he was finally able to speak. "If I wasn't the male I am now, you might not have tethered me. I'm not sorry for my life or how it shaped me. Not anymore."

Nothing more needed to be said as their mouths met. Jenner had used his insecurities to push Bria away. He'd made excuses, painted himself as some sort of monster in his own mind. He'd resurrected a wall between them and Bria had torn it down. Bria, so strong, so sure, so unafraid. His Bria.

His, forever.

Jenner rolled them and settled Bria beneath him. Her legs came around his thighs and he buried his fangs in her throat as he drove his cock deep inside of her. Bria's sweet impassioned sounds filled Jenner's ears. She rolled her hips to meet every drive of his and her knees fell to the side as she opened herself fully to him. Her blood, thick and sweet, filled his mouth; her pussy, hot and tight, squeezed his shaft. Jenner had never known such bliss and the rightness of it all caused his heart to stutter in his chest.

Bria's cries grew louder, the motion of her hips desperate and wild. Jenner sealed the punctures in her throat and kissed her hard and deep, swallowing the sounds of her passion and taking them into himself. His need for her crested and Jenner drove harder, deeper, until the cavernous emptiness in his chest became so full of Bria that he felt close to bursting.

Bria broke their kiss and threw her head back as she arched into him. "More, Jenner. Harder. I need you deeper."

He'd thought her made of glass, but his mate had been forged with steel. A growl built in Jenner's throat as he cupped her ass in his palm and angled her hips upward. He pounded into her, their panting breaths and the sound of their bodies meeting echoed in the dark room.

"Yes," Bria gasped.

She gripped on to his forearms and the bite of her nails caused Jenner's cock to grow even stiffer. It throbbed in time with his racing pulse and every deep thrust into Bria's tight heat brought him closer to the edge. Her luscious breasts bounced in time with every powerful drive of his hips and Jenner watched the erotic show, rapt, before he scooped her up in his embrace and sat up on the

bed. He swung his legs over the mattress and Bria straddled him. He continued to pound into her as he sealed his
mouth over the swell of her breast and bit down.

Bria's moan of pleasure rippled over his skin as she
bent over him and latched on to his throat. Delicious heat
raced through his veins, ignited his skin. A shiver of sensation vibrated through him and tightened his sac. He
fucked her with wild abandon, every bit the animal he'd
professed himself to be. Bria didn't shy from the aggression. His mate met him with equal fervor as she bit down
harder on Jenner's throat, giving him the shock of pain
that only served to intensify his pleasure.

Bria sealed the wounds at his throat as she continued
to ride him. The wet heat of her tongue lashing out at his
skin caused Jenner to shudder. He disengaged his fangs
from her breast and leaned back, his arms braced behind
him on the mattress. The sight of Bria's blood as it trickled over her breast in four tiny rivulets ignited his lust to
white-hot proportions. His ass came off the mattress as
he levered his hips upward. His jaw clamped down with
the force of his thrusts and a wild snarl tore from between
his pulled-back lips.

"Come for me, Bria." He pushed the words from between his teeth. "Now, *viaton.*"

Her pussy clenched around him in powerful pulses as
she came. Bria's back bowed and she threw her head back.
Sobs of pleasure filled Jenner's ears, the erotic sound so
sweet that it pushed him over the edge of his own release.
He came with a shout. His cock twitched with powerful
spasms that swept him up in waves of pleasure so intense
it stole his breath. He fucked her hard and deep until they
collapsed against each other, completely spent. The room
quieted until all that remained was shallow, mingled
breaths.

"No night will compare to this," Bria whispered close to his ear. "I'm sure of it."

Jenner smiled against her cheek. He was never one to back down from a challenge. "I'll make sure to prove you wrong. Every night after this one will be better than the last."

"Jenner, you are a male without comparison," Bria said on a contented sigh.

No. You are the one without comparison.

And she belonged to him.

CHAPTER
25

"Has it been forty-eight hours already?" Bria stretched along the mattress, more content than she'd ever been in her life. She'd never felt more sated. So utterly comfortable in her own skin. "I'm not ready to leave the room yet."

"I'm actually surprised Mikhail left us alone for this long."

Jenner tugged his jeans over the perfect curve of his ass. Bria let out a quiet sigh as she drank in the perfection of her mate's body. The tattoos that covered his torso, back, and upper arms drew her attention, and Bria traced the patterns with her gaze. Her fingers itched to follow the path. Over the course of their time closeted in the guest bedroom, Bria had acquainted herself with every minute detail of Jenner's remarkable body. Every hill and valley that constructed him. She was particularly fond of the cut that slashed down either side of his hips at the juncture of his thighs. She'd traced the grooves with her tongue, following the path to the stiff length of his erection. Her body heated at the memory and her lower abdomen clenched.

Their hours spent together had been a lesson in passion and Jenner had been a very, *very* thorough instructor.

"If you don't stop looking at me like that, I'll have to fuck you at least once more before I go downstairs to meet with Mikhail."

Bria smiled, pleased with the effect she had on him. She rolled onto her back, drawing his gaze to her breasts. She idly caressed over the top of one swell up to her throat. Jenner's eyes flashed brilliant silver and he let out a tortured groan. "I could wait here," she suggested. "Naked. Until you've finished talking with him." She let her fingers tease the pulse point at her throat.

"You're a much crueler female than I gave you credit for to torture me with that image."

Her lips spread into a slow smile. "I think a little torture is exactly what you need."

She'd learned a great deal about her mate over the course of their erotic play. Jenner wasn't simply a voracious lover. His pleasure was heightened with the slightest bit of pain. A nip of her fangs, the bite of her nails across his back or chest. He'd fucked her with the assertion of a male who wasn't afraid to take what he wanted, and yet Bria sensed his reservation. He still hadn't let go of the tightly reined control he pretended not to have a grasp of. It would take time to convince him that he didn't have to hold any aspect of himself from her. But Bria welcomed the challenge. Soon she'd tear down the final bricks in the wall of his restraint.

Until then, she was content to learn. Jenner was an amazing teacher, after all.

"Get dressed." Jenner crossed the room and bent over Bria to place a kiss to her mouth. His hand cupped her breast, lingered for a long moment as he brushed her nipple with his thumb and coaxed it to a stiff peak.

"Are you sure that's what you want?" Bria pressed into

his touch. A low moan rose in her throat and Jenner's eyes flashed even brighter at the sound.

"No, but it's what's going to happen," he growled close to her ear. "Get ready and come downstairs. After my meeting with Mikhail, we'll eat before I go out."

Bria's brows knitted. "Go out?"

"I'll be playing catch up from the last couple of nights. Ronan's mate, Naya, is going to help me track the necromancer." Jenner slipped on his socks and boots—still shirtless since Claire had cut the garment from his body two nights ago—and headed for the door. "See you downstairs. Don't keep me waiting, *viaton*."

The door closed behind him and Bria stared after him, dumbstruck. After everything that had happened . . . the club, his wounds, his admission that she was a strong and capable fighter, his own admissions about his past and why he'd kept his distance from her, the hours they'd spent together . . . Jenner still insisted on treating Bria as though she were something too fragile to be let out. She'd proved she could take care of herself. He still considered her *innocent*. A tiny bird confined to the nest. Bria's chest burned with indignant anger and she launched herself from the bed with purpose.

There was always another obstacle to overcome with Jenner, it seemed. One more mountain to climb. How many times would she have to prove herself to him before he quit trying to put her behind him and allowed her to stand beside him as an equal?

She marched into the bathroom and turned on the shower. Any passionate inclinations she'd felt evaporated under her annoyance at being disregarded yet again. If Jenner thought to keep her complacent with the artful way he fucked her he should think again. Jenner was her mate, not her jailer. And Bria would do whatever the hell she wanted from here on out.

Her step faltered. *No.* Those were the thoughts of a spoiled girl. The words she'd spoken to Jenner in the darkness had been true. She was sorry for her selfish behavior. Jenner wanted to protect her. She couldn't begrudge him that, just like she wouldn't begrudge her uncle and mother their decisions.

Jenner was a reasonable male. He'd apologized for his own stubbornness as well. He'd revealed so much of himself to her over the past two days. He was mastered by his worries and she had to convince him that there was no need for concern. Surely they could come to a solution that would please them both. If Bria promised to follow his instructions to the letter, if she promised not to run headlong into danger, perhaps he'd let her come along as he hunted the necromancer. Compromise could be found. With that upbeat thought her anger vanished as though blown away by a cleansing breeze. A smile curved her lips as Bria stepped under the warm spray of the shower. Today was a new day. Her tether with Jenner was stronger than ever. She would do whatever it took to convince him that together they could shape their future.

"It seems all that needed to happen for you to pull your head out of your ass was a silver bullet in your back. I'll remember that for the next time you need a wake-up call." Ronan tossed Jenner a black T-shirt and he swiped it out of the air to tug it on. "According to Mikhail, no one's seen hide nor hair of you for almost two days." Ronan's expression turned mischievous. "Seriously, Jenner, there's a kid living here. Hardly appropriate for your sex-fest."

He cut Ronan a look. The first thing Jenner planned to do was move Bria out of Mikhail's house and into his apartment. This no-privacy bullshit was going to get old, fast. And he didn't need either male giving him shit over the amount of time he spent in bed with his mate or the means by which he'd finally succumbed to his want of her. Though, he had to admit, the silver bullet that had been lodged close to his heart had been one hell of a fucking wake-up call.

"Do you want to know what Gregor's up to?" Jenner asked. "Or would you rather I paint your fucking nails while we discuss my love life?"

Ronan had the nerve to act as though he was contemplating his options. "I don't know." He examined his nails. "I could probably use a mani."

Jenner snorted his amusement and headed for the king's study. "I want to start tracking the necromancer tonight. Can you make Naya available?"

Ronan let out a disbelieving bark of laughter. "I can't *make* my mate do anything." He gave a sad shake of his head that Jenner suspected was meant to convey Ronan's pity for his stupidity. "She likes to pretend that she's deferring to me, or at the very least allowing me an opinion in the matter, but the truth is, she's a headstrong female who's more than capable of taking care of herself. That doesn't mean I'm going to let her get within two hundred yards of the necromancer, though."

Bria shared that same headstrong will and it scared the shit out of Jenner. She still hadn't told him what she'd been doing at Ultra the other night. Alone. Without even Alex as an escort. Despite the fact that Jenner had spent the last two days sating his lust for Bria, every muscle in his body stretched taut with renewed tension. The relaxed, boneless state he'd found in her arms evaporated the moment he'd stepped through the door and out into the hallway. He wouldn't—couldn't—let down his guard until the necromancer was dead.

Her expression when he'd told her he was going out stuck in Jenner's mind like a burr. The disappointment etched on her features tugged at his chest still. She was too precious to him to lose over something as trivial as a little freedom. He'd make her understand that all of this was temporary. He wouldn't treat Bria the way her uncle had, but if she could be patient with him, let him focus on hunting the necromancer without the distraction of worrying for her, she could finally have the life she'd always wanted. One that didn't require her to be closeted away.

"I told you, I don't need her that close. I just need her to pinpoint a location."

"Naya was ready to roll the second you mentioned it," Ronan said. "If Mikhail doesn't have anything pressing, we can start tonight."

"Good."

Mikhail waited for them in the study. Along with a male Jenner hoped he'd never come face-to-face with for a good, long while. A territorial growl built in Jenner's chest as his eyes locked with Lucas's. His fangs throbbed in his gums with the urge to tear out the dhampir's throat.

Ronan leaned in and spoke from the corner of his mouth. "Apparently, Bria did little to domesticate you over the past couple of days."

Hilarious. He doubted Ronan would be much more civil if a male who wanted Naya showed up at the front door. "What in hell is he doing here?"

Mikhail raised a brow and a sizzle of power sparked in the air. Jenner averted his gaze and deferred to his king, though what he really wanted to do was draw a little blood.

Lucas shot a superior smirk Jenner's way and it was all he could do not to take the son of a bitch down right then and there. The dhampir rose from his seat and turned toward Mikhail. "Thank you for seeing me. I hope we'll speak again soon."

Mikhail gave a shallow nod of his head. Jenner refused

to budge from the doorway as Lucas headed toward him. Bria's scent clung to Jenner's skin and he wanted the male to be *very* aware of whom she was mated to. Lucas brought his gaze to Jenner's as he neared the doorway and his lips formed a hard line as he brushed past him.

A long-suffering sigh broke the silence and Jenner turned his attention to see Mikhail pinch the bridge of his nose between his thumb and finger. "Gods, I'd forgotten what it was like to be in the company of mated males." His exasperation drew a chuckle from Ronan. Jenner simply scowled.

He opened his mouth to speak and Mikhail raised a staying hand. "No. I absolutely will not discuss the matter of Lucas's presence here with you. In case you've forgotten, Jenner, this is *my* house. I am the king and I'll see whoever the hell I please, whenever I please. Do you understand me?"

Jenner clamped his jaw down so tight that his fangs punctured his lower lip. He flicked out with his tongue and sealed the punctures before giving a sharp nod of his head.

"Now, tell me about the slayers."

"I was headed for my bike to catch up with—" Jenner bit the words off before he admitted he'd been chasing Bria. "When I spotted Gregor and at least a dozen other berserkers. They'd congregated in an alley outside of Ultra. From what I heard, he's decided to pull back on the attacks on the covens. He's got a tracker looking for someone. A dhampir, I think. Gregor called her the daughter of Réamonn. I thought you said Gregor was looking for Siobhan."

"He is," Mikhail answered darkly, though he offered no further explanation. "Who do you think he's using as a tracker? The werewolf?"

Jenner nodded. "That's my guess. Called him Whalen. From what I heard, his loyalty was purchased. If we have to, we could probably buy his allegiance as well."

Mikhail let out an annoyed chuff of breath. "I want no male who has to be bought. We'll continue on our path," he said. "We'll keep an eye on Siobhan. Even with a tracker, it'll be hard for Gregor to find her. She's done a good job of hiding who she is." Jenner met Ronan's curious gaze and the male shrugged. Mikhail was older than all of them. And even through the Collective, Jenner had never seen a memory that might have included the female to let him in on what her sordid history with the berserker might be. "Gregor's obviously hell-bent on finding her. We'll just wait for him to do it."

"There's more," Jenner said. Mikhail quirked a curious brow. "They're planning a coup against the Sortiari."

Mikhail's eyes widened a fraction of an inch, but it might as well have been a gaping stare. "An insurrection?"

"Gregor claims to have a weapon that'll lay McAlister low."

Ronan took a step forward. "Like what?"

"A female," Jenner replied.

Ronan let out a burst of incredulous laughter. "You're joking? Gregor thinks to overthrow the entire Sortiari— an entity of unimaginable membership—with a single female. Who is she, the Dark fucking Phoenix?"

Ronan's X-Men humor aside, his guess was as good as anyone's. "I didn't hear much more. Gregor sensed my presence and that's when they came after me. I ditched my bike and got the fuck out of there."

"It's a good thing you did," Mikhail said. "I doubt that even you would have withstood a dozen slayers, Jenner."

"No doubt," Ronan added. "We need to be more on guard from now on. It's obvious that Gregor isn't going to leave anytime soon. And if he's planning a hostile take-over, you can damned well bet he'll call in reinforce-ments."

Mikhail's jaw squared and he gave a shallow nod of his head. "We'll need to bump up our own security as well."

"I can have Naya place a few protection charms on the property," Ronan suggested. "Jenner, want me to have her do your place, too?"

"Yeah." If he was going to move Bria to his apartment he wanted to make sure the place was better protected than Fort fucking Knox.

"Tell me about the werewolf." Mikhail swiveled in his chair, his elbows on the armrest, fingers steepled in front of him. "What more do you know?"

"Not enough," Jenner replied. "Like I said, he's a male who's easily bought. Up to his eyeballs in debt and more than willing to flip his allegiances for whoever has the deeper pockets."

Mikhail scowled. "Do you think the wolf is one of McAlister's?"

Jenner shrugged. "Could be. That's the way Gregor made it sound. Either way, the bastard's got a hard-on for Siobhan. The closer we watch her, the more we're bound to find out."

A stretch of silence passed and Mikhail said, "Saeed has made a petition to be turned."

Saeed's coven was the second largest in the city next to Siobhan's. The male was also the oldest dhampir in ex-istence as far as anyone knew, though some speculated that Siobhan was older. Few dhampirs could boast more than three centuries. It was no coincidence that the two oldest dhampirs managed the two largest covens. Jenner didn't know the male well, but he had a more-than-formidable reputation. "What did you tell him?"

Mikhail fixed Jenner and Ronan with a contemplative stare. "I told him I'd consider his request. But with this new information about Gregor, I think it might be wise to turn him sooner rather than later."

The impact of turning an actual coven leader was huge. "I think you should do it," Jenner replied. "As soon as possible."

"Turning Saeed could have an impact that we're not ready for, Mikhail." Ronan, always the voice of reason. "If left unchecked, he could easily turn his entire coven in a matter of weeks."

"And if you drag your feet and continue on with this bullshit vetting process, you're going to be seen as classist and Siobhan's disdain for what you represent will only gain traction." Jenner didn't share Ronan's opinion. "You were born into the aristocracy, Mikhail. And likewise, Ronan has kept company with you for long enough to have adopted your way of thinking. Transition can't be only for the upper class. You can't rebuild the race by adhering to out-of-date doctrine." He knew he was pushing his luck with his flapping lips, but it needed to be said.

"You're kidding yourself, Jenner, if you think Siobhan is any less the aristocrat than I am."

Jenner regarded his king with narrowed eyes. If that was true, then Siobhan had indeed done a damned good job of burying her true identity. "Either way, I think you should grant Saeed's request whether he turns his entire coven or not. We need fighters strong enough to fight the berserkers."

"Whether he wants to turn the members of his coven is a moot point for now," Mikhail said. "Without a mate, Saeed won't be strong enough to turn a dhampir."

"Who's to say Saeed's soul won't be tethered as quickly as ours were?" Ronan suggested. "Seems like

Fate is making up for lost time, if you know what I mean. Is it a variable we can afford to ignore?"

"I don't think we have a choice," Mikhail said with a sigh. "Jenner's right. We need vampires with the strength to fight. To survive. The dhampirs need protection as much as we do. I've decided to turn one member of each coven who's sworn fealty. It's a starting point."

Jenner's eyes narrowed. "Is that why Lucas was here?"

Mikhail's gaze flitted to Ronan. "Lucas made a request. But I'm not sure if I trust any members of Thomas Fairchild's coven yet. He's going to attend to Chelle until I decide what to do with him."

Ronan let out a disbelieving bark of laughter. "You've got to be fucking kidding me. You're throwing a lamb to the lion, you do realize that?"

Jenner snorted. He might have wanted to beat the dhampir to a bloody pulp, but Ronan had a point. Chelle had been given the guesthouse at the edge of Mikhail's property for a reason. Her bloodlust was still out of control. As an offshoot of the race, disconnected from the Collective, Chelle was an anomaly. Completely unpredictable. "If you want the male dead"—Jenner smirked—"then by all means, feed him to Ronan's sister."

"I can't keep her locked up forever." Mikhail gave Jenner a pointed look and a wave of guilt washed over him. "And likewise, I won't isolate her out of fear. Fairchild's coven is . . . decidedly naïve."

Wasn't that the fucking truth? He wondered if Mikhail realized how naïve. That they were forbidden from taking the vein at the throat and were only allowed to feed when it became necessity. Not to mention that the lot of them were as virginal as a bunch of nuns. Lucas would be in way over his head with Ronan's wild twin.

"I think Lucas's innocence will have a calming effect

on Chelle," Mikhail continued. "It's better not to pair her with a dhampir who shares a like personality."

"Makes sense," Ronan agreed. "I'll keep an on eye on her as well. Make sure she plays nice."

"Good," Mikhail said. "In the meantime, I'll contact Saeed. My own power will only stretch so far and I can't exhaust myself turning dhampirs when Claire is so close to the end of her pregnancy."

Most of this was bureaucratic red tape that didn't concern Jenner. Mikhail was the king after all. These decisions were ultimately his to make.

"Now that that's settled"—Mikhail turned his attention back to Jenner—"let's discuss this necromancer. . . ."

CHAPTER
26

"I fold. *Fuck*."

Christian tossed his cards down on the felt table with disgust. He was down two grand and they'd only played five hands. The private game had seemed like a decent prospect, a way to make back the money he owed to Marac and free him from his obligation to the berserker. Christian could throw the bastard's generous down payment in his face and be on his way. So far, all he had managed to do was dig a deeper gods-damned hole.

He waited as another hand was dealt and scooped up his cards. Two, seven . . . not a single matching suit and no fucking face cards. *Great*. Another shitty hand. He set three cards down on the table and waited for three new ones. What he got in exchange wasn't a hell of a lot better—an ace and ten of clubs and a suicide king—but maybe he could bluff his way to the pot. He tossed in three hundred dollars' worth of chips. "Raise."

Around the table, the other players tossed in their chips. The shifter beside him folded and pushed away from the table with an angry growl. *Thank the gods*. The sooner he was out of the game, the better. The bastard's strong, musky scent drove Christian's wolf bat-shit crazy. At least he wasn't a bear shifter, though. Those fuckers were scary. Christian threw in another three hundred and met the gaze of every player at the table, daring them each to call his bluff. One by one they tossed in their cards, and Christian flashed a satisfied grin as he scooped up the chips. A zing of adrenaline rushed through his bloodstream. In one hand he was flush.

Fuck. Yeah.

It was as hot as a hooker's crotch in the secret back room at Onyx. Not a lick of ventilation, and the watered-down whiskey tasted like piss. The lack of windows, low lighting, and haze of smoke made Christian damn near claustrophobic. His wolf growled in the recess of his psyche. The squatter that resided under the surface of his skin didn't enjoy being kept in a room with only one way in or out. Made a quick escape tough to accomplish if shit got dicey.

Still, he wasn't about to leave until he'd accumulated some serious green. He couldn't be sure that Siobhan was the dhampir Gregor was looking for but didn't want to be the one to hand her over to the berserker either way. What Christian wanted from the female would satisfy no one's needs but his own, and it would require her to be wearing a hell of a lot less clothes. A vision of her, thighs spread, skirt hiked up, and an expression of bliss softening her usually stern expression, flashed in his mind. Maybe her state of undress didn't matter so much.

A firm hand came down on Christian's shoulder with enough force to push him a couple of inches lower in his chair. His wolf rose to the surface and a snarl built in his chest. His gut clenched and his muscles bunched as he prepared to pounce. He was getting gods-damned sick of being pushed around and the sorry bastard behind him was unfortunate enough to be the straw that broke his wolf's back.

"Take it easy, werewolf." A head bent close to his, the words meant for Christian's ears alone. "My mistress would like the pleasure of your company."

Christian angled his gaze to the left to get a look at the male whose hand was damn near large enough to palm a pumpkin. He recognized the male as the dhampir who'd pleasured Siobhan for his benefit a few weeks ago. His wolf clawed at the back of his mind, more than ready to tear the bastard's throat out.

Take it easy? How 'bout I take your head off, fucker?

Christian calmed his wolf as best he could. It didn't help that the moon would be full in a few days, giving the animal more sway over him. The bastard was as eager as a pup at its mother's tit to get to the fiery female. "And what if I'm not interested in seeing your mistress?"

The dhampir leaned over him. "You act as though you have a choice in the matter."

Again, Christian was reminded that he was virtually trapped in a closet of a room with no alternate exit. The dhampir was built like a fucking redwood. He'd take Christian to the concrete floor before he managed to take two steps. Without even glancing at the cards he'd been dealt he slid them toward the dealer. "Sorry, gents, but it looks like I've got to call it a night."

"Typical." The shifter snorted and jerked his chin toward the dhampir. "Is there a night of the week that someone's not shakin' you down for what you owe them, Whalen?"

Lately? Nope. "Don't worry, I'll be back to take your money tomorrow night." The traveling game would only be at Onyx for one more night and Christian would be damned if he missed out on an opportunity to hit the table again. He had forty large to scrounge together before

Gregor got impatient. Christian pushed out his chair and stood. Slowly. No telling what the dhampir might do to him. One quick move and he could easily snap Christian's neck. He wasn't quite ready to check out. Especially now that he was about to get a face-to-face with the female who'd occupied his every waking thought for months.

Close enough to touch . . .

Christian turned to face the big motherfucker and actually had to tilt his head up to get a good look at him. *Jesus.* The dhampir looked Christian over with a disdainful sneer. His light blue eyes were downright fucking creepy up close. Nearly translucent, and they lent a menacing air to his expression. Christian swore he felt the chill from the male's gaze.

His wolf wasn't a damned bit intimidated. A snarl rose in Christian's throat and he swallowed it down. All he could think of was the dhampir's hands on Siobhan. Touching all of the places that Christian longed to explore. This male had taken what Christian coveted. His wolf continued to grow more agitated as a single word echoed in his mind: *Mine.*

He held out a hand, inviting the dhampir to lead the way. Gregor would shit a brick if he knew that Christian not only had a credible lead on the female he was after but also was being taken straight to her. So it was a damned good thing that the berserker had been too busy to check in with him for a few days.

"You first."

Apparently the dhampir wasn't the trusting sort. *Go figure.* Christian stepped out in front of him and headed for the door. The hairs at the back of his neck stood on end. His inner animal didn't like having the threat at their back, and for once Christian agreed. Wherever he was about to be taken, he'd be stupid not to stay on guard. The situation was bound to be hostile. Siobhan hardly appeared domesticated. His wolf howled at the prospect of seeing her again. Getting within touching distance.

The dhampir marched Christian through the club and out the front door. He filled his lungs with clean air—well, as clean as L.A. air could be—and cleared a bit of the angry haze from his mind. He directed Christian to a car down the block, nothing to write home about, a few years old and a little banged up.

"Get in." He gave Christian a not-so-gentle nudge.

"Do I get to know where we're going, or are you gonna blindfold me first?" The dhampir jerked open the passenger side door and waited. "I don't mind a little mystery."

"Do yourself a favor, werewolf, and keep your mouth shut until we get where we're going. Your voice annoys the fuck out of me and I've been given instructions to bring you to my mistress in one piece."

After getting up close and personal with Siobhan's henchman, Christian was beginning to think of bear shifters as cute and fluffy. He zipped his fingers across his mouth and got in the car without saying another word. If he was going to die tonight he could be thankful that he'd get one last look at those beautiful emerald eyes.

At least, he hoped.

Thirty minutes later, they pulled up to a house in a run-down part of the Valley. Christian got out of the car and brought his nose up to scent the breeze. Disappointment settled in his gut like a stone. Either the dhampir was talking a lot of shit and had lured him into a trap or Siobhan had arranged for a meeting far from where she hung her hat. Her jasmine scent was absent from this place. She'd probably never even been there before.

Before he could take a step toward the cracked concrete walkway, the dhampir gripped Christian by the throat and slammed him back against the car with enough force to leave a dent. *Ouch.* That was going to hurt in the morning.

"If you so much as cast a caustic eye her way, I'll gut you," the dhampir snarled, an inch from Christian's face. "Do you understand me, wolf?"

The threat of a loyal follower or something more? From the way he'd touched her, Christian assumed that the male felt particularly possessive of Siobhan. Guess that made two of them. "Not even a squint," Christian rasped through the constriction of his throat. "You have my word."

The male pulled back and hauled Christian away from the car. He pushed Christian out in front and once again he was forced to walk with a threat at his back. The front door loomed in the darkness, a gaping maw that waited to swallow him whole. A single light illuminated the interior and Christian stepped past the foyer, his footsteps whispering over the bare hardwood floors, and he walked into an equally bare living room. His earlier suspicion was about to be confirmed. No doubt the dhampir meant to kill him and leave his body to bleed out on the floor.

Hope you're packing silver, asshole.

He allowed his wolf to the forefront of his psyche and readied himself for the impending attack when the *click-clack* of footsteps echoed from his left. A waft of fragrant jasmine hit his nostrils and Christian's gut knotted with anticipation.

"I'm disappointed you didn't put up more of a fight." Siobhan stepped from the shadows, her smoky voice a caress that Christian felt on every inch of his body. His wolf growled its approval and he swallowed the sound. She might have given him an instant hard-on, but the female was still unpredictable and dangerous. The sway of her hips as she entered the room drew Christian's undivided attention. She took a seat in a lone armchair situated near the faux stone façade of the gas fireplace and crossed one leg over the other. "Tell me, werewolf, why have you been following me?"

Mine. Mine, mine, mine. His wolf practically yipped when her sultry scent hit his nostrils. She managed to work him into a lather and she'd barely spoken two sentences. Christian was more determined than ever to scrape up the money he needed to pay Marac in order to get Gregor off his back. Because he wasn't anywhere close to being ready to reveal Siobhan's existence and her possible link to the female he hunted for the berserker. They'd barely started this game they played.

Siobhan crossed her legs, every inch of her aware of the powerful male who stood before her. She'd hoped that by having Carrig bring the werewolf to her the spell would be broken. That her memory of him would prove to be better than the reality. His scent, spicy with a dark earthy undertone, swam in her head. His eyes were every bit as gray and brooding as she remembered. And his mouth, sinful and inviting, curved up into a sardonic smirk that made her want to master him and surrender to him all at once.

He was her only weakness. One she needed to squash before he became her undoing.

Her question went unanswered. He simply studied her with that damnable smirk. It's not as though she expected him to spill his secrets. For the first time in centuries, Siobhan wished she had the power to compel. Rather than press him, she cocked her head to one side and asked, "What's your name, werewolf?"

"Christian Whalen. But I doubt a female as well informed as yourself didn't already know that."

His voice was as decadent and rich as melted chocolate. The deep timbre enveloped her in warmth and Siobhan suppressed a pleasant shudder. He told the truth; his words didn't smell of a lie. Had she been more diligent, Siobhan would indeed have learned everything about him that she could. Though with Gregor still in the city and Mikhail keeping a close eye on her she'd decided to err on the side of caution. There was no use drawing undue attention to herself or her coven.

"Did you like what you saw at Onyx last week?" No need to clarify. At the vague mention of the night he'd watched Carrig pleasure her, Christian's eyes heated with lust and his nostrils flared. Siobhan's body answered in kind. Her blood raced through her veins and a spark of excitement flared low in her abdomen.

She uncrossed and recrossed her legs, let her fingers trail from her cocked hip down one leather-clad thigh. Christian's gaze followed her path as the moon followed the sun across the sky. "I didn't like the sight of another male's hands on you." The rough, possessive edge to his words sent another thrill of excitement chasing through her.

"I think you liked watching Carrig pleasure me," Siobhan said. She let her voice go low and husky, little more than a murmur. "And I think you'd like to watch again."

He fixed her with a hard stare. "Do you."

It wasn't a question. No, there was a challenge inherent in the werewolf's tone. One that Siobhan was sorely tempted to accept. What would he do if she called Carrig in right now and asked him to service her while she made Christian watch? Would he simply stand there and take in the sight with that infuriating smirk affixed to his face, or would he let more of that possessiveness out?

A charge of electricity spanned the space between them. If she continued her line of questioning there wouldn't be much to keep her from fucking him right there in the armchair. Siobhan shifted, slumping down in her seat as she flung one leg over the arm of the chair. Her relaxed posture was intended to show him that he had no effect on her whatsoever. That she couldn't be bothered to perceive him as a threat or anything else. His eyes tracked the movement and his fists clenched at his sides as his gaze settled between her thighs. A rush of delicious heat bloomed where he stared and Siobhan suppressed a shudder. Gods, he could get to her with a look.

"You have no pack?" She'd draw out the conversation, learn as much as she could in the brief time she planned to keep him there.

Christian shrugged. "I'm not much of a people person."

A rogue then. Carrig had been right about him. "A rogue in the city," she mused. "If any of the local packs knew you were here, they'd hunt you down and kill you."

His expression remained calm and the corner of his delectable mouth hinted at a smile. "Probably. But lucky for me that won't be a problem."

Siobhan's eyes narrowed. "And why is that?"

He fixed a pleasant expression to his face and simply stared. It would take more than dragging the werewolf to her feet to uncover his secrets. And no doubt he had many. "Who do you work for, wolf? The Sortiari?" His scent changed slightly. Almost too faint to recognize. "What do you do for them? I suppose a rogue wolf could be considered useful to the guardians of Fate."

Christian took a step closer. And another. Siobhan sat upright; the tiny hairs on her arms tingled with awareness of him. "Why not say what you really want to ask me?" Gold flecks sparked in the gray depths of his eyes, transforming his expression to something wild and untamed.

"And what exactly is it that I really want to ask?" Siobhan's fingers curled around the armrests, anchoring her to her seat lest she be tempted to reach out and touch.

"You don't care about who I work for or what I'm doing in the city."

She kept her tone as bland and disinterested as he had: "Don't I."

"No." A corner of his mouth quirked in a confident grin. "You don't."

"Then tell me," Siobhan purred. "What do I want to know, werewolf?"

He took another step toward her. So close that the heat from his body caressed her in gentle waves. She leaned back in the chair and canted her head up to look at him. The dominant positioning of his body wasn't lost on her as he leaned down and braced his arms on the rests at either side of her. "You want to know why I haven't fucked you five ways north of Sunday yet."

A lick of heat traveled the length of Siobhan's spine and her pussy clenched around nothing. Her lips thinned as she regarded him. "Don't flatter yourself."

Christian leaned in closer and ran the tip of his nose along the length of Siobhan's neck. A riot of chills broke out on her skin and her breath caught in her throat as a wave of want crashed over her. He stopped below her earlobe and made a dramatic show of inhaling a deep breath. A low, seductive growl rumbled in his chest. "I can't help but be flattered." He nuzzled her skin and Siobhan was reminded that this male was every bit an animal. "Your scent tells me everything I need to know."

Hiding emotions—anything really—from another supernatural being was problematic. With their heightened senses, changes in scent, body temperature, the dilation of pupils, and an increased pulse rate were much more noticeable. Siobhan cursed her weakness. That her want of this male was so easily betrayed. "I'm certainly too much for you, werewolf. I doubt you could handle me."

When he pulled away, his eyes were no longer stormy gray but brilliant gold. "You won't give that big bastard outside a second thought once I've had you."

She found his overconfidence amusing. "Don't be so sure," Siobhan purred. "My appetites are voracious."

"I'm more than capable of giving you what you need," Christian assured her.

Siobhan quirked a challenging brow.

Christian moved in until his mouth hovered a hair's breadth from hers. A slight shift would be enough to press their lips together. His heated breath mingled with hers as he whispered, "Try me."

Gods, how she wanted to. What she needed was to get him out of her system so she could once again lend her focus to matters that deserved her attention. He was an itch that required scratching, just under the surface of her skin. Siobhan made no move to close the slight distance between them. "Tell me who you *really* work for, and why you're following me, and I'll consider it."

His lips brushed against hers, a whisper of contact. Siobhan's muscles went rigid and a rush of wetness spread between her thighs. "I think I like some secrets between us," Christian growled as he pulled away. "So I suppose that for now, I'll have to be content to watch."

He pushed himself away from her and Siobhan felt herself lean forward as though unwilling to put even an inch of distance between them. The male's effect on her was as powerful as it was disturbing. Siobhan forced her body to relax back in the chair and affixed a cold, emotionless expression to her face. "I'll be sure to keep you entertained. For now. My offer to you will only be extended for so long, however. And I don't like to be kept waiting."

"I'll take that under advisement." Though he appeared to be unaffected by the moment that passed between them, Christian's eyes remained bright gold. "I'll see you soon, then?"

"Yes," Siobhan replied. She resumed her relaxed position, letting her arms flop over the armrests. He turned to leave and Siobhan let out a shuddering breath. She'd see him soon, and often. She could play his game. Seduce him. And once she'd snared him, once she made him irrevocably hers, Siobhan would cut his strings.

"Watch your back, werewolf. I'd hate for anything to happen to you between now and our next meeting."

"And you watch yours," he said too earnestly for Siobhan's peace of mind.

Perhaps Carrig was right. Maybe she should leave Los Angeles in her wake and put as much distance between her and Gregor as possible. But as she watched Christian walk away his rolling predatory gait held her rapt. How could she possibly flee if it meant leaving the one thing she wanted behind?

CHAPTER
27

"Lucas, what are you doing here?"

Bria stopped midstep on her way out of the kitchen. Lucas flashed her a wide grin as he headed toward her from the hallway that led from the king's study, all too pleased for someone whose life had been threatened mere weeks ago by one of the vampires currently in the house. "I had business with the king," he said.

She fixed him with a suspicious stare. "What sort of business?"

"You're not the only one who wants a life outside the coven," Lucas replied.

No, she supposed she wasn't. Her uncle had ruled over them all with a heavy hand. It would be selfish of her to not want the same freedom for the members of the coven that she'd found outside of it. Though she supposed "freedom" was stretching it a bit. At least, for now. "I'm sure whatever task Mikhail has set out for you, you're more than capable of performing."

Lucas beamed. A quiet moment passed between them and Bria shifted on her feet. Lucas's gaze was too full of emotion; his expression conveyed too many unspoken words. She hated to see him like this, but there was nothing to be done for it. She was tethered. To Jenner. And over the past couple of nights, their bond had become even stronger.

"I'll be seeing you more often, then. Give my love to my uncle when you see him."

Lucas's brow puckered and he took a tentative step away from her. "I will. Have a good night, Bria."

"You too, Lucas." She gave him a soft smile and continued on toward Mikhail's study.

She hated that she'd just treated a male who had been her dearest and closest friend as nothing more than a casual acquaintance. Her transition and tethering had changed so much in her life in such a short time. Lucas would understand . . . someday. And once she and Jenner settled more comfortably into their relationship she was sure that the tension between the two males would disappear entirely. Until then, Bria would have to endure more awkward moments like the one she and Lucas had just shared.

Curiosity burned through her as she made her way down the hall. What could Lucas possibly be doing for the king? And what reward did Lucas hope to reap in return? Her thoughts refocused on the low voices that came from the other side of the doors that led to the study, too low for her to discern their words. Which meant that whatever they talked about, they wanted to make sure none of the other supernatural inhabitants of the house would overhear.

What could the topic of their discussion be? she wondered. *Lucas?*

The doors slid open and Bria looked up to find Jenner's eyes on her. The heat in his expression nearly melted her where she stood. There was nothing playful or even mildly pleasant about it. Instead, he devoured her with his gaze as it raked her from head to toe. Bria felt naked as his eyes wandered over parts of her body that his hands had touched mere hours ago. A rush of excitement chased through her and her fangs tingled in her gums. Why did either of them ever have to leave at all? They could simply stay in the guest bedroom forever. Naked. Bodies entwined, with nothing more than each other's blood to sustain them.

Jenner's dark and brooding perusal of her body left Bria addled and breathless, but she needed to stand strong against his seductive assault. It would be an easy thing for him to coax her back upstairs. A few kisses, the glide of his fingers through her sex, and Bria would gladly stay right where he wanted her to. The thrust of his thick erection inside of her would surely convince Bria to agree to anything. Even if it meant extending her own jail sentence.

She gave her head a shake. Why was she worried about Jenner's power of seduction when her own traitorous mind worked against her? A narrow hallway separated them, though it might as well have been a vast canyon. He was much too far away from her.

"Bria."

Gods, when he said her name in that dark and rumbling voice it unraveled her. She leaned against the wall—it was the only thing keeping her upright at this point—and affixed what she hoped was a seductive smile on her face. "Jenner."

Silver reflected in his eyes. The power she felt at knowing she could so easily affect him was almost as heady as his kisses. He crossed the hallway—two wide steps—and pressed his body against hers. His arms came up on either side of her, braced against the wall to box her in, and Bria's breath raced in her chest. Such a male. And he belonged to *her*.

She looked up to find his expression tense. Almost pained. That intensity in Jenner never ceased and that aspect of his personality held her in thrall. "I'm dressed and ready to go," she said in a honeyed tone. She'd win him over with sweet compliance. Show him that she could be agreeable to his demands. And then she'd tell him, just as sweetly, that from here on out their relationship would be a partnership.

Surely he'd be thrilled by the mandate.

A wry smile curved Bria's lips. She reached around and scraped her nails along the back of Jenner's neck. His lids drooped almost imperceptibly, but the rapid beat of his heart was all Bria needed to hear to know that he enjoyed the contact.

"Are you hungry?" she asked. Jenner had promised her a meal before he set out for the night. She planned to use the opportunity to convince him to bring her along.

He leaned in close and Bria shuddered as his mouth brushed the outer shell of her ear. "I'm *starving.*"

"For the love of the gods, get a room!"

Ronan's booming voice broke the spell and Jenner pulled away. An arrogant smirk tugged at his mouth. He kept his gaze locked on Bria, so full of heat that she began to sweat. He reached out and feathered his thumb over her bottom lip before he turned to face the other male.

"I'll be ready to roll in a couple of hours. Where do you wanna meet?"

A wide, mischievous grin spread across Ronan's face. "Just a couple of hours, huh?" He cocked his head to one side and gave a cluck of his tongue. "We can't all be rock stars in the bedroom, I suppose."

Bria's cheeks flushed with the innuendo. If only Ronan knew how they'd spent the bulk of the past two days she bet he wouldn't be quite so smug. Jenner didn't take the other male's bait. He simply stared him down until Ronan squirmed. "You know, I liked you better when you weren't so gods-damned broody. Let's meet at your place. That way Naya can work her mojo on your apartment."

"You like me just the way I am, Ronan," Jenner replied with a smirk. "A cranky bastard who doesn't mind knocking heads together when you need it done."

"Eh. You've got a point." He flashed Bria a devilish smile and winked. "See you in a couple of hours."

Jenner turned to Bria. He held out his hand in invitation. Bria placed her palm in his, reveling in the heat that soaked through her skin, the way his fingers wound with hers. "Where are we going?" She already suspected where, but she could barely contain her excitement that Jenner would actually let her leave with him. Threat of necromancers be damned.

"My place," he said as he led the way to the foyer. "*Our* place. Go upstairs and grab the rest of your things. You won't be staying here anymore."

Ours. The word sent an unexpected burst of joy through Bria. She's never had a place that she felt she could truly call her own. That Jenner would finally take her to his home, that he considered it something they would share, caused her chest to swell with emotion. *Such a male.* With every passing day Bria lost another piece of her heart to him.

Sadness tugged at her that she'd be so excited simply to be taken from point A to point B. A sad reflection on the sorry state of her life up until this point. But like the gradual way that Jenner continued to win her affection, she counted these small victories as a step in the right direction.

The rest of her things turned out to not be much. Her backpack with her geocaching gear, a few clothes and books her uncle had brought, and that was about it. Her worldly possessions could fill the cargo box on the back of Jenner's Ducati. When she followed Jenner out to the driveway, she noticed that Alex waited with the town car. "Where's your motorcycle?"

"Left it parked at Ultra." Jenner opened the car door and waited for Bria to climb in the backseat. "I had to ditch it when the slayers spotted me."

Bria wished she could erase that entire night from her memory. "Should we go get it? I hope nothing's happened to it."

Jenner gave an unconcerned grunt. "I'll have Ronan take me to get it later tonight." He climbed in beside her and Alex pulled out of the driveway, slowing as the large wrought-iron gate glided open.

"How far is your house from here?"

"Apartment," Jenner said. "About thirty minutes. Forty if traffic is shitty."

A long drive. Plenty of time to broach the subject of her independence. Plus, she had the benefit of Jenner being a captive audience. He'd have no choice but to hear her out. She turned to face him, ready to state her case. The words died on her tongue, though, as Jenner leaned in and put his mouth to hers.

Jenner's hungers hadn't abated with his tethering. Instead, they'd merely shifted focus. The drinking of blood and the search for a body to fuck had commanded his focus for months. Now his thirst raged for only Bria's blood and it was her body that he craved above all others. The past forty-eight hours had only served to intensify those needs. His satiation only temporary. Gods, she drove him to the very brink of his restraint. He no longer feared those urges, however. Bria trusted him. Understood him. And through her, he could better understand himself. They'd soon find a rhythm, an ebb and flow to their tether. Until then, Jenner knew that he'd need to take Bria often. Both her body and her blood. Thank the gods his mate wanted him with the same ferocity. He planned to keep her by his side for as long as he could safely do so. The thought of leaving her nearly brought him to his fucking knees.

Her scent enveloped Jenner as he kissed her. Lilacs and honey. Her dewy mouth tasted sweeter than any nectar. Jenner wound his fist in the length of her hair as he deepened the kiss, thrusting his tongue between her lips. He wanted her to feel the kiss everywhere as he lewdly fucked her mouth with his tongue in the same way he wished his cock was moving inside of her right now.

Bria let out a quiet moan that vibrated through Jenner and settled in his balls. He'd take her in the backseat of Mikhail's fancy fucking town car if he thought she'd let him. Her hand settled in his lap and she cupped his cock through his jeans. Almost idly she stroked along its length with the tips of her nails, and a shiver of intense sensation rocked through him, calling to mind the way it had felt to have her fangs scrape against his shaft.

Jenner pulled away and buried his face in her hair. He inhaled her scent and held it in his lungs before he rested his lips against her ear. "If I don't fuck you soon, I'll go out of my mind." Bria gripped him through his jeans and a rumble gathered in his chest. He put his mouth to her neck, nipped her flesh with his fangs light enough not to break the skin. She shuddered against him and a rush of pure lust burned through him. "I need to see your pussy. To taste it. I need to bury my cock inside of you. Bite you."

She whimpered at his words and the scent of her arousal bloomed around him. "You don't have to wait, you know. You could bite me, Jenner. You can touch me. Right now."

He needed no other invitation. He slipped his hand past the elastic of her stretchy leggings and plunged inside of her underwear. His cock throbbed against his fly as he found her pussy nearly dripping wet, the tight bud of her clit already swollen as though in want of his attention. Bria wound her fists into his T-shirt. Tight little gasps of breath left her lips as she tucked her face against his shoulder.

The way he touched her was a dare. A test of her control. Beside him, her body went rigid. Her thighs trembled on either side of his hand as he worked her into a frenzy. Her grip on his T-shirt tightened to the point that the fabric ripped. And still she didn't cry out. Didn't so much as whimper. His fiery mate was a wanton creature, allowing him to bring her to orgasm in the backseat of the car with nothing but a few feet separating them from Alex.

Jenner nuzzled Bria's throat. He sealed his mouth over the vein and gently sucked to coax it nearer the surface of her skin. Using the pad of his finger, he continued to circle her clit. With each pass he increased the pressure and Bria's quick breaths became disjointed and shuddered out of her. Her thighs tightened around his hand and Jenner bit down, piercing her flesh with the sharp points of his fangs. Bria's breath stalled and a violent tremor shook her from head to toe as she came. Her orgasm vibrated through her, into him, and Jenner swore he could go off from nothing more than the evidence of her pleasure. He carried her through every clenching spasm of her pussy, stroking her swollen clit as he took deep, languorous pulls from her vein.

It still amazed him how much he enjoyed simply giving Bria pleasure. His own needs didn't even register when she was so willing, so responsive in his arms. He scored his tongue and closed the punctures at her throat. The hitching breaths that had driven him crazy resumed and slowed to a soft, easy rhythm that brushed over Jenner's collarbone.

He put his arm around her and gathered her close.

Bria's head came to rest on his chest and Jenner shifted so as to relieve some of the discomfort of his still erect cock from pressing against the restrictive fabric of his jeans. As Alex steered the car toward downtown, Jenner watched the lights of passing cars and took note of the foot traffic that clogged the sidewalks. Nearly 4 million people inhabited Los Angeles and he had to weed through those millions for a single necromancer. He hoped to hell that Naya was as skilled as Ronan bragged she was. Because if Jenner couldn't secure Bria's safety soon he'd crack. The thought of losing her constricted his chest to the point of pain and sent an anxious burst of adrenaline through his veins. He held her closer, pressed her body into his, and she let out a gentle sigh.

"Jenner?"

"Bria?"

"I think . . ." Bria's voice trailed off, her tone unsure.

"Yes . . . ?" A smile tugged at his lips.

"Never mind," she whispered so quietly he almost didn't hear the words.

His amusement faded into concern. After a moment Jenner gave her a squeeze. "What is it, *viaton*? Are you all right?"

"I'm fine."

Curiosity gnawed at his gut. Anxiety tightened his muscles until he squirmed in the plush leather seat to release the tension. What had she wanted to say to him? Before he could press her on the matter, Alex pulled up to Jenner's building. He gave Bria a gentle nudge. "We're home."

We're home. Two simple words, and yet they were the most important words he'd spoken in a long damned time. He hadn't given Bria any choice in the matter. Once again, he'd made an edict that he expected her to accept without argument or input. Really, Jenner hadn't once considered his apartment home in all of the years that he'd lived there. Since his transition he'd crashed at the places of whatever females he'd fucked or he'd stayed at Mikhail's. Rather than a haven, the modern three-bedroom on the edge of downtown had made Jenner feel trapped.

Would Bria consider it a haven or a prison? He supposed that depended on whether or not he intended to treat her as his mate—his equal—or his captive. Even if he managed to kill the necromancer could he let go of the cloying fear that prompted him to keep her hidden from the world? If he couldn't Jenner knew his overwhelming protectiveness would do nothing but push her away.

She tilted her head up to look at him, a seductive smile curving her luscious mouth. "How much time do we have before Ronan shows up?"

"An hour and a half or so."

She brought his hand up to her mouth and kissed each one of his knuckles. "Good. Because I think you need to make good on those promises you made to me earlier." She leaned in until her mouth brushed his ear. "The ones about fucking me."

Holy fuck. How could he be expected to think clearly when she spoke to him that way? Jenner said a quick good-bye to Alex and climbed out of the backseat. He helped Bria out and pulled her against him before he shut the door. The car drove away and he kissed her with every bit of the longing that burned bright in his soul. "Let's go inside. I plan to use every minute of our time before Ronan darkens our door."

Bria giggled. "I can't think of a better use of our time."

Neither could he.

CHAPTER
28

True to her promise, Bria had let Jenner lead her straight into his bedroom. She'd paid so little attention to their surroundings that they could have made love in an alley for all she might have known—or cared. Jenner's appetite for pleasure was insatiable. His fervor as he took her *almost* without restraint. He'd made her come for him again, coaxing it from her with slow, deep thrusts that made her cry out and beg him to take her deeper still. When the storm of their passion subsided, Bria rested her head on his pillow and inhaled Jenner's scent. The thought that they'd be sharing this bed for many days to come filled her with a euphoric sense of peace that softened her bones to mush. After they'd both come down from the high that seemed to sweep them up every time they lost themselves in each other, Bria followed her mate out into the living room for her first honest-to-goodness look at the apartment that was her new home.

Jenner's apartment couldn't have been further from what Bria expected. Her jaw hung slack at the spacious apartment with picture windows that looked out over the city and the understated, post-modern decorating. Such a juxtaposition to the male she thought she knew.

"Jenner, this place is gorgeous."

A rush of happiness-infused pleasure rippled through their tether and he bestowed upon her a rare smile that showcased the wicked points of his fangs. Fangs that had been buried deep in her throat only minutes before. A molten jolt of pleasure shot through her at the memory and his gaze heated. Bria forced herself to look away. He was the sun, blinding her with his brilliance. Instead, she focused her attention on the subtle gray furniture and deep turquoise–colored walls. Ronan obviously paid him well.

"Are you hungry?" Jenner headed toward the pristine kitchen that looked as though a single meal had never been cooked there. "I haven't been here much over the past several months." He opened the refrigerator and turned to face her with a sheepish grin. "And when I am here, I usually just sleep. We can order out."

Where had he spent his days before they'd become tethered? Bria's hackles rose at the suspicion that he might have spent his time with the female she'd seen at The Dragon's Den and then again with him at Ultra. Just as quickly as the jealousy surfaced, she squashed it.

There was no point in trying to capture water that had already slipped downstream. Bria wanted to look forward, not back. Her fingers glided over the polished concrete countertops as she walked into the kitchen. She planned to cook in this kitchen. To stock the refrigerator with food and to make this place her home. She planned to have a life outside of these walls as well. And the independence to carve out her own life in tandem to the one she shared with her mate. Bria wanted it all and there was no reason for her to believe that she couldn't have it.

She thought back to those wonderful stolen moments in the backseat of the car and the shuddering orgasm that

Jenner had coaxed from her with so little effort. The tenderness she'd felt for him afterward—the all-consuming want of him—had nearly prompted her to say the words she'd somehow managed to bite back. *I think I'm falling in love with you.*

It was too soon for words like that, wasn't it? Jenner hadn't professed any deep feelings for her and she worried that revealing hers too soon would make her more vulnerable to hurt. So much was still unresolved between them. They'd crossed the barrier of their sexual issues and that was a huge step forward, but they were far from the finish line.

The low reverberation of the doorbell echoed through the apartment. Her eyes met Jenner's, and in his gaze Bria saw a tome of unspoken words. He strode through the kitchen, their conversation all but forgotten, and Bria followed.

"I'm ready to lay the mojo down." Ronan's mate breezed through the door like a force of nature. Magic prickled along Bria's skin and her step faltered. *A witch?* Bria hadn't given much thought to what sort of female had tethered Ronan. "Let's get this apartment good and protected so we can hit the town."

Whatever "hitting the town" entailed, Bria suspected that Ronan wasn't happy about it. His tawny brows gathered over his eyes and his lips thinned to form a hard line.

"Naya is still under the impression that she'll be on the front lines," Ronan remarked in a sour tone.

"And Ronan is still under the impression that I enjoy being used as a bloodhound and kept far away from the real action." She countered his words with a smile that coaxed her mate's dour expression to relax. She reached out and he took her hand in his for a brief moment as though the simple touch had brokered an unspoken peace between them.

"The front lines of what?" Bria spoke up, no longer content with watching from the background. Naya flashed a confident smile, her dark eyes showing an intelligence and fire that Bria found admirable.

"We're hunting big game tonight," Naya said as she outstretched her hand. "I'm Naya. Nice to finally meet you, Bria."

Naya was a warrior. She walked straight and tall, her shoulders thrown back. A sheathed dagger rested at the small of her back and another dangled low at her hip. Every ounce of her exuded strength. A perfect match for Ronan. Bria felt pitifully small compared to the stature of Naya's presence. Had Fate gotten it wrong with her and Jenner? He was equally powerful, a force of raw strength and violence. Though she'd learned how to fight, how to compel, and how to protect herself if she had to, she was hardly Jenner's match. At least, not yet.

Bria returned Naya's smile. Her gaze slid to Jenner, who stood near the foyer, arms crossed over his massive chest and a scowl set on his expression. He obviously wasn't happy that Naya seemed eager to share tonight's plans. "Sounds exciting," Bria remarked. "I can't wait."

"You're not going." Jenner's dark tone brooked no argument. He was an immovable statue all but blocking the doorway as though Bria would try to slip past him and break out.

Naya looked from Bria to Ronan. She cringed, as if only now realizing that she'd said too much. As far as Bria was concerned, she hadn't said enough.

An uncomfortable silence settled on the group. Naya cleared her throat and turned to her mate. "We're burning dark. I'll get to work with the protection charms."

Ronan cast a nervous glance Jenner's way. "I'll help you. Let's start on the balcony."

No doubt he figured it was the safest place to avoid

being caught in the impending cross fire. Bria let out a derisive snort. Jenner's gaze finally met hers. She wasn't a bit surprised to see the flash of angry silver swallow his usually dark irises.

"I thought we'd moved past this," Bria said. Rather than cross the room to where Jenner stood rooted to the floor, she kept the wide living room between them. "You admitted yourself that I was a skilled fighter. So why make me stay here while the rest of you go out and hunt? Finding the necromancer is just as much my responsibility as it is yours."

Chagrin showed in his expression for a split second before Jenner recovered. The male was all hardness and steel. Immovable. No one challenged him.

Until now.

Jenner's jaw squared and a hint of fear skittered in Bria's chest. There was a reason why no one dared to argue with him. "You're not going."

That's it? That was all he had to say to her? Indignation scalded a path up Bria's throat. "Give me a reason why not."

He simply stared at her.

Realization dawned and her temper flared white-hot. "So those things you said to me, that I was strong, fierce, capable . . . Those were lies?"

Jenner's shoulders slumped and a deep groove cut into his brow. "Of course not. You know I spoke the truth."

He hunted the thing that hunted her. Used one witch to find another. And while he put his life at risk—put Naya and Ronan at risk—he expected Bria to sit in his living room, the dutiful mate, and wait for them to return. They'd resolved nothing, it seemed. He still meant to control her. To keep her. And Bria refused to continue her existence as a kept thing.

"The thought of losing you—" The words stalled as

though lodged in Jenner's throat. "I don't know that I'd survive it, *viaton*."

"And what if something happened to you?" Bria countered. "Don't you think it would destroy me, too?"

"You're mine to protect, Bria." Jenner's arms came down to his sides and he leaned forward with emphasis. *"Mine."*

"What does that have to do with *anything*?" Bria was sick and tired of hearing that same excuse over and again. "What about you, Jenner? Aren't you mine as much as I'm yours? Doesn't it fall on me to protect you, too? Our tether isn't one-sided! You can't keep me on a shelf until you're ready to take me down and play with me!"

Heat rose to her cheeks and her chest heaved with anger. He opened his mouth to speak and took a step forward. If anything, his expression grew even more enraged, but Bria cut him off before he could launch his tirade against her. "Don't do this to me. Don't treat me as though I'm inconsequential. That our tether is inconsequential. Trust me to be capable, Jenner. Trust *us*."

How could she not see that the thought of losing her scared the shit out of him? It choked the air from Jenner's lungs, stilled his heart in his fucking chest. He loved her too damned much to risk her safety for something as ridiculous as her perceived captivity.

Hold up. Love?

Jenner took a stumbling step forward. The realization that he'd fallen in love with Bria felled him like a tree. As did her accusation that she was nothing more than his prisoner. Again, he was reminded that he was no better than her uncle, allowing his fear to master him. Bria had suffered her entire life because of someone's fear. Bria wasn't afraid. His mate was *fearless*. When she finally thought she'd found the freedom she longed for, Jenner had tethered her soul and shackled her as surely as her uncle had.

Jenner had always known he was a lousy asshole. Further confirmation from his mate's lips stabbed through him like a slayer's stake to his chest.

"Jenner, we need to go!" Naya pulled the heavy glass patio doors aside and rushed into the living room. Her eyes lit with excitement and the sound of her heart beating madly in her chest carried to Jenner's ears. "I heard her music, Jenner. She's close." Behind Naya, Ronan's expression of concern held a new meaning that Jenner understood far too well. "I've only secured a couple of protection charms on the apartment, but if we don't move now, we could lose her." Naya headed for the door with Ronan close on her heels. She flung open the door and disappeared out into the hallway.

Ronan paused at the threshold. His expression plainly said, *It's now or never.*

Jenner might as well have been standing there with his dick in his hands, as much use he was to anyone. "I need to gear up." No way was he going out unarmed. "Go with Naya. I'll be right behind you."

Ronan gave a sharp nod of his head and took off after his mate. His urgency had nothing to do with Jenner's crisis and everything to do with protecting Naya.

Jenner's gaze met Bria's. If he didn't get his ass in gear he might lose the one opportunity to free her from the evil that had stalked her for two centuries. She was safer within these walls. Even a couple of protection charms were better than nothing. Out there, the only thing standing between Bria and the thing that wanted her was Jenner. He couldn't take the risk that he'd fail her.

"I won't have the presence of mind to kill the necromancer if I'm preoccupied with worry for you." Jenner wanted her to hear in his tone the desperation of his request. He needed every ounce of focus he could muster. He got his ass in gear and rushed for the bedroom closet, Bria only a few steps behind. He grabbed his Ruger, a set of throwing knives, and two daggers that he quickly sheathed.

"What about me?" Bria's voice was no longer angry. Fear dug with sharp talons into Jenner's heart. It was resignation he heard in her words. The same resignation that had prompted her to tell him she was leaving two nights ago. Indecision warred within him. "What about my concern for you? We're stronger together, Jenner. Why can't you understand that?"

There were too many variables outside that door. He knew that forcing her to stay might be the thing that finally pushed her away, but if she died . . . Jenner shuddered. If the necromancer took her—killed her—it would open up a hole in him so deep and so dark that it would make his earlier soulless state a cakewalk in comparison.

Jenner crossed the room to where she stood, her bright amethyst eyes shining like jewels. He brought his mouth to hers and kissed her, hoping like hell that he could convey every single emotion, everything that had gone unspoken between them because he was too much of a fucking coward to say the words.

He pulled away to find her expression devoid of emotion and it chilled him to the bone. "Please, *viaton,* do this one thing for me. Let me know that you're safe so I can go out there and do what I have to do."

She averted her gaze and her lips thinned. Already Ronan and Naya had a significant head start, and there was no way Ronan would let Naya pursue the necromancer if there was any chance she'd put herself at risk. It felt as though Jenner left his own beating heart behind as he turned his back on his mate yet again and left her confined to her cell while he ran headlong into the path of danger.

Jenner's text alert went off and he pulled his phone out of his pocket to find a message from Ronan with their location. He took off in the direction of South Hill and Ninth, careful to keep out of the shadows and out of sight. The tether that bound his soul to Bria's gave an uncomfortable tug. The tension between them stretched to the point of breaking. There had been very few things in Jenner's life that he gave a shit about. And his existence up until he'd met Ronan had been nothing but endless toil and hardship. In the short time he'd known her Bria had become precious to him. Invaluable. He coveted her with a ferocity that bordered on obsession.

She wanted him to release his hold on her, to allow her to decide for herself what she could handle and what she couldn't. How could he possibly do that? Let go when all he wanted was to hold her tighter.

An arm reached out and snagged Jenner by the collar of his T-shirt to haul him into an alley at his left. He drew his dagger, prepared to stab first and ask questions later when Ronan's angry face came into view. "Jesus fucking Christ, Jenner. Do you know nothing about stealth?"

Clearly on edge, Ronan let his fingers relax from Jenner's shirt, though it did little to soften the rigidity of his body. A deep groove marred his brow and he kept Naya tucked behind him as though he could single-handedly shield her from all of the evil in the world.

That's all Jenner wanted to do for Bria. Protect her. Shield her from anything that might harm her. *But you left her confined to your apartment while Ronan keeps Naya by his side.* A pang of regret stabbed at Jenner's chest. He needed to keep his fucking head straight. Now wasn't the time for deep reflection.

"Where's the necromancer?"

Frustration built in him until Jenner thought he might burst. He itched for a fight, and the urge to commit violence was a palpable thing that stretched his muscles taut with unspent energy. Naya sidled out from behind Ronan and he gripped her wrist to keep her close.

"Relax, vampire," Naya chided. Ronan let go of her wrist, but he angled his body so that his shoulder remained in front of her. "She gave me the slip," Naya said with disgust. "I can barely hear her magic now. If I had to guess, I'd say that she's put at least five miles or more between us."

"Fuck!" Jenner's jaw clamped down on the word. He flicked out with his tongue to seal the punctures he'd made in his lower lip and laid his fist into the alley wall. He stared at the deep indentation he'd made and then down at his bleeding knuckles. The splits in his skin slowly healed and he wiped the blood on his jeans. *"Gods fucking damn it!"*

He'd been *so* close!

"Don't get worked up, Jenner." Naya's words fell on deaf ears. His anger built to a near-unmanageable level. "If I heard her magic once, I can do it again."

"You're sure it was the necromancer you sensed?" Ronan turned to face his mate, his expression pinched.

Naya gave him a look at though to say, *You dare to doubt my power?* "I'm sure. There are a lot of magic users in the city. The music of that magic distracts the hell out of me, but each song shares a common trait if the magic is natural to the user. The necromancer's song is unique because the magic she wields is dark. Taboo. I'd recognize it even with a million distractions."

"Do you think she knows that Bria is close?" If the necromancer had managed to track her down where would she possibly be safe?

"Not exactly. There are millions of people in the city, Jenner. It's harder than you'd think to find a single body. Chances are, she has a sense of where Bria is but can't discern an exact location. The protection charms on your apartment will further help to mask her presence. I think she's safe."

"Could you put a charm on Bria?" Jenner had never considered the possibility. "Like camouflage?"

Bria pursed her lips. "I've never done that before, but I don't think it's impossible."

If Naya could provide Bria with a portable bubble of protection that followed her wherever she went the freedom his mate wanted was a hopeful possibility. She'd be safer. He'd be more at ease. He could stalk the necromancer with patience instead of this damnable sense of urgency that opened the door for all sorts of mistakes to be made.

"Let's head back to your place," Naya suggested. "I can finish placing the wards on your apartment and then I'll see what I can do for Bria."

For the first time in more weeks than he could count, Jenner finally found a reason for cautious optimism.

CHAPTER
29

"I still think you should come home."

Bria kept her gaze straight ahead. She and Lucas had been over this a million times. That part of her life was over. "No. Didn't you just tell me that you wanted a life away from the coven? Why would you even suggest I go back?"

A stretch of silence spread between them and Lucas let out a sigh. "You can't live out of a hotel forever, Bria."

True, and she didn't plan to. She'd asked Lucas to make the reservation for her when she'd called him to come pick her up. The moment Jenner walked out the door and left her behind he'd made the decision for her. She couldn't stay there with him if he planned to treat her no better than her uncle did. If she'd stayed, her earlier ultimatum would have lost all credibility. Jenner would have known that her threats were idle and it would have made her needs inconsequential. If she was going to talk the talk she had to walk the walk. And that's what she'd done. She'd walked right out of Jenner's life.

A hollow ache opened up in her chest, the pain so deep

and sharp that she feared it would never subside. She'd left
her heart behind in Jenner's apartment. And she felt the
absence even deeper than she had the loss of her own soul.
She was sick and tired of being *dependent,* though. She
didn't even have money, her own damned credit card, to
reserve a hotel room! *Pathetic.* Jenner might have been
okay with continuing to keep Bria as a pet, but she wanted
more. And she'd come to the realization that she'd only
get what she wanted if she went out and seized it.

"What will you do, Bria?" Lucas's concern broke her
from her reverie. "You have to feed."

Bria pulled her bottom lip between her teeth. The
thought of drinking from anyone but Jenner further tore
at her composure. *Dependence.* That need for him—his
body, his blood—nearly prompted her to order Lucas to
turn the car around. "You could feed me." The suggestion soured on Bria's tongue. She didn't want to take
anyone's vein but Jenner's.

A pregnant pause answered her. "I don't think I can,"
Lucas said with chagrin. "I've offered to feed Chelle,
Ronan's sister."

Bria turned toward Lucas. He kept his eyes on the road
as he negotiated traffic, his expression tense. How had she
not known that Ronan had a sister? "When did you agree
to this?" Lucas's visit to Mikhail's house and his mysterious dealings with the king made so much more sense now.

"I've asked the king to turn me." Bria opened her
mouth to protest, but Lucas cut her off. "This is what I
want, Bria. I've sworn fealty to him. He doesn't trust
Thomas or any member of the coven, and to be honest, I
don't blame him. We both know your uncle's loyalty lies
with only himself. I'm going to prove myself worthy.
Ronan's sister is . . ." He paused as if trying to find the
right word. "An anomaly. Mikhail said that they needed
a strong dhampir to feed her, and I'm more than strong

enough to do it. Mikhail has put his trust in me and I'm going to show him that it wasn't misplaced. He's promised to turn me if I prove myself."

Who was Bria to judge Lucas's decisions? All she wanted was for him to be happy.

"If Mikhail turns you," Bria began. She swallowed down the lump of emotion that rose in her throat. "I hope that your soul is tethered soon after."

Lucas reached over and squeezed Bria's hand. "I'm starting to think I might be better off untethered."

"I'm sorry if I've hurt you." Her uncle had made promises that Bria couldn't keep. Even if she'd remained a dhampir, she never could have been Lucas's. Her soul belonged to Jenner. It always had and it always would.

"You haven't." Lucas's voice tightened with the words. He pulled the car up to The Standard, Downtown L.A. and put it in park. "Call me if you need anything. I'll come right over." He handed her a shiny silver credit card and she tucked it into her pocket.

"I will," she said. "Thank you, Lucas."

"And be careful. I know that you think Jenner's treatment of you is harsh, but Bria, if I were your mate I'd do far more than he has to keep you safe."

Bria's brow creased. Had she judged Jenner too harshly? "I'll call you before sunrise to check in."

He gave her a smile that didn't reach his brilliant blue eyes before she climbed out, backpack in hand, and shut the door. She watched from under the awning as Lucas pulled out into traffic and disappeared in the steady stream.

She didn't blame Jenner for wanting to protect her. The thought of any harm coming to him froze her with fear. But there had to be compromise. Without it she was nothing more than his possession. Bria wanted to be considered an equal. And if leaving Jenner—whether

temporarily or not—was the only way she could get him
to see that, then so be it. She hadn't made this decision
lightly. She needed a few days to think, that was all. And
when Jenner was close—his gaze burning with its
intensity, his hands wandering over her flesh—Bria
couldn't think. Nothing mattered but him and the want
that never loosened its hold.

A tingle of electricity brushed Bria's senses as she
headed for the entrance. Her step faltered and she rubbed
at her bare arms as if to banish the sensation. Magic? It
was almost too faint to tell. It could have been nerves or
the guilt that slowly crept over her skin. Gods, she hoped
she'd made the right decision. If not, she'd have to live
with the knowledge that she'd given up the one thing she
couldn't afford to lose.

Jenner brought his Ducati to a screeching stop in Mikhail's
driveway. Wilder than he'd ever been, his thoughts a tangled mass of black matter, he barged through the front
door, intent on tearing the house off of the foundation if
that's what it took to get his hands on that traitorous son
of a bitch who'd stolen Bria from him.

He'd never regretted his decision to order Bria to stay
put as much as he had the moment he'd walked into his
apartment to find it empty. She'd left him a note to let him
know that she was safe and that she'd asked Lucas to take
her somewhere she could think. *I hope you understand
that I have to do this, Jenner. I can't be a prisoner, not
anymore. I hope this time apart will help you to realize
what I've been trying to tell you: We are stronger together
than we will ever be apart.* He'd pushed her too far. *Gods.*
Given her no other choice. She'd bared herself to him,
confessed her disdain of being sheltered, kept. This was
his fault. He might as well have pushed her out the door.
The blame might have fallen on him, but that son of a

bitch Lucas had helped her. Hell, probably encouraged her. When Jenner got his hands on the dhampir, he was going to beat him to a bloody pulp.

Reason tugged at the back of Jenner's consciousness, a voice that reminded him no male had stolen Bria from him. She'd left. Walked out the door of her own volition. Because he'd opted to make her a prisoner. Because he'd refused to listen to what she wanted and had treated her like something in his keeping. He stuffed that levelheaded reason and buried it deeper even than the Collective that took up residence in the darkest corner of his mind.

He wasn't interested in logic or reason. He wanted someone to pay for what he'd lost. He wanted Lucas to *bleed*.

Fear pounded through Jenner's chest. Something wasn't right. He'd had enough of Bria's blood and she'd taken enough of his for him to easily track her. He had no sense of her at all save the tether that bound them. It wasn't possible, and yet some unknown force kept her hidden from him. How? What? The grim realization that the very thing that hunted Bria might have blocked their connection shredded Jenner's composure. He needed to find her before he lost his gods-damned mind.

Jenner had lost precious hours during the day. The oblivion of daytime sleep had eluded him and his anger only mounted with every passing hour. He knew Bria's frustration firsthand, as he'd been confined by the sun to his apartment, incapable of doing a damned thing about it. At sunset he'd taken off for Fairchild's compound, hoping that Bria had sought his protection. Instead, Jenner learned that she'd refused to return home, which meant that dhampir bastard was the only one who knew where she was. Fairchild had nearly pissed his pants with fear at the sight of Jenner enraged and bloodthirsty. It hadn't taken much for the male to splutter out Lucas's location.

Jenner shouldn't have been surprised to learn that Lucas had gone to Mikhail's. The son of a bitch was worse than a needy pup.

"Where is he?" Jenner's voice boomed through the expanse of Mikhail's mansion. "Where the fuck is he?"

Mikhail and Ronan came down the hallway ready to take Jenner to the ground much the same way they had the night of his tethering. Unlike that first night, he'd die before they kept him from what he wanted. "Get the fuck out of my way!" he railed.

"Jenner!" Ronan barked. "Calm down."

"The fuck I will! Where did you take her?" Jenner shouted to the cowardly fuck who was no doubt hiding from him. "Where is Bria?"

Ronan took a step toward him, hands outstretched. "Don't," Jenner growled. "Don't come near me. I'm so far out of fucking control, I don't know what I'll do."

"You'd better get yourself under control." Power sizzled in the tenor of Mikhail's warning. "Now. Lucas is under my protection and you won't be allowed to touch a hair on his head."

Jenner let out a bellow that ripped through him. Pain. Betrayal. Frustration. He felt it all to the marrow of his bones, as though his skin and muscles had been torn from his frame. Mikhail protected the male who had helped to spirit his mate away while he was out hunting for the creature that threatened her existence. Jenner wanted him to pay for what he'd done and Mikhail had offered him sanctuary?

Jenner's breath sawed in and out of his chest. White lights swam in his vision and his fangs throbbed painfully in his gums. His throat burned with unquenched thirst and his soul cried out in agony for Bria. He'd rather someone ran a stake through his fucking heart right here and now. Anything to put an end to this seemingly endless suffering.

"Get a grip." Ronan took a tentative step toward him and Jenner snarled. His expression turned from one of anger to exasperation. "Jesus fucking Christ, Jenner. Lucas is here for Chelle. She needs someone strong to feed her. Dhampir females aren't cutting it. Lucas is."

Jenner took off toward the rear of the house. Mikhail grabbed him by the arm and Jenner stilled. He might have had a death wish, but he wouldn't disrespect his king. "She's volatile, Jenner. You know that. If you startle her, she might kill you before she's even realized what she's done."

He gave Mikhail a sharp nod of acknowledgment and continued on his track. If he couldn't find Bria and convince her to forgive him and come home with him he'd rather be dead.

Jenner exited through the media room and stepped out onto the paver path that would lead him to the guesthouse at the far end of the property. He approached the small cottage with considerably more care than he'd entered Mikhail's house. The fine hairs stood up on the back of his neck and the predator in him rose to the surface, ready to defend against a potential threat. Chelle's power rivaled Mikhail's. It unnerved Jenner, felt unnatural as it brushed against his senses and banished the mindless haze of violent rage that had clouded his vision since he'd come home at sunrise to find Bria gone.

Chelle had always set Jenner on edge and that was before she'd been made into a vampire. Her mystical transition had cranked that strange energy of hers all the way up. No matter his unease, Jenner was determined to go into that room and get some fucking answers from Lucas if it killed him.

Hell, for all he knew, it might.

Rather than barge in, Jenner knocked on the door. He was answered with silence, and a renewed wave of anger burned through his chest. If Chelle had drained Lucas and killed him before Jenner could get his answers he was going to go *off*. He eased open the door and stepped inside the guesthouse. The place was dark and quiet as a tomb, the eerie stillness sending a chill over Jenner's skin.

"Chelle?"

"Jenner." Chelle's voice slithered over him, sweet and sinister at once. She strode into the room from a dark hallway, her blond hair and bright green eyes hidden by shadow. "Did Ronan send his enforcer to make sure I didn't kill the tasty dhampir he sent to feed me?"

He didn't see any sign of Lucas, and for a second Jenner feared for the male's safety. It was good that Siobhan hadn't been allowed to see Chelle. No doubt she would waste no time in finding a way to exploit Ronan's sister to her benefit. "I came to find my mate."

Chelle's amused laughter tinkled like wind chimes. "And you think I have her?"

"No. Lucas knows where she is."

"I have to admit, you're the last male I'd ever expect to be domesticated. Being tethered agrees with you," she said offhandedly. "From the wild fire burning in your gaze, I'd be willing to bet it's made you even more lethal."

Only where Bria was concerned. "Can I talk to him?" Chelle had managed to chill Jenner out in a way that Ronan and Mikhail had failed to do. She was enough of a threat to put him on alert rather than being the aggressor.

"He's asleep." Her gaze met Jenner's, cold and emotionless. "It seems I've taken a lot out of him."

What had Mikhail been thinking to turn an innocent like Lucas over to Chelle? Lucas might have been physically formidable, but he was the lamb to Chelle's lion.

She'd been practically raised by Siobhan, which made Chelle a certifiable badass to begin with. Her vampiric nature and soulless state had obviously enhanced that feral side of her personality.

"Then wake him." Chelle might have made Jenner nervous, but he wasn't about to back down.

She stepped fully into the small living room and flipped on a light. The tightness in Jenner's chest relaxed by a small degree. Not much had changed since the last time he'd seen her. Still tall, lithe, powerfully built. Her gaze still pierced him with its intensity and the dimples in her cheeks still made her look like a child when she grinned. To see her relatively unchanged put Jenner more at ease. He didn't know what he'd expected. Perhaps an ethereal creature. A shining goddess, ready to unleash her wrath on the world. The coffin that created her had transformed a god into the first vampire. Nothing about her transition would have surprised him at this point.

"No," she replied idly. "I don't think I will."

"Chelle, I'm not in the mood to play games."

"I can tell." Her transition sure as hell hadn't affected her snark. "Don't get your boxers in a bunch. Mated males," she said on a dramatic sigh. "So *intense*."

Jenner's patience hung by the barest of frayed threads. The control he'd regained when he stepped onto the walkway that led to the guesthouse tattered under the gale force of Chelle's sarcasm. "Get his ass out of bed," Jenner grated. "I won't tell you again."

"I like you better mated." Her eyes flashed with silver, different from those of any vampire or dhampir he'd ever seen. It pooled in her irises like a swirling storm of quicksilver. "Before you were an asshole just because you could be. Now you're an asshole with purpose."

Jenner took a step forward, ready to rip Lucas out of Chelle's bed by the scruff of his neck.

"I know where your mate is."

He stopped dead in his tracks. Fear coursed through his veins hot and thick. A corner of Chelle's mouth hinted at a smile. She'd no doubt picked up on the change of his scent and liked that she'd managed to rattle him.

"Lucas told you where Bria is?"

"More or less," Chelle said with a shrug.

"What does that mean?"

"I plucked the thought right out of his head," Chelle replied. "Cool trick, huh?"

Jenner's eyes grew wide. "That's impossible."

"Not for me." The tenor of her voice changed, almost sad. "I'm a freak, remember?"

Mikhail had made a mistake by keeping Chelle's transition a secret. Jenner let out a slow sigh. It seemed they'd all kept too tight a grip on things lately. "You can't stay shut up in this house forever."

Chelle cocked her head. The action made her appear wild. "Are you talking to me, Jenner, or should those words be meant for someone else?"

His own damned stupidity had forced Bria to make good on her ultimatum. "You said it yourself. I've never been anything but an asshole."

"True," she said. "But anyone can change."

Jenner hoped so. If he was going to win Bria's trust he'd have to convince her that he could quit with the controlling psycho mate routine. He'd have to let go of his own crippling fear and have a little fucking faith.

Chelle's chin tilted down and to the left, as though she'd picked up on some faint sound. "Time for round two," she said with a devilish grin that was identical to Ronan's. "Lucas took your mate to The Standard, Downtown L.A. But that's all I know."

Chelle turned to head back down the hallway and Jenner paused. "Go easy on him, Chelle. The members of his coven are—"

"Adorably innocent?" Chelle finished for him. The points of her fangs were fully visible in her wide smile. "Don't worry; I know how to take care of him."

That's what Jenner was afraid of.

CHAPTER
30

The joy of Bria's freedom soured with Jenner's absence. So far, her trek through downtown L.A. hadn't offered the sort of entertainment or thrill that she thought it would. From the hotel's roof she'd leapt to the next building and the next. She'd flipped, dove, tumbled, and launched herself from obstacle to obstacle with such grace and ease that her flow state had no equal. She could outparkour the most skilled traceur and still she found no joy in it. Even when she'd followed her GPS to the geocache not far from the Standard and signed the logbook inside, she felt hollow. Unfulfilled. Nothing held her interest as Jenner had only last night, his powerful body moving over her as he thrust deep inside of her. This separation wasn't what she wanted. Not really. But she couldn't be the sort of female who didn't stand by her convictions. She'd warned Jenner. Asked him to treat her as though she was his tethered mate and not a prisoner in the home he'd declared as *theirs*.

Loneliness ate away at her and it had only been twenty-four hours since she'd left the apartment. She missed him so much it hurt. His gruff voice and sharp expression. The deep groove that cut into his brow, and his large, imposing form. The way he could be both gentle and fierce. His thinly veiled restraint. Half of her soul seemed to be missing. In fact, since the moment Lucas had dropped her off at the hotel she could no longer sense Jenner past their tether, and she'd taken enough blood from him that it shouldn't have been a problem to find him if she'd wanted. The absence of any sense of him frightened her more than any possible threat against her could.

After her uneventful geocaching adventure, Bria decided to roam downtown L.A. simply because she could. She carried two daggers and a set of throwing knives for protection and kept them sheathed beneath her light jacket and at her back. Bria might have been free to do as she pleased, but she wasn't stupid. The sensation that someone—or something—watched her hadn't subsided since last night. Invisible insects traveled the length of her spine and her fangs tingled in her gums. Instinct clawed at the back of her mind, a part of her vampiric nature that Jenner had helped her to hone. Rather than subside, that need to be vigilant, to stay on her toes, had only increased. Bria wanted to make a point to Jenner, but she didn't want to die, either. The necromancer had been close to Jenner's apartment last night, and for all Bria knew she could still be close.

Bria continued to walk down Flower Street, careful to keep her pace slow and to stay as close to the edge of the brightly lit sidewalk as possible. Her unease grew and with it shame over what she'd done. Gods, she'd been every bit as stubborn as Jenner. Where he'd insisted she stay cooped up so he could guarantee her protection, she'd insisted that she be free to traverse the city without a single thought to her own security. The threat against her was very real. *Bria, how could you be so foolish?*

Her decision might have been foolish, but she wasn't afraid. In fact, she welcomed an attack. If anything, to end the anticipation. She hadn't gone out unarmed. If the necromancer wanted her she should have shown herself and fought Bria fair and square. Bria had to prove to herself, to Jenner, that she could take care of herself. Protect herself if she had to. Otherwise, she'd never be anything other than a yoke around his neck. Their tether had to be equal in all things; Bria refused to be nothing more than a responsibility to him.

A tingle of sensation danced along Bria's skin and she shuddered. A spark of magic. She stole a glance around her in search of the magic user. It could have been her own stupid paranoia that got the better of her. Witches and fae were both magic users and were for the most part benevolent. Naya was certainly an example of a witch who distanced herself from black magic. *Shake it off. Don't let your unease distract you.* Yet instead of heading toward the hotel, a dark energy urged her away and Bria changed her track and crossed to the other side of West Sixth. She abandoned well-lit and crowded main streets for darker, vacant alleys and side streets as some foreign force goaded her from her intended path. Her heart began to pound with her mounting anxiety and her fangs no longer tingled but throbbed. The fine hairs on her arms stood on end and a low growl built unbidden in her chest.

Without even realizing it she'd been herded. Directed away from the safety of the lights and crowds and forced onto a narrow road that dead-ended at a tall concrete wall. She'd been corralled as easily as a mindless sheep. It appeared as though the attack she welcomed would happen sooner than she'd thought.

Trapped.

A pair of eyes peeked out from behind a Dumpster and studied her. Low to the ground, they glistened with an almost metallic sheen. A dog? Coyote? Mutant tomcat? No. Bria's stomach rippled with fear. It rose hot and thick in her throat. Whatever watched her now was much, much worse than a hungry wild animal.

Bria had grown up believing that wendigoes were the equivalent of supernatural boogeymen. Something to scare petulant dhampir children into minding their parents. This one was every bit as intimidating and terrifying as the stories depicted. The only difference between the myth and the wendigo that watched her now was that this particular one had at one time been her father.

She'd lived her entire life up until this point believing that her father had died during the Sortiari attacks. She hadn't even been born when he'd fallen in battle. Her heart clenched at the thought that her own father had become a creature of nightmares. Before he'd ever had a chance to cradle her in his arms, to nurture and coddle her, he'd been commanded to hunt her down.

The wendigo snarled as it shifted its weight. As far as she could tell, there was nothing left of the male who'd sired her. Bria's heart pounded in her chest. She'd managed to cheat death not once but twice so far since her birth. Maybe she should stop trying to thwart fate and hand herself over.

No! The thought rang through her mind with the impact of a battle cry. Bria had too much to live for to give up now. She might have thought at one time that the only way to escape her lot in life was to die, but not anymore. The possibilities of her future were endless and she was mated to a male she couldn't wait to experience those possibilities with. She refused to leave this world until she was damned good and ready.

Slowly, she deposited her backpack on the ground and drew the daggers from their sheaths. The wendigo canted its head as it continued to watch her, the motion almost avian. Its lips pulled back to reveal tusk-like teeth that glistened with dripping saliva. Bria swallowed down the fear that threatened to choke her and gripped the handles tight to keep her hands from shaking. She'd never known her father, but this creature wasn't him. She'd do whatever she had to do to save herself. Even if that meant killing the very male who'd sired her.

The air pressure changed. Bria's shoulders felt weighted down, her lungs compressed, and her skin tightened on her frame. A sharp pain shot through her ears as though she'd been plunged hundreds of feet below the water and she'd yet to decompress. Swallowing, taking a breath, even focusing her vision, became problematic as the silhouette of a body came around the corner. The wendigo let out a mewling whine and rushed to its mistress's side, coming to heel like any obedient pet.

As Bria struggled to breathe she tried to remind herself that she didn't need the air in her lungs. The function was a reaction to the panic that gripped her, and if she couldn't get a handle on her fear she'd be dead before she made a single move to fight.

"You're not much use to me now." The necromancer's voice slithered toward Bria, coating her senses as though with thick oil. "But a bargain made is a bargain kept. No one, not even the niece of Thomas Fairchild, is allowed to escape her fate."

A chill shivered down Bria's spine. It would do no good to ask for mercy. None would be afforded. "Only a coward enslaves another and forces him to do her bidding. Perhaps you should fight your own battles, witch? Otherwise I can't be convinced that you're as formidable as I've been told you are."

Bravado? Oh, absolutely. If Bria didn't do something to bolster her confidence she'd surely crack. Her vision cleared by slow degrees, and soon Astrid's face came clearly into focus. Bria never would have guessed the lithe beauty standing before her practiced such dark and forbidden magic. Her long hair was nearly silver, the strands shining in the low light. A serene expression rested on her eternally youthful face and not a single blemish marred her flawless skin. Teeth white and straight became visible as a slow smile spread across her dark pink lips, and her eyes, wide and blue as a pool under the summer sun, watched Bria with not much more than mild interest. Astrid could have passed for nineteen, if that. And she was beautiful enough to be a model or a movie star. The necromancer must have fit in quite well in L.A.

"Do you think I roll out of bed looking like this?" Laughter filled the air, light and euphonious. Had she heard Bria's thoughts? Astrid reached down with one perfectly manicured hand and stroked the top of the wendigo's head. "Dark magic takes a toll on the body. Fortunately for me, I've found a way to counteract its effects."

Bria's stomach turned. It hadn't been enough that her mother had sacrificed a member of their coven to resurrect her father. Astrid had exacted a higher price. "The blood of an infant," Bria murmured more to herself. She didn't need confirmation to know the truth of it.

"It does wonders," Astrid replied with a smirk. "Better than Botox."

Bria choked up on the daggers and kept her weight on the balls of her feet. Static energy charged the air and instinct, coupled with weeks of Jenner's instruction, clawed at the back of her mind. Astrid brought her finger gently down on the wendigo's head. *Tap, tap, tap.* And Bria braced for the impending attack.

Jenner hustled down the walkway toward the front of Mikhail's property where he'd left his bike. His tether with Bria had become increasing slack to the point that he could no longer feel the presence of her soul. Panic welled hot and thick in his throat and Jenner swallowed it down. Gods-damn it, if he'd just compromised—not treated her as though she had no choices—he wouldn't be tracking her all over the fucking city, worried over the fact that something, or someone, had managed to block their bond.

His cell rang and Jenner dug it from his pocket as he straddled the worn leather seat of his bike. Ronan's name popped up on the ID and Jenner swiped his finger across the screen as he turned the key. "You need to check on your sister, dude." The bike roared to life and Jenner spoke over the growl of the engine: "I think she might break her new toy." He revved the engine and coasted down the driveway. The metal gates slid open and with every inch Jenner's impatience mounted.

"Later." Ronan replied. "Lucas is on his own for now. Get downtown. Now. Naya's got a bead on your necromancer."

Fuck. Jenner hit the gas and sped through the gate. He was at least twenty minutes away if he put the pedal to the metal. Fifteen if he ignored traffic lights. His gut twisted into an unyielding knot and he damn near broke the hunk of plastic in his hand with the tension that stretched out through his fingers. He held the phone closer to his ear, the sound of wind rushing past him nearly drowning out the sound of his own voice. "Where?"

"We were driving past Flower when Naya picked up on the magic. Mikhail sent me to pick up Saeed before sunrise and I'm on a time crunch."

Jenner's heart rate kicked into overdrive. He pushed the bike as fast as it would go, one hand steering while the other held the phone to his ear. "Lucas took Bria to The Standard on Flower last night."

"Fuck," Ronan spat. "That's only a few blocks from where we are now."

Agitation churned like acid in Jenner's gut. He weaved between two cars, nearly clipping the rearview mirror of a Corvette before he righted the tottering bike. "I'm about ten minutes out." Less if he could help it. "Saeed can wait. I can't sense Bria. There's not even a blood bond between us anymore."

Another sharp expletive came through the receiver. In the background Naya said something to Ronan and he replied, "Absolutely not."

"So what, you're just going to fucking abandon her?" Jenner had no way of knowing if the necromancer had found Bria, but the coincidence of her location didn't give him hope that his mate was safe. "Bria could die by the time I get to her and you're just gonna drive by like a gods-damned punk and put Mikhail's political agenda ahead of my mate's life?"

In all the years he'd known Ronan, Jenner had never talked to his friend with such disrespect. Nothing mattered more than Bria. *Nothing.* Ronan could coldcock him later if he wanted. Right now Jenner couldn't be bothered to give a single fuck.

"No one fucking said that." Clearly Jenner wasn't the only one riled up. "I'm turning around now, but I've told you already, Naya isn't getting within a stone's throw of that evil bitch. We'll keep her in our sights. Just hurry up and get your ass down here."

Ronan disconnected the call without another word, which was fine by Jenner. He shoved the phone into his back pocket, bent low over the handlebars, and sped toward downtown.

Ten minutes and one near-head-on collision later, Jenner hopped off his bike and hustled to where Naya and Jenner waited for him.

"I think she knows we're tracking her." Naya blew out

a frustrated breath. Her brows drew together over her dark eyes. Her agitation nearly matched Jenner's. "I can hear her music, but I can't track her. It's crazy. Dark magic is already unpredictable, but a necromancer is like dark magic times a thousand. She's close, though. A block, maybe two at the most."

It was still too much ground to cover.

"We'll head south," Ronan said. "You go north."

Jenner took off at a slow jog, careful to keep to the shadows. He headed down Flower, past Wilshire, and managed to cover four blocks when he stopped dead in his tracks. He couldn't explain it, but somehow he felt as though something was leading him away from Bria. Like a dog gathering up sheep, that force pushed and directed Jenner where it wanted him to go. This was wrong. *Damn it!* How could he have let his own instinct take a backseat to the magic that manipulated him now?

With a snarl he turned and backtracked the way he'd come. Jenner's feet pounded on the pavement as he ran at what might have been an acceptable human speed but still far too slow for his vampiric peace of mind. The false impression that he'd gone the wrong way pushed at his mind, filling Jenner with an unease that made him sick to his stomach. Instead of allowing that sensation to repel him, he forced himself to run headlong toward it. Magic pulsed hot and thick around him, weighing down the air until his lungs refused to take in oxygen.

It wouldn't have mattered, but Jenner needed to scent the air for any trace of Bria. His lungs worked overtime as he dragged the heavy air in through his nose only to find it void of the familiar honeyed lilac scent. He hooked a right and headed down Sixth. Jenner stumbled as an invisible force pressed against him. His head throbbed and his vision blurred. His secondary fangs ripped down from his gums as a sense of danger overtook him. His gut twisted as every inch of him screamed to turn around and go the opposite direction. Jenner fought the urge and pushed forward. His steps slowed as his feet became lead weights that scraped along the sidewalk.

Someone put a lot of gods-damned energy into making sure Jenner stayed the hell away from this part of the city. He wondered if Ronan and Naya had encountered the same issue. If so, they'd been led away from the epicenter of the witch's power. Then again, Naya had an advantage that Jenner didn't. With any luck, Ronan's mate hadn't been fooled. Bria was close. Jenner *knew* it.

Jenner's stomach heaved as he crossed South Grand over to Seventh. His eyes watered, tears streamed down his cheeks. Pain exploded in his skull and vibrated through his limbs. He dragged in ragged gulps of breath through his nose, the air so thick to his keen senses it might as well have been sludge. It soured on his tongue and Jenner choked. He breathed in again and his muscles twitched as he caught the barest of scents.

Bria.

The unmistakable sweetness of his mate's scent was a godsend. Jenner fortified himself against the pull of magic and continued down Seventh toward two large buildings that flanked a narrow alleyway. Heat burst in his chest and a bright light ignited in his soul. Relief cascaded over him, banishing the darkness that fought to keep Jenner at bay. He'd found her. *Thank the gods.* And the witch who'd tried to keep him from her was going to pay with her life.

CHAPTER
31

Jenner had never been so relieved to feel Bria's presence. It burned through him, igniting his soul with a heat that rivaled that of the sun. His fangs throbbed in his gums; his bloodlust mounted with every step. His mate was close, but even worse, the evil that hunted her was closer. How Bria had wound up in this dimly lit, quiet portion of the city was beyond him. Had the necromancer lured her out? Drawn Bria from the safety she might have found in the press of people who crowded downtown in the same way she'd tried to push Jenner away? An enraged shriek rent the night air, causing the hackles to rise on his neck.

His pace increased as Jenner pushed himself harder. The magic that bound him melted away and he ran until the sidewalk blurred beneath his feet. He rounded the corner and came to a stop where a high concrete wall dead-ended the street. Bathed in moonlight, his mate swung out with her right arm, a glint reflecting off the steel of her dagger with the motion. A woman, tall and lean, with unnaturally silver hair, parried the thrust with nothing more than a flick of her hand. Jenner rushed forward, ready to tear the necromancer's head from her shoulders, when a low warning growl sounded from his left.

Son of a bitch. The wendigo emerged from the shadows and snarled. Its scaly, grayish skin quivered and the accompanying sound reminded him of a rattlesnake's warning. Jenner didn't bother to draw his Ruger. The wendigo was already dead; it wouldn't matter how many bullets he drilled into its body. If he wanted the damned thing gone once and for all he'd have to kill the one who commanded it. He'd cut the bitch's black heart from her chest and show it to her while it still beat in his palm.

Bria's gaze flitted to him. Silver flashed in her eyes and she bared her fangs as she swung out with her dagger once again. Jenner rushed to her aid, but the wendigo blocked his path. Its jaws snapped down and the sheen of its milky eyes followed his every movement. It would be impossible to take down an unbeatable foe. He didn't need to beat it, though. All he needed was a momentary distraction.

"Bria, focus, damn it!" Until he could get to her she had to defend herself. He'd trained her well, but she wouldn't be worth a damn if she didn't keep her head in the fight. Worrying about him would only get her killed.

The wendigo lunged at him and Jenner jumped back. A low growl rumbled in its chest and another strange shiver vibrated its scaly skin. Their battle dance ensued as they walked a wide circle around each other. Jenner transferred the dagger from one hand to the other. He was proficient with both and the repetitive motion helped to center him. The wendigo feinted left, but Jenner didn't take the bait. He followed the creature's movement, gauged its eyes, the shift of its limbs, and mirrored his opponent's actions.

Hang on, Bria. You can do this. He'd ordered her to focus, but he found it difficult to follow his own advice. He kept the wendigo in the periphery of his vision so that he could be assured that Bria hadn't been hurt in the fight. Trepidation tightened Jenner's muscles until they twitched. The witch hadn't made a truly aggressive move yet. She played with Bria. Taunted her. It would only be a matter of time before Astrid unleashed the full force of her power upon his mate.

He couldn't allow that to happen.

In all of his years Jenner had never had the misfortune to cross a wendigo. As rare as the witches who controlled them, the beasts were rumored to contain a deadly venom in their claws and sharp incisors. He wasn't interested in testing that theory out, though. The wendigo lunged at him again, but this time it wasn't for show. Jenner braced for impact, his dagger at the ready, as its large frame crashed into him, taking him down to the pavement.

"Oh my gods. Jenner!"

"Bria!" Jenner grunted as all 250 pounds of his assailant landed on his chest. "Keep your head . . . in the game!"

If the witch was indeed the master she instructed her puppet well, creating the distraction needed to draw Bria's focus from defending herself. Jenner brought his dagger up and the blade deflected off the wendigo's armored flesh. An indestructible creature created by magic. How could he hope to gain the upper hand?

The blade might not have been effective, but Jenner wasn't above reducing the fight to brute force. His inability to see Bria—to assure himself that she was safe—sent a renewed surge of panic through him. He pulled his arm back and threw every ounce of force he could into the punch. His fist connected with the wendigo's chin, narrowly missing the sharp points of its teeth. The beast reeled back and a snarl tore from its throat.

With a roar the wendigo came up on its legs as it prepared to pounce on top of him. Jenner rolled to the side, his legs tangling in the wendigo's. He avoided the

razor-like tips of its claws by inches as its open palms
smacked down. The pavement gave way under the force
and the wendigo pulled one hand and then the other from
the fissures it created in the asphalt. It came at Jenner
again, but he was ready and dodged out of the way.

Fucking bullshit.

Bria's panted breaths grated in Jenner's ears and his
rage mounted with every one of her pained grunts, every
frustrated cry. He threw another punch and then an up-
percut that managed to knock the wendigo from on top
of him. It rolled away but recovered in an instant, ready
to renew its attack and take Jenner down once and for all.

He bent low at the knees to help with his center of grav-
ity and braced for the attack. Arms held wide, the dagger
clutched in his right hand, he'd be damned if he died in
some dirty back alley at the hand of a creature created
from murder. "Come on, you fucker!" Jenner railed. "Let's
see what you've got!"

A force of raw energy barreled over Jenner, taking him
to the ground. It hit the wendigo with the same intensity.
The creature rolled like tumbleweed in a strong wind and
came to a stop some thirty yards away. The necromancer
paused as well. She held out a hand and Bria froze as
though suspended in time. *Fucking bitch!* Jenner knew
that she'd been playing with Bria all along. Entertaining
herself while his mate fought to save her own life.

"I have to admit, I hadn't realized you were even here,
vampire." Astrid gave him a slow appraisal, her cold blue
gaze raking over him. "Come out, little white witch!" Astrid crooned into the night. Silence answered. Not even a
breeze stirred the air and she turned toward Jenner with
a superior smirk. "Your friend must be shy."

Jenner took a step toward Bria. Astrid held out her
other hand and stopped him dead in his tracks. His muscles seized up. His blood boiled in his veins. He gritted

his teeth against the pain and fought like he'd never fought before to move even his little toe. How could he possibly kill Astrid if he couldn't even get to her?

"William. Come." The command was merely a murmur, but the wendigo rushed to its mistress as though on punishment of death. It nuzzled her leg almost lovingly before it raised its head to her and snarled. Astrid looked down on the pathetic creature, her eyes narrowed. "Find the witch," she said with venom. "And kill her."

He took off like a shot, but it did him no good. Another wave of energy crested over them like a tidal wave. The force of it knocked them all on their asses—Astrid included—and the break in her concentration was enough to free both Jenner and Bria from her control.

He rushed to Bria's side and tucked her behind his body. It might not have done him a damned bit of good, but he'd do whatever he could to protect her. Magic tingled over his skin and Jenner said a silent prayer. Ronan might not have wanted his mate in the thick of the action, but Naya had given them aid nonetheless. She was more powerful than Jenner had given her credit for.

Ronan rounded the corner, fangs bared, his eyes alight with silver. The wendigo crouched and regarded him for a single moment before throwing its head back to let loose a vengeful roar. Naya stepped out of the shadows behind him. In her right hand she held a dagger with a strange blade. The citrine glow of the weapon illuminated her face, casting sinister shadows on her usually calm expression. A sphere of energy hovered just above her left palm, pulsing with a cold golden light.

Equal parts concern and relief swirled within Jenner. They were now a force of four versus an immortal killer and a witch whose power seemed immeasurable. Their odds of success were pretty gods-damned bleak.

But Jenner would take bleak over impossible any fuck-

ing day of the week. Astrid regained her footing and a
fiery rage reflected in her gaze. "I'm going to consume
your souls," she seethed.

Jenner leveled his gaze and his lip curled back into a
sneer. "I'd like to see you try."

Bria should have felt relief that Jenner placed his body in
front of hers. Protected her. That Ronan and Naya had
come to help. Instead, fear coursed cold through her veins.
The thought of losing any one of them was unbearable.
The thought of losing Jenner crippled her. She wouldn't
allow them to potentially sacrifice themselves for her.
Again, Bria was struck with the notion that she'd been living on borrowed time. Running from an outcome she
couldn't escape.

But maybe . . . just *maybe* it was time that she take control of her own fate.

She rose on her tiptoes and placed a kiss to the back of
his neck. "I love you," she murmured against his heated
flesh.

Every muscle in Jenner's body went taut and he said,
"Bria, whatever you're thinking, *don't* do it."

Bria smiled. *My mate is so fierce.* "You can have me!"
she called out to Astrid. Bria stepped out from behind
Jenner and dropped her daggers to the pavement. They
landed with a clatter of metal, the sound stark in the quiet
that descended with her words. Jenner reached for Bria
and Astrid raised her palm, stilling him in an instant. His
rage, his worry, reached out through their tether and Bria
steeled herself against his emotions lest she change her
mind. "You said it yourself; a bargain struck must be hon-
ored. I only ask that you let the others live."

"You're more honorable than both your mother and her
cowardly brother," Astrid remarked. "Come closer, Bria."

Bria cast a tentative gaze at her mate. Jenner's

expression bespoke murder and retribution and for a moment she wondered if it would be her or Astrid on the receiving end of his rage. Surely he was ready to throttle her. A wan smile curved her lips. He'd have plenty of time to berate her for her choices later. At least she hoped so.

"Bria, don't do this!" Naya's concerned shout sent a ripple of anxiety through Bria's bloodstream. Naya knew Astrid's power better than anyone.

Her worry nearly sent Bria back to Jenner, to the protection of his hulking body. *No.* She refused to be anything but brave. "It's okay, Naya." Bria held out a hand to stay any further argument. "Take Ronan and back away."

Naya hesitated. Her brow furrowed with concern and Bria turned her gaze away. In the periphery of her vision she watched as Ronan gripped his mate by her upper arm and slowly pulled her away from the epicenter of the danger. The wendigo growled but made no move to pursue them. Bria let out a sigh of relief. *Be brave. Be brave.*

She did this for Jenner as much as for herself. If she couldn't take care of herself—couldn't protect herself when she needed to—she wouldn't be a worthy mate for him. She couldn't remain tethered to him forever knowing that he felt as though she needed his constant protection. She didn't want to simply be some pathetic creature who needed looking after. Bria wanted to be Jenner's equal. A mate he could be proud of and stand beside. If she wanted a future with him she had to have faith. To trust that Fate knew what was best.

"I'll come closer." Bria infused her voice with confidence she didn't necessarily feel. "If you give me your word that you won't harm my mate."

"Your mate?" Astrid arched a delicate silver brow. "Not simply a vampire, but a *tethered* vampire? I'm almost glad your mother and uncle hid you from me. Your life essence must be brimming with power."

That was Bria's hope. She needed every ounce of power she could get right now. She took another step closer to Astrid and paused. "Do I have your word Jenner and the others will be spared? You've made no bargains for their lives."

"True," Astrid said on a dramatic sigh. "Fine. Your mate and your friends will be spared." She snapped her fingers and the wendigo came to heel, ignoring Naya and Ronan completely.

Bria studied the creature that had once been her father. She looked past its armored skin, mirrored, milky eyes, and expressionless face for any sign of the male who'd once thrived in that same body. Tears gathered in her eyes as grief welled within her. She'd never been given the chance to know him.

"Father?" The very word sounded foreign in Bria's ears.

The wendigo studied her, canted its head to one side. A low, sad whimper left its lips and it shied away as though afraid. Afraid of what? Her? Or the evil witch who controlled it?

Was there any small part of the male it once was trapped in that hideous form? Bria bent low until she was at eye level with it. The tether that bound her to Jenner pulled taut and she sensed his distress. With any luck this would all be over soon. "Father," she said again. "Do you know who I am?"

The wendigo thrashed its head as though trying to dislodge a thought. Astrid's gaze narrowed and her lip curled back into a sneer. "This"—she grabbed the wendigo's neck and gave it a rough shake—"belongs to *me*. As you soon will, Bria."

A snarl tore from the wendigo's mouth and Astrid increased the pressure on its neck, sending it lower to the ground. It fought against her hold but ultimately went down at her feet with a low, tortured whine that shredded Bria's heart. She might not have ever been afforded the chance to know her father, but she was going to make sure that he was set free.

She took another step toward Astrid. Bria's limbs quaked, her heart raced, and the breath stalled in her chest. Her vision darkened at the periphery and her head swam. Could she do this? Was she capable of saving her own life? *Yes.* The thought resounded with perfect clarity. She wasn't the same female who'd hung limp in her uncle's arms mere weeks ago wishing like hell that she'd die. Bria wanted a life! She wanted Jenner! And she'd be damned if anyone stood in the way of her happiness ever again.

The final step that brought her within inches of her worst nightmare felt as though it spanned miles.

Magic pricked at Bria's skin, the sensation like pins and needles. It increased in intensity until her flesh practically burned and Bria fought the urge to claw at herself. A light blue glow shone from beneath Astrid's skin, giving her a luminescent quality. Power swirled around Bria. Surrounded her. It pulsed and built until she was cocooned within a force that tightened her skin and caused her heart to thunder in her chest. Astrid flicked her wrist and Bria's left hand rose as though she were nothing more than a puppet on a string.

Astrid took Bria's wrist in an iron grip. She brought the sharp, pointed nail of her thumb to Bria's flesh and made a puncture. Pain sizzled through her and bloomed with the blood that ran in a rivulet down her outstretched arm. Astrid watched the crimson path with fanatic interest, her eyes glued to the sight of Bria's blood.

"There's so much power in blood," Astrid mused. "Aside from witches, I suppose vampires and dhampirs are the only other creatures in the world who realize it.

The blood of an innocent is the most potent, which is why I wanted yours to begin with. But a mated female . . ." Her gaze shifted to Jenner, still suspended by her magic. "Do you love him, Bria? Nothing is more powerful than a self-less love."

"I love him," Bria said loud enough for Jenner to hear. She slowly brought her right hand down to her side and let it wander behind her back to where she'd sheathed the trio of short knives. "More than anything or anyone else in this world."

Astrid bestowed upon Bria a slow, indulgent smile. "I'm so glad to hear it. And what about you, vampire?" Her shrewd gaze went to Jenner. "Would you sacrifice yourself for her? There's power in sacrifice as well."

"I would," Jenner said. "Anything for her."

His words punched through Bria and caused her chest to ache with a swell of emotion. Astrid bent over Bria's wrist, her mouth poised to latch over the puncture she'd made. Bria seized one of the knives from its sheath and brought her arm around whip quick. With a forceful up-ward stab she speared the witch's throat. Astrid took a stumbling step back, clawing at the knife still protruding from her skin. Bria retrieved a second knife and in a blur of motion drove it into Astrid's chest.

"I love Jenner," Bria snarled close to the necromancer's astonished face. "And not you or anyone else is *ever* going to take me from him."

CHAPTER
32

The force that held Jenner immobile released him the second Bria ran her petite blade into Astrid's chest. Though the witch was momentarily stunned, she was far from impotent and still had the wendigo at her command. Bria . . . his brave, clever mate had bought him the distraction that he needed to end this once and for all. Jenner wasn't about to let her moment of bravery go to waste.

Within seconds Jenner was surrounded by activity. Bria held her last knife out in front of her as though the blade would deter the wendigo from attacking. Ronan rushed forward, gun drawn and a long dagger in his opposite hand. Naya remained behind him, but magic gathered in her palm and her own dagger was held aloft. No longer at a disadvantage, Jenner was more than ready to put the necromancer down once and for all.

Astrid let out an enraged shriek. She plucked the blade from her throat. Blood welled from her mouth as she coughed and spluttered. Jenner didn't waste a second throwing his body over hers, pinning her to the pavement. The wendigo let out a tortured bellow and lurched forward, but Naya managed to keep the thing immobile through the use of her own magic so it couldn't get to Jenner.

"Father, please," Bria urged. "Be still. This will all be over soon."

The wendigo turned toward Bria, its baleful eyes almost sad. Astrid struggled against Jenner, clawed with the sharp tips of her nails until blood ran from the wounds and down his forearms. He remembered what she'd said about the power that blood contained. If she managed to ingest it, to draw on its power somehow, they'd all be fucked.

Without hesitation Jenner stabbed down into the witch's chest. Power exploded from her, nearly knocking him from her body. The sensation of knives piercing his skin, of flames blistering him with their heat, seized him, but Jenner fought against the blinding pain and stabbed down again, harder, until he'd opened her up. Gods, he hoped that Bria looked away, that she'd shielded her eyes from the sheer violence of this moment. This wasn't what Jenner wanted for her, but he wouldn't shy from what had to be done to protect her.

"Father, no!" Bria reached out and caught the wendigo round the neck as it lunged once again for Jenner.

"Gods-damn it, Bria! Run! Get the hell out of here!" If the creature bit her, managed to give her even a scratch, it would surely kill her.

"No! I'm not leaving you!"

The desperation of her tone sent chills down Jenner's spine. He cut down again and again, his stomach turning with every downward stroke until nothing stood between him and the witch's beating heart. There wasn't anything he wouldn't do for Bria. *Nothing.* He severed the organ from Astrid's body in a single forceful stroke and tossed it away with disgust.

Jenner watched as Naya pushed forward despite the grip Ronan had on her wrist. She took the strange citrine dagger and ran it through the witch's discarded heart. Another blast of power exploded around them, this time knocking them all to the ground. Jenner landed a good ten feet from the witch's still body and watched as her heart shriveled into a blackened mass and then crumbled into a pile of ash. *Jesus fucking Christ.* Her body soon followed. Her alabaster skin darkened and charred. The fine strands of her silver hair turned to midnight black and then stark white. Her bright eyes dulled with lifelessness and sank away as her body disintegrated and crumbled into nothing but black bits of ash.

The wendigo crumpled not far from Bria. It let out a series of painful whines before it brought its head up and howled. Bria threw herself on top of its body as mournful sobs racked her. Her grief broke Jenner's heart into myriad shards. Her pain was his own and it cut him to the bone.

He went to his mate's side. Gently, he put his arms around her and urged her away. Despite her feelings, despite the hurt she felt, she was still in harm's way and Jenner had to keep her safe even if that meant taking her away from a father she'd never gotten the chance to meet.

"No, Jenner." Bria's refusal of him carried little weight as she relaxed against him. "No!"

He slumped back and pulled Bria tight against him. His arms came around her and he rocked her as he whispered words of reassurance and love in her ear. "I know, love. I know. I've got you, Bria. Everything's going to be okay. I love you. I love you so much."

The wendigo brought its milky gaze to Bria. For the briefest moment its eyes lit with recognition and affection. A peaceful calm settled over William's expression, and with one last chuff of breath its body disintegrated into ash.

Two centuries of vengeance, pain, and fear dissipated in the cool midnight breeze, swirling about their bodies in a morbid cloud of dark particles. Bria turned in Jenner's embrace and clung to him as her tears flowed freely. Powerful sobs shook her and with each one Jenner held her a little tighter, as though his love for her could single-handedly banish the pain that she endured.

"I love you, Bria." The words tumbled from Jenner's mouth in a whisper. He'd never loved anything as much as he did this brave female in his arms. "I love you." She clutched at him, holding on as though her life depended on it. "I love you."

It shouldn't have hurt so much. She'd never known her father. Hadn't even known the truth of what had become of him until a few short weeks ago. And yet the pain of losing him, of realizing that she'd never get to know this male who was worth her mother's rash sacrifices, was almost more than Bria could bear.

"I love you, Bria. I love you. I love you."

Jenner's softly spoken endearments washed over in a rush of warmth. She'd done what she'd set out to do. She'd *survived*. Her future no longer loomed bleak and frightening before her. Threats no longer hung over her head. Bria was finally *free*.

"I love you, too." The words pushed past the thickness of emotion that clogged her throat. "I'm so sorry I left, Jenner. I'll never do it again."

"That's good." The slightest lilt of humor accented Jenner's gruff voice. "Because if you do, I'll hunt you to the ends of the earth. You scared the shit out of me, *viaton*. Don't ever scare me again."

Viaton. Bria used to think that when Jenner called her that he insinuated that her innocence made her weak. Now she knew better. When called her *viaton,* his dark voice so full of emotion, she felt *cherished.* "I won't," she promised. "As long as you promise me the same."

"I promise. And no life-or-death situations. For now at least."

She knew avoiding danger was a promise neither of them could keep. The future was an uncertain thing and Fate could be fickle. Still Bria could accept *for now.* "As long as we're together," she murmured against his strong chest, "nothing else matters."

"Nothing," Jenner agreed.

Bria's life couldn't be more perfect. Whatever else happened, she was loved.

The sound of footsteps approaching drew Bria's attention. She looked up through the blur of tears to see Ronan and Naya stop close to where she and Jenner sat. Ronan surveyed their surroundings and let out a slow breath. "That shit was *intense,*" he said. "Everyone all right?"

Bria nodded.

"Yeah," Jenner rasped. "You?"

"We're all good."

"Thank you," Bria managed to say through a fresh bout of tears. "I don't think we would have managed without your help."

"Yeah, well, you obviously didn't need me," Ronan remarked. "Naya is the real badass in this situation. Though"—he turned to his mate—"I think we're going to have a nice long talk about *not* running balls out into dangerous situations from here on out."

"Please," Naya scoffed. "Jenner and Bria did all of the heavy lifting. I'm just glad I was here to absorb the residual magic in the necromancer's heart. It's dark as hell. I need to get home and discharge it from my dagger. I don't want it contained in the blade for any longer than necessary."

"It's going to have to wait a while longer, unfortunately." Ronan checked his phone and stuffed it back in his pocket. "I'm two hours late to pick up Saeed. If I don't get my ass in gear, Mikhail is going to blow a blood vessel."

"Go," Jenner said. "I'll explain to Mikhail."

Ronan reached down to give Jenner a robust pat on the back. "Later."

Jenner jerked his chin in response.

"Bria," Naya said. "If you need anything, call me." She turned and took off at a slow jog to catch up with her mate.

Minutes passed and Bria remained still, held tight in Jenner's arms. The security she felt, the peace and contentment, calmed her by slow degrees until her breaths no longer hitched in her chest. Weariness stole over her. A bone-deep exhaustion of both body and spirit. She wanted to sleep, right here and now with nothing more than Jenner's strength to support her.

"I never should have left," she said again quietly against his chest. "I'm sorry."

"I knew I'd pushed you too far." Jenner's gruff voice washed over her. "The second I walked out the door, I regretted laying down that mandate."

"I should have trusted you," Bria countered. "You were only trying to protect me."

"And I should have known that you're strong enough to protect yourself. I underestimated you, and I promise that I never will again."

Bria's heart swelled with emotion. So many highs and lows in one night. "Let's agree to never underestimate each other again," she said.

"Sounds good to me." A space of silence passed and Jenner lowered his mouth close to Bria's ear. His warm breath brushed the outer shell and she shivered. "Let me take you home."

She nearly asked him for another minute. The thought of leaving this place where she'd watched the creature that had once been her father die filled her with sorrow. It was all she had of him, no matter how morbid the memory, and she wasn't sure she was ready to leave it behind. Jenner brushed her hair away from her face and laid his lips to her temple.

There was nothing here for Bria but sadness and death. From the moment she'd woken a vampire Bria had sought nothing but happiness and life. It was about damned time she got on with it.

She pulled back to look at her mate. He was her strength. Her happiness. Her love. "Let's go home."

CHAPTER
33

Mikhail paced the confines of his study. It was nearly sunrise and the night had gotten so damned far out of hand,
there seemed no hope of reining it back in. He'd planned
to turn Saeed, to take the first step toward resurrecting
the infrastructure of power within the covens. Saeed
would be the first coven master to be turned, but if Ronan
didn't hurry the hell up and get him to the house they'd
have to wait until sunset tomorrow to begin the process.
Mikhail wasn't interested in wasting another minute, let
alone another hour.

From the sounds of Ronan's phone call, Mikhail would
be in for an earful when they arrived. Gods, was there to
be no peace for any of them? Danger lurked around every
corner. He laughed at the thought that the Sortiari was no
longer at the top of their list of concerns.

The sound of his cell phone distracted Mikhail from
his thoughts and he circled back around to his desk to
retrieve it. The "unknown" that flashed on the caller ID
gave him pause as he swiped his finger across the screen
and brought the phone to his ear. "Yes?"

"This is Tristan McAlister."

Gods-damn it. Perhaps Mikhail had counted his birds before they'd hatched. The director of the Sortiari couldn't have called at a worse time. And how had the bastard gotten Mikhail's number? McAlister was certainly crafty. Mikhail expected Ronan at any minute. The urge to tell the director to fuck off burned in Mikhail's throat, but he swallowed it down. He could be civilized. For now. "What can I do for you, Mr. McAlister?"

The director gave a short laugh. "Call me Tristan."

That he thought they could be cordial after centuries of war and genocide truly spoke to the director's arrogance. The utter destruction of his race might have been water under the bridge for the guardians of Fate, but Mikhail wasn't so forgiving. "What can I do for you, Mr. McAlister?" Mikhail repeated.

The director cleared his throat on the other end of the line. "All right then, I'll get straight to business. We'd like to see the child."

A finger of dread stroked down Mikhail's spine. He already had so much to worry about. Saeed, Jenner, Gregor . . . *gods, Chelle*. Not to mention his pregnant mate, who was due to give birth at any moment. This wasn't a development he was even remotely interested in addressing yet. "I'm not sure that will be possible at this time." There was no use in pretending that he didn't know what child McAlister referred to. Vanessa had been on the Sortiari's radar for months.

"I think that the both of us are interested in maintaining peace. Why undo all of the progress we've made to that end by turning down a simple invitation?"

Progress? Is that how the Sortiari saw it? Mikhail wanted to laugh. "Are you saying that if I deny you access to the child you'll consider it an act of aggression?"

McAlister huffed. "I'm not interested in fighting with

you. It's a simple request, wouldn't you agree? Besides, you can't keep her from us, Aristov. Fate will not be denied."

Of course not. And that's what worried Mikhail. Soon Vanessa's mother would be fit enough to care for her. What then? His resources weren't what he needed them to be. His forces, scant. He simply didn't have the bodies to protect Claire and their child, his property, covens of dhampirs from slayer attacks, *and* a human child and her mother.

"You can't possibly think we'd harm her?"

McAlister's question hung in the air. Mikhail knew that the Sortiari had ordered that Vanessa be spared when Gregor had taken Claire. The guardians of Fate seemed to change their minds on a whim, however, and that had Mikhail worried. He swallowed down a derisive snort. For something that should be carved in stone, Fate certainly was a fickle bitch.

"You'll forgive me if I'm inclined to make my own conclusions as to your motives."

"We've made no move to remove her from your custody."

This time Mikhail did nothing to hide his derision. "As though you could have." Gods, he wished the Sortiari would remove themselves from the city once and for all. The world was vast. Why set up shop in his backyard?

"You forget who we are, Mikhail."

"Don't think I'll *ever* forget who you are or what you're capable of!" Mikhail snapped. "What of your slayers, McAlister? Will you be bringing them along?"

McAlister sighed on the other end of the line. "You have no reason to worry about the berserkers. They answer to me and they're under control. There will be no more attacks on any dhampir covens." Either McAlister was bluffing or he had no idea that Gregor was planning a coup. "Surely we can compromise. I'm amicable to meeting in a neutral location. You may bring your mate, and one other representative besides yourself. And likewise, I will bring two members of our organization with me. The playing field will be level and after I've had a chance to meet the child and speak with her—in your presence of course—we can go our separate ways."

Claire would *not* be in attendance. For all Mikhail knew, McAlister was using Vanessa as an excuse to learn more about his mate. Rumors swirled about her uniqueness. No doubt the Sortiari's curiosity had been piqued as well. "I will bring two representatives along with myself and the child. I will meet with you in one month's time at a location of *my* choosing, at sunset."

McAlister harrumphed. The bastard actually had the nerve to act offended by Mikhail's demands. "Why a month?"

Mikhail wasn't about to leave Claire's side until well after their child was born. "I have other matters that require my attention. Surely a man in a position such as yours understands that?"

Silence stretched between them. "All right, then. One month. I'll contact you one week prior to finalize the arrangements."

"Very well," Mikhail responded. The sound of the front door opening and closing drew his attention. "If there's nothing else, I'll bid you a good day."

"No," McAlister said. "I think we've settled everything for now. Good day."

He disconnected the call and Mikhail tossed his phone down on the desk.

A long sigh slipped from between his lips and he pinched the bridge of his nose between his thumb and finger. *One more potential crisis to worry about—*

"Better late than never, huh?" Ronan strode into

Mikhail's office with Saeed and two other dhampirs behind him.

"You're certainly cutting it close," Mikhail groused. "The sun's about to rise."

"Blame Jenner," Ronan said with a grin. "He's the one out killing necromancers and wendigoes hours before dawn."

Mikhail raised a brow. It certainly had been a busy night. "Where is Jenner?" He'd no doubt be receiving another call from Thomas Fairchild, since Jenner had nearly turned the male's coven upside down in search of his mate earlier in the night. "Is Bria with him?"

"She is," Ronan replied. "You probably won't see him until sunset tomorrow, though. Believe me when I tell you it's been one hell of a night."

Mikhail had no doubt.

He turned to Saeed. The male exuded strength. His dark eyes met Mikhail's and he gave a shallow nod of his head. Mikhail mused that Saeed must have looked much like Osiris, the vampire who'd sired them all. The male had strength, intelligence, and a quick temper that made him a formidable dhampir. No doubt he'd make a truly fearsome vampire. Thank the gods, he'd sworn allegiance to Mikhail.

"I apologize for the delay," Mikhail said. "As you can see, our small numbers make for complications when trouble arises."

"Then hopefully my presence here will put you on the road to righting that weakness," Saeed answered in his smooth, deep voice.

"I think it will," Mikhail said.

"This is Sasha and Diego." Saeed indicated the dhampirs who'd come in behind him.

Mikhail offered them both a nod of acknowledgment. Saeed had brought the male and female to feed him once his transition was complete. Mikhail had warned him that his need for blood would be ravenous and was glad to see that he had taken the words to heart.

"I don't see any point in wasting more time; do you? Sunrise isn't far off, so I think we'd better get to it."

Saeed nodded. "I'm ready."

"You'll stay?" Mikhail asked Ronan.

"Yeah. Naya's wiped, I'm sure she's already in bed and I told her that I wouldn't be home until sundown."

"Good." Mikhail held his hand out to indicate the doorway, and Saeed and his coven members stepped out into the hallway. Mikhail followed after them. "Let me know when Jenner shows up."

"Will do," Ronan said.

Another vampire would soon fill their ranks. Mikhail couldn't help but be pleased.

The blackout blinds would come down over the windows in Jenner's apartment in less than an hour to shut out the sun for the rest of the day. He wasn't tired, though. Didn't feel the onset of exhaustion that usually weighed upon him in the moments before daybreak. A dry burn chafed his throat and unsatisfied need built within him.

They'd been separated for little more than twenty-four hours, but if you'd asked Jenner he hadn't seen his mate— felt the comfort of her body or tasted the sweet nectar of her blood—for years. His emotions had run the gamut: fear, rage, despair, sorrow. . . . His chest ached from the buildup. Jenner's limbs quaked, his hands balled into fists. If he didn't purge soon he'd fucking explode.

He needed Bria to survive. And he'd almost lost her tonight.

She stood at the living room window and looked out at the city lights below. Her dark hair tumbled over her shoulders in a riot of curls that Jenner couldn't help but want to comb his fingers through. With her shoulders thrown back, her spine straight, she was the very picture of strength. His Bria. *His.* For the hundredth time he marveled that Fate had seen fit to tether his soul to such an extraordinary female.

Jenner came up behind her and buried his face in her hair, inhaling the intoxicating lilac scent. His arms came around her and he hugged her tight against his chest. Bria's hands came to rest on his forearms and she let her head fall back against his shoulder, baring the delicate column of her throat to him. Jenner's thirst blazed and his secondary fangs throbbed in his gums.

He put his lips to the creamy skin at her neck. A soft kiss followed with a slow flick of his tongue that caused Bria to sigh. The sweet sound tightened his sac and hardened his cock in an instant. There wouldn't be a day of his existence that his body didn't yearn for hers. One hand ventured up to cup her breast and Bria arched into his touch. Through the fabric of her shirt her nipple hardened beneath his palm, and Jenner stroked the peak, swirled his fingers over it until it further pearled under his ministrations.

Bria let out a low whimper and her muscles tightened against him. Jenner released his grip on her long enough to strip off her shirt and remove her bra. He brought his gaze up to the large picture window and stared with appreciation at her reflection in the glass. Her eyes met his and a rush of molten lust shot through Jenner's system. Cupping both of her breasts, he teased her, plucking at the rosy tips until Bria's breath came in quick pants and her moans of pleasure grew louder.

He reached down and slid her pants and her underwear down her thighs. Bria kicked the garments from around her ankles and Jenner sucked in a sharp breath at the sight of his mate's naked reflection in the glass. So brazen. So unashamed. The complete opposite of the female her uncle had hoped to raise. Jenner reached down between her thighs. His fingers met her slick arousal and an appreciative groan built in his chest. She was ready for him, dripping, and it caused his cock to throb hot and hard behind his fly.

Bria's expression melted into one of ecstasy. Her lips parted with her quickened breaths and her eyes held his through the reflection in the darkened window. Jenner couldn't remember a time he'd ever been so gods-damned aroused just watching Bria's expression, her body as she reacted to his touch. She opened her legs wider and Jenner found her clit with the tip of his finger. He swirled a slow circle while he rolled her nipple with his other hand. Bria gasped and her knees buckled, but Jenner's grasp on her kept her upright.

She reached around to cup the back of his neck and her nails dug into his skin. *Gods, yes.* The bite of pain amped him up, got him even harder. He continued to stroke her, gentle swirls of his finger and light flicks that would bring Bria close to the edge, but not enough to allow her to topple over it. The sweet sounds of her whimpers graduated into passionate cries. Her thighs trembled around his hand. She was so damned slick that her wetness spread over his palm and dripped down her thighs.

"I need you inside of me," Bria gasped. She took a handful of his short hair into her fist and tugged. "Please, Jenner."

"Not yet, love." He wanted nothing more than to pound into her tight heat, but Jenner enjoyed watching her through the reflection too damned much to stop. Her stomach muscles flexed and released beneath his forearm as Jenner increased the pressure on her clit. The quaver in her thighs intensified. He bent over her and sank his fangs into the delicate flesh at Bria's throat.

He brought his gaze to the window as he drank from her. Bria cried out as the orgasm took her. An expression of pure bliss settled on her beautiful face and her muscles bunched and flexed with every powerful spasm. Her thighs tightened around Jenner's hand and he stroked her slowly, light, gentle passes that brought her down from the high by small degrees. He continued to suckle at her throat, each deep pull bringing with it the heady nectar of her blood that coated his tongue like honey.

When he'd had his fill Jenner closed the punctures. He'd never seen anything so lovely as Bria's reflection as she came for him. He enjoyed it so much that he considered outfitting the bedroom with floor-to-ceiling mirrors so that he could watch her from every angle imaginable.

His own need crested to the point that Jenner could no longer control it. He pressed Bria fully against the pane of glass. He jerked her hips back and she spread her legs wide for him, bracing herself by placing her palms flush to the window. With shaking fingers Jenner unfastened his pants. His cock sprang free and he shoved his jeans down around his ass. He took the heavy length of his erection in his hand and squeezed before stroking himself. Just once to relieve some of the built-up pressure. A growl gathered in Jenner's chest. He guided the head of his cock to Bria's pussy and ran the sensitive head through her slick folds. They both let out a sound that was equal parts pleasure and torture and Jenner slid home in a single deep thrust.

"Oh, gods!"

Bria's impassioned cry nearly caused Jenner to go off. He breathed through the sensation, willing his body to hold off. He wasn't about to come the second he entered her. His fingers gripped her hips, sinking into Bria's yielding flesh. She pushed against him and rolled her hips. The angle put pressure on the head of his cock and Jenner pushed deeper to intensify it.

"Bria," Jenner growled close to her ear as he bent over her. He pulled out to the tip and plunged back in, pressing Bria hard against the window. "You feel so fucking good." He repeated the motion and she cried out. "So gods-damned tight." She reached back with one hand and gripped his thigh as Jenner's thrusts increased in pace and force. "So wet."

"Harder," Bria said on a gasp of breath. "Please, Jenner. I need you deeper."

Her pleading words sent him into a frenzy. He fucked her with abandon; the sound of her palms slapping against the glass with every deep thrust only added to his pleasure as he took her with all of the force he could muster. He held nothing back from her, and still it didn't seem like enough. He cupped one of her breasts in his palm and squeezed and teased the already swollen nipple. Bria's pussy clenched around his cock, pinching the head just right. Unable to keep himself from tasting her while he fucked her, Jenner buried his fangs at the juncture of where her shoulder met her neck.

Bria came again with a strangled cry. Her pussy squeezed him tight and Jenner toppled over the edge. He pulled away from her throat with a roar as wave after wave of pleasure stole over him. His cock jerked as Bria milked him with every tight contraction and he continued to thrust deep inside of her until he had nothing more to give. Jenner scored his tongue and sealed the punctures he made at her neck before resting his forehead on Bria's shoulder. Deep shuddering breaths rocked them both as they slowly came down from the high.

A light sheen of sweat glistened on Bria's skin, giving her an almost luminescent quality in the early-morning light. The eastern sky brightened to a burnt orange and the daylight shutters came down over the windows as though closing the curtain on their sensual performance.

Jenner cradled Bria in his arms and collapsed into a nearby chair. He gathered her close and breathed her scent deep into his lungs. He'd never felt more content. So *right*. Bria was what he needed to make him feel complete. Sated, despite his constant want of her. She filled the endless void, anchored him against the restlessness that had possessed him after his transition. Bria hadn't simply tethered his soul. She *was* his soul. His everything. His love.

"If that's the welcome home I can expect, maybe I'll take a day away more often." Her lazy, contented voice brushed his senses like myriad feathers.

"I'll never give you reason to go if you promise never to leave my side for even an hour."

"Not even an hour?" Bria teased. "You'll get sick of me if I cling to you like that."

"Never." Jenner pulled her tighter against his body and laid a kiss to her temple. "I want you by my side every second of every minute for the rest of my existence."

"Okay," Bria said with a dramatic sigh. "You asked for it."

Bria turned in his embrace. She kissed him, a slow, sensual caress ending with a flick of her tongue that stirred his cock once again. Jenner raised a brow in question and Bria responded with a deep, throaty chuckle. "What? Did you think we were done so soon? I'm not even close to being ready to call it a day."

Gods, she was extraordinary.

CHAPTER
34

Bria lay beneath the covers, snuggled against the heat of Jenner's body. A contented smile curved her lips as she recalled the hours they'd spent pleasuring each another. Jenner had made love to her slowly with agonizing precision and lazy, shallow thrusts of his hips that drew out her pleasure and had Bria growling her frustration before he brought her to orgasm. He'd fucked her hard and deep, each violent thrust a claim on her body that sent her to dizzying heights of ecstasy that left her breathless and begging for more.

He'd taken the vein at her throat and at her thigh. He'd suckled from punctures in her breasts, her wrists, the back of her neck. And she'd taken her fill from him, giving in to her animal nature as she clamped her jaws down hard enough to tear Jenner's flesh from the impact of her bite. Jenner wanted her wild and unfettered and he'd encouraged Bria to give herself over to that abandon. She'd never felt more comfortable in her own skin, as though she was finally who she was meant to be.

Events of the previous night flickered through Bria's

THE DARK VAMPIRE · 367

mind and she tucked herself closer to her mate's big body. There had been so much sorrow, so much fear, but also love unlike anything she thought she could ever feel for another. Bria had faced her trials and come through them a stronger female. A better female. And if given the opportunity to do it all over again she wouldn't have changed a thing.

The sound of the blinds retracting from the windows echoed around the apartment and Jenner stirred beside her. His arms came around her and he rolled Bria until she lay fully on top of him. "Did you sleep well?" Voice still thick and husky with sleep, the sound sent a dark, delicious shiver over Bria's skin.

"I did," she murmured. "Did you?"

The hard, silky length of his erection pressed against the crease of her ass and he rolled his hips before letting out a low groan. "Mmmm. Yes."

Another gentle thrust of his hips further ignited Bria's lust and a rush of wetness spread between her thighs. Jenner's eyes remained closed. Bria reached up and braced her palms against his wrists that rested on the pillow above his head. She levered herself up and slid down over his erection, taking him deep inside of her. Bria let out a contented purr and Jenner's eyes opened to reveal pupils rimmed with brilliant silver.

His heated gaze raked over her before he reached up to cup her breasts. Bria arched into his touch as she moved her hips over him and let her head fall back on her shoulders. Jenner filled her, stretched her inner walls. With every roll of her hips he seemed to swell inside of her, creating delicious friction that turned her bones soft and set her blood on fire.

Bria took him as deep as she could and increased her pace. Jenner shifted, gripping her hip in one hand as he took the other and wrapped his long fingers around her throat. He held her not tightly but with just enough pressure to convey his intent. He'd finally let the wall of his restraint crumble and it thrilled Bria to no end.

Rough. Wild. Intense. Focused. Jenner fucked like he lived: without shame or apology. Gods, how she loved it! Bria brought her legs up and braced her feet on the mattress in order to take him deeper still. She ground her hips into his as a frustrated growl built in her throat. She teetered on the edge and she was desperate to topple over it.

"Fuck me, Bria," Jenner grated from between clenched teeth. "Take it all."

She took everything he could give her. He was so deep, filled her so completely, that Bria didn't know how much more of the blinding pleasure she could take. She threw her head back on her shoulders and rode him harder, faster, until the orgasm exploded through her. A supernova of sensation that caused her muscles to seize and her breath to catch.

Jenner's orgasm stole over him not a second later. His back bowed off the mattress and his shout echoed in the quiet bedroom. A deep groove cut into his brow and his muscles flexed as he thrust his hips up wildly to meet hers. Bria stared, intoxicated by the sight of him. Jenner was the most magnificent male she'd ever known. She'd spend the rest of her life thankful for the gift she'd been given.

Bria was the luckiest female alive.

Jenner wanted nothing more than to be back at his apartment with Bria. Naked. Spending the night enjoying her body until sunrise and exhaustion put them both down. Duty called, however, and Mikhail needed him. Balance between his want of his mate and, you know, everyday life was still not quite within his grasp. Now that the evil that hunted Bria had been taken care of and he no longer feared for her safety, he hoped that they'd soon fall into a rhythm that would put him more at ease. Until then, he was bound to remain on edge and stay a cranky son of a bitch whenever anything took him from his mate's side.

Mikhail's house was quiet when Jenner walked in. He found Claire in the kitchen with Vanessa. The girl sat on one of the high bar stools, schoolbooks and papers strewn about the bar. She worked on her homework while Claire flipped her finger across the screen of her iPad.

"Hey." She looked up from what she was doing and greeted Jenner. "Everything okay?"

"Yeah. Bria doesn't have anything to worry about anymore."

"That's good," Claire said as though an evil necromancer hunting his mate was as tame as her having a run-in with a bill collector. "But what I meant was, is everything okay between the two of you?"

Jenner appreciated her concern. He knew that Claire was fond of Bria and it warmed his heart that she'd been so eagerly accepted by those Jenner now considered his family. "It is," he said. He wasn't a share-his-feelings sort of male. Claire was just going to have to take his word for it.

"I'm glad." Her tone held genuine affection. "Everyone's upstairs. You hungry? There's some leftover fried chicken."

"Nah." Truth be told, the only thing Jenner hungered for right now was his mate's blood. Part of that whole lack of balance he'd been trying to come to terms with. "I'm good. I'll just head upstairs."

"All right," Claire said with mocking disappointment. "You don't know what you're missing, though. If you change your mind, there's plenty."

Jenner nodded and then backtracked to the foyer. He hit the stairs two at a time. He should have been here sooner, but it had been so hard to tear himself away from his mate. Bria had offered to come along, and for a moment Jenner nearly dragged her along simply so he wouldn't be bereft of her company. But he knew she was exhausted. The emotional and physical toll of the past couple of days had worn her down. So he told her to rest, to enjoy a little downtime, and he'd come home as soon as he could.

Soon wasn't soon enough.

Ronan waited at the top of the second-story landing, one massive shoulder propped against the wall. He jerked his chin in greeting and Jenner returned the gesture. "What'd I miss?"

"Not much." Ronan pushed himself away from the wall. "Saeed is in the room at the end of the hall. He brought two members of his coven to feed him once the transition is complete."

Smart male. Jenner had been ravenous after his turning. So much so that it felt as though Mikhail had a revolving door of blood donors ready to take care of him. "This is a turning point," Jenner said.

"It is." Ronan nodded. "And it's about damned time."

"Did you check on your sister?" Jenner didn't want to admit that he was worried about Lucas. The male had feelings for Bria, after all. But after seeing Chelle for the first time since her transition and witnessing the wildness it had bred in her, Jenner couldn't help but worry that the naïve male was in way over his head.

"Not yet. Saeed's been a bit of a handful. Pretty combative and disoriented. Mikhail says he's having a hard time meshing with the Collective."

Jenner snorted. "Yeah, well, it's a total mind fuck at first. No one should have that many memories stuffed inside their heads."

"No shit."

"I thought once Mikhail gave the okay on Saeed I'd head over to the guesthouse. Wanna come with?"

The sudden tang of Ronan's scent betrayed his nerves. Jenner suspected that Ronan sensed more about his twin's current state than he let on to the rest of them. In which case, he understood Ronan's trepidation in paying a visit to Chelle. "Yeah, sure."

Ronan's gaze slid toward the closed door at the end of the hall as an uncomfortable silence stretched between them. Jenner cupped the back of his neck and he tried to rub some of the tension away that pulled his muscles taut. "Look, I know you're not happy about what went down last night. But if Naya hadn't been there I don't know—"

"Don't sweat it." Ronan didn't make eye contact and his tone stiffened with the words. Jenner knew all too well the fierce protective instinct of a mated male and it must have nearly broken Ronan to see his mate throw herself into the thick of the action. Any one of them could have died and it was a gods-damned miracle they'd come out of it safely. "Believe me, it's not the first time Naya's dove into danger without realizing how bad it rattles me. Maybe I'm the one who needs to loosen up," he said with a laugh. "She knows what she can handle and what she can't. I have to trust in that."

Jenner found himself in the same situation with Bria. She'd left him because he hadn't trusted her to know what she could and couldn't handle. He'd never even given her the opportunity to prove it to him. Never again, though. As much as it might kill him to see her put herself in what could be a possibly dangerous situation, he had to trust that she wouldn't be there if she didn't think she could hack it. All he could do was support her in all things. Remain by her side and be her strength when she needed him to be.

Before either one of them was forced to further explore his feelings, Mikhail emerged from the guest room. The vampire king's drawn face and pallor were enough to tell Jenner that the male had yet to feed since turning Saeed.

"How goes?" Ronan asked.

"I'm glad we've turned him," Mikhail said on a long sigh. "There's no way I can continue to do this by myself. It's too gods-damned exhausting. Now let's hope he becomes tethered soon. If we turn the coven masters who've been vetted, they can make appeals to turn their members. The system will soon run like a well-oiled machine."

"Don't be so sure," Jenner said.

Mikhail raised a brow. Jenner knew that he should keep his mouth shut, but the reality of this elitist system needed to be drilled into the male's head.

"It's a flawed system. It's not going to run smoothly."

"I realize you think it's classist—"

"It *is* classist," Jenner stressed. "Elitist. Dhampirs who are denied transition will rise up against you. They'll leave their covens. Maybe join Siobhan. By setting stringent rules, you'll do nothing but build up your detractors."

"That will be the coven masters' jobs. To keep order and squash rebellion."

"Your father was a high king, Mikhail. Did that system work for him?"

Mikhail pursed his lips and pinned Jenner with narrowed eyes. "You've pleaded your case," he said. "And I'll take it under advisement. I don't want strife, but we *need* order."

"That's what Ronan and I are here for," Jenner said. "Order."

Mikhail gave him a robust pat on the shoulder. "True." He cast a glance toward the guest room. "We might need Lucas. The dhampirs that Saeed brought along will need to eat, to take blood, and replenish their strength before they can feed him again. I've asked Lucas to tend to Chelle, but perhaps he'll come if we ask."

"My guess is he's still here," Jenner remarked. "Chelle's pretty damned pleased with him. Ronan and I were about to go check on her."

"Good idea. Saeed is resting and he's past the worst of it. I don't think we need to keep quite as close an eye on him."

"What will you do when he's calmed?" Jenner asked. "Cut him loose?"

Mikhail held out his hand and they proceeded down the stairs. Mikhail led the way toward his study and Ronan and Jenner followed him inside.

"I have contractors coming tomorrow to soundproof this room. I've found I don't have quite the privacy I used to."

Ronan snorted. "Isn't that the fucking truth. This place went from tomb to Grand Central in nothing flat."

"I am cutting Saeed loose." Mikhail lowered his voice to below a whisper. "That's not to say we won't be keeping an eye on him. He seems to be handling the Collective now, but . . ." He raked his fingers through his hair. "I'm worried about him maintaining the grip on his sanity."

"He'll be all right," Ronan said with a shrug. "We all know how hard it is in the beginning. He just needs time."

"That's my hope," Mikhail said. "Until I know for sure, we need to keep him on a short leash."

Jenner nodded his agreement. The last thing they needed was a crazed vampire running around. Jenner himself had been starved for blood and sex post-transition, but thank the gods his mind had remained intact. He'd been on the very verge of losing his control and he had no doubt Mikhail would have put him down if he hadn't gotten his shit together.

"I think we're all on the same page. If you don't need anything else, we'll go check on Chelle," Ronan said.

"Let me know how she's doing," Mikhail said. "It's been much too quiet over there."

No shit. Time to check on the wild female. If Jenner let anything happen to Lucas he doubted Bria would ever let him live it down.

CHAPTER
35

"What's up, Bro?" Chelle said as she answered the door. "Jenner? Another minute and you guys might not have caught me at home."

Ronan stiffened beside Jenner, his anxiety palpable. It was a good thing they'd come together.

"You know you're not supposed to leave the property, Chelle," Ronan said. "Not until your thirst is more under control."

She laughed and tossed her mane of golden hair over one shoulder. Her green eyes sparked with mischief. "It's been *months*. I'm bored and want to go out. Besides, you don't need to worry about me anymore. I'm the epitome of control."

Somehow, Jenner doubted that.

Chelle turned her attention to him and flashed a sly smile. "Did you find your mate, Jenner?"

The hairs stood on the back of his neck. "I did."

"Good. Lucas will be glad to hear it. He used to worry about her, you know."

Used to. Jenner's nerves cranked up another notch.

"Where is Lucas, Chelle? Mikhail would like to speak with him."

She opened the door wide and turned. Jenner and Ronan followed her into the modest guesthouse and down the dark hallway toward the bedroom. Power radiated from Chelle, sending little jolts of electricity over Jenner's skin. Ronan looked at him from the corner of his eye, making it obvious that the male shared in Jenner's worry over his sister.

Chelle pushed the bedroom door open and stepped to one side. Lucas lay stretched out on the bed, naked. One arm was slung over his head and the other stretched over his bare chest that rose and fell with breath. Jenner relaxed by a small degree until his eye caught sight of a second set of fangs protruding from beneath the male's upper lip.

Fucking hell.

Ronan looked close to blowing his head right off his gods-damned shoulders. Anger vibrated off of him and he tensed. Chelle put her finger to her lips and closed the door. "Don't wake him," she chided her brother with a coy grin. "He's been through a lot."

Chelle had turned Lucas.

This was a fucking disaster. Jenner had known all along that not Mikhail or Chelle's own brother would have been able to control her. She'd turned Lucas without a thought to her actions. She'd probably done the deed before Jenner had come here last night. *Gods-damn it.* Had he known she'd be so impetuous, he would have demanded to see Lucas before he'd gone after Bria. He was as much to blame as anyone. They never should have left Chelle alone and unchecked. Mikhail had indeed thrown the lamb to the lion and it could never be undone.

"Get Bria," Ronan said on a breath. "I have a feeling we're going to need her."

"Yeah." Jenner was inclined to agree.

* * *

"Are you ready?"

Bria took a deep breath. "Yes."

Her own transition had been violent. She'd suffered so much pain before her uncle brought her to Mikhail's door and she'd been awoken from the bliss of death with fire coursing through her veins. Claire, Mikhail, even Lucas had seen her through those first three days when her mind wandered and her thirst raged. Had Lucas's transition been so violent? Had Ronan's sister comforted him? Had she even given him a choice in the matter?

Anger swelled within Bria like a tide. Lucas had made an arrangement with Mikhail, and Bria was positive that agreement hadn't involved his being turned at Ronan's sister's hand. Making accusations and starting fights weren't going to change what had already been done, though. Jenner warned her that Chelle was volatile. A vampire unlike any other and very powerful. Bria felt that power as a thickness in the air when she entered the guest-house at the back of Mikhail's property.

"Bria," Chelle said pleasantly as she walked through the door. Ronan's twin was quite beautiful, with long blond hair, striking green eyes, and sharp features. She sat in an overstuffed chair in the cozy living room, the remote control held aloft as she surfed through channels. "How's it hanging?"

Bria had never met Ronan's sister, but Chelle seemed comfortably familiar with her. "I'm fine." Bria bucked her chin up a notch, threw her shoulders back. "I'm here to see Lucas."

"You've already got one virile male," Chelle eyed Jenner up and down as though he were her next meal. "Now you want mine?"

"Watch it, Chelle."

She shot Jenner a petulant pout. "You're no fun, Jenner."

"And you're not funny."

"You all worry too much." Chelle tossed the remote aside and shifted her position in the chair with a flounce. "He's fine. You act as though he's going to sprout horns or mutate into a mindless, murdering beast." Her expression grew almost said and her voice dropped an octave. "Is that how you all see me?"

Bria sighed. If she'd been in Chelle's position she supposed she'd feel the same way. From what little she'd learned about Chelle, her existence must have been incredibly lonely. Bria knew all too well how disconnected the female must have felt. How isolated. Better precautions should have been taken before they'd allowed Lucas to come here, but that couldn't be changed now. She didn't sense a bit of malice from Chelle. Simply . . . loneliness.

"You're right, Chelle," Bria said. "I'm sure we're all being overly cautious. I'm just here to check on my friend. That's all."

"I knew I'd like you," Chelle replied. "All of Lucas's memories of you are happy ones."

Bria looked to Jenner. If Lucas had been turned by Mikhail the only memories that would have entered into the Collective would have been the ones from the day of his turning, on. Chelle certainly was an anomaly.

"I'm glad," Bria said without missing a beat. "Where is he?"

"Sleeping." Chelle indicated the hallway.

"For how long?"

"Since last night."

Chelle wasn't much of a conversationalist. Bria had a feeling that having her, Jenner, and Ronan standing in Chelle's living room, staring at her as though she were an animal at the zoo, wasn't doing much to put her at ease. "You and Ronan should go back to the main house," Bria suggested. "See if Mikhail needs your help with anything." Jenner opened his mouth to protest and Bria held up a hand. "I'll be fine. Trust me."

A few quiet moments passed. Jenner's gaze locked with Bria's. She sensed his doubt, the tension that pulled his muscles taut. With a gust of breath his shoulders relaxed. "All right." He leaned in and placed a slow kiss on her mouth. "I'll be close."

Bria beamed. That he'd trust her to take care of herself in this situation spoke volumes as to how far they'd come so quickly. "I'll be fine."

Once Ronan and Jenner left, Bria went into the living room and plopped down on the couch. "What are you watching?"

"*Mob Wives*," Chelle said. "These women are cuh-ray-zy."

Chelle was powerful, there was no doubt about it, but there wasn't a malicious bone in her body. She exuded life and positivity. No wonder Lucas had been drawn to her. "I like *The Bachelor*," Bria responded. "And *So You Think You Can Dance*."

"Oh my gods! Did you watch last season?" Chelle's expression became animated and a wide smile lit her face, revealing the wicked points of her fangs. "Last year's group was *so* good."

"They were," Bria agreed.

"I've gotta be honest with you, Bria. I'm going stir-crazy. If I don't get out of this house, my head's going to explode. I would kill for a caramel macchiato right now."

Bria didn't know much about Chelle's situation, but she was a pro when it came to feeling cooped up. "You seem fine to me. I don't know why everyone is so nervous."

"Maybe because I was made into a vampire by a magic coffin and now I've turned your BFF so he could join my wacked-out little coven?"

Jenner had filled Bria in on how Chelle had been turned, but she still had a hard time wrapping her mind around it.

"Crazy, right?" Chelle said to Bria's astonished expression. "Looks like all of those rumors of how we were created happen to be true."

"Did—" Bria cleared her throat. "Did Lucas ask you to turn him?"

Chelle continued to stare at the TV, watching as the group of women screamed at one another in the middle of a restaurant. Moments passed and Bria gave Chelle the time she needed to respond. "No," Chelle said. "It was an accident."

Bria's heart sank. Had Lucas asked Chelle to turn him, Bria wouldn't have worried as much. Lucas had expected Mikhail to turn him after he proved his worth. Instead, his transition had been a matter of circumstance, just like hers. "Did you hurt him?"

Chelle didn't seem offended by Bria's bluntness. A half smile quirked one corner of her full lips. "Believe me, Bria, he wasn't hurting when it happened."

A flush rose to Bria's cheeks. "I shouldn't have . . . I mean . . ."

"Relax. I know how it seems. That I seduced him, brought him over to the dark side," Chelle quirked a brow and gave a mischievous grin that made her look so much like Ronan. "It wasn't like that, though. I know about your coven. How you were raised. I hadn't planned to turn Lucas or do anything else with him." She averted her gaze back to the TV. "It just happened. It was an accident."

Bria didn't push Chelle for details. To be honest, she didn't think she wanted to hear them. She believed that Ronan's sister hadn't meant to turn Lucas. Her scent hadn't soured in the slightest with her words. "You are more than your own coven," Bria remarked. Chelle glanced at her from the corner of her eye but didn't acknowledge her. "You're your own race."

Like Chelle, Lucas would not be a part of the Collective. Maybe that was for the best. Perhaps it would mend Lucas's broken heart. Chelle could give him purpose. The life outside of Bria's uncle's coven that he'd hoped for.

"A one-man wolf pack no longer," Chelle said with a laugh. Her expression turned serious and her tone softened, "It scares the shit out of me. I've felt so alone ever since—" Her words cut off. "It's nice *not* to feel that way anymore."

Bria's heart went out to Chelle. She knew the crippling pain of isolation. Of being surrounded by people and still being utterly alone.

Chelle's head snapped up. The action made her appear wild and predatory. She'd sensed something—heard something—that even Bria's vampiric senses hadn't picked up on. "Lucas is awake," Chelle murmured. "You can go talk to him if you want."

Bria missed their earlier lighthearted banter about reality TV. The current turn of conversation had quickly become far too morose. She couldn't ignore the sudden sadness that Chelle exuded or the way it weighed down the air and made it hard to breathe. "Thank you, Chelle. I'll bring you a caramel macchiato if you'd like. For what it's worth, though, I don't think you need to stay cooped up here. Isolation isn't going to strengthen your control. You need to get back out into the world."

"You're a good egg, Bria," Chelle said. "No wonder Jenner's so into you." Chelle went back to channel surfing, all but dismissing her.

Bria turned and headed down the narrow hallway that went past the dining room and kitchen. A shiver of anticipation danced down her spine. Not necessarily a warning of danger, just a tickle against her senses that convinced her it would be a good idea to stay on her toes. She passed the bathroom and a small office and came to a stop in front of a closed oak door. Her fist rapped on the surface, three light taps, and she leaned in toward the wood. "Lucas? It's Bria. Can I come in?"

"Bria?" His voice roughened when he spoke her name. "It doesn't sound like you."

Vampiric senses were hard to get used to. Nothing sounded like it should, looked like it should. The transition was certainly a rebirth, and it took time to adjust to the change. Bria eased open the door and stepped into the room. "It's me. You just need to get used to hearing with new ears."

Bria remained close to the door. The room wasn't big, but the space she kept between herself and the bed gave her a small amount of comfort. If she sensed Lucas didn't have a grip on his control she could easily slip out the door.

"Are you all right, Lucas?" The tentative question was answered with an eerie silence that pressed down on Bria's shoulders. "Is there anything you need?"

He responded with a bitter chuff of breath that chilled Bria. She wrapped her arms around her middle as though to warm herself. Soullessness was a heavy price to pay for being turned. And though hers had been brief, Bria remembered the apathy, the dark, empty hole that had opened up inside of her.

"I didn't know the thirst would be like this," Lucas rasped. "I didn't know that I could experience need with such intensity. How is it possible to feel that and be so empty, Bria?"

She didn't have the answers for him. None of them, save Mikhail, could answer that and maybe even he couldn't articulate to Lucas what he was going through.

"Soon, you'll be tethered and that emptiness will go away."

"I'd hoped that Chelle would tether me. If I'm being honest, I'd hoped—" He choked the word off on a bitter laugh. "My hopes were foolish."

"You are anything but foolish, Lucas."

Bria took a step forward and another. Lucas sat with his back propped against the headboard, his chest bared, a sheet slung over his narrow hips. He raked a hand through the tangles of his blond hair and let out a ragged gust of breath.

"Chelle wants you to think that we slept together." Lucas spoke so low that Bria had to strain to hear him even with her superior senses. "Well, we did, but we only slept. We kissed. I held her. We comforted each other in our loneliness. But that's all." Lucas's gaze hardened; his irises shone like silver disks in the darkness. "She said she couldn't bring herself to take my virginity as well as my soul."

For as long as Bria could remember, Lucas had been her confidant and she had been his. The hollowness of his words echoed a pain that she knew he couldn't feel and yet she felt all of it for him. It bit into her heart with sharp claws. Lucas's vulnerability lent a sharp tang to his scent and Bria wrinkled her nose. He would have seen it as a rejection, but Chelle's gesture proved further to Bria that everyone's assumptions about the female were wrong.

"I think you should go, Bria." Lucas's voice further roughened and his hands clenched into fists at his sides. "My thirst isn't under control yet and your scent is making me forget that you belong to another male."

"All right, Lucas." Bria knew better than to tempt him. "But if you need me, I'm here for you."

"Good-bye, Bria."

The coldness of Lucas's parting words sent a chill over Bria's skin. She left the bedroom as quietly as she'd entered and headed back down the hallway. Chelle still sat in the living room, sprawled out on the chair. *Mob Wives* had apparently lost its appeal and now she watched a re-run of *Modern Family*.

"I was thinking," Bria said as she entered the room. Chelle made no move to acknowledge her, but she knew the female listened. "Instead of me bringing you a macchiato, why don't we go out and get one together?"

"Sure," Chelle said. She kept her attention focused on the screen. "After Lucas's thirst levels out, though. I'd thought about going out earlier, but I probably shouldn't leave him here alone."

"Of course." Chelle wasn't half as fearsome as everyone gave her credit for.

"Yes, I am," Chelle replied. "But I like you."

Bria's jaw dropped with astonishment. Chelle had heard her thoughts as surely as if Bria had spoken them. "I like you, too."

"I bet you're a good secret keeper, aren't you, Bria?"

Bria recognized the undertone of Chelle's words. "In the vault," she replied.

"I'd better go check on Lucas." Chelle pushed herself out of the chair. "His thirst is burning *my* throat."

"Thanks for letting me see him." Bria headed for the door.

"We might be a two-man wolf pack now, but Lucas doesn't belong to me, Bria. I know you're friends. Come whenever you want." She turned and flashed Bria a wicked smile. "In fact, come just to push Jenner's buttons." With a wave Chelle turned toward the hallway. "See ya around."

"Yes," Bria replied. "See ya around."

CHAPTER
36

"So much for maintaining order."

Mikhail shot a disgusted look in the direction where the guest cottage was situated. Anxiety pulled Jenner's muscles taut, but he refused to give in to his fear that Lucas—or Chelle—might harm Bria. She could take care of herself. Jenner knew that. But it would be a while before he could truly relax. The events of last night still weighed heavily on his mind, as did the realization that he could have lost her.

"What's done is done." Ronan didn't sound any happier with his sister than Mikhail did. "Honestly, Mikhail, it was bound to happen."

"I sent Lucas to her to help assuage her thirst. I did not give him to her to turn. *Gods*," Mikhail spat the word. "You know how sheltered the members of Fairchild's coven are."

"Lucas is a big boy," Jenner grumbled. Gods, the male wasn't some skinny, weak child. Nor was he so young to imply that Chelle had taken advantage of him. "I'm sure he can take care of himself."

"You saw him?"

"Bria is with him now." Jenner tried to keep the scowl from his face. He knew too well the drive of post-transition thirst. The thought of Lucas's mouth anywhere near Bria sent Jenner into a jealous rage that caused his secondary fangs to punch down violently from his gums. He dug his feet into his boots in an effort to keep from sprinting over there and coldcocking the son of a bitch on principle.

"We'll wait and see what she has to say then," Mikhail said.

"How's Saeed?" Maybe if Jenner changed the subject he'd be able to keep his shit tight.

"Good." Mikhail's demeanor relaxed as he sat back in his chair. "His control is better than I thought it would be, and now that his thirst is sated the Collective seems to have quieted in his mind. I doubt he'll need to spend another day here. I plan to send him back to his coven before sunrise."

Probably a good idea. Mikhail's property was becoming overcrowded with vampires lately and Jenner knew that having so many variables so close to his pregnant mate had begun to wear on him.

"Saeed is the least of my concerns right now," Mikhail remarked. "And strangely enough, so is Chelle. Tristan McAlister contacted me just before sunrise yesterday."

Ronan's eyes widened. "What did that fucker want?"

"Vanessa," Mikhail said. "He wants to get a glimpse of the girl and so he's brokering a tentative peace to get it done."

"Right," Ronan spat. "As if the Sortiari has any interest in peace."

"He agreed to a location of my choosing. Him. Me. Two representatives each and Vanessa. He wanted to meet immediately, but I pushed him back to a month."

"You can't be seriously considering his request?" Ronan said.

Mikhail smirked. "He claims to have the slayers in check."

Jenner snorted. "That's reason enough not to trust the bastard. We know it's a lie."

"True, but our knowing gives us the upper hand, don't you think?"

Jenner regarded his king. Mikhail was an intelligent male, though perhaps a little too eager to get his eyes on the Sortiari's enigmatic director. "Or you could be giving those berserker bastards exactly what they want: an opportunity to take out the both of you in one fell swoop."

Mikhail nodded as though he'd considered the possibility. "Regardless, we won't be able to keep McAlister from the girl forever. And I think we've learned over the course of the past month that locking someone away from the world in the name of protecting them can have disastrous effects."

A lesson hard learned by all of them. Jenner had tried to keep Bria locked away and he'd almost lost her because of it. They'd isolated Chelle and she'd been forced to turn Lucas in order to have another creature with which to share a connection.

"The longer we keep Vanessa from him, the more his obsession with her will grow." Mikhail paused, thoughtful. "I must admit, I'm curious myself. Perhaps McAlister will give something away that might clue us in as to why she's so special."

"Does Claire know?" Ronan asked the most important question. Claire loved the child like she was her own. Surely Claire wouldn't allow for Mikhail to take Vanessa to McAlister.

Mikhail kept his gaze focused on some far-off point.

"No. She has enough to worry about right now. The girl's mother will be released from the facility she's in soon and Claire will have the baby to think about. She's already too worried over things she has no control over. I don't want to add to that stress."

"If you take that girl out from under her nose, you'll have more than McAlister to worry about." Claire was a feisty female. No doubt she'd lay Mikhail out if he practiced subversion with her.

Mikhail sighed. He turned to look at Jenner, lips pursed. "You're probably right. Which is why I put McAlister off for a month. It gives us time to do our own recon, find out what we can about Gregor's plot to overthrow the Sortiari, and perhaps learn more about this rogue wolf that's been sniffing Siobhan out."

A lot of fucking work to accomplish over a scant four weeks.

"We can worry about all of that later," Mikhail said as though the subject of McAlister and Gregor no longer held his attention. "Tell me more about what happened with the necromancer."

For the next half hour Jenner filled Mikhail in on what had happened after he and Bria had left for his apartment. Mikhail listened intently and only Ronan interrupted to add his own details to the story. The words Jenner spoke began to bleed into one another in his mind as he regurgitated the story. His mind wasn't in the moment anymore. It was across the property where Bria more than likely sat with Lucas.

"Has anyone notified Fairchild?" Mikhail asked.

Jenner came back to the moment and shook his head. "No. There hasn't been time."

"I'd like to see the look on that smug bastard's face when he finds out that you've managed to rectify in a matter of weeks something he took centuries to fuck up," Mikhail said.

"You're welcome to deliver the news yourself if you want." Jenner wasn't interested in seeing Thomas Fairchild ever again.

"No," Mikhail replied. "I think it's best he hear it from you. I would appreciate it, though, if you offered him a gentle reminder of where he agreed to place his allegiance. Especially now that Lucas has been turned. It's been suggested that the male has fickle tendencies."

Thomas had certainly made that apparent the night Jenner had shown up at his compound looking for Bria. The male had the nerve to act offended that his privacy had been violated and proclaimed to Jenner that members of Mikhail's household were no longer welcome, since the king had seen fit to "steal" members of his coven. Jenner wouldn't mind rattling the male's chain a bit.

"I can do that. I'll tell him about Lucas, too, if you want." The idea gave Jenner a perverse sense of satisfaction. "I have to warn you, though. Don't expect to see much of Fairchild in the future. And if you ever need him for anything, he'll more than likely have to be pushed into doing it."

Mikhail sighed. "Not the way I'd like to conduct business with him, but so be it. He needs to learn to honor his obligations."

A knot twisted and then unfurled in Jenner's gut. He was glad that, at least once, Fairchild had seen fit to run away from familial obligations.

Bria crossed the grounds back to the main house. So much had changed in her life over the course of a few short weeks. She had trouble wrapping her mind around it all. She'd be glad to put the whirlwind of change behind her and settle into a rhythm. Jenner had given her the opportunity for a life she never thought she'd have. Such a magnificent male. Bria had never loved anyone more than she did him.

A presence to her right drew Bria's attention and she started. A male stepped from the shadows. His bright smile stood in stark contrast to his dark skin and even darker eyes. The wicked points of his fangs came down over his bottom lip to nip the skin before he licked the blood away. His gaze burned with curiosity, one brow arched as he regarded her.

"You're Jenner's mate." His midnight voice shivered over her, almost sinister. "I smell him on you."

What a completely creepy way to greet someone. Bria didn't know who this male was, but she sensed he could be dangerous when he wanted to be. Vampires seemed to be coming out of the woodwork tonight. How many more, she wondered, would she encounter before sunrise?

"I am." She wanted to follow that up with, *And he'll rip your arms off if you try anything shady.*

He flashed a deadly smile. For a moment he studied her before recognition lit in his eyes. "I know who you are," the male said. "You belong to Thomas Fairchild's coven. You're his niece, if I'm not mistaken."

"Yes."

Low laughter rumbled in his chest. "Your transition must have been quite a blow to him. I've seen your father." His words gave Bria pause. Her heart rate increased as a manic light shone in the male's eyes. "In the Collective. So many vampires. So many memories that whisper to me."

Bria didn't bother responding. Whoever he was, she didn't like the wild glint in his gaze. "I need to get back to the house," she said. "Mikhail and Jenner are waiting."

He bent low and swept his hand out in front of him. "May the rest of the night treat you well."

Bria cast him one last furtive look before she hustled back to the house.

A wave of relief washed over Bria when she entered Mikhail's study. Jenner's relief. He turned to face her and his hard expression softened the moment he laid eyes on her. She smiled and crossed the room toward him, allowing herself to be wrapped in his embrace.

"Do I even want to hear the sordid details?" Ronan asked.

"First, you *all* worry too much." Jenner's grip around her torso tightened and she bit back a grin. "Chelle isn't half as volatile as you all make her out to be. She's been shut up in that tiny house for the gods know how long and she's going stir-crazy. I think she's been more than accommodating by staying put, but there's no reason why she has to remain locked up like an animal that hasn't been housebroken."

Ronan and Mikhail dropped their gazes. Though Bria couldn't see Jenner behind her, she hoped that he was just as ashamed as the other two. She shook her head. *High-handed males.*

"You're right, Bria," Mikhail said. "We've been unfair with Chelle. I'll be sure to apologize to her."

Score a point for ladies! Bria tried not to feel too smug, since she was going to follow up her championing of Chelle with a ding to her control. "She claims that she turned Lucas on accident. That she became . . . overzealous."

Ronan let out a chuff of breath. "Not volatile? Jesus fucking Christ."

Bria expected Ronan to be hard on his sister. She wasn't going to let it slide, though. "Aside from throwing dhampirs to her like fresh meat to tigers at the zoo, what have any of you done to help her learn to exercise control?" She turned to look up at Jenner and then Mikhail, pinning each of them with her accusing gaze. "It doesn't surprise me that something like this has happened. I hope you don't intend to cut the other male loose in the same way." When no one responded she said, "The one I met on the back of the property. The male with the dark skin and eyes."

"Saeed?" Jenner asked. He tipped Bria's face up to his before looking to Mikhail. "He shouldn't be wandering the property."

"No," Mikhail agreed. "He shouldn't."

So that was Saeed. Bria wondered at their worry. Though, with Claire's pregnancy and Vanessa running around the house, she could see cause for a certain level of caution.

"You can deal with him later," she said. "Lucas is going to need guidance as well. I don't think that Chelle is going to be able to give that to him, since she's had very little herself. I admit that I don't know enough about my own nature; I'm still adjusting, too. But if you want someone to help them, to act as an envoy between the coven Chelle will inevitably form and your own, I'd like to volunteer." Jenner took a big breath, but she cut him off before he could protest. "Of course, I don't want you to make a decision right now. This is something that should be discussed between Claire, Mikhail, and of course the king's counsel." Bria squeezed Jenner's hand in her own. "I just ask that you consider my request. In fact . . ." Was she ready to offer herself up for this responsibility? *Yes*. This was exactly what she needed to start living her life. "I'd like to act as an envoy between you and all of the covens, Mikhail. I can help those who are newly turned. Sort of like community outreach. A new-vampire guidance counselor."

Mikhail regarded her with narrowed eyes, his lips pursed. "Once again, it's been pointed out to me that the way I've gone about replenishing the race might be a bit misguided."

"Not misguided." Bria dropped her gaze in a show of respect to her maker and her king. "You had to start somewhere. I think everyone is doing the best they can."

"But *we* can do better," Mikhail emphasized. "Tell me, Bria, how did Saeed seem to you?"

Her uncle had always spoken of the male with fear. Obviously formidable. He was famed for his temper but also for his sharp wit and fighting prowess. She'd never met him until tonight. Hell, she hadn't met any dhampirs from outside of her coven before the day the slayers came.

"He was . . ." She searched for the right words. "Under control. I didn't sense that his thirst mastered him. His mind was not so clear, though. I found him wistful and perhaps disoriented."

Mikhail swore under his breath. "He didn't resist the pull of the Collective after his turning," Mikhail said. "Instead, he dove willingly into the memories."

"So he'll need some coaching," Bria suggested.

"And Lucas?" Mikhail asked.

"His mind is very clear," Bria replied. "But I suspect there's no Collective memory besides his and Chelle's." Bria thought of Chelle, the way she sensed things, heard Bria's thoughts. She kept that information to herself for now. She didn't want to plant a kernel of fear if there was no need. Plus, she'd promised to keep Chelle's secrets. "Lucas admitted to me that his thirst is not under control and Chelle told me that she wouldn't take him out into the city until his thirst was mastered."

"Do you really think Chelle accidentally turned him?"

Bria had sensed no lie from Chelle. Still . . . she wondered if Chella's "accident" had more to do with her loneliness than anything else. Had she seen in Lucas a chance for camaraderie? Perhaps a replacement for the brother she felt disconnected from? "I don't think there was any malice in her actions," Bria responded. She turned to Ronan and said, "You should visit her more often, though. She's lonely."

"Yeah," he said. "You're right. There's just been so gods-damned much going on since—"

"Holy shit!" Claire's shout echoed through the house. "Oh my god! Ohmygodohmygodohmygod! *Miiikkkaaiil!*"

The king shot from his desk and then left his study in a blur of motion. Bria, with Jenner and Ronan, was close behind. They followed the sounds of Claire's startled shouts to the kitchen. She stood in the middle of the tiled floor, legs spread slightly as she clutched her stomach. Mikhail was at her side, his arms around her, concern and fear etched on every line of his face.

"What is it, love? What's wrong?"

She brought her gaze to his. "My water just broke."

CHAPTER
37

Bria sat in the living room with Vanessa. Mikhail refused to take Claire from the protection of the house, and his private doctor—a dhampir who'd been tasked with Claire's prenatal care—had rushed over with a small team of assistants to perform the delivery.

Bria marveled at the way everyone had come together to prepare for the birth. Though it had happened ahead of schedule, Ronan had taken Saeed and his companions back to their coven with a not-so-gentle reminder that what they'd seen and heard at Mikhail's house tonight was not to be shared with *anyone*. Jenner had gone to Chelle's and advised her of the situation and asked her to keep a low profile for a couple of days as well. Bria hadn't found that necessary, but she knew that when it came to protecting their mates vampire males were relentless. Mikhail would soon have a mate and a child to look after. It was a wonder the property wasn't surrounded by electric fences and razor wire.

Alex had come over as well. She wasn't sure what the human's responsibilities entailed, but whatever tasks

Mikhail had set out for him, he completed them discreetly. In fact, he'd been so quiet that Bria nearly forgot he was there.

"The baby's a boy, you know." Vanessa didn't turn to Bria; she merely kept her eyes glued to the TV. "His name's going to be Braeden."

"That's a good name," Bria replied. "Did Claire pick it out?"

"Claire doesn't know," Vanessa said without guile. "She wants to name him Andrew and Mikhail wants to name him Dimitri. But they're going to call him Braeden instead."

A tingle danced down Bria's spine. Everyone knew that Vanessa was unusual, but her words were far too confident for a child making fanciful guesses. "How do you know that, Vanessa?"

"I dreamed about it." Again, the words came out so matter-of-fact. "He's going to have lots of dark hair and blue eyes like Mikhail." She turned to Bria and smiled. "So cute. I can't wait to cuddle him."

"Do you have dreams like that often, Vanessa?"

She shrugged her little shoulders. "Sometimes."

"Do all of your dreams come true?"

She shook her head and the end of her ponytail swung. "No. I know the difference between a sleep dream and an awake dream."

Bria's brow furrowed. "What's an awake dream?"

"I don't know," Vanessa said. She obviously had as much trouble articulating her visions as Bria did understanding them. "Sort of like a daydream, I guess. Like a movie I see in my head."

"So you're not asleep in bed when you have awake dreams?"

"Nope."

"Have you always had awake dreams?"

Vanessa was quite for a moment. "No. I just started having them. Maybe six . . . or three weeks ago."

Bria bit back her amusement at Vanessa's perception of time. It was clear that the visions had started only recently, though. *Interesting.* Bria couldn't help but wonder what had triggered the onset. Vanessa's confidence and absolute lack of guile made Bria believe that the visions were real. She supposed when the baby was born and named would be the true test to what Vanessa proclaimed.

"Do you tell Claire about your awake dreams?"

"No," Vanessa answered. "She's got enough to worry about."

Bria let their discussion trail off. She didn't want to pry, and even if she did she wasn't sure what good coaxing this information from Vanessa would do. They remained on the couch and watched TV for another half hour before Vanessa spoke again.

"What's a mage?"

An odd question. One Bria wasn't sure she could answer. "A magic user, I think. Sort of like a witch, but different. Why?"

"Tristan is a mage."

Another anxious chill settled over Bria's skin. "Who's Tristan?"

"I don't know," Vanessa said. "But Mikhail is going to take me to meet him."

"Another awake dream?" Bria ventured.

"Uh-huh."

Before Bria could question Vanessa more about her visions, Jenner walked into the living room. For some reason the child had seen fit to confide in Bria, and she didn't want to betray that confidence. At least, not unless it became absolutely necessary.

"You hungry?" Bria shifted so that Vanessa no longer rested against her shoulder and she pushed herself up from the couch. "Alex made pasta and chicken, and I'm pretty sure there's a pizza in the oven."

"Pizza!" Vanessa exclaimed. "Can I have root beer, too?"

"I'll see what I can do."

Bria headed for the kitchen and Jenner followed her. Her heartbeat kicked into overdrive as the thrill of pursuit raced through her veins. The heat from Jenner's body overwhelmed her and his breath brushed the back of her neck as he stopped her at the counter and swept her hair over one shoulder. His mouth came down on her bare flesh, wet and scorching. She shivered.

"I don't want to be here," he murmured against her flesh. "I want to be home. In bed with you. Naked."

A secretive smile curved Bria's lips. "Mmmm. That sounds perfect." His tongue flicked out at the sensitive skin near her pulse point and Bria's stomach clenched. Want rose within her and ribbons of heat unfurled inside of her. "I have to keep an eye on Vanessa, though."

Jenner reached around and cupped her breasts through the thin fabric of her T-shirt. Bria arched into his touch, hungry for the contact. Her nipples pearled in anticipation and her breath raced in her chest. "Maybe we could slip into one of the bedrooms later?"

Her suggestion was met with a growl of agreement. Jenner's fangs scraped against her skin. His fingertips played with the waistband of her jeans as though he was contemplating plunging his hand inside.

The oven timer put an end to their play and Jenner pulled away. Empty disappointment settled in Bria's gut. She didn't mind watching Vanessa, especially with Claire in labor, but yearned to be alone with Jenner in their home. *Theirs.* The thought seemed so foreign, the changes in her life still so sudden that her head swam. She was ready for it all, though. Never had she been so happy for the blow of the slayer's blade. Her almost death had brought her here. And though Mikhail had given her this new life, it was through Jenner that she'd been reborn.

Bria grabbed a pair of oven mitts and removed the pizza from the oven. Alex had truly outdone himself—the steaming pie looked better than any she'd ever eaten. She placed the pizza stone on the counter and grabbed a wheel to cut Vanessa a couple of slices. Jenner plucked the utensil from Bria's grip and set it on the counter before whirling her around into his arms.

"It needs to cool." The gruffness of his voice touched every part of her and Bria's lust resurfaced. His scent enveloped her, warm, spicy, and clean. His blood called to her and the vein in his throat pulsed as though begging for her bite.

He lifted Bria up and set her down on the counter. His dark gaze delved into hers. The intensity of it stole her breath. "I love you, Jenner." She reached up and laid her palm along his strong jaw. He was everything she could ever want and she'd spend the rest of her existence making sure that he knew it.

Tender emotion surged in Jenner's chest. Bria was a light in the darkness, the strength to his weakness. She was a fire that burned bright in his soul. "I love you. So gods-damned much."

He settled himself in the cradle of her legs and they wrapped around his torso, welcoming him closer. Jenner cupped Bria's face in his palms and brought his mouth to hers. The kiss sizzled through him, set his blood on fire, and hardened his cock. He thrust at her core, groaning against her lips. If he didn't get Bria into one of the guest rooms soon he was going to explode.

"I need to fuck you," he murmured against her lips. "Need to sink my fangs into your throat."

Bria pressed her body against his. A delicate purr gathered in her throat. "Yes." The word was nothing more than a desperate whisper, but it set Jenner ablaze. She slanted her mouth over his, hungry and demanding. Her tongue flicked out at the seam of his lips and Jenner deepened the kiss, his own tongue acting out on her mouth what he intended to do with his cock as soon as they were behind closed doors. The thought of her mouth on him, silky lips sliding over his shaft, sent a lick of heat up Jenner's spine. Gods, he could come just thinking about it. About her. His perfect Bria.

He never could have imagined that Fate would have graced him with a such a mate. Bria was everything he could have ever wanted and more. She was made for him, her soul the piece that he'd needed to make his whole. He loved her so much that it hurt and he couldn't wait to make a life with her, to make beautiful, perfect babies with her.

"It's a boy!"

The exclamation came from the foot of the stairs. Bria pulled away to look at Jenner. Her expression shone with excitement, her amethyst eyes sparkling with happiness and her lush mouth upturned in a wide smile. His heart clenched at the sight of her. So beautiful in her joy.

He helped Bria hop down from the counter. She and Vanessa hit the foyer at the same time, both of them bouncing impatiently at the prospect of a baby. Jenner's lips stretched into a smile. Gods, how he loved Bria.

"A boy! A boy!" Vanessa sang. "Can we see him?"

The dhampir, a female whose name Jenner didn't know, bent low to meet Vanessa's gaze. "You can, if you promise to be very calm and quiet."

Vanessa settled in an instant. "I can. Promise."

The dhampir looked at Bria. "You can come, too, if you want."

Bria grabbed Jenner's hand and urged him to follow

her up the stairs. He'd gladly follow wherever she led. To the ends of the fucking earth if that's what she wanted. The third story of the house was dark and quiet. His footsteps fell far too loudly as he made his way down the carpeted hallway. Jenner wasn't comfortable with intruding on what was no doubt a very intimate moment between Mikhail and Claire. He wondered, as the dhampir gently pushed open the door to Mikhail's private suite, how he would react to a crowd of well-wishers if it was Bria who'd just given birth to his son.

They were all a family of sorts, though, weren't they? Jenner realized as he stepped into the darkened bedroom that he would want to share his joy with Mikhail and Claire, with Ronan and Naya. He'd proudly show off the perfect little bundle as Mikhail did now, holding up his son for everyone to admire and croon to.

"He's soooo cute!" Vanessa exclaimed in a whisper. "And he's sort of like my little brother, isn't he?"

"Of course he is," Mikhail said. He brought the baby down for Vanessa to see more closely. She caressed her finger over his ruddy cheek as she spoke low in a singsong tone.

"What's his name?" Bria stepped away from Jenner to admire the little pink bundle, but she kept hold of his hand.

Mikhail's chest puffed out, 100 percent the proud father. "Braeden," he replied in a robust tone. "We both agreed it suited him."

Bria's grip on Jenner's hand tightened and a wave of anxiety crested over him. He stepped up behind her, unsure of the reason for her sudden discomfort, but he wanted to do whatever he could to assuage it. "A good name," he said to Mikhail. "Strong."

Mikhail beamed. Jenner had never seen the male so damned happy.

Ronan stepped into the room a few moments later. "Naya's on her way over. Baby fever's going to spread, I think." He leaned over Jenner's shoulder to get a peek. "Damn," he said as though disappointed. "I was hoping he'd look like Claire."

Mikhail didn't seem a bit fazed by the playful dig. Instead, he said, "So was I. But I think we'll keep him, regardless."

Good humor abounded and congratulations were offered. Claire was obviously tired, but her expression shone with pure bliss as she lay tucked under the covers of the bed. After a while the baby began to fuss and Mikhail returned him to his mother. "I think he's hungry," Mikhail said low.

Jenner took that as their cue to clear the room. He gave a gentle tug on Bria's hand and she turned to him with a dreamy smile. *Baby fever indeed.*

"How about that pizza, Vanessa?" Bria said. "I'm pretty sure it's cooled enough."

"Oh man," she said with a pout. "I wanna stay in here and play with the baby."

"Later," Bria said. "Let him eat and rest. I'm sure you can come up and visit him later."

The girl grumped but complied and followed Jenner, Ronan, and Bria from the room. "Bye, Braeden!" she called in a stage whisper from the doorway. "I'll be back soon."

Once back in the kitchen, Bria set about getting everyone fed. Jenner watched his mate with awe and admiration as she took charge, becoming the head of the household while Mikhail and Claire enjoyed their son. Jenner's mate was remarkable. So strong. So confident. Again, he was struck by his luck that fate had sent her into his life. She brought him the balance that he'd sought for months. Through Bria, Jenner had found peace.

She served Vanessa a plate with a couple of slices of pizza and slid a glass of root beer across the bar to where she sat. A furrow marred Bria's brow and Jenner couldn't help but think that the girl had rattled Bria somehow. Vanessa was a strange little human; they all knew it. But Jenner sensed that Bria knew something more about her than anyone else did.

Conversation flowed. Ronan grabbed containers of chicken and pasta from the fridge and popped them in the microwave. He and Bria talked about nothing and everything. Small talk that they included Vanessa in as the girl dug into her pizza with gusto. Bria's earlier unease dissipated like clouds under the heat of the sun and a warm rush of pure happiness stretched out between their tether to bathe Jenner in warmth. Whatever her thoughts about the girl, they weren't enough to trouble Bria any further.

So much to consider. Especially with the meeting with McAlister looming in their future. Jenner knew, though, that whatever obstacles were thrown in their path, he could handle it. He could handle anything as long as Bria was by his side. They were two halves of a whole. The perfect team. And there was no one he'd rather experience all of life's adventures with. She was his. And he was inexorably hers.

Forever.

Don't miss the first two novels in
Kate Baxter's True Vampire series!

THE LAST TRUE VAMPIRE
THE WARRIOR VAMPIRE

Available from St. Martin's Paperbacks

And look for her sensational e-novella about an
alpha shifter and the woman he can *bearly* resist . . .

STRIPPED BEAR

www.stmartins.com